EVENMERE TALES AND OTHER STORIES

COME WITH US TO WORLDS OF WONDER

A collection of Fantasy and Science Fiction stories from the author of the *Evenmere* trilogy, including Stoddard's celebrated *The Battle of York* and his previously unpublished Evenmere novella, *The Leechmont*.

Within these pages you will find:

The history of the United States remembered only as myth.

A wizard who changes his victims into books.

An astronomer who regulates the stars.

A grand hotel whose guests determine the fate of the universe.

All these and other realms of the fantastic.

"Stoddard's an incredibly gifted stylist who happens to have a knack for character and pacing as well, so that you end up surrounded in glowing prose while you're frantically turning pages to see what happens next."

—Howard Andrew Jones, author of *For the Killing of Kings*

On *The Evenmere Chronicles* Series:

"Stoddard tells a thrilling story... that features not only a unique and powerful family, but a magnificent edifice filled with mysterious doors and passageways that link kingdoms and unite the universe."

—Publishers Weekly

"The language is rich and whimsical... Evenmere is what you would get if you dropped the Winchester Mystery House into a giant mirror maze, and left it alone for a few decades."

—Michael M. Jones, Green Man Review

"Without question, *The High House* is one of my favorite books of the year."

—Charles DeLint, Magazine of Fantasy and Science Fiction

On *Liberty Bell and the Last American*:

"Liberty Bell is a delightful post-apocalyptic Dorothy Gale, dropped into a country every bit as strange as Oz. This fun, fast-paced science fiction adventure gives hope that, while America may be broken, it can be put back together again, better than before."

—Josh Rountree, author of *Fantastic Americana: Stories*

On *The Back of the Beyond*:

"... the author has captured the very essence of fantasy, rife with magic, quest archetypes, greed and treachery, panoramic battles, chivalric romance, megalomania... and an endearing puppy named Blunder."

—Lone Star Literary Life

EVENMERE TALES AND OTHER STORIES

JAMES STODDARD

Ransom Books

This is a work of fiction. All events portrayed in this book are fictitious, and any resemblance to real people or events is purely coincidental.

Print Edition

Cover illustration and design by Mimer E.

Visit www.james-stoddard.com to learn more about the author.
To contact James Stoddard email: evenmere@gmail.com

A Ransom Book
Printed in the United States of America.

First Printing: October 2023
10 9 8 7 6 5 4 3 2 1

TO THE CHAMPIONS OF THE PEN

THE EDITORS

WHO HELPED ME ALONG THE WAY

George H. Scithers

Rachel E. Holmen

Betsy Mitchell

Jaime Levine

Gordon Van Gelder

Andy Robertson

Howard Andrew Jones

Dr. Robert B. Finegold

TABLE OF CONTENTS

THE IFS OF TIME

EVENMERE IS A house of infinite proportions. Within its gabled halls, beneath its countless roofs, are countries and kingdoms, dominions and principalities, walled fields and farmed courtyards. The manor is the mechanism that regulates the universe, and its many servants light the lamps, wind the clocks, repair the walls, polish the doorknobs—a thousand tasks—so light and time and space, the stars and the worlds, continue.

Enoch, the Windkeep, the immortal Hebrew who has been with Evenmere nearly since its beginning, made his way down benighted halls, lantern in hand, traveling through forgotten passages in the land of Querny. He did not sing or whistle as was his usual wont; his face was lined with care.

"Who am I, a country boy from Aram, to be doing this?" he muttered. "What do I know about such things? The Master should be here; he'd know what to do."

The echoes of the Windkeep's boots pattered up and down the passage.

"Time I know," Enoch said. "I know time. I like time. It moves forward. It's steady. I wind the clocks, time goes; I don't wind the clocks, it doesn't go. It's a good job, a steady job. Am I a diplomat? If I had gone to school, maybe. They didn't have schools when I was growing up."

He wore a greatcoat against the chill. His Assyrian curls bobbed as he ascended a spiral stair; the worn boards creaked beneath his boots. The smell of dust set him sneezing.

Up and up he went, a long, steady climb past floor after floor, never once hearing a sound, save for his own footfalls and the settling of the structure.

"Not even a mouse," Enoch said. "You'd think I wouldn't miss mice. I had one once for a pet. Samuel, I called him. I haven't thought of him in centuries. Cute little fellow. I wonder what happened to him? I don't remember."

Far above in the highest heights, the faintest speck, a single light, glowed. Enoch craned his neck to see it. He licked his thick lips and continued his climb.

Two hours later he reached a landing at the top of the stairs. The light came through the window of a red door with peeling paint. He took a deep breath and stepped inside.

The room was comfortable as a pub, unicorn tapestries on the paneled walls and floor, flickering gas-lamps, the brown aroma of tobacco, a roaring fire in the hearth. Three men and a woman, all exceedingly ancient, sat around a claw-foot table; four pairs of elderly eyes stared at the newcomer.

"Hello," Enoch said, waving a hand. "I saw your light. Is there room for one more?"

They looked uneasily at one another. A gentleman in a tweed frock coat, the tallest of them and the most gaunt and frail with age, pulled his pipe from between his lips and said, "I fear you have stumbled on the meeting of a rather exclusive club. We are not currently open to new members."

Enoch pulled up a chair. "Who am I to want to join? I was never a joiner, anyway. I'll just sit a minute. You go ahead with what you're doing."

Again, the four exchanged glances.

"This is highly irregular," said a corpulent fellow in a black double-breasted vest. "Really, sir, we don't mean to be rude—"

"Then don't be," Enoch said, still smiling. "My mother, she said there was never a good reason. My father, he took a different approach. He said discourtesy was an insult. He killed a man for it, once."

"Well I never—" the corpulent gentleman began.

"Now, Jonas," the woman said. "Let's not be hasty. I'm sure after our guest has rested a moment, he'll be on his way. Would you like something to drink, sir? We haven't any beer, I'm afraid, nothing to blur the senses, you see. But we have tea. There isn't a servant, if you don't mind getting it yourself?"

"Easily done," Enoch said.

A moment later, he was back at the table. No one had spoken during his absence, and the silence continued awhile. The four traded nervous glances as it became obvious Enoch had no intention of leaving.

"We really must be about our business," the woman finally said. Her eyes were a piercing blue, her face mummy-wrinkles; her silk dress wrapped her other wrinkles in a sheath smooth as ice. "We are an association of tale-tellers, who meet to exchange amusing little stories of our own invention. A harmless hobby."

"Totally harmless," the gaunt man said.

"But our time is fleeting," the woman said hurriedly, "and we must continue."

Enoch waved his arms. "Don't mind me. I like a good story as well as the next fellow. I'll be like a little bird. Won't say a word."

"I believe it was Tremor's turn," the heavy-set Jonas said.

"Is it?" the third man asked. His aged voice quavered like a warbler's. "Very well. For this round, I have chosen as our topic 'Stories of the Future.'"

Tremor gave a rasping cough and began.

✧ ✧ ✧

It was one of those nights where the rain comes down in sheets and everyone stays home, leaving the roads blank and deserted. Edward, alone in the small apartment he had leased for the spring semester, sat at the window watching the lightning flashes, his thoughts turbulent as the tempest outside. Earlier that evening, he had broken off his engagement with Janet.

It had not been an impulsive decision, was in fact one of the few things about their relationship that wasn't impulsive. Literally falling in love at first sight, they had courted only three weeks before he proposed. Thereafter, the excitement and complexity of the wedding plans had swamped their lives. But in the end, two weeks before the blessed union, Edward had realized he was marrying a woman he scarcely knew.

He glanced back at the open books on the kitchen table. The next day began examination week of his final semester, and he needed to do well; the whirlwind romance had taken a toll on his concentration. A student of the sciences could not afford to ignore his classes if he wanted favorable employment.

He needed to forget Janet and get to work. He strode resolutely to the table, sat down, and tried to read, but his mind wandered. Had he done the right thing? Was this merely a case of cold feet?

A knock sounded at the door, causing him to start.

"Who the devil could be out on a night like this?" he muttered, though undoubtedly it was Janet come to talk him back to his senses.

He went to the door, paused, and took a deep breath. He had to be strong. He couldn't vacillate; it would only hurt her more.

He opened the door and gaped in surprise. A slender man, dripping wet, with shoulder-length hair, stood back from the door, partially hidden in shadow.

"You are Edward Monroe," the stranger said. "There is little time and we must talk. Your future depends on it."

He stepped into the light. With a shock, Edward saw the man could be his older twin, so closely did they resemble one another.

"Are you a relative?" Edward blurted.

"In four years, you will become part of Project Time," the man said. "I am you, twelve years in the future."

"What?"

"There is not a moment for explanations. I came here to tell you to follow your heart. If you desert Janet now, you will always regret it. Despite your accomplishments, your life is incomplete without her. This is your one chance for happiness. Go to her. Don't be afraid."

The man was gone, there one instant, vanished the next. Edward staggered back against the apartment wall.

For a moment, he couldn't think. He had always had an interest in the conundrums of time. Was it possible he would soon work for a company that would discover the means of traveling its byways?

Suddenly, he laughed. His doubts were ended. He had been given reassurance from the future. He couldn't go wrong! He had to see Janet at once.

As he was reaching for his coat, another knock sounded at the door.

"He's come back," Edward said.

He had left the front door open, and a figure leaned over the threshold. It was the previous traveler, yet it was not. This time the man wore a dark slicker, as if he had known to expect the rain. He was in his mid-forties.

"Has he been here?" the older Edward demanded.

Edward nodded, speechless.

"He was wrong, Edward. Janet and I—and you—it won't work out in the end. You'll come to resent one another. The two of you will do everything wrong. Don't contact her. Don't go back to her. Do you understand?"

"I understand," Edward said. "But—"

The figure was gone, vanished like the first one.

Edward shut the door and sat down in a chair. That was it, then. The words of his older, wiser self showed his original instincts had been correct. If he had followed the first one's advice. . . He shook his head. Dangerous stuff, this time-travel, giving counsel before one has the full perspective. He would have to remember that.

A knock sounded on the door. Edward gave a sharp intake of breath and flung it wide.

An old man stood there, wearing a heavy sweater and carrying an umbrella, his frame stooped, his face so changed it took a moment for Edward to recognize his elder self.

"It doesn't matter, Edward," his voice rasped. "Do what you think best, the best you can, with the knowledge you have at the moment. It all works out in the end. What we do during the journey is what's important."

When the figure disappeared, Edward stood staring out at the rain. He was no better off than before.

"They never should have come," he said. The instant the words escaped his lips he realized he had made a decision of a different kind, and knew, for the briefest instant before his memory went, that none of his future selves had ever been there at all.

✧ ✧ ✧

"EXCELLENT STORY," JONAS said.

"Refreshing," the gaunt man added.

"Bravo!" The woman clapped her hands.

They all looked at Enoch.

He returned their stares before clearing his throat. "I liked it. It had a nice ending."

The four storytellers beamed.

"I believe you are next, Lady Chandless," Jonas said.

The woman nodded and began.

✧ ✧ ✧

AHN AND SHUSHANA had come to the Cinnamon Sea to cease.

They stood close together beside its serene, sienna waters and listened to its languid lapping against the shore. Russet *tegets* rose and dove along its surface, ripping with claws and mandibles their protesting prey from its chestnut fathoms. Ebon *dartbirds* veered and capered against an ocher sky dotted with wisps of flaxen clouds. From the safety of golden water-rushes, amphibians crooned their parchment-rustle songs.

The red sun lay low on the horizon, the drawing of the dusk on the tablet of the sky. A slow breeze stirred the copper-tanged air. Silver stones glimmered along the saffron bank. From the nearby forests, Ahn heard shadowed animal cries, low and deep and high and clear, ringing like funeral bells for the last day of his people.

Ahn and Shushana were alone but not alone on that dulcet shore. The others of their kind stood apart from them in groups of two or four. They had already ceased a few hours before, and now stood still as the scattered trees on the surrounding hills. These were the last of their race, and Ahn and Shushana were the last of the last.

"I wish. . . we had created offspring," she said, staring into his scarlet eyes.

"The decision was made long ago," he said. "We did as we did."

The secret that had made them immortal had come with the price of sterility. They had grieved, but unwilling to forsake the gift of the ages, had reconciled themselves.

"We were too selfish," Ahn said.

They had lived for eons. The planet of their birth had perished, but still they continued, finding new worlds. They traveled through space on bands of energy, stood on barren moons and birthing planets. Eventually, they created this place, not a world but a disk on a cosmic plane, as enduring as themselves.

When they first began to cease, none had understood why.

He glanced at his wrist-indicator. Time was fleeting. With alarm, he noticed her own indicator showed she would proceed him. He would be the very last, then. For a moment, he was dismayed, then saw it was for the best. He would be her guide.

"We must speak of happy things," he said.

"I remember the first time I saw you," she said. "Upon the Cliffs of Consu, in your flecked mantle."

"I hunted the white *feral,*" he replied. They had spoken the words many times before, but now they were the sweetest wine. "I broke across your Festive Camp. Your father was angry."

"My father? My mother was furious! Your *geetdogs* trampled everything. You came through the underbrush, muddy and sweating. My sister said you were a wild beast, but I thought you handsome."

"And you were the loveliest woman I had ever seen. So are you still."

She looked away fearfully, but he whispered in her ear. "We are together. I will always be with you. Not in trepidation but in joy. I will not let you go alone."

She wept a little while he watched her indicator with concern.

By the time she composed herself, dusk was falling. The red sun was but a rim along the horizon, and her time was nearly done. A minute, perhaps. How had it come so quickly? She realized it, too, and terror filled her eyes.

He spoke rapidly, hoping to keep the desperation from his voice. "Do not think of it. You must not think of it. Think of me. Think of our times together. Think how much I love you. Look into my eyes. You are very beautiful. You are all I ever wished. Remember the night we danced the *tyrinhee* across the Maukish Canyons? What was the music?"

"*The Temporinum* by Zezree," she said. "You were striking that night, dressed in evening dark, your eyes burned like twin coals. I remember. . ."

Her words fell away. The warmth in her gaze remained, but she no longer moved. Her indicator wrote the fatal words across the air.

He gave a stifled sob, afraid to disturb her even then. Finally, he touched her hand, grimly satisfied by her expression. So would she smile through the ages.

He was glad he had so little time to grieve. He steeled himself, vowing to look at the indicator no more. He would study her golden eyes, feel the warmth of her hands—she would never grow cold—and remember their love.

When he tried to think of the good times, none would come.

A momentary panic filled him that he would be thinking of death at the moment of ceasing. If that happened, his eternity would be dreadful. He calmed his thoughts, reassuring himself that he could perform this final act. Briefly, he hovered between confidence and terror.

He quit trying to think of the past. He thought only of her, and the past came to meet him. Her presence filled him. Even after so much time, there was much he did not know of her. That was the wonder of it, that he could bask forever in awe of her mysterious, loving otherness. He caressed her cheek, kissed her lips.

He did not know when the time came; his wonder of her had enfolded him. He ceased gently, passing from one state to another.

The indicator on his wrist wrote the words in the air above him: *Brain capacity filled. Further memory unavailable.*

Standing together, looking into one another's eyes, they stood enraptured, unable to think beyond their final thought, unable to recall any instant before it. Ahn had been successful; their ceasing was not one of fear. So they would remain, lost in themselves, living only in that moment of love while the ages drifted by.

✧ ✧ ✧

"LOVELY," THE GAUNT man said.

"Splendid. Such imagination," Jonas said.

"Well done," Tremor quavered.

Again they looked to Enoch. His eyes had narrowed in thought, but he gave an innocent smile. "A story of the far future. Like you're seeing all the ifs of time."

"Thank you," Lady Chandless said.

"Am I giving you a compliment?" Enoch asked. "Maybe. Maybe not. I know time pretty well. We get along, time and I. But you're playing a different dance with her."

"I think we'd best move on," Jonas said, eyeing Enoch sharply. "Our tales cannot wait."

"I'm sure they can't," Enoch murmured.

"You are next, Mr. Howell," Tremor told the gaunt man.

✧ ✧ ✧

TOM WATCHED THE sunset die in purple and orange across the grassy plains. He had already built his nightly campfire from the tough, fibrous wood that smoldered but never burned. Despite its oily odor, it cheered him. He sat down on a homemade stool and took out his worn reader. He was studying a particularly difficult problem on the lifter conversion rates. It had taken him nearly a week of diligent analysis, but he saw a glimmer of understanding. His delight grew as he pondered the ratios.

A streak lit the dusk, running like molten silver down the azure sky, the glowing trail of a ship. He stood and watched dully, mouth agape, as the vehicle descended toward him, its patterned lights flashing red and gold.

It landed less than three hundred meters away, and still Tom remained motionless, clutching his reader close while a lone figure left the craft.

"Greetings," the stranger called.

"H. . . Hello." Tom's voice croaked from disuse.

The tall, blonde visitor approached warily, his hand close to the holster of his weapon. "I'm Captain John White. Just passing through this sector. You been shipwrecked long?"

Tom glanced back at the rusting wreckage of his vessel. "Yeah, I. . . it's been a while. I'm Tom, eh Lieutenant Tom Moyers. I was on reconnaissance for the *Artemis* when my central pods blew. Communications don't work down here. Too much interference. Never found me."

"*Artemis.* I don't know an *Artemis.*"

"It was part of the Celsis expedition."

White's mouth fell open. "That was over thirty years ago!"

"So long?" Tom stared at the man, then shuffled his feet in the short, brown grass.

"Can I look at your ship?" the captain asked. "It's a '36 Spangler, isn't it?"

"Thirty-seven," Tom said proudly. "Dual engine, 504 Vorzes with a midshift drive. Point zero zero zero five four micro rate."

The captain chuckled. "I recognize these babies." He walked over and tapped the ripped hull. Most of the forward section lay buried under the impact. Part of the quarters remained, though holes pocked the roof.

"I spent time training on Spanglers," White said. "Even worked on a few myself." His smile slipped away. "How did you survive?"

"Mostly off fish. Some other things are edible—types of roots. I had no computer. No video. Nothing to write on or dictate to. Only this." He held up his reader.

"Hey, that's a real antique. Still work?"

"It's solar powered." Tom grinned. "I lost all the data except the ship's manual. It's all in here. Mechanical, electrical, life systems. Everything. Been reading it... thirty years, I guess. I know this craft inside out." He patted the rusty hull. "I could build one if I had the parts."

The captain gave him a strange, sympathetic look and glanced up at the sky. "I've got some provisions back in the hold. Let's add some variety to your diet."

As they ate dinner, the captain asked a number of questions, making it difficult to talk and eat at the same time, but Tom didn't care. It was vegetables and solid meat, and it wasn't fish, and he had never tasted anything so good.

"Is there anything you'd like to know about Earth?" White asked. "Things have changed while you were gone."

Tom thought a moment. "Do they still fly ships... like mine?"

The captain's gaze moved toward the ground. He shook his head. "They haven't flown ships like those in twenty years. Why, you won't believe mine." He gestured toward his craft. "We call it a *streamer*. It's sleek, smooth, operates on voice command. I'm the only one programmed to fly it. You couldn't take off in it if you wanted to. Intricate. Single capstan, not triple like yours."

Tom shook his head. "Mine's not triple. The '37 Spangler has a dual capstan, dual pin-up rotator with intertwining tapers and a fully automated seysin, operating at twelve-thousand telebeats per nanosecond. Non-lockup thin charger, full swelled rinature."

The captain chuckled. "You do know the manual. But—can I see that?"

Tom looked down at the battered reader, its red case faded over time. He handed it over reluctantly.

White laughed again as he looked through it. Tom suddenly realized he was young for a captain.

"Like I thought," White said. "We studied these pretty thoroughly in flight school; their fundamental design remains the basis for modern spacecraft. This manual is wrong. There was quite a controversy over it years ago. It's in all the histories.

Several pilots died because of it. It might even be why you were stranded. There was never a dual capstan model in any of the Spangler line."

"What?" Tom said slowly. "What did you say?"

"Not a one. They intended to manufacture them and printed the manuals that way. If you could see your engine below the wreckage, you'd find out."

Tom's head spun. "But, if that were true, the lifter conversion rates would be different. All the charts. Why, everything would be wrong!"

"Well, yes, that's true." The captain spooned more potatoes into his mouth.

"Just a minute," Tom said, rising slowly. "Let me go back and show you something from my gear. I need to show you."

He stumbled over to the ship's partially intact living quarters and returned a moment later. The captain looked up as Tom pointed the pistol at his chest and fired. The man was dead before he hit the ground.

Tom walked over and pried the reader from his hands, thankful it hadn't been damaged. "It's a shame. But you shouldn't have said it."

He looked down at the pages. Triple capstan! He nearly had the conversion tables done.

✧ ✧ ✧

"TREMENDOUS," LADY CHANDLESS said.

"Lovely," Jonas added.

"Very artful," Tremor interjected.

Enoch said nothing. He was listening not to the story but to the pulse of time, feeling it stagger and stammer as Mr. Howell told his tale.

Seeing that the Hebrew refrained from comment, Jonas began his turn.

✧ ✧ ✧

"I JUST HATE to live a lie," Michael said, his haggard eyes looking into the haggard eyes of his wife. The light from the table lamp cast shadows across her dark hair and high cheekbones.

"We can't put it off any longer," Kristen said. "It's been three weeks already."

He put his hand to his brow, rubbed it methodically, and gave a grim laugh. "I knew my thirtieth birthday was supposed to be a benchmark, but I never thought—has it really been three weeks?"

"We went home to your parents on the sixth; we were there nearly a week, and this is April fourth."

Michael glanced helplessly around his house, thinking of the strange meeting with his parents and friends and neighbors, people he had known all his life in the small town where he was raised. They had told Kristen and him The Secret. If it had been one or two, instead of all of them, he never would have believed it.

Kristen sat beside him on the bed and tucked her smooth hand into his rough one. "I know its hard, but we have to adjust."

"It just sounds so. . . conspiratorial. I wish my parents had been allowed to write it down, so I could remember the sequence better." He stared out the bedroom at the door across the hall, the door he dreaded entering. "When did they say Columbus discovered America? The twelve hundreds?"

"1136."

His mouth went dry. All the history since the tenth century was completely different from what he had been taught—electric light bulb invented in 1435, automobile in 1447, airplane, 1450. First man walked on the moon in 1482—there had been four others before Neil Armstrong. The time of British rule of the colonies, the lengths of presidential terms, all had been changed to conform to the supposed facts.

"Each generation passes away," he said. "If they lied to us, how would we know? You're handling this much better than I am."

"The video from the nuclear wars in the fifteen hundreds was what finally convinced me," she said. "We can't let that happen again."

Michael glanced at the dreaded door, as solid as the Knowledge Barrier. Computer programmers had been the first to discover that learning was finite; humanity could never progress beyond its current level of advancement. The other sciences had hit the Barrier soon after. Despair had gripped the world until a plan was devised to reshuffle old technologies.

"Michael, we have to go through with this. Louise came by this morning, wanting to know if we had done it yet."

"Louise? She knows, too? Doug Barker mentioned it to me at the office today."

"I'm scared, Michael. They're both over thirty; we shouldn't be surprised. And they're just looking after us, making sure we don't do anything stupid. You know what happens to people who resist."

"We should call the newspapers," he said, "get it out in the open."

Kristen looked horrified. "We will *not* tell anyone! Don't even say it. We will not become an example. We can do this, Michael. They've shown us the old things. The words will come. You have to try."

"So we can continue the lie?"

"Yes! Because the next generation must believe in progress."

He felt the tears gathering around his eyes. "But. . . if the technology fails us, what's left?"

Kristen smiled slightly. "What we've always had. One another. Faith. Hope. We always have hope."

He sighed, tired of fighting it, tired of hating it, tired of trying to accept it. It was no use. Maybe after it was done, he could see it was for the best. "Let's get it over with."

They slowly rose, hand in hand, and went to the door. He grasped the knob and turned it.

The light from the hall lit the small, trusting face of their five-year-old daughter, her eyes expectant, her soft, dark hair haloed against her pillow.

"I thought you were never coming to kiss me goodnight," she said, with a pretty pout.

His mouth felt bone-dry; his voice shook as he began. "Tonight, honey, we want to tell you a bedtime story about when your mom and I were your age. Back then, you see. . . there weren't any refrigerators, or televisions, or electric lights. We made butter by hand. And we didn't ride the bus; we walked to school every day, three whole miles. . .

✧ ✧ ✧

"MOST INSIGHTFUL," LADY Chandless said.

"An interesting twist," Mr. Howell said.

"Good as gold," Tremor confirmed.

"Shall we begin another round?" Jonas asked.

Enoch pulled out an ancient brass pocket watch. "Maybe you should stop for lunch. It should be nearly noon. It's funny, my watch must be broken; it only says 9:30."

"We don't usually have lunch," Tremor said. "We practice austerity throughout our meetings."

"How long do your little gatherings last?" Enoch asked.

"We don't limit our time," Mr. Howell said.

"I think you do," Enoch said. "I'll tell you what. How about I tell a story of my own? Just as a guest."

"Well," Tremor said, "I suppose—"

"Mr. Tremor!" Jonas said. "You know how stringent are our requirements."

"Highly irregular," Mr. Howell said.

"Most extraordinary," Lady Chandless said.

Enoch smiled as he spoke, but Jonas looked into his eyes and did not seem to like what he saw there.

"I think it would be best if we let our guest tell his tale," Jonas said. "Perhaps he will then have the good grace to depart."

"I'll give it a try," Enoch said. "Maybe it will be as good as yours, maybe it won't, but it will pass the time."

✧ ✧ ✧

"THERE WAS ONCE a man who was the Windkeep of Evenmere, the Keeper of Time. He kept the clocks wound, the little clocks in the Inner Chambers, the Eternity Clock in the Clock Tower, the Hundred Years Clock in the Land of Twelve, all the clocks great and small, so time continued running. Time is important, you know, because everything happens inside it. A person lives and dies between the brackets of the hours.

"Time can be cruel. It's implacable. You think you have a moment to yourself and it's gone, slipped right through your hands. You're playing in the woods with your little sister, climbing trees, having the time of your life; you turn around and you're an old man watching your grandchildren play. Your sister is gone and you can't climb so well anymore. I could tell you stories about how time gets away from you. And when it does, you start thinking about death."

"I have a sudden headache," Mr. Howell said, rubbing his temple.

"Death," Enoch continued, "it's dark and scary, full of mystery. Anyway, this Keeper of Time, he notices one day things aren't running so smooth. Time is like your second cousin—all relative—a cousin of seconds and minutes, days and years and centuries. It's like a river—sometimes it goes fast, sometimes slow; it's never the same for anyone. So it takes a little time for the Windkeep to see time isn't running right. He realizes it's getting slower and slower, and he can't understand why. So he starts looking. But time gets so slow, it's nearly crawling. The Keeper of Time, he can ride the crests of time; he can stay above it if he needs to. That's why he's lived so long—it's a gift."

"I'm really not feeling well at all," Mr. Howell said.

Enoch felt the slight throbbing of time, a gentle pulsing like a heart restarting itself. He ignored Mr. Howell. "It comes to a point where time stops. The Master of the house, he sits in the Inner Chambers, unable to lift a finger. Everything stops; everything and everyone except for the poor Keeper of Time.

"He looks around. It's easier now to track the source of the problem, because all he has to find are the only ones still moving. He listens and hears a small disturbance in a high tower in Querny. When he goes there he finds four people sitting around a table.

"All kinds of folk live in Evenmere, talented and not-so-talented, smart and not-so-smart. Men and women of science and of sorcery, with all sorts of ideas, some good, some not-so-good. The Keeper finds four brilliant people who know a lot about science and a little about enchantment. Four people who don't want to die, who found a way to keep death at bay.

"Our reality is created by the stories we tell; these four use stories to change theirs. The stories are all different but always on the same subject: changeless times—visits from the future that don't alter anything, people living forever in a moment of time, a traveler stranded on a timeless planet, a civilization that repeats itself over and over. They tell their tales as they sit in their high tower. As long as they keep telling them, time and death hover like vultures, never landing, never touching them.

"Most people would run out of things to say, but they've learned to look through time into the might-be's and could-be's and will-be's and won't-be's, so they have an endless supply of stories."

Enoch glanced at the four octogenarians, their faces filled with weary fear. "So they live while everyone else sits paralyzed in time."

A single, papyrus exhalation escaped Mr. Howell. He lolled in his chair, head back, eyes staring.

"What did you do to him?" Jonas cried, voice high with terror.

"Me? I didn't do anything. That's the surprise ending of my story. When the Keeper of Time comes to the tower and tells *his* tale, time starts moving again. Your friend's hour was up, that's all. He was overdue."

Enoch licked his lips as he studied their horrified faces. "How long can you stave it off? How long have I sat here? Ten minutes? A thousand years? Who knows?"

"You could join us," Mr. Tremor said. "Even you won't live forever."

"You think I want to? I had a wife and children back in Aram. I haven't seen them in three thousand years. Everybody I ever love dies and I go on. I didn't choose this. You, you decided on it. You thought you were the center of the universe."

Mr. Jonas reached into his pocket and produced a small revolver, aimed at Enoch's heart. His voice trembled. "I think our guest best be going."

"I don't think so. I've dealt myself in. This kind of magic requires symmetry. Even I know that. Four people, four stories, each in turn. You go ahead and tell your tales. You'll stop time during your turn, I'll start it during mine."

"You're giving us a death sentence," Lady Chandless said.

Enoch shrugged. "No more than anybody else."

The three storytellers and the corpse stared at Enoch. Somewhere a clock was ticking. In the house below, the Windkeep sensed hearts beating, blood running, lungs pulling air in and out. A minute passed, two more.

"I am so very weary," Mr. Tremor said. "I am sick of all of you, sick of sitting here scared to death of death, telling stories in this endless purgatory. I want to return to the world. I want to laugh and cry and do some good for someone, do some good for myself."

Lady Chandless began to weep. "We didn't mean for it to affect everyone else. We didn't know!"

Jonas placed the revolver on the table. "It was pleasant at first, like sitting in a little coffee shop. But it's terrible now. We can't leave, you see. We're trapped. We can't even rise from the table."

"An unforeseen side effect of the magic," Lady Chandless said. "We ourselves have become a story, one from which we cannot escape. Yet now you have entered our little tale. What will you do?"

Enoch studied their blanched faces for several minutes, trying to think. Finally, he said, "I like stories. I tell them all the time. Stories of my boyhood, stories of people I knew. True stories. It's said the truth can set you free. If you really want to escape, why don't you tell *your* stories?"

The three sat silent. Gradually, like the lifting of a mist, their faces brightened.

"That's just the thing!" Tremor's eyes glistened. "I want to tell about what happened to *me*."

"Yes," Lady Chandless said, growing excited. "I want to talk about what it was like when I was young. I was a lovely woman once, you know. Everyone said so. My husband and I met when we were twenty. He was so handsome and so good. We were married for fifty-seven years. We worked hard, but on Saturdays we used to love to go to the dances. I miss him so."

The pulse of time grew stronger.

"I had a wonderful childhood," Tremor said. "We lived in the country. My parents were so kind. I had a little dog named Hercules and we used to run and play in the fields. My two brothers were both older than I. They're gone now. All my family is gone. I am the last. The very last. Only I am left to remember how happy it was. Only I can tell the tale."

Far away, ringing through distant chambers, a tower clock gonged the hour.

"I was in the war," Jonas said. "I was young and stout, not fat like now. My friend, Billy, and I used to play cards in the barracks. A sniper killed him when we were on reconnaissance. I held him as he died; his blood ran down my hands. When I got home, I found his wife and told her how he once saved my life. He was my best friend. He's been gone sixty years while I still walk the Earth."

As the house below them gradually came to life, breathing in and out the dust of time, the three told the stories of their lives, their eyes burning with the memories. Hour by hour they spoke, and with each hour the hours grew stronger, until time was time again. Far in the distance, the clock sounded once more, a long, echoing gong.

When its reverberations died, the three silently rose and stepped from the room. Enoch, coming last, paused long enough to close Mr. Howell's eyes and bless his passing. He turned off the lamps before closing the door.

Outside, he was met by Time. It circled around him, its pulsing breath sweet as cool wind on his face.

"You go down the stairs," he told the three, pointing the way. "You go down the stairs and live."

✧ ✧ ✧

Afterword

AS I NOTE later in the book, I stopped writing for a few years to pursue a career in music. When I returned to writing, I thought the best way to break back into the magazine markets was to write stories under five-hundred words. What I didn't realize is that super short stories are terribly difficult to write.

As I recall, I only wrote three of them. I submitted one, sending it to the *Magazine of Fantasy and Science Fiction*. It was promptly rejected, and I abandoned the whole short short story plan.

Fast forward to 2009. The stories were sitting on my hard drive, and—following my motto that nothing is ever lost—I decided to incorporate them into a single piece of prose, having characters within the tale tell the stories, an old technique borrowed from Lord Dunsany's *Jorkens* and Fletcher and Pratt's *Tales from Gavagan's Bar*. To round out the group, I added the time travel one, an idea that had been wandering in my brain for some time. I chose Enoch from my Evenmere novels as the protagonist.

Writing the rough draft, I realized that in order to make the ending work, I had to figure out what the four stories had in common. And I was stumped, unable to see any relationship between them.

Writing is weird. It's rare for me to begin a short story knowing where it will go. It's the same when plotting a novel. You can't surprise your reader if your plot is obvious. You have to put your protagonists into situations you don't know how to get them out of, then let your subconscious mind discover the answer.

Sometimes that takes a while. With *The Ifs of Time,* it required a year or two. During that duration, I would occasionally think about it, always failing to see the connection I needed. Then, while driving my car one day, it was suddenly clear that—as Enoch says—each of the little yarns is about resistance to change. Once I saw it, it seemed obvious; it was also disturbing since I wasn't sure what it said about myself. But that's an entirely different question.

I finished the story; Gordon Van Gelder bought it for *The Magazine of Fantasy and Science Fiction,* and I had the secret pleasure of selling him a piece that the previous editor had rejected, albeit in a much different form. But let's keep that between ourselves, shall we?

THE BATTLE OF YORK

THREE THOUSAND YEARS have elapsed since the passing of America. Though scholars have uncovered multitudes of valuable archaeological evidence, little written literature exists from that era. It is indeed unfortunate that books made of paper were replaced by magneto-optical storage by the middle of the twenty-first century. The world-wide magnetic field disaster of the last decades of that century did more than herald a new Dark Age—it erased the literature and history of the world, even as the accompanying geological disruptions obliterated cities and landmarks.

Fortunately, near the end of the twenty-fourth century, an unknown scholar passed through the American regions, collecting the stories and legends we now call "The Americana." Though we can expect little accuracy from a people dependent on electronic data storage rather than oral tradition, we believe there is always a grain of truth concealed within the tales. But to quote one of the figures from The Americana itself: "When the Legend becomes fact, print the Legend."

✧ ✧ ✧

YOUNG GENERAL WASHINGTON rode alone on his white stallion through the vast forest of Yoosemitee. His battle-axe, Valleyforge, hung glistening from the pommel of his saddle, the blood fresh-scrubbed from its edge. He had slain too many soldiers in the war against the Gauls and American Natives and was glad to be going home.

I will never fight again, he thought, *but will return to the Mount of Vernon to become a surveyor and farmer*. There was no pursuit more important to any country than to improve its agriculture and its breed of useful animals. How he longed for the simple cares of a husbandman.

He brooded on the horrors of war, his dead comrades, and

the American Native maid, Pocahontas, whom he had loved. He loved her still, though she had betrayed him to the Gauls.

In his people's language his name, *General,* meant *pertaining in common to all,* and that was what he had become, a leader to the American tribes in Virginia. As a youth, an enchantment had been laid on him by the Wise Woman, Betsee Ross, the Star Weaver, that he could never tell a lie. Because of this, some called him "Honest Gen."

As the last rays of twilight turned the ancient American forest golden with dust and sent the shadows streaming east, he heard the cry of the hawk and the distant howls of wolves. He shivered uneasily. The sequoias rose all around, hundreds of feet tall, the trees the American Natives called the Silent Giants. His men had accompanied him through most of his journey, until he had chosen to shorten his trip by going through the woods. Even the bravest had refused to follow him then, for the forest was said to be haunted. At the time he had thought it just as well; he had wanted to be alone, to try to forget. He had intended to pass through the woods and into the safety of Virginia before nightfall, but weariness had overtaken both him and his mount, and in his brooding he had dawdled.

He dared ride no farther that night for fear of losing his way. Already shapes grew gray and indistinct. The howling of the wolves sounded nearer.

If I continue, I will lame Silver, he thought. He stroked the stallion's neck, then reined him to a stop. He dismounted, then led him forward a few paces, intending to make camp beneath one of the great trees. The shadows seemed to close around him.

The hoot of an owl overhead startled him. "My nerves are frayed," he muttered.

General removed Silver's bridle and saddle and let him go free. He was unconcerned about the stallion wandering off; the horse was loyal as a hound. Silver nickered uneasily, as if he, too, distrusted the woods.

"Easy, boy," General murmured automatically. Though he preferred traveling unseen through Yoosemitee, he needed to start a fire to ward off the wolves. Picking up twigs and dead limbs, he soon had enough wood to last the night.

He knelt with flint and steel. Sparks flew and a tiny flame sprang up. Before he could fan it into a full fire, Silver nickered again.

General looked up, then stood, his hand to Valleyforge. A spectral green light haloed the enormous tree trunk. Washington crept around it and looked across the forest floor.

A man approached, a tall, inhumanly broad figure carrying a lantern that glowed with an unearthly luminance. Washington felt his mouth go dry; his heart pounded against his chest, for he thought he recognized the intruder. He wanted to hide, but there was nowhere to go if the Pilgrim sought him. He drew Valleyforge and held it close.

The figure paused a few feet from Washington. The lantern light spread at General's feet, turning the ground emerald and olive.

"General Washington," the figure said, his voice a deep drawl. "I am Waynejon. Some call me the Pilgrim."

"Have you come for me?" General asked. Despite his best effort, his voice trembled.

The Pilgrim rumbled a laugh. "I'm not Death, if that's what you mean. I'm a man. I put my pants on one leg at a time."

Washington remained unconvinced. According to legend, the Pilgrim had died many times, but death could not keep him, for he was cursed to walk the earth until the end of the age because of an ancient wrong. He stood a head taller than Washington, who was a tall man himself, and wore a square, black hat with a buckle at its front, a black cloak, and ebony riding chaps. A black eye-patch covered one eye, and a rooster stood on his left shoulder. He carried an ancient blunderbuss.

"You look like you're getting ready to eat. If you'll share your fire, I have some salted beef in my pack."

General nodded, then finding his voice, tried to sound confident. "What brings you to the woods?"

"As a matter of fact, I've been looking for you."

✧ ✧ ✧

"AND THEN," WAYNEJON concluded, "the boys got the cattle to the railhead."

Washington laughed and sighed. The fire crackled warmly before the pair. They sat across from one another, the flames between them. In the last hour, General had lost most of his fear. "An excellent tale. Whatever happened to the lads?"

"They turned out to be good men, most of 'em. But they're all long gone to their reward on Boot Hill by now."

In the subsequent silence Washington asked, "Why were you looking for me?"

"You get to the point. I like that."

The Pilgrim took a drink of coffee from a tin cup, then gestured with it toward the woods. "This country, this new land, it's wild, untamed. It could be a great nation, different from any other, a place where people could come from all over the world. A place of freedom."

"We all want that. It's why my forefathers came."

"Mine did the same. They fled the dark realm of the Old World to escape the tyrants. But it's not enough, General. The people aren't free."

"We've driven the Gauls back to France."

"But you didn't get Bone Apart, the Skeleton Man."

Washington shrugged. "He escaped to Mexico. No American can cross the Rio Grande and live. An enchantment prevents it."

"He's done more than escape. He's made alliance with the Huns."

Washington drew a deep breath. This was bad news. The Huns, led by their leader, Hitler, the Wolf Prince, were a constant threat, raiding the coasts on their dragon-headed ships, striking and then fleeing. Was there never an end to peril?

"And it's not just Bone Apart and Hitler," Waynejon said. "There's a powerful wizard living in the dark regions of the Canadian north, whose heart is cold as the bitter winds that blow there. The Mounties can't stop him because he's conjured a giant from the Old World, tall as a mountain. They're climbing down the steep cliffs from the ice fields with their armies, preparing to march to York. The Huns, whose longships wait outside York Harbor, have promised the wizard great rewards if he helps them conquer America. The Gauls are reforming along the Rio Grande. We're in danger, General."

"What can we do?"

"Only the Words of Power in the iron box on Mount Rushmore can stop the giant. The titan has no strength against them."

"Mount Rushmore!" A chill ran along Washington's spine. "None have ever gone there and returned."

"It doesn't matter what others have done, General. I'm asking you."

"It was not my intention to seek further adventures."

"You gained a reputation in your battles against the Gauls."

"I heard bullets whistle, and believe me, there is something charming in the sound."

Waynejon laughed. "Sarcasm doesn't suit you."

"I meant none. By the miraculous care of Providence, I was protected beyond all human expectation, for I had four bullets through my coat and two horses shot under me, yet escaped unhurt. It was an exhilarating experience, but one I have little desire to repeat." He shook his head. "I fear you have chosen the wrong man."

"How do you figure?"

Washington hesitated, not wanting to say the words. "My men love me, but though we seem to return from the war in triumph, it isn't true, at least not for me. I was the one who began the war against Gaul, when I urged the Virginian governor, Dimwiddie, to build Fort Necessity at the joining of the Ohio and Allegheny rivers. Had we not confronted the Gauls there, the colonies might have been spared much bloodshed. There should have been another way.

"Under my leadership, we struck out to attack Fort Duquesne. Though I knew better, out of my own vanity, we went like soldiers on parade, for I thought our movements were unknown. In my pride, I had told our plans to. . . someone. . . I cared for deeply, someone who betrayed us. We were unexpectedly attacked by three thousand Gauls and American Natives, and though our numbers were nearly thrice their own, my men were struck with such a deadly panic that nothing but confusion and disobedience of orders prevailed amongst them. We broke and ran as sheep before the hounds. If Braggart had not reinforced us at the end, the final battle would have been lost. Braggart himself, a mighty commander, was wounded behind the shoulder and into the breast. He died three days after.

"No, Pilgrim. I, a failure in all I have undertaken, am not the man to perform this deed. You must place your trust elsewhere."

Waynejon took a long sip of coffee. "Seems to me that's the thing about this country, General. It's a land of second chances. Someone must go or America is lost."

Washington, who had ducked his head in shame, looked up into the Pilgrim's steady eyes, and for a long moment they held each other's gaze. Finally, General murmured, "If I make the attempt, who will help me?"

"Near the slopes of Rushmore waits the Iron Hewer. Go to him. He will show you the way."

Washington stared into the fire and sighed. War had found him again and he could not refuse. Human happiness and moral duty were inseparably connected. "I suppose it is easier to prevent an evil than to rectify mistakes," he said. "I will set out tomorrow morning."

"That's good. That's mighty fine." Waynejon set his tin cup down. "I have to be on my way. Thanks for the grub."

Without another word, the Pilgrim rose and strode into the woods, his broad back disappearing into the shadows. Washington shivered, feeling very much alone.

✧ ✧ ✧

FOR SEVEN DAYS General rode through the forest of Yoosemitee, and on the eighth reached the wheat-covered plains of Kansas. The whole earth shook with the pounding hooves of herds of buffalo pursued by the valiant Comanches, who looked dreadful in their war paint. To escape their notice—for they had no love of the white man—Washington hid himself among the amber waves of grain. At night, storm clouds built in the south and swept over the plains, the lightning tearing at the sky, the tumult of the thunder reminding Washington that should he survive Rushmore, he would have to face the wizard and his giant.

He crossed the country of Mount Ana, a stark land, all sky and earth, and came in the evening to the banks of the Little Bighorn, where sat a rider on a white horse caparisoned in midnight blue. The rider, too, who had a golden moustache and penetrating blue eyes, wore blue and gold, with a deep blue cape. His curling hair, falling down to the middle of his back, shone like ripe wheat in the sun. But Washington did not believe fine clothes necessarily made for fine men, any more than fine feathers made fine birds.

"Hurrah, good sir," the stranger called. "What brings you to the banks of the Bighorn?"

"I am Washington, who cannot tell a lie, a son of Virginia. I seek the Iron Hewer on the slopes of Rushmore."

"Then you seek death," the stranger replied. "I am Custard, named for the creamy white of my skin and my golden hair. I am called Arm Strong for my might, Lord of Horsemen, Captain of the Seventh Cavalry."

Washington perceived this Custard had no lack of vanity, though he was indeed a mighty warrior. But General said, "I have never been to Rushmore before. Perhaps, if you know the way?"

"Why do you want to go there?"

"I seek the Words of Power to defeat the Wizard of Canada."

Custard gave Washington a long look before replying. "I will take you at least part of the journey, though I cannot tarry long. I have unfinished business here. The Sioux have risen against me."

Washington nodded. "I thank you for your kindness."

Together the two set off toward Rushmore. Along the way, Arm Strong told tales of his many deeds. Though he listened politely, Washington found such boasting distasteful, for it had always been his motto to show his intentions through his works rather than his speech.

"And someday," Custard said, "I will be the President of all this country, from east to west, and men everywhere will praise my name."

"I am unfamiliar with the word, *president*," Washington said.

"Like a king, but even greater, presiding as judge over the land."

"Perhaps, if the Huns and Gauls can be driven back," Washington said, thoughtfully, "but even a president should answer to the people."

"The people should answer to their liege lord, not the other way around."

"That is the old way, the manner of royalty," Washington said, as he stared out at the endless horizon. "Like all the dark necromancy of the Old World, it should best be forgotten. It will not be like that here. The purpose of all government, as best promoted by the practice of virtuous policies, ought to be the aggregate happiness of society. As the Pilgrim told me, America should be a place where everyone has a voice."

"You have seen the Pilgrim?" Custard asked.

"Yes. He was the one who sent me."

Arm Strong fell silent then, and dared brag no more of his

own accomplishments.

After two days' travel they reached the Black Hills of Dakota, where they rode through the gloom of perpetual twilight and eternal shadows, for the sun never shone in that dismal country.

As they struggled through the gloaming, Washington spied a great eagle watching them from the back of the carcass of a bull buffalo, which the bird had apparently slain. As the travelers passed, General gave a respectful bow from his saddle and called out, "Greetings, Master of the Air. I see you will have a fine feast." But the eagle only watched the men with unwinking eyes.

That evening, they came to a valley ringed in jutting peaks, and had traveled only a short distance when a cold voice called to them from the heights. "Who dares trespass on the aeries of the eagles?"

High overhead, its talons clinging to the tallest peaks, stood an eagle twice the size of a stallion.

"I am Washington," General said, "with my companion Arm Strong, seeking passage to the Mount of Rushmore."

"This day we will surely break your bones," the eagle screeched, "for I am E. Perilous Union, mother of the eagles who make their homes both in the Peaks of Usps and the Mountains of the Moon."

Other, smaller eagles, lurking on the lesser crags encircling the travelers, raised their voices in agreement.

"Hear us, I beg you," General called, in as brave a tone as he could muster. "Spare us, not for ourselves, but for the sake of our mission, for we are on a journey for the freedom of our countrymen."

A ruffling of wings passed around the heights.

"Freedom!" E. Perilous cried. "Freedom! You speak the sacred word of the eagles. What is the meaning?"

"It is a word sacred to us as well," Washington replied.

"Mother," another eagle called across the heights. "Let us spare these men who speak of Freedom, for when I met them on the plains, the pale-faced one bowed and addressed me with respect."

"Is this so?" E. Perilous Union asked. "Tell us then, children of men, the purpose of your journey."

Washington did so, and when he was done, E. Perilous said, "We have heard of this evil wizard and despise his ways. Because my son, Apollo Leven, asks it, I will permit your passage. More, in the sacred name of Freedom, I will send him as your guide."

Washington and Custard thanked the mother of the eagles, and Apollo Leven lifted himself above the crags to accompany them.

As they continued through the Black Hills, wolves and evil spirits tried to destroy them, and more than once they battled for their lives, but Washington, his face grim and terrible to behold, fought with his great axe, Valleyforge, that shone silver in the darkness; and Arm Strong, wielding a golden blade, proved dreadful in combat. Apollo Leven strove beside them as well, and his terrible beak and talons slew many a foe.

The eagle led them true, and they finally saw Mount Rushmore looming in the distance, awful and majestic, a living monster shaped like a mountain with four heads. The heads were craggy and ill-formed, and shifted from side to side, guarding the treasure.

"The Iron Hewer lives at the base of Rushmore," Arm Strong said, "where the behemoth cannot reach him."

They came by twilight to a house made of iron. As they approached, a figure stepped out dressed in simple gray garments and bearing no arms. Around his bald head he wore a circlet with five silver stars that glistened in the dusk.

Washington expected to be challenged, but the man raised his hand in salute and gave a slow smile. "Welcome, strangers, and be at ease. I am Eisenhower Iron Hewer, but my friends call me Ike."

Washington found he liked Ike immediately, and the two travelers dismounted and introduced themselves. When General told Eisenhower why he had come, the Old Commander shrugged. "Though I have never liked war, I won't shirk from a fight, especially if Waynejon sent you."

From out of his larder, Eisenhower prepared a fine meal, though where he got his victuals Washington could not guess. Afterward, full and content, they sat before the hearth, drinking hot coffee and smoking tobacco from wooden pipes, listening to the wind whistling around the iron eaves, while Apollo Leven stood in a corner, his eyes reflecting golden in the flames.

"There is only one way to approach the creature," Ike said. "All its heads face south, except for the fourth one, which looks to the north. But that head is blind in one eye. If we're careful, we can creep up the northwestern slope. The box containing the Words of Power is hidden in a cave below the monster's chins. We'll know if it sees us, for its faces, which normally resemble rough stone, always take on the features of its victims."

"Can the monster be slain?" Custard asked.

"A single blow to the mountain's heart can kill the beast," Eisenhower replied, "if the warrior who delivers it is pure of soul."

"Who knows if such a man is among us?" Washington asked.

"I would like to try my hand at it," Custard said, "if the chance arises."

"Such a task is not for me," Eisenhower said. "I am unworthy. I've sent too many men to their deaths."

"Is that why you live here alone?" Custard asked. "A warrior such as yourself would be highly honored in York."

"I live here to serve and have had all the honors I need. I have led good men."

"You display great modesty," Washington said. "Humility must always be the portion of any man who receives acclaim earned in the blood of his followers and the sacrifices of his friends."

"I have not fought for such, sir," Custard said, "but for the glory of combat. You give me much to consider. Still I would like to set my good right arm against the monster."

"The Pilgrim sent me here many years ago, to act as a guide. There is a prophecy that one day a man will destroy the creature and use the Words of Power to preserve the land. I hope you are that one, but many have scaled those slopes. None have lived to tell of it."

"These are strange times," Washington said, "filled with magic."

"True," Ike replied, sagely, "but things are more like they are now than they have ever been before."

Washington nodded his head and stared into the fire. It was good to befriend a man of Ike's wisdom.

✧ ✧ ✧

THE THREE COMPANIONS rose with the morning light. They left

their horses in Eisenhower's stables and went on foot, angling toward the west, while Apollo Leven wheeled away to watch from a distance, lest his presence alert the four faces. If the monster saw them, it gave no sign. By midday they reached a region strewn with boulders, near enough that they could see the heads closely. Washington gaped up at them. Three faced toward the men, one away. They were large as houses, and all looked identical, with gray eyes, weather-beaten noses, and thin lines for mouths. Their guttural voices rose and fell as they murmured among themselves in an ancient tongue.

The travelers headed north until they came to a point behind the mount, where only the easternmost face kept watch, its left eye staring vacantly down the slope.

"We begin the assault here, just before sundown," Eisenhower said.

"Shouldn't we wait until dark?" Arm Strong asked.

"No. They see as well at night as in the day, but at twilight the setting sun will be in their eyes."

For three restless hours the companions waited for sunset, saying little, thinking of the coming encounter. Custard stared fixedly at the mount.

"Ike," Arm Strong finally said, "exactly where would the killing blow have to be struck? I cannot rightly determine the location of the beast's heart."

Eisenhower pointed. "There, just between the two central heads. Front or back makes no difference."

"And the Words of Power?" Washington asked.

"A few yards farther down in a narrow cave. It's hard to see from here."

"You have guided us well," Washington said. "You need not accompany us."

"I don't have to, but I will. I've always stood with anyone who made the attempt."

When the sun was still three finger-widths above the horizon, Eisenhower ordered the travelers to move out. They crept between the boulders, keeping always to the blind side of the head, and were soon scrambling up the mountain slope. Pine trees provided concealment until they were two-thirds of the way up, but after that the mount lay barren.

Washington's heart pounded in his chest as he climbed. He

tried not to look up at the terrible face above him. At first, he could not see the cave, but then he spied it, a narrow opening half-covered by an overhanging shelf. If they could reach it, the head would be unable to see them.

Abruptly, the terrible visage turned with the sound of rock scraping on stone, and the three flattened themselves against the boulders, scarcely daring to breathe. For a moment the good eye swept along the slope, but the sunlight blinded it, making it squint and look away. The men kept climbing.

Custard was the first to reach the cave, and he helped the others under the protection of the ledge. They clapped one another on the back and turned toward the opening.

It was little more than a niche in the rocks, and Washington searched only a short while before finding the iron box set in a recess. It proved neither long nor heavy, and he drew it out easily and opened the lid, which needed no lock with such a terrible monster guarding it. Within lay a brown parchment.

"The Words of Power," Washington whispered. He placed the scroll within his breast pocket and slipped the box back into its place.

"Have any ever come this far before?" Custard asked softly.

"Only two," Ike said. "Their bones are strewn across the slope."

Shuddering at Eisenhower's words, Washington told the Old Commander to lead them back down.

They were nearly to the tree line again before Washington realized Custard was not behind him. He turned to discover Arm Strong ascending the mount. General clutched Eisenhower's shoulder and pointed to their comrade.

"That vain-glorious fool!" Eisenhower hissed.

Reaching the region above the monster's heart, Custard raised his sword high above his head, shouting, "Die, beast, in the name of Arm Strong, Captain of the Seventh Cavalry!"

He looked magnificent at that moment, his cape billowing, his golden hair sweeping back behind his head, the last rays of the sun glinting on his blade. With all his power, he thrust downward.

The sword snapped beneath the weight of the blow, leaving Custard gaping at it in astonishment.

A scraping noise filled the heavens as all four of the monster's heads swiveled toward the captain. General gasped, for the faces had transformed into the features of Custard, Washington, and Eisenhower. Only the head with the blind eye remained unchanged.

The air filled with roaring as the heads screamed their rage. The whole mount trembled as vast arms rose from either side, reaching toward Custard.

"Let's go!" Eisenhower ordered. "He won't make it."

"No!" Washington cried, handing Ike the parchment. "Take it and flee!"

General did not hear Eisenhower's reply; he was already sprinting toward Custard, Valleyforge unsheathed. Though it had taken several minutes to creep down the mount, he ascended in seconds and was beside Arm Strong as the giant arms groped toward both of them. Washington saw his own face, filled with hatred, glowering down upon him.

Do I really look like that? he thought. *My nose seems so large.*

At that moment, Apollo Leven streaked from the sky to harrow the faces with his talons. But the action bought the men only an instant before the rocks erupted around them, lifting them off the ground and sending them sprawling down the incline. Custard's expression was wild, but he held a knife in his hand as he rolled to his feet. Washington scrambled back toward the mountain's heart, axe upraised, staring straight into his own seething eyes.

The mount rippled beneath him, but as he fell he brought his axe down on his target with all his strength. He expected nothing but the destruction of his weapon, followed by his own death, but Valleyforge cut easily through the rock.

The whole mount screamed, a deafening blast. Blood rilled from the wound, covering General in ichor. He rolled on his back and saw the faces above him, including his own, writhing in their death struggles. He watched himself expire, the light leaving the eyes, the head lolling downward.

The mountain shuddered and sank. The four dead faces stared across the plain.

For a moment, Washington could hear nothing, but finally Custard's voice came to him, as the captain helped him up. "You have shamed me, sir, and saved my life. I am forever in your debt."

Reaching them, Eisenhower fell to his knees before Washington. "You are the one," Ike cried, taking the circlet of five stars from his forehead and casting it at Washington's feet. "The one who was to come. You have ended my vigil. Accept my service. Wherever you go, I will go also, and will serve you until my death."

"I, too, will follow you," Custard said, though he did not kneel. "Accept my service as well, General."

Scarcely understanding their words, Washington stared up at his defeated foe. "But how?" he exclaimed. "How could a failure such as I be worthy to destroy the beast when Arm Strong could not?"

Apollo Leven glided to a landing and placed his large head under General's hand. "Do not question the turn of events, Washington Paleface, but accept the fealty of these men, and mine as well, for I also would follow you."

Still overwhelmed, Washington laid his hands on the shoulders of the two men. "I do not understand, nor know where this will lead, but I cannot refuse the service of such brave warriors, nor of this great eagle. Now rise. We have a giant to kill."

"Another?" Ike asked.

They spent the night in Eisenhower's house, where Washington cleaned the blood from himself and his garments. In the morning they left Rushmore far behind, and the four dead heads gaped at them to the edge of the horizon.

✧ ✧ ✧

THEY RODE ONCE more across the darkness of the Black Hills, and as they went Eisenhower asked, "General, why did you go back for Custard? You had the scroll. If you and I had died, there would have been no one to stop the wizard."

"I could not leave him behind."

"If a commander thinks expending ten thousand lives will save twenty thousand later, it is up to him to do it."

"Custard was not ten thousand, but one," Washington said. "And though you have a point, I labor to keep alive in my breast that little spark of celestial fire called Conscience. I could not desert him and live with myself."

They passed back into Mount Ana, where Custard seemed to

grow increasingly nervous. At last they came once more to the banks of the Bighorn River, where they topped a hill and found a giant American Native standing before them. Behind him sat a creature with the head of a stallion and another with the head of a bull.

"I am Bitter Gall," the native said. "The appointed time is come." He raised his arms and hundreds of warriors appeared over the hills, dressed in feathers and skins, war-paint covering their fierce faces.

Sweat broke across Arm Strong's brow, but he said nothing.

"What do you want?" Washington asked.

"Your people have sinned and there must be death," the sitting bull said.

"I have done it!" Arm Strong burst forth. "I am not what you think me, General. I admit it, now. I have shed the blood of children. I spoke before of unfinished business. Long ago, it was prophesied that I would meet my death by the banks of the Little Bighorn. I hoped to redeem myself in the slaying of Rushmore, but I failed there, too."

"Only one life is required," the stallion said. "One of you three. But none shall pass until the deed is done."

"I have accepted the fealty of this man," Washington said, "and I cannot tell a lie. I am responsible for him. I will accept the punishment in his stead."

For a moment, Arm Strong's eyes became crafty. But he looked at Washington and shook his head. "No, General. I have been a villain, but you returned for me on Mount Rushmore when I would not have done the same for you. You must live to fight the wizard. My fate is sealed. You have shown me the way to restore my honor, and I will go with the sun shining on my face."

Custard bowed low to Washington, then strode down the hill toward Bitter Gall, passing out of the story and into history. But Washington wondered if someday, he, too, would have to pay for the deaths of so many of his men in the battle of Fort Duquesne.

✧ ✧ ✧

WASHINGTON AND EISENHOWER, grieving at Custard's loss, made their way through the forest of Yoosemitee, where they had many adventures. At last they came to York, a city of magnificent spires. Others heard of Washington's heroism on Mount Rushmore, and warriors came to him offering him their service, so that he gathered a group of America's finest around him. Of these, Lafayette DeGaul was one of the greatest. Though a Gaul, he had vowed to follow Washington when General had saved his life many years before and had been with him through the Gaul and American Native War.

"Mon General," Lafayette said, "it is good to see your face. The wizard, accompanied by his giant, approaches the city and is encamped beyond the banks of the Mighty Delaware. Those sent to stop it have been smashed to bits. I was just preparing to go myself, to die for the cause of freedom."

DeGaul was a wild-eyed man, with a moustache and plumed hat. Until he met Washington, he had been a member of the famous Musketeers, who had fought against the powers of darkness and evil in the Old World.

Washington assembled his company, which had grown to over five hundred men, just inside the gates of York. As he looked upon them, despair ran through him, for they were poorly armored and had little supplies, the Hun's blockade of the harbor preventing needed goods from entering the city. Despite his reservations, he drew a deep breath and addressed them briefly, explaining the situation.

He ended with: "The time is now near at hand which must determine whether Americans are to be Freemen or Slaves. The fate of untold millions will now depend, under God, on the courage and conduct of this army. Our cruel and unrelenting enemy leaves us no choice but a brave resistance or the most abject submission; this is all we can expect. We have, therefore, to resolve to conquer or die."

The men gave a ragged cheer while Apollo Leven wheeled and cried overhead.

Knowing how few warriors he had, Washington ordered a special surprise in the form of large, mysterious crates loaded onto the supply wagons.

As they rode out through the gates of York toward the Canadian Ice Fields, a crowd assembled to watch them go, young women pinning flowers and kisses on the warriors. Washington was approached by one of the most beautiful ladies he had ever seen, with pouting lips and eyes that flashed like fireworks. Her dark hair flared long and wild over a necklace hung with wooden teeth, suspended over a dress of forest green. She handed him a red, white, and blue standard covered with thirteen stars and stripes.

"Take this, General," she said, "and fight for York. The Star Weaver herself has enchanted it, washing it in the tears she sheds for those who die beneath the titan's heels. Tie it to your axe-handle in your moment of need, and its magic will give your blade power."

He reached down from the heights of Silver's back to take the cloth. Their hands and eyes met. "What is your name?" he asked.

"Martha Custis."

"I thank you for this," Washington said.

She smiled and watched him ride away.

"She is a beauty, that one," Lafayette said.

"There is no time for such things," Washington replied, but his hand felt warm where she had touched it, and he raised the standard high.

✧ ✧ ✧

FOR THREE DAYS the company traveled north, and by the second afternoon icy winds began to blow. Snow flurried at evening, and the warriors soon rode through banks of white. It was bitterly cold, and Washington's men lacked sufficient clothing.

By midafternoon the company reached the edge of a valley, where ran the Mighty Delaware River. In the vale's center stood the giant, Britannia the Great, hundreds of feet tall, an enormous creature with the face of a woman, wearing a crown and carrying a heavy mace that it used to pound the earth. Wherever it walked or struck, it flattened houses, fields, and living things, a brutality that came to be known as the Stamp Act. The wizard stood upon the titan's shoulders, and an army of ten thousand red-clad warriors followed behind.

"How can we face them?" Lafayette asked.

"I have a plan," General said. "But the Words of Power will not work unless the monster hears them, so I must be very close. We will wait until nightfall."

The snow fell harder as evening progressed. The men carried

half-shrouded lanterns, but it was still difficult to see through the storm. Everyone shivered with the cold, but Washington led them to the banks of the Delaware, accompanied by the wagon filled with the mysterious crates. They found boats upon the shore, left there at Washington's request by his American Native friend, Massasoit. In the dead of night, scarcely able to find their way, the company crossed the torrent of the Mighty Delaware, Washington standing upright, holding the red, white, and blue banner before him. He shivered from more than the cold, knowing that if the wizard or Britannia discovered them upon the waters, they would be doomed.

After a long hour, they reached the farther shore. Washington divided the men into three sections under the command of Eisenhower Iron Hewer, Ulysses Grant, and Benedict Arnold, three of his greatest warriors. Giving them their orders, General turned to Lafayette. "The rest is up to us, I fear. Come with me." Washington took the banner Martha Custis had given him and tucked it beneath his cloak.

Together, the two comrades crept toward the titan, whose gigantic form blocked the stars. They slipped through the sentries, then waited until moonrise. As the first rays lit the land, Lafayette called in a loud voice just outside the tent of the Wizard Cornwallis. "Come out, great magician, for we have seen your might and know we have no chance against you. Come and accept our surrender."

The sentries around Cornwallis's camp leapt to their feet, but Lafayette drew his bow and covered them. "Stand back, my friends. We surrender to Cornwallis alone." As the guards hesitated, the wizard appeared at the tent door, a dazzling lantern in his hand. Lafayette lowered his weapon.

The wizard wore a bulky red robe and a white, pointed hood, which allowed only his dark eyes to show. His voice was grating as he spoke. "Who dares interrupt the slumber of Cornwallis, Grand Wizard of the Empire?"

"It is I, Lafayette DeGaul, with the great General Washington, who asks you to accept his surrender."

The giant, Britannia, gave a low rumble and raised its mace, but Cornwallis bid it stay its hand.

"Why do you come slinking to me in darkness?" Cornwallis demanded.

"We came as quickly as we could, to end the bloodshed, for who knows what this behemoth of yours will do?" Lafayette replied.

Cornwallis laughed. "I almost believe it. How like your people, the wretched refuse of the Old World, vermin sent to pollute these fair shores, fit to be nothing but slaves. When York is overthrown, I will show you how such should be treated."

"We are willing to do as you say," Lafayette said through gritted teeth. "Only accept our surrender."

"I have heard of you, Washington. It is said you cannot tell a lie. Answer me then, Commander, is that truly why you have come? I will believe it from your lips."

Washington dared not answer, knowing the truth would spring unbidden from his mouth.

"I thought so," Cornwallis said, signaling to the giant.

"Scatter!" Washington ordered.

The Americans moved just in time to avoid a shattering blow as Britannia brought its mace down with all its force. The impact tossed Washington off his feet, but even before he hit the ground he was unrolling the scroll containing the Words of Power, for this had all been part of his plan to bring the giant close to the earth in striking. Landing, Washington sprang up and began reading in a mighty voice.

At the first word, everything seemed to freeze in place as if time had stopped. Britannia remained immobile as Washington spoke:

We hold these truths to be self-evident, that all men are created equal, that they are endowed by their Creator with certain unalienable rights, that among these are Life, Liberty, and the Pursuit of Happiness. That to secure these rights. . .

On and on Washington read, his voice growing stronger with the reading, his delight rising as he saw the wizard and the giant both helpless against the words. He raised his arms as he ended: *And for the support of this Declaration, with a firm reliance on the Protection of Divine Providence, we mutually pledge to each other*

our Lives,

our Fortunes,

and our sacred Honor.

The moment General finished, Cornwallis fell to his knees. When he tried to rise, Lafayette, with the speed of thought, raised his bow and placed an arrow through the wizard's evil heart.

"Liberty, Equality, Fraternity!" Lafayette cried.

Britannia gave a terrible scream, for the Words of Power began to turn its feet to stone. Snarling, it fled toward the south, stomping away on increasingly clumsy members.

A roar rose from the valley's edge as hundreds of fireworks, the contents of the mysterious crates, were released at once. The sky erupted in red, white, and blue flares as Eisenhower, Grant, and Arnold led the Americans toward the Red Army, which milled in confusion, stunned at being attacked from a direction they thought safe.

"The giant!" Washington cried. "It heads toward York."

Washington and Lafayette captured two of their enemies' horses and sped after the titan, but the mounts could not keep up. As soon as they reached their camp, Washington leapt off his steed and onto Silver, who stood waiting for his master, impatiently pawing the earth.

"Go on!" Lafayette shouted to Washington. "Go on, Mon General! I will catch up."

Faster than the wind, Silver ran, while Washington kept his eyes upon the giant. But when he reached the banks of the Mighty Delaware, General found the titan had already crossed. He nearly despaired until Apollo Leven streaked out of the sky and landed before him.

"You must ride upon my back," the eagle screeched.

Still bearing the banner Martha Custis had given him, Washington climbed in front of Apollo Leven's wings. The eagle took a single bound and streaked over the great river.

Yet fast as they were, the monster strode far ahead. It steadily approached the gates of York, dwarfing the city's gleaming spires. Washington was still some distance behind it as it raised its mace, preparing to sweep the metropolis away.

In desperation, General lifted Valleyforge and tied the banner to its pommel. As he let it fly, the weapon streaked toward the giant, the flag streaming behind, and as it flew it grew, powered by the flag's enchantment. It struck Britannia full in the back, and the monster writhed away, stumbling as it went, its massive feet missing the gates of York.

In its frenzy, it thrashed into the water. Most of its lower body was stone, and it moved with awkward, hesitant jerks.

Crossing the bay, it pulled itself onto a massive rock rising out of the harbor. By the time it reached the top, its waist had turned to stone, leaving it unable to move its legs. The effect crept up its body. It raised its enormous mace in defiance and turned its face toward the sea, looking for its home across the waters.

Washington's axe, returned to its former size, fell from the giant's back and clattered down the rocks.

✧ ✧ ✧

WITH THE GIANT and the wizard destroyed, the Red Army, thinking the fireworks the beginning of an enormous assault, fled in terror. Washington returned to his men and led them back into the city in triumph, the whole company singing *When General comes marching home again*. Washington was declared a great hero. Some wanted to make him king, but he refused, remembering Custard's words of a new office of *president*.

He recalled what the Pilgrim had said as well and realized that America was indeed a place of second chances.

The Gauls retreated from Mexico, and Hitler drew his boats back across the sea. Although Washington searched through all of York for many weeks, he found no sign of Martha Custis, nor anyone who knew her. However, he did find his axe with the flag still tied to its pommel, on the shores of the rock where the giant stood.

Afterward, a great Convention was held in honor of Washington's victory. A tremendous plan was conceived to build an enormous door, gilded with gold, across York harbor, to prevent the Huns from ever attacking again.

There was talk of tearing down the stone titan, but Lafayette had the last word. "Let it rather be a symbol, this vanquished foe. And we will call it Lady Liberty, for with its defeat we have won our freedom."

Being a poet as well as a warrior, in mockery of the words the wizard had spoken, Lafayette etched the following lines upon the base of the rock where the giant stood:

Give me your tired, your poor,
Your huddled masses yearning to breathe free,
The wretched refuse of your teeming shore,

Send these, the homeless, tempest-tossed to me,
I lift my lamp beside the golden door!

The Convention ordered a flame lit atop the statue's mace that became a torch burning across the waters, so bright it could be seen from the shores of the Old World. And when the kings and emperors of that shadowy realm looked upon it, they trembled.

✧ ✧ ✧

AFTERWORD

IDEAS COME TO writers in unpredictable ways. In the case of *The Battle of York,* two sources converged for me. I read a satirical story—*Letter from a Higher Critic* by Stewart Robb—in an old *Analog 6* Science Fiction anthology, in which a future scholar uses Higher Literary Criticism to prove that World War II never happened. I was also reading about the controversy surrounding *The Poems of Ossian,* the lost heroic literature of the Gaels of Scotland "discovered" by James Macpherson in 1762, now believed to be his clever forgeries. These two influences suggested the question of how American history would be remembered if we lost all record of it.

Much of the dialogue and thoughts of Washington and Eisenhower are taken from actual quotations spoken by those two American heroes. The idea of adding the eagles and George Washington's wooden teeth came from editor Gordon Van Gelder.

Since it's publication in the *Magazine of Fantasy and Science Fiction, The Battle of York* has become my most reprinted story, appearing in Eos Books' *Year's Best SF 10, Lightspeed Magazine,* and most recently, in a Spark and Fizz Books anthology. The short story would later become part of the mythology of my novel, *Liberty Bell and the Last American.*

THE PERFECT DAY

A LADYBUG WAS crawling on his ear. At least, Billy hoped it was a ladybug. If it was a wasp, he would probably get stung. He wanted to reach up and find out for sure, but that might be the wrong thing to do, so he pretended to concentrate on his *Tommy Tomorrow* comic book. Maybe if he kept reading he would forget about the ladybug (surely it wasn't a wasp; the feet felt too close together).

That reminded him of his own feet, which were caked with bits of mud from his earlier romp through the sprinkler. He wiggled his toes experimentally and felt the half-dried ooze crumble away in parts. He grinned and leaned back against the trunk of the Chinese elm. With his eyes closed he could better hear the rushing of the hot Kansas wind through the branches above, but he was safe and comfortable in the tree's shade. Sanctuary. Cool warmth.

Keith Taylor would be over soon. The two boys had been planning the occasion for nearly a week. As Billy stared out across the distant heat waves passing between himself and the ripening fields of wheat, he clapped his hands in anticipation. It had been a good day so far, the perfect afternoon, and he and Keith were to be allowed to camp out in the backyard that night. Billy had saved a half-dozen sparklers from the Fourth of July, and they were to be part of the evening festivities, along with the hot dogs and ice cream his mother had promised.

The ladybug flew away while he was thinking, but he didn't notice until it was already gone. He had decided to walk out to the billboard located in the field beside his house; it gave a better view of the highway, and he could watch for the red Rambler station wagon Keith's mother always drove. His dog, Sam, deserted the bone he had been chewing to accompany his master. Sam was gold and white, too small to be a real collie and too lanky to be a terrier. The boy half-skipped his way toward the sign, Sam leading and alert for rabbits and field mice. Billy became more cautious as he came to the heads of golden wheat. His dad had warned him often enough not to go trampling Mr. Kinney's crop. The boy slid carefully between the rows and made Sam follow him.

He was nearly to the billboard when he noticed a small cloud just peeping over the southern horizon. A frown crossed his face.

"That kinda bothers me, Sam. Sure hope it doesn't rain to-night."

The dog was inspecting a suspicious burrow and didn't seem to hear, so Billy continued toward the billboard. Someone had recently covered up the old ad with a shiny red *Phillips 66* slogan. It was real neat. Billy was proud because he thought of it as *his* billboard, it being the only one along the highway for several miles. It was tall and long, huge up close. When he reached it, he sat down in its shade and began digging clods out of the field to throw into the drainage ditch.

Each time a vehicle topped the distant hill, he studied it. A truck passed, and a bus, then a green Chevrolet pickup with a German shepherd riding in the back. Then the road was vacant for a long time.

"Sure hope it doesn't rain, Sam," Billy said again. "Wish Keith would get here."

Four more cars passed before Billy caught sight of the red Rambler. He jumped up and ran waving toward home, Sam close to his heels, and managed to intercept the car half-way down the long dirt drive that circled the house. The two boys met in a rush and immediately headed toward the garage to dust off the tent, leaving Keith's mother to make arrangements for her son's return the next day.

✧ ✧ ✧

THE BOYS STEPPED back to survey their handiwork.

"It doesn't look just right," Keith said.

"It's pretty close, though."

"They never look that way on *Rat Patrol.*"

The tent had a definite sag in the middle, and the stakes on the right side were pulled tighter than those on the left.

"Dad can help us when he gets home," Billy said.

Something made him turn just then toward the south. The cloud he had noticed earlier had been joined by a handful of others. These were darker than the first.

At about the same time, a car came over the hill, looking for all the world as if it had popped out of one of those clouds. Billy watched the onrushing auto and tried to make out its color. From a distance it looked the same hue as the gray of the approaching rainstorm.

"What's the matter?" Keith asked. "How come you look so scared?"

"I ain't scared. I'm just watching that car."

"What about it?"

The vehicle activated its left blinker and came up the drive. Billy had never seen anything like it. It was real long and fancy, and sort of funny-looking, like something out of a comic book. And it wasn't gray. It was black. Coffin black. Outer space black.

It stopped short of the house. It was impossible to see inside it; the windows were black, too, but pretty soon the one on the driver's side rolled down, accompanied by a funny electric hum. A gloved hand reached out and beckoned the boys.

"Come over here, lads," a deep, raspy voice said.

The two complied, though Billy kept a pace behind Keith. They were right next to the car before they could see the driver, and when they did Billy almost ran away. He would have, if his friend hadn't spoken.

"Hi, mister. Who are you?"

"Libby's the name. You must be Keith."

The man was like the vehicle itself, made more of blackness than anything else. The whole right side of his face was shadow. Deep darkness. It covered his features, so Billy could barely see his eyes. His nose was sharp and cruel, and he had a black moustache that curled around into two tight circles above his mouth. He wore a tall hat, which cast most of the shadows. It was a top hat, like the ringmaster at a circus might wear, except it, too, was black. He was wearing some sort of riding cloak.

"Billy, don't you know who I am?" Mr. Libby asked.

Billy had trouble finding his voice. He tried not to look at the dark face or think about the rasping voice. He looked out toward the gathering storm. "Yeah, I know. You're the Shadow Man."

"Why do you call me that, Billy?"

The boy shrugged and took a step away from the car.

"How would you lads like to ride in my new automobile?" the Shadow Man asked.

"Wow! That'd be neat!" Keith said.

Billy looked at his friend in horror. Didn't Keith see how evil the Shadow Man was? Couldn't he tell? "We better not," he said hurriedly. "My folks told me never to ride with people I don't know."

"But you know me, Billy. I'm from the Syntaps Company. You've surely heard of it."

"No, mister, I haven't. You must be confused or something. Me and Keith got to go now."

"Stay awhile and talk. It won't hurt."

"We gotta go!" Billy yelled and sped off toward the back of the house.

Bewildered, Keith followed. "What's with you?" he demanded, when he caught up with his friend.

"You some kind of dope or something? Didn't you see his hat and moustache? Don't you recognize a bad man when you see one?"

"You're crazy," Keith said. "He wasn't wearin' no hat. And he didn't have a moustache."

"He must be a magician, then. He's got you fooled. He's a bad man, and he's come to take me away!"

"He looked all right, more like a salesman, but if you want to pretend he's the bad guy, it's okay with me. This tent can be our fortress where we plan how to stop him."

The car had pulled up to Billy's house, and the Shadow Man stepped out. Sam barked at him and nipped at his heels as he went up to the door, but the Shadow Man wore heavy, black boots.

"He'll get mom!" Billy cried, but he didn't dare take a step toward the house. He was too afraid. For long, awful moments he waited out in the yard while Keith tried to straighten the tent.

After a short time, Billy's mother stepped from the house. The relieved boy ran to her, but he skidded to a halt when she said, "Billy, there's a man here to see you."

He tried to back towards the tent, but she already had a hold on his hand. "Ma, me and Keith were playin'."

"Well, you'll have to stop your play for a minute."

Billy was led into the house. Inside, the kitchen was filled with the aroma of chocolate chip cookies, but he scarcely noticed. His stomach was crawling.

The Shadow Man sat on the couch in the living room.

"Billy, I want you to meet Mr. Libby. He works with Doug Randell, your scout leader."

"I've heard a lot about you, Billy. Mr. Randell has nominated you for a special Order of the Arrow camping trip. It will include a tour of Washington D.C."

"I don't want to go! I want to stay right here."

"Billy!" his mother warned.

"Let me talk with him, Mrs. Martin. He probably doesn't understand the offer."

The last thing Billy wanted was to be left alone with the Shadow Man. He looked huge sitting there, dark as darkness. But it was too late. His mother had already retreated. When she was out of earshot, the Shadow Man leaned toward him and said quietly in his harsh voice, "Billy, I haven't much time. Deep down I think you know why I've come all the way to Kansas."

"To take me away," the boy whispered. "Forever."

"Now, Billy, maybe not forever. You can always come back and visit. Syntaps might allow that. It's my job to fetch you, and I've come through a great deal of danger to do it."

"You won't! My dad won't let you."

"Your parents have nothing to do with this, Billy. It's between you and me. You must decide to come back with me. People are depending on you."

"What people?"

"Many, many people. Those at Syntaps, others you have known. Do you remember, Billy Martin?"

"What if I decide not to go? This is my home."

"Billy, we no longer have the power to remove you. We lost that. That's why I've been sent, to reason with you. Please, you must leave with me. I'm not even certain I can find my way out alone."

"That's a lie, I'll bet. You better leave me alone, mister, or my dad'll knock you flat."

"I'll tell you what, Mr. Martin, why don't you enjoy the afternoon. Go play. We will talk again this evening."

The Shadow Man's last words didn't matter much because Billy had already bolted for the door. He skidded through the kitchen and plunged outside. His mother's call echoed behind him, but he pretended not to hear.

A few moments later the Shadow Man left the house, got in his car, and drove away.

"Looks like your worries are over," Keith said.

Billy watched the vanishing cloud of dust and shook his head.

✧ ✧ ✧

DURING THE REMAINDER of the afternoon, the two boys played army. Billy had nearly forgotten about the Shadow Man when he noticed the storm clouds had drawn nearer. They were rolling fiercely and covered the southern sky.

About the same time Keith pointed toward the billboard. The Shadow Man was there, standing in its shade. Watching. His car was nowhere in sight. They watched him until Billy's mother called them in for supper. The hot dogs were ready, and while the pair ate, Billy's dad drove up in the company car. Billy jumped from his chair and rushed into his father's arms.

"Dad, Dad! You gotta stop the Shadow Man. He's come to get me!"

"Whoa, son," Mr. Martin said, lifting the boy up. "What's all this about?"

"*I'll* tell your father about Mr. Libby," Mrs. Martin said.

"No! He's got mom fooled. Let me!"

"Billy, that will be all!" his mother said. "You've embarrassed me about enough for the day! Now I want you to go eat right this minute! Let's go in the living room, Poppa, and I'll tell you how your son has been acting."

After a few moments quiet discussion, Billy's father came out of the living room and went outside.

"Dad will recognize the Shadow Man. You'll see," he whispered to Keith.

Billy couldn't resist peeking out the screen door. When he did, he saw his father shaking hands with the Shadow Man. Both were smiling and talking. Billy moaned.

When Mr. Martin came back, his expression was stern, but his eyes were twinkling. "I'm proud of you, son. Mr. Libby is giving you quite an honor. Wouldn't you like to go to Washington D.C. with a bunch of other scouts? You could see where the president lives."

"Dad, he won't ever let me come back. Didn't you see how bad he was?"

"What kind of games have you boys been playing? What makes you think Mr. Libby is a bad man?"

"I just know it, Daddy! I just know! He'll carry me off and I'll never see any of you again!"

"Now listen, Billy. I don't know where you got such an idea. Your mother called your scoutmaster, and he said he had contacted Mr. Libby."

"Mom couldn't have called Mr. Randell!" Billy insisted.

"What do you mean, son, couldn't?"

A thick silence fell upon the room, broken only by Sam, who was at the screen door whimpering. Billy felt as if he stood over a great emptiness. Tears started to flow down his cheeks. "She just couldn't, that's all," he muttered, staring down at his feet.

"Now, none of that. Let's act like a man, son. I'll make a deal with you. You go outside and play now, but you think about this trip. I believe when you see what Mr. Libby is offering, you may change your mind."

After dinner, Mr. Martin brought out the bucket for making homemade ice cream. Billy and Keith helped crush the ice, and both boys took turns turning the crank until it got so hard that even together they couldn't budge it. Billy's dad took over, and while the ice cream was making, he allowed them to light up their sparklers.

For a time Billy forgot his worries beneath the glow of the forgotten gaudies from Independence Day. The boys ran in circles in the yard, each carrying a pair of sparklers, while Sam chased them, barking, his animal eyes glowing with the flames. The lights twirled until both boys were breathless and dizzy, but they ran around and around the house, laughing and chasing one another. In the end, with all their torches extinguished, they began to wrestle. The darkness held only their gasping giggles, as they took turns throwing each other to the grass.

Finally, Billy had Keith pinned, and both were too out of breath to continue. Or to move. They were sweat and grass, the pumping of lungs, and sweet laughter. They shook hands and went to check the ice cream.

They sat with their backs to a tree, eating their chocolate swirl. Billy was full, happy, and tired. Sam nuzzled his elbow, and the crickets sang beneath the umbrella of the Milky Way. He didn't notice that most of the stars were covered with cloud.

"This has been the best day, the most perfect day." Keith said.

Billy nodded and let Sam lick his face. "Yeah, I know. I wish it would last forever."

✧ ✧ ✧

"ARE YOU BOYS certain you wouldn't rather stay inside tonight?" his mother asked as they bundled their sleeping bags into the tent. "It looks like rain."

"We don't mind," Billy said. "Now that dad has the tent up straight, it should keep us dry."

"Well, if it starts to lightning, you better come in."

"Leave the boys alone, Eloise," his dad said. "Lightning won't strike a tent. They'll be fine."

"Thanks, Mr. Martin," Keith said, as they wormed their way into the comfortable darkness. Once Sam and the sleeping bags were comfortably situated, Billy hung one of the flashlights from the roof of the tent.

"This is neat!" Keith said.

"Yeah. Hey, you want to play *Submarine Fleet*?"

"Sure. That's a keen game."

Billy had stowed the board game in the tent earlier in the day, and they dug the contents out of the box eagerly. The game involved the capturing of submarines, and the children became quickly lost in the play.

"Dive, dive, dive," Keith called as an imaginary torpedo barely missed one of his boats. "Hey, Billy, you think the Shadow Man is still outside?" As quickly as he said it, a bit of fear touched his eyes.

"Yeah, but I don't want to talk about it. Okay?"

"You don't think he'll try to take you away while we're asleep, do you?"

Just then, the thunder rolled overhead, and the boys both jumped.

"Let's play some more, Keith. He can't come get me. He said so. I have to agree to go with him."

"But what if you don't agree?"

"It's your move. Just play the game, all right?"

✧ ✧ ✧

AFTER *SUBMARINE FLEET*, they got in their sleeping bags and started playing flashlight tag, a game of chase using the two beams of light as men and the roof of the tent as the field. Around and around the bright hunters went, and by the time they were through, Billy and Keith were giggling and sleepy.

Billy put aside all thoughts of the Shadow Man, despite the thunder and falling rain outside the tent. It had been a long day, and he fell asleep quickly.

When he awoke, the door of the tent had come unzipped. Cold rain was blowing on his face. He caught a glimpse of Keith during a lightning flash, but his friend was still asleep. He was afraid but decided to be brave and shut the flap.

Just when he was about to bring the zipper down, the lightning flashed again. He saw a split-second of clouds and grass. And he saw the Shadow Man standing beneath the old Chinese elm a few feet from the tent. Just standing. And watching, while the rain ran off his hat.

Billy wanted to close the flap, but for some reason he didn't. Sam had risen to join him and began to softly whine. He petted the animal. Then, with sudden resolve, he dressed and went out to meet the Shadow Man. Sam followed.

The Shadow Man was even more horrible in the night. He stood with his unwinking eyes and his darkness. The rain seemed to lessen as Billy approached him.

"Billy," the hoarse voice said. "It's nearly midnight. Do you know what that means?"

"No," Billy quavered. "The end of the day, I guess."

"Yes. Do you remember what Syntaps is, Mr. Martin?"

"Sorta. And don't call me Mr. Martin. I don't like it."

"I will tell you, Mr. Martin. Syntaps was created just a few years ago. Brain cell manipulation is used extensively as part of its work. Do you understand?"

Billy shook his head desperately.

"I think you do. You've known from the moment I arrived here, at least subconsciously. Billy, Syntaps offers people incredible vacations. Syntaps taps into memories, locates those areas that hold the individual's most wonderful fantasies or their most precious remembrances. Now do you see?"

"I won't. I won't! You're a wicked man!"

"Only because you see me that way. You've put me in this form, the shadowy figure of a cartoon villain. You know it's true. If this were real, do you believe your parents would let me stand in the rain all night? They can react only as you recall them, slightly different if I impose my presence on them as I did this afternoon.

"You have to face it, Billy. Your mother and father have been dead for over fifteen years. This is just a vacation."

Billy tried to run, but Libby caught him by the arm, causing the boy to stumble. He fell on the wet grass, his arms clutching at Sam. "Leave me alone. *Leave me alone!*"

"I can't. Your time is up. Your day is over."

"You're the one who brought the rain, aren't you?"

"Of course. It takes a great deal of expense and time for Syntaps to cause changes in the fantasy. You've been at the lab for the last thirty-seven days. They had to do something to spoil your perfect day. Otherwise you would relive it, over and over again, for the rest of your life."

"It's the money, isn't it?" Billy was crying and holding Sam.

"Syntaps accepts the full blame. They try to screen out individuals such as yourself, but occasionally one gets by. Insurance covers their losses, but they can't shut off the machines without killing you in the process. You have to agree to come back."

Billy's crying ceased. His voice took on an adult tone that part of him didn't recognize. One that frightened him. "I want to stay. This is better. Did you know that Sam lived to be thirteen years old? Thirteen years! That's a long time for a dog. I've never forgotten him. And now he's back. They're all back! I want to stay."

"It's no good. It's all ruined for you, Billy. And it's nearly midnight, when the cycle starts again. Come with me. Come away."

"I won't!" Billy cried. High overhead the clouds were boiling; the lightning flashed continuously. Billy jumped up and began to run, head down. At his back he could hear the sound of the Shadow Man's boots splashing through the rain.

He darted around the corner of the house and headed toward Mr. Kinney's wheat field, but the rain made it hard to gain traction. Like a dream he had dreamt once, where he could only run in slow motion, each inch a desperate effort, he turned to see the Shadow Man hurrying behind him, coming closer and closer.

The dark, gloved hands were closing on his collar when Sam darted between Libby's legs. He stumbled over the dog and fell headlong into a mud puddle. He cursed. Billy ran.

The wheat was tall. It looked frightening in the darkness, for the wind made it hiss, but Billy welcomed its touch around his waist. He knew from the games he and Keith had played, on warm days when his parents hadn't been outside to see them, the best way to hide in a wheat field. He knew to travel up the furrows instead of running across them, so he wouldn't leave a trail of broken stalks.

The Shadow Man had just entered the field when Billy dropped to his knees on the damp earth. In the darkness and rain, his footprints were invisible; he couldn't be tracked. He wormed his way in the opposite direction the Shadow Man would expect him to go, back toward the house.

Soon, he heard Libby thrashing through the wheat. He was quite close, searching desperately. Billy tried not to breathe. His heart pounded at his temples, and the panting of the dog beside him sounded louder than the wind running through the field.

The Shadow Man was almost upon him. Just beside him. Passing behind him. Moving away.

Billy began to crawl again.

"Billy," the Shadow Man called out. The boy smiled. His voice sounded worried. "It's nearly midnight, Billy. Almost time for it to begin again, just as it does every midnight. Don't make me come back tomorrow. You can't win. I'll come back every day. Come out, Billy. Come home."

Once he got far enough away, Libby could never find him. It was a big field. All he had to do was hide until midnight.

He went several yards before the Shadow Man suddenly grew quiet. He raised up slightly to peer between the heads of wheat.

The Shadow Man was gone!

It was a trick. The worst kind of trick. It made him want to jump up and run. But he knew that was what the Shadow Man wanted. He was about to hide again when he noticed the sky changing colors. He held his hand over his mouth to keep from crying out. They were changing things again! They were making something horrible light up the eastern sky. To ruin his perfect day. He didn't want to look, but he couldn't help it. He turned his head almost painfully in the direction of the light.

The clouds were thinning, but in their place an evil, blood-red moon was rising. What he had always thought they meant when they said, a hunting moon. A moon meant for hunting him. He shuddered.

A dark hand touched his shoulders.

He screamed and bit and clawed until the Shadow Man yelled in pain. Billy ran free. He fled down the long furrows as hard as he could go.

The wheat field was changing around him. Ahead of him were tall rows of hedges. He didn't recognize them for the maze they were until he had already plunged between them. He would have turned back then, but the Shadow Man was too close. So he ran, between the high, dense columns of shrubbery. The path twisted and turned, opened up, then became more narrow. He encountered walls of the growth and had to brake often to avoid crashing into the thorns. Sometimes as many as four individual paths presented themselves. Each time he chose one at random, never the same twice.

Then the thing he had feared occurred. He found himself in a cul-de-sac. He searched frantically for an opening. He tried to tear through the hedges, but the thorns drove him back.

"Billy, do you know who I really am?" a voice behind him said. He turned to face his enemy.

"I am more than you imagine," Libby said. "Behold my face."

Billy looked into the darkness of the Shadow Man's face. At first, he could see nothing, except that it was terrible. Then the deep blackness seemed to shift and lighten. It became a new face, one that made Billy cry out.

"Not just a shadow has invaded your perfect day, Bill," a voice that was not Libby's said.

"Mr. Smothers, sir," Billy said. "You go away. You don't belong here. You're not a part of this."

"Oh, but I am. After all, I've been your employer for better than fifteen years. I've put up with you that long. I should be like family."

"You stay away from me. You go back out there where you should be."

The neck of the Shadow Man's body slowly shook the face of Mr. Smothers. "I'll never leave, Bill, now that I've found you. What's the matter, anyway? Can't handle the pressure?"

The Shadow Man lurched at the boy, throwing him to the ground. Billy managed to grab a rock. He struck out blindly. The Shadow Man gave a cry and crumpled onto the child.

Billy pulled himself out from under his enemy. He would have run, but the Shadow Man lay very still.

"You can't trick me, Mr. Libby."

Billy kicked at him. When there was still no response, he started to leave. Even as he did so, the Shadow Man turned his head upward. Billy screamed and backed into the shrubs.

Libby's face had changed again. It was Susan now. His wife, Susan.

"You shouldn't have left us, Bill," a woman's soft voice said. "How could you do this to me and the kids? I don't know why I married you. You're such a loser!"

"How can you say that?" the boy asked. "I thought you'd understand. Of all people, I believed you at least would."

"Because I always have? Well, I'm tired of making excuses for you. I despise you for what you've done. Why can't you be more of a man?"

He didn't hear the rest. He was running. Blindly, without hope. He stumbled into shrubs and emerged bleeding. He tripped over stones and tree roots and fell without feeling the pain. Each time he glanced back he saw another face: his children, his friends, all accusing him, all shouting in their own voices words he had hoped never to hear.

The maze opened into a large arena, one filled with crumbling, half-legible grave markers. He circled around them, along the wall of shrubbery, looking for an opening. When he had nearly completed the circuit, he halted, for the Shadow Man was walking slowly toward him.

He dropped to his knees. "Please."

"Billy," a new voice said as the face changed again. "Answer me, Billy."

Billy fell face down in the cold grass. It was raining again, though he couldn't remember when it had begun.

"Answer me, Billy."

"Yes, dad," he finally said.

"You know I'm dead, don't you, son?"

"Yes. But I don't want you to be," he said through a sob.

"We all die, Billy. But I have something I want to tell you."

Billy looked up.

"I never loved you, son."

A look of pain crossed the boy's face. "That's not true. My dad would never tell me that."

"What of the things those other people said? Your wife. Your friends. Your children. Were they true?"

Billy looked down at the ground. He shrugged.

"Then why should it be a lie when I say I never loved you?"

Tears began to fill Billy's eyes, but the flow abruptly stopped. A look of anger rushed across his face.

"No," he whispered.

"Yes."

"No." He stood. "You're wrong and you're trying to take everything from me. My father always loved me! I know that better than I know anything! You can't lie to me about that, Mr. Libby." The thunder rumbled just overhead.

"It's true," Libby said, still with the voice of Billy's father. He took a step forward. "It's completely true."

"No!" Billy screamed. He was burning with anger now, filled with hate for the Shadow Man. "You leave me alone!"

The Shadow Man came closer. Billy backed up until he felt the thorns of the hedge digging into his back.

"I wish I had never had a son," the Shadow Man said.

The thunder was booming everywhere. The lightning crossed the sky in multiple forkings. Billy's anger filled him. He reached up, up into the sky he had created, into the world of his making, to call down the lightning.

It came with a brilliant flash and the smell of sulphur. It coursed into the body of the Shadow Man, whose scream rent the air. Billy fell to his knees. When he could see again, the Shadow Man was gone. All that remained was a lingering blue cloud.

Sobbing, the boy turned away, back toward the exit. "I

warned you," he muttered to the rain. "I warned you. You should have left me alone. And it's nearly midnight."

He walked between the rows of grave markers, the sullen accusing stones. He tried not to look at them. It seemed a long way back to the beginning of the circle. He sped up his pace. Sometimes his eyes drifted over the etchings on the tombs, but he tried not to read any of them.

A gust of wind whirled by, and something black went running to Billy's right. He jumped to the left, tripped over a narrow marker and fell face down directly before a grave. As he lifted his eyes, he couldn't help but read the letters.

Dearest Mother, Eloise Martin.

He backed away from the marker on his hands and knees and hurriedly stood. "You don't belong here, either," he said.

Turning, he saw the black object that had startled him. It was the Shadow Man's hat. He looked all around and started walking again. He was too tired to run or even trot. But he went as fast as he could go.

A meadowlark cried to his left, and he jumped again. When he looked at it, the marker on which it stood hurried to his eyes. **Charles Martin, Beloved Father.**

He began to run despite the pain in his side. But when he came to the opening of the arena, a tombstone, cracked at the top and much smaller than any of the others, barred his way. Moss grew along one side, and it had no flowers.

"I won't read it," he said. "I won't read it."

He looked at the hedge, stared at each individual leaf, trying to count them as he walked past.

"I won't read it." He was nearly beyond it. A moment more and he would never, ever have to read the lettering on the grave.

His eyes betrayed him with a glance. He tried to lie to himself, to say he hadn't understood, but his eyes filled with tears, and he fell down before the grave.

KEITH TAYLOR
Beloved Son
1955–1966

"No, please. No!"

"It will occur in less than a year, Billy," the Shadow Man said. He stood beyond the grave, his hat on his head again.

Billy was too tired to run, too filled with grief. "It was never the same after that. Never! Mother got sick later that year. My parents changed. It was all over. All the perfect days. I didn't know about it until then—about death. About anything. I don't know why Keith had to die!"

He cried for long moments until the Shadow Man spoke again.

"Billy, did your father love you?"

"Yes. Very much."

"I could not lie to you about that, could I? Does Susan love you?"

"Yes, she does," he said softly.

"Does your employer hate you?"

"No. I guess not."

"But you feared he would. Finally, you imagined he did."

"There was so much pressure. I felt I was failing. . . all of them."

Billy felt the touch of a hand on his shoulder. He looked up in surprise, for there were tears in the eyes of the Shadow Man.

"Billy, do you know who I am?"

Billy looked down at the ground. "I think so."

"When left to its own devices, sometimes the mind will heal itself," the Shadow Man said.

"You're me," Billy said, looking back up. "The part that knows we have to go back. The part that showed me my own fears. . ."

"So you could face them with the lightning," the Shadow Man whispered. "Only I understand you. Come here, Billy."

The little boy ran into the big arms of the Shadow Man, and they wept, both together, among the gravestones.

They talked for a long time, it seemed to Billy, though the moon did not change positions all the while. They spoke of old friends and relatives, of days lost and Easter eggs found. They talked of Christmas, of jokes in the rain, secret forts and magic rings. Of the Day of the Dust Storm and Cousin Jimmy's birthday. And when they were done talking, it seemed they had said it all, there in the cemetery beneath the summer sky.

When they walked through the exit of the arena, they found themselves beside the driveway. The black car was waiting, and Sam sat beside it.

"It's past midnight, isn't it?" Billy asked.

"Yes. Are you ready?"

"Shouldn't I go tell my folks goodbye?"

The words caught in the Shadow Man's throat, but he said, "No. They could never understand, and it would only make it more difficult. There is only old Sam. He will know."

The boy and the man went to the dog and petted him together.

"Goodbye, Sam," Billy said.

"He is the hardest because he never changed, not in all the years of his life," the man said. "But what a glorious life he had here, Billy."

Billy hugged the animal. "I know. But I'll never forget you, old dog. I'll never forget any of this."

He turned and climbed into the passenger side. The car started with a whirr.

A modern whirr.

It eased out of the driveway. He looked back, just once, at the old house and the dog who was already trotting back to the yard.

"There's one more thing I'd like to tell you before this journey ends," the Shadow Man said.

"What's that?"

"Just that I think we can make it now. And I'm glad we had this chance to talk."

The two looked at one another, and both exchanged sudden, sad smiles.

"Me, too."

The car hurried through the night toward the piercing light of the present.

✧ ✧ ✧

Afterword

The Perfect Day was my first published short story, appearing in *Amazing Stories* magazine when I was twenty-five years old. It would never have seen print if not for George H. Scithers' generosity to a young writer. He was editor at *Isaac Asimov's Science Fiction Magazine* when I first submitted it, and he rejected it because the hero remained in his virtual world. Because I've always kept my rejection letters, I can report that he said in part: *Syntaps is obviously not going to give up, so the story isn't over. And the general problem of what to do about people who want to live in the past like this hasn't been directly addressed... The problem has been posed, but it hasn't been solved.* He invited me to resubmit the story if I could fix it.

I did a rewrite and sent it back. Again, he rejected it, taking the time to write a critique of the new ending, insisting that "*Billy has to work out his problems in a way that's dramatically effective...*" Again, he invited me to resubmit.

Back to the keyboard and a final version. I submitted it again, only to receive a nice letter from Managing Editor Shawna McCarthy explaining that George had left, and although the new editor liked the story, she wasn't yet certain what direction she would take the magazine.

Fortunately, George soon reappeared at *Amazing Stories.* I sent in the rewrite, and to my wonder, he accepted it for publication.

I've always been torn between a passion for music and writing. When I wrote this story, I was working a full-time job, remodeling a house myself, taking audio recording classes at a nearby college, and recording original songs at home. Being a less-than-brilliant self-promoter, rather than build on my small success with the major publication that Steven Spielberg had just licensed for his *Amazing Stories* TV show, I decided to stop writing to concentrate on music.

Those were difficult times, ones I now equate with waiting in a cave for some good to come. One of the things that kept me going, however, was the publication of *The Perfect Day,* and the knowledge that a professional editor thought my work had value. I have never forgotten George's kindness.

My forays in music bore unexpected fruition a few years later when I was invited to teach Sound Technology at the college I had attended, a job that gave me a terrific career and the time to return to writing.

Reading this story, you may recognize the influence of Ray Bradbury. Writers learn by imitation. Though I eventually developed my own style, a bit of Bradbury still intentionally appears in an occasional line or two of my work. In my Evenmere novels, I modeled the rapid-fire dialogue of Jormungand, the Last Dinosaur, on Ray's prose.

CAGE OF HONOR

FOR FOUR DAYS Tanager had wandered across the Desert of Sonora, following the remnants of US 80 from Gila Bend toward the Yuma Sea. There was nothing to eat in the wasteland, even the fruit of the gnarl-cacti having failed this year; he had drunk his last sip of water by late afternoon.

Normally he would have flown on his black avian wings. He *had* flown during most of the trip, until weariness and the breathless air kept him from remaining aloft. Now he trudged over brown sand that scorched his feet through his boots, despite the sun having set three hours before.

Topping a hill, he found a town stretching below him. Though the place lay dark beneath the rising moon, he gave a grim smile. These were surely the ruins of Tacna, a prosperous suburb before the Great Blackout. The Gila River had vanished with the catastrophe, but with any luck he might find a cistern or working well. He ran reassuring hands over the hilt of his sword before descending the hill.

He passed low, silent buildings disintegrating beneath the elements. Cracks lined the *metaphalt* surface of the sand-strewn streets; traffic signals lay broken and rusting. Scattered clumps of petrol-barrel bushes, the genetically-engineered wonders that had once brought prosperity to the region, grew wild in abandoned lots. No more would fashionable Americans wear their shadow-mantles here, their biomed tech caressing their skin; never again would they visit their *virtch* playrooms and gyms, or laugh and toast in holoed restaurants.

Tanager strode grimly on, inured yet never wholly unmoved by such sights. By the light of the moon, he searched for signs of water but found only sand and stone. He began to despair until he stepped past the edge of a building onto the town square. A fountain stood in an open courtyard, its spray reflecting the frail moonlight in piercing swords of silver brilliance. He wondered why he hadn't heard its splashing before, for it cascaded from a height of three meters.

Beside the fountain stood a woman wearing trousers and a tunic the same blue as the water, with long hair flowing to her waist. But her eyes, strangely visible in the moonlight, were all he truly saw, their color shifting from emerald to iron gray to frost blue.

He gave a low, graceful bow, for though weak from thirst, he was still one whose DNA had been programmed, and whose nature could not change, so he was always polite. "Good evening. I am Tanager, a traveler in need of water, if you would kindly share?"

"I am Rapunzel," she said. "Do you see my long locks? Come to me, that I may use them to climb down the tower into your arms."

He gave a slow, cautious smile. "There is no tower, lady."

But suddenly there was, smooth and white, in a forest of towering trees. A witch rushed from beneath the boughs toward him, screeching and casting bolts of power from her fingertips. The fountain had disappeared, while the woman who had stood beside it now descended from the tower's height on a rope braided from strands of hair.

Without hesitation, he sent his knife whistling through the air, striking the witch full in the throat. She clutched at the bleeding wound, tried to speak, and fell writhing to the ground.

Ignoring her, he turned to the woman. She dropped the last few feet; he caught her in his arms, and she was everything to him all at once, everything he ever wanted. Her clothes had changed to silk soft as her skin. He kissed her full red lips.

He stood upon the flagstones once more, and she, several paces from him. The fountain sang its soft song. The witch and tower—if they had ever been—were gone.

"Rapunzel," he said, shaking himself from his desire and retrieving his knife. "A fairy tale told by my old nurse."

"What brings you to this desert place?"

Bewildered, he could but answer. "The ruler of Gila Bend demanded to know my opinion of his court. Taking umbrage at my honesty, his soldiers drove me into the desert. I was lucky to escape alive."

"You should have lied."

"Unfortunately, I cannot tell a lie."

A smile touched her lips. "Pure as George Washington! Until I saw you, I thought the stories of the gene-dabblers only legends. You're one of the Nobles." She laughed in delight. "An admirable experiment. Humans bred like pedigreed dogs with all the best traits. You're surely the last of your kind. A collector's item, I suppose."

"Some have tried to add me to their collection."

"Do you know who I am?"

"I'm not certain knowing would be advantageous. I would rather know *what* you are, and how you caused the holo of the witch."

"She would have killed you if you'd let her. And I am Helen, who launched a thousand ships."

He stood on the rolling deck of a wooden vessel, blue sky and blue sea surrounding him, before a warrior tanned by the Aegean, his fiery crest rising gold as the comb of a fighting cock, his bronze blade glittering with reflected light. From the corner of his eye Tanager saw the woman, golden-eyed and golden-haired, standing behind him to his right. Though he knew she was impossibly beautiful, he dared not look upon her, for the Greek's blade was close and sharp.

She whispered in his ear, her breath sweet as roses, the enchantment full upon him. "Only you stand between me and death."

She was the rising sun, the newborn moon; he would have suffered a hundred torments for her. Shield upraised, the Greek warrior unleashed a furious assault. Despite being hollow, Tanager's bones were strong, but it was not his way to stand toe to toe. He dodged skillfully, parrying a handful of times before arching his back, his angular wings rising on the sea breeze. From above his foe, he struck downward, a killing stroke to the side of the neck.

She rushed into his arms, her blonde hair covering his eyes. Their lips touched.

They stood once more before the fountain, the sea and corpse gone. Tanager recovered himself and backed away.

The woman stepped toward him. "Please stay. We've only begun our conversation. I want to know more about you."

He continued his slow retreat. Weak from his trek through the desert, he could not survive extended combat. "I no longer desire to speak, good lady." As he stepped backward, his foot crushed the dried bones of a human forearm.

"Don't you want to know who I am?"

"Whether you are real or otherwise, you're part of a powerful enchantment. I prefer to withdraw."

"A fraction of electricity remains in this place," she said, "and the old magics have returned, augmented by the drapings of science: pheromones, holos, sonic stimulators. Have you ever wondered what it would be like to know the love of the women of legend? To walk with those whose beauty and goodness surpasses all others? A man such as you, bred to nobility? Haven't you longed for one of your own kind?"

Tanager glanced around, searching for something to aid him. He needed to get to the water without triggering whatever caused his loss of reason. Perhaps he could persuade her. "Because I am whom I was made to be, there is no room in my heart for dalliance. I cannot be fickle. My engineered genes make me a creature of high honor. Those I love, I love with all my heart. Some have called this a weakness. I see now they were right. My lady, spare me from too much passion."

She smiled sweetly but shook her head. "Do you know who I am?" Her voice dropped to a whisper. "I'm Sleeping Beauty."

He stood before a great castle guarded by three soldiers. They came at him one at a time, else they would have surely overwhelmed him. Lunging, he took the first in the chest. The second was a better swordsman, and for several long seconds they parried and thrust, moving back and forth before the gates of the castle. With a twisting motion, Tanager entangled his opponent's sword, locking it against his own and tearing it from the man's grasp. A final thrust ended his life.

Before the remaining soldier could engage, Tanager pulled his sling from the holder at his back, chose a smooth stone from the pouch at his belt, and sent the projectile flying in one smooth motion. It struck the man in the forehead, sending him to the ground, dying beneath the summer sun.

Panting for breath, Tanager rushed into the upper chambers of the castle, where lay a woman pale but lovely. He kissed her lips. Her eyes opened. He lost himself in her arms.

They faced one another upon the flagstones, he on his knees, too breathless to stand, sweat pouring from his brow, his limbs like water. His throat burned; his breath came in gasps. His retreat had been stymied; in his delirium he had returned to his previous position. He could not bear another such battle without crumbling into unconsciousness. Nor would he ever awaken from that sleep. His bones would bleach under the morning sun, his thirst unslaked before the mocking fountain.

Yet, the enchantment came and went, perhaps as a failsafe to provide its designers a means of escape. There had to be a way to bring an end to it. The woman was either an illusion or the one controlling the enchantment. Either way, she was assaulting him, giving his innate code of conduct permission to strike back.

He drew his long knife and cast it at her, but though his aim was true, it missed her and fell to the flagstones. Her sweet voice echoed around the courtyard, her tone puzzled, reproachful. "Why do you seek to harm one who offers you the gift of love?"

A new thought struck him, and with it a faint hope. *If all that I do fails, I must try something else. If I'm wrong, at least I won't live long to regret it.*

Taking his sword and sling, he cast them as far as he could, his blade clattering in the stillness against the side of a building.

"I am all that is Woman," she said. "And that is more than any man can bear. Call me Guinevere."

A warrior stood between him and a lady bright and lovely as the sun, a regal man a head taller than Tanager, with the branches of a rowen tree for a crown and the sword Excalibur in his hand—Arthur himself, filled with rage; and beside the king, five other men.

Again he wanted only her, again he raised his arm to fight his way to his beloved, but his blade was gone. He sought another weapon but found none. His attackers approached, their swords glistening, their cruel eyes victorious.

He raised his bare hands to defend himself, but no blade struck. The warriors stood uncertain, their swords pointed at his heart.

He took a step toward them, so close a sword-tip touched his chest. The warriors retreated, backing toward the woman.

He pursued them, still under the spell, an unarmed man, shouting, threatening stout men with his fists, and as they retreated, so, too, did she. At last he backed them against the fountain. She sat at its lip, beckoning.

He leapt at his foes, parting them like rows of ripe wheat, and fell into her arms.

The spell ended, and he found he had crawled to the edge of the well. The woman, now holding him, brought a cup of water to his lips. Tears glistened in her eyes. "So brave," she murmured.

After he had drunk a long time, she asked, "How did you know?"

"Because I am Tanager, whose nature cannot change, I understand my own limitations. I knew I couldn't have defeated that many men in my diminished state, so I assumed they were allowing me the victory. The trap is cunning. What man is willing to throw away his weapons? Yet, only through surrender can one reach the fountain."

She kissed him, a long kiss, her mouth hot on his. "Two years I've waited, a prisoner here. A woman is required to maintain the fountain. A score of men have perished seeking the water."

"Why is it guarded?"

"It is controlled by merchants from Tombstone. An underground spring feeds it, but the supply is limited. Unless the waters are protected, other traders will establish a caravan route between Tucson and Yuma, disrupting the merchants' profits. They kidnapped me and left me here."

"How have you survived?"

"The merchants bring food and supplies."

"Why didn't you flee? Scattered among the victims' bones, I see containers you could have used for water."

She shuddered. "A woman traveling alone would find herself in low estate. But I'm glad you are the one who survived. I hoped you would." She spread her hands at the field of bones. "Unlike yourself, most of these were men of common, vulgar blood."

"And if I had been of vulgar blood as well?"

"Then you would still have the fountain, but I wouldn't accompany you."

"If you had truly wanted me to survive, you could have told me how to escape the trap."

"But if you failed and the merchants learned what I had done, they would have punished me. They have ways of knowing."

He stared at her until she grew uncomfortable. "What's wrong?"

"You came here willingly, didn't you?"

Her eyes grew wide. "Of course not! How can you think that?

You don't know how lonely it's been. I—"

"How much do they pay you? Enough to live comfortably for the rest of your life?"

She shook her head in denial, then, as if struck by a realization, her expression changed, her voice grew smooth. "All right, my noble friend, I admit it, but you don't understand the circumstances. I am the daughter of a wealthy house left destitute by mischance. If I hadn't accepted, the merchants would have found someone else, and it was either this or common labor. It's been horrible watching men suffer and die. I'm just glad it's over."

Tanager shuddered. "The men who brought you here read your passions well."

She stepped away, beautiful but angry, tears springing from her eyes; and he saw she knew how to use her anger. "So you think poorly of me? And I, so long in the desert! Have you no pity?"

"I can always pity."

"Then pity me. Take me with you. Half the wealth I earned can be yours, if you want it."

"The desire for opulence is not within my nature."

"Then what of the desire for desire?" She parted her lips. She was very lovely.

He turned away. "You don't understand what you've done to me. You are indeed beautiful, and as I told you, when I give my heart the giving is total. I am Tanager, whose nature cannot change."

She laughed haughtily, her eyes filled with scorn. "I thought you a hawk; I see you're a parrot, mouthing the same speech over and over. For the sake of the treasure, anyone else would have pretended to befriend me until we reached the cities. Will you take me with you?"

"I won't take you. Assuming you don't try to kill me yourself, your orders are undoubtedly to bring anyone who survives the trap to the merchants, who would silence me lest I inform others how to escape the snare."

She studied him a moment, then shrugged. "Too bad. We could have had some fun along the way, and at least I knew you wouldn't steal from me. Get your water and go! My contract ends in six months. The merchants will free me then."

"Yet, if I leave you, you will only entrap others."

Her eyes became mirthful. "And earn that much more wealth. But don't look so! You can't frighten me. I know the stories about your kind. Poor bird-man! Yes, I've done what I had to in order to survive, but you're a prisoner of your own genetics, incapable of harming an unarmed woman, your virtue bred into you like loyalty into a sheepdog. Pathetic creature! A bird in a cage! Fly away then. Take your honor and leave." She shooed him as if he were a bothersome insect, then turned and swaggered toward the fountain.

Tanager watched her go, his expression bleak. And because he was who he was, he did what he had to do swiftly, before she even knew what happened.

✧ ✧ ✧

HE BURIED HER with the bones of those she had slain, crooning a soft dirge above her grave. In his song was his sorrow for being one whose nature could not change, who because he had once felt love for her, would love her forever despite her wickedness. Sorrow that the word branded foremost on his genetic code cursed him to roam the earth. Sorrow that the word was not *Virtue* as she had supposed, but *Justice.*

Weeping, he filled his water bags and left the town behind.

✧ ✧ ✧

AFTERWORD

A YEAR OUT of high school I wrote a novelette, which still sits in a notebook, about a winged man much different than Tanager. When the idea for *Cage of Honor* came to me, I remembered my bird-man and decided to use his physical characteristics. I sent the story to a magazine or two, was rejected, and ran out of professional markets where I could submit it.

It was originally set in a nebulous far future. When Howard Andrew Jones, editor of *Tales from the Magician's Skull* asked for a story, I decided to rework it, using the same universe as the Great Blackout from my *Battle of York* yarn. A bit of research on Arizona gave me a setting. Howard liked it. I find I rather like it myself.

A STAR TO EVERY WANDERING BARQUE

THE AGE OF Conscience arrived on a Thursday evening in June, as Greg Stoll sat in the twilight on his front porch in a suburb of Houston. His house overlooked a small lake, and after work he liked to rest in his porch swing and watch the trees cast their long shadows across the water. Sometimes his wife, Michelle, sat with him, but on this particular evening he was alone, the swing gently creaking.

The shards of the day remained with him, the myriad noises of the broadcast booth at NASA, where Greg worked as a video and audio supervisor, handling everything from interviews to launches to public relations spots. He had been hired in time to witness the original shuttle launch firsthand and had been there ever since. It was a good job, easy in some ways, fun in others, but the last decade had been difficult. Budget cuts, personnel changes, mission failures, faltering morale; sometimes it was hard to remain optimistic. Though his was a support position, he loved NASA. But the politics could be overwhelming; in his position, he saw too much of it. The organization could do so much more if only everyone would forget their personal agendas, stick to the task, and just get along.

As the sun fell below the horizon and the first stars came out, he remembered the taped interviews he had done with the crew of the ill-fated *Columbia*. He could still recall their bright, hopeful faces, their quick wit and ready smiles, some arrogant, some humble, all confident. It had been the same before the *Challenger* accident. He stared at the clouds, orange and pink with the setting sun—especially lovely that evening—and sorrowed for those brave souls, gone forever from the Earth.

Even as he watched the gathering gloom, his own thoughts desolate, something inside him abruptly *lifted*. A weight seemed to rise from the center of his chest. He gasped, the breath pouring immeasurably sweet into his lungs. Forever after, he would associate the sensation with the beauty of the clouds.

In that moment, he *understood*, though several days would pass before he could totally comprehend his understanding. A great oppression had departed from him, one he had carried unknowing throughout his life. He understood.

All the pain borne of his fifty-odd years, the misunderstandings, hurt feelings, slights, griefs, disappointments, the little agonies of living, fell from him. A tremendous sense of forgiveness overwhelmed him, for himself and for others. A love for everyone and everything suffused him, the kind of love he must have had as a small child. He felt abruptly whole.

The experience came with rocket speed, a hundred thoughts and sensations pouring through him. Before he even recognized what he was doing, he found himself weeping in the porch swing overlooking the little lake, gasping sobs, crying as he had not cried since he was ten years old.

Eventually, he fell silent, and a part of him recognized that his brain no longer rattled away as it had done for so many years, chugging along like a broken steam engine fueled by a thousand useless, random thoughts. The silence of a sanctuary, of a cathedral. The silence of peace.

Night fell, a glorious night, the darkening of the sky, the shifting of the shades, the beating of the stars seen through the haze of the streetlights. He had always appreciated a good night sky, yet this time was different. Now, he truly saw its splendor.

At last, when the songs of the crickets filled the air, he staggered to his feet. He had to tell his wife what had happened. He had to tell everyone!

Turning to his front door, he found every light in the house extinguished, as if no one had bothered to turn them on. He hurried inside, calling several times before finding Michelle upstairs, seated in a wooden chair, looking out the window.

She turned to him, her face lit by the dull glow of the street lamps. She had always been beautiful; now she looked holy, her eyes twin lamps, radiant with love. In wonder, he realized he must look the same.

"Why didn't I ever see how incredible life is?" she asked.

He took her in his arms, rejoicing.

✧ ✧ ✧

OUT OF A lifetime of habit, they turned on the TV to see if they were the only ones. Mindless entertainments played, stories without meaning. Most of the news stations were off the air. One had a camera rolling on a news desk empty except for a woman sitting and smiling at her hands, half her face outside the range of the lens.

Greg and Michelle went outside, intending to knock on their neighbors' doors, but people were already in the street, talking in soft, excited voices. When the couple joined the crowd, everyone greeted them with a hug. Introductions were made all around, as if this were the first time they had met their neighbors. Despite having lived there many years, this was mostly true. People laughed and cried, but notwithstanding the festive air, Greg noticed how little anyone said, how little *he* said. There was too much going on in his mind.

In their excitement, Greg and his wife stayed up late that night, falling asleep curled together as when they were young.

✧ ✧ ✧

THE NEXT MORNING no one went to work. The world, as one, began a day of reflection. Greg spent the morning with Michelle.

"I never appreciated you enough," they told one another. They spoke of their early life together, the good and bad, and for the first time, looking at his wife, Greg truly understood what Yeats meant when he wrote: *But one man loved the pilgrim soul in you, and loved the sorrows of your changing face.*

"Is it a dream?" Michelle asked. "Will we wake up tomorrow and be the way we were before? So. . . limited?"

"It's not that I feel any smarter," Greg told her. "But I understand more. My thinking before was. . . disturbed. The things I worried about. It was all so. . . so—"

"Evil," Michelle said.

The word hung in the air between them.

"An old, unused term," Greg said. "Out of date, I would have called it before. Never would have applied it to myself. I mean, I thought I was basically a good person. But there was so much selfishness, so many times when I was petty or cruel."

He called his daughter in California later that day.

"I'm sorry I wasn't a better father," he said.

"I'm sorry I wasn't a better daughter," she said.

"It's all right," they both said together. They laughed and fell silent.

"It's like everything I ever blamed you for is gone," she finally said. "Not that you were a bad dad or anything, but now I understand you did the best you could, for what we were then."

They talked about moving closer, so they could see each other more often.

Afterward, Greg had a similar conversation with his son in Wisconsin.

Throughout the day, by mutual consent, every television station remained off the air until six o'clock that evening when the President gave a message. For the first time in years, every station carried it; for the first time in decades, everyone considered the business of the nation more important than The Home Shopping Network and reruns of *Gilligan's Island*. Nor was it the same beleaguered man who had faced the cameras dozens of times before. His usually penetrating eyes were calm, his face relaxed. He didn't read a speech; he just talked.

"Something has happened," his smooth, warm voice said. "Something wonderful. A New Reasoning. We don't know how or why, and it will take time to understand the ramifications. There is much to be done. This is a new beginning. A great work lies before us. We will do it together. All of us. A world of us.

"I have been duplicitous; I will be duplicitous no more. I have been arrogant; I will be arrogant no more. I have catered to private interests for the sake of personal power. From now on, I will put the good of the country ahead of my own concerns.

"There is one thing you should know," he ended. "Not a single weapon has been fired anywhere in the world since yesterday evening."

✧ ✧ ✧

Even though he had the day off, Greg went to work on Saturday. He had a lot of ideas he wanted to share. When he arrived, he discovered the entire staff had done the same. A big meeting was held, and Greg's video crew recorded it for posterity.

Abe Feinstein, the Director of NASA, addressed the audience.

"Given the week's changes, I think there are three questions we should ask. Number one: Is our work important, or should we petition Congress to eliminate NASA? Two: If our work *is* important, have we been pursuing it in the best manner? Three: If not, how should we change? I want us to break into small groups, each no larger than ten, and discuss these questions."

With his crew's hand-cam's rolling, Greg walked among the participants, listening to them talk. Some were fellow workers he had once disliked; one was a woman he had loathed. Now, he wondered how he could have ever felt that way. It seemed so unreasonable.

"Greg," a man told him, pointing to a chair. "You should be in on this. Join our group."

No one had ever asked Greg's opinion on the direction of NASA before, but he had ideas and took a seat.

Everyone in the group spoke softly, taking turns, considerate of one another. Though many were passionate, no voices were raised, despite differing opinions. Gone were the needs for attention, the rivalries, the childishness. People said what they meant. No offense was given; none taken.

They quickly agreed that the exploration of space *was* important. Curiosity, rather than being dulled by the New Reasoning, had been intensified. The old, child-like sense of wonder permeated the discussions, the thirst to see the marvels of the universe. It was decided that NASA must be managed in a new way, with greater freedom for input in all areas. Simple logic dictated the necessity to ask for increased funding.

Greg drove home that night whistling.

✧ ✧ ✧

ON MONDAY MORNING, several important announcements were made. The Grand Wizard of the Ku Klux Klan dissolved the organization. Forty-seven terrorist groups renounced violence. People who had committed crimes began turning themselves in to authorities, overwhelming the resources of the penal system. Four major hotel chains agreed to house the overflow for free until the courts could determine whether incarceration remained a social necessity.

China recognized Taiwan as an independent nation. Israel and Palestine began serious peace talks. South American and Middle Eastern countries vowed to plow up their poppy fields.

Major magazine publishers met with advertisers to determine whether the content of their periodicals was truly meaningful, resulting in a suspension of more than seventy-five percent of their offerings and a revamping of the remainder.

With the drive for self-promotion extinguished, producers, directors, and actors walked away from movies made purely for profit. The studios agreed and tore up their contracts.

The pharmaceutical, insurance, and healthcare industries began a series of talks with the World Health Organization to discuss providing a standard of care for every citizen on Earth.

Thousands of companies announced a restructuring of remuneration policies to provide more equitable salaries to their employees. Hundreds of CEOs voluntarily returned the bulk of their benefits.

Bookstores noted a marked increase in the sale of poetry.

A phrase appeared that would become the slogan of the world: *Do no harm to others or yourself.*

✧ ✧ ✧

ON TUESDAY, GREG realized the importance of silence. He had filled his life with the constant yammering of TV, movies, the Internet, audio books—anything to keep from thinking. Now he basked in the solitudes. No longer did he spend his time regretting the past or brooding over the future. The present surrounded him. He could finally appreciate happy moments without analyzing his own appreciation, without comparing it to the happy times of his childhood.

To sit in a car and meditate became a joy. He drove slower, no longer in a hurry. So did everyone else, and the speed limit found its natural equilibrium at forty-five miles per hour on the freeway and twenty in the city. With the highways less dangerous, Greg contemplated riding a bicycle to work.

On his way home that evening, he realized that though death and disease remained on the Earth, he no longer feared either one. How strange that he ever had.

The news that evening announced that every country in the

Middle East had agreed to the joint Israeli/Palestinian peace plan. The United Nations voted unanimously to adopt democratic reforms and to abolish trade sanctions worldwide. Ending hunger by the end of the year became *the* international priority. A list was made of the key points of the treaties and resolutions, but no papers were signed. A country's word had become its bond.

In India, the people voted to eliminate the caste system.

The lotteries closed after giving away their last few millions to people who donated the money to the food-relief effort.

Across the world, street people and those placed in institutions because of mental rather than physical causes awoke to sanity. Millions of alcoholics and drug addicts turned themselves in to treatment centers.

✧ ✧ ✧

BY THE SECOND week, all weapons of war were abolished.

Ben Thomas, Greg and Michelle's next-door neighbor, appeared at their door at five that evening.

"Greg, we're having a block party tonight to celebrate. You coming?"

"Wouldn't miss it," Greg replied.

By seven o'clock, everyone in the neighborhood was in the streets. This was a different kind of party, a different type of revelry—quiet, joyous. Greg discovered he no longer needed a couple of beers to feel comfortable in a crowd. He could be himself. He said things that were meaningful, encouraging, or playful. He listened when others spoke. No one talked about the weather just for something to say.

He noticed that people laughed more than they used to but told fewer jokes. Humor itself had changed. The ironic or sarcastic didn't seem funny anymore. The idea of making light of others seemed ludicrous.

Earlier that week, with safety no longer an issue and energy conservation a priority, the city council had voted to discontinue using street lights. As twilight fell, everyone in the neighborhood sat in lawn chairs or on blankets in front of Ben Thomas' place, to watch an event many hadn't witnessed in over twenty years, a tableau some had *never* seen.

They watched the stars come out.

One by one, the tiny, enormous suns appeared, and the children *ooohed* and *ahhhed* as if they watched fireworks.

"There's one!" a little girl shouted.

"I see another," a little boy cried.

"Awesome!" a teenager said.

"Daddy," another boy said, "tell me about the constellations."

But no one knew the names of the constellations except Greg, so he pointed them out, one by one: the North Star, the Big and Little Dippers, the Teapot, Scorpio, the Swan, Hercules, the tiny Pleiades. He showed them the Milky Way and the planets; he told them the distances, and his listeners—who had never cared before—sat riveted by the telling.

When he was done, Greg and his neighbors lit candles and stood in a circle, looking up at the millions of stars, the great wheel passing overhead.

We shall overcome, they sang. *We shall overcome someday.*

✧ ✧ ✧

A TIME POPULARLY called *The Big Reshuffle* began. With the Criminal Code abolished and everyone rethinking their lives, hundreds of job categories either changed or ceased to exist. Psychiatrists, prostitutes, professional models, district attorneys, security guards—thousands had to find other work. The word *policeman* was changed to *helper*. Most lawyers lost their clientele.

Droves of people quit their jobs to find meaningful work, many moving from management to service industries: plumbers, electricians, carpenters. The Peace Corp and several other charity organizations soon had more volunteers than they could use.

The economic restructuring was difficult at first, but many of those whose jobs had become obsolete joined either the World Hunger Organization or the World Housing Authority.

"TV doesn't interest me much anymore," Michelle said.

"They're coming out with new programming," Greg replied. "I read about it in the paper. Speculative series about what we might accomplish. History and Natural History. Game shows without prizes. Puzzle shows. And the camera shots are going to be a lot slower."

✧ ✧ ✧

WITH NO CONCERNS of bribery, blockades, or kickbacks, the World Hunger Organization, powered by farmers' wheat donations from Kansas to the Ukraine, soon announced it had enough distribution centers in place to feed the world.

Millions volunteered to give twenty percent of their income for the construction of basic housing. The standard of living in the developed countries dropped slightly, as its citizens rid themselves of things they had once considered necessities, the status symbols of neighborhood and nation.

The automobile and petroleum industries retooled. Radical engine designs, uncovered in corporate vaults, were put into production. The car, no longer a symbol of prestige, became both more functional and more beautiful. The popularity of public transportation soared. With profits a secondary concern, measures were taken to protect the environment. A plan was implemented to end strip mining within three years.

Socialism resurfaced, a system too idealistic for a selfish people. The European Union decided that people were responsible enough to use only the supplies, food, and clothing they needed, and to work to support the public good with no thought of income. A referendum was passed to abolish currency. Within two months, the other nations followed suit, and the strange, abstract system of monetary compensation that had ruled the world for so long was finally laid to rest. A short ceremony was held as the New York Stock Exchange closed for the final time.

✧ ✧ ✧

AT NASA, GREG began to see big changes. The world's resources, no longer required to wage war, were turned to research and public works. Materials poured into the space agency; countries shared knowledge indiscriminately.

More importantly, people's minds were finally free. Greg no longer wasted time on company politics and personal animosities. The joy of his career filled him, the *play* of handling the NASA broadcasts. Mistakes were made but easily forgiven, both by his bosses and his own conscience. There were no misgivings. Projects proceeded at astonishing speed.

Given full range of their imaginations, NASA dreamed big. In an astounding breakthrough, a group of physicists in Zurich discovered a method to overcome Einstein's limits on space travel. The problems that had baffled scientists for half a century were suddenly solved: ships' weight, shielding, propulsion, the health of the crew. Plans were drawn to build an interstellar craft.

✧ ✧ ✧

ACROSS THE WORLD, epidemic outbreaks became controllable as concern for others overcame all other considerations. New vaccines appeared. Unwanted pregnancies dropped to nearly zero, reason finally overcoming the drive for procreation. To reduce overpopulation, everyone agreed that couples should have no more than two children. Families that wanted more than that adopted from the dwindling numbers in orphanages.

The pace of life slowed, yet more was accomplished. Through no edict, the workday gradually diminished to six hours with a one-hour lunch. More people began to garden.

✧ ✧ ✧

ON THE SECOND anniversary of the New Reasoning, millions gathered in New York City at the site of the Memorial Museum erected to commemorate the destruction of the World Trade Center. Former members of terrorist organizations were in attendance. The centerpiece of the ceremony was the bronze sculpture entitled *The Sphere,* which had survived the September 11 attack. A new band was added to the piece, with the words of Martin Luther King, Jr. inscribed upon it.

Free at last! Free at last! Thank God almighty, we are free at last!

✧ ✧ ✧

IN THE FIFTH year of the New Reasoning, Greg sat at the mixing console at the broadcast facility at NASA, watching a sleek, white ship preparing to launch. The unmanned test flights had gone well. He smiled. This was to be a *short* flight to Proxima Centauri, the closest star. How he would have laughed if anyone had called it that five years before.

He had spent the last month taping interviews of the seven-person crew, another group of bright, hopeful astronauts about to take the trip of a lifetime. He thought again of the recordings of the *Challenger* and *Columbia* crews. Once, such memories would have evoked only sorrow. But not today. Death was part of life; the sacrifices had not been in vain. No sacrifices were ever in vain.

The countdown began. No one was nervous; no one afraid. Fear was in the past. As the numbers rolled down and the engines began their roar, Greg adjusted the volume on his monitor feed, smiling down at the faders.

"Now," he whispered, *"we're ready."*

✧ ✧ ✧

AFTERWORD

MY PHILOSOPHY ON writing is that a writer writes even when he doesn't feel like it. I've only suffered once from Writer's Block, that mysterious mental aberration that prevents a writer from putting down the words.

During the years I taught at a local junior college, I was fortunate to have summers off, allowing me time to write. I don't recall anything particularly stressful in my personal life the summer I wrote *A Star to Every Wandering Barque,* but I couldn't write much of anything else. I couldn't *bring* myself to write. Mostly, I hung out at the house with my West Highland Terrier after my wife went to work, wondering what was wrong with me. The why of it remains a mystery. I only know that the story came from a longing for a better world, one I hope to someday see once I've departed the Earth.

The title comes from Shakespeare. He spelled it *A Star to Every Wandering Bark,* which sounds like a story about a lost dog, so I changed it to *Barque,* a later term for a sailing ship. I must admit that amending the Bard left me fidgety.

There is a humorous incident concerning the story. The main character's name is a combination of the first and last names of two of my former students who work at NASA, done as a tribute to their accomplishments. One of their surnames is "Wiseman," and I had originally used that. When Gordon Van Gelder accepted the story, he suggested I change the name because it was "a bit too on-point." We had a laugh together when I explained the coincidence, one I hadn't even thought of. I altered it for the final draft.

THE LEECHMONT

I CAME HERE three years ago in February. I came because of a broken heart. And because of the murders. But I don't dwell on that. I am the night clerk of the Leechmont Hotel.

Guests arrive sporadically during my shift, making the nights long and dull, often leaving me time to read and reflect after checking the register and putting everything in order. This suits me well, for I am of a solitary nature. On this particular evening, I had indulged in my sole infringement of the Rules of Deportment by polishing my fingernails at my station, unconcerned of reprimand, as the Night Manager never enters the lobby.

If you have not been to the Leechmont, you should know that much written about it is true. It comes from a grand and ancient tradition. The lobby is cavernous, its high-timbered ceiling lost to the shadows, its crystal chandeliers yellowed by time. Sitting behind the long cherry desk, I can look across the sweep of the room to the enormous stuffed head of the Fenris Wolf above the entrance doors. Carved, winged lions adorn the dark walls, matched by twin rearing statues in the central fountain. A fresco of the tigers of Naleewuath fills the left side of the chamber, the ruby eyes of the great cats gleaming crimson in the light of the ensconced gas lamps. A side stair to the right leads to the Observation Deck, and it is often my wont to ascend and gaze out its high windows. This allows me a certain measure of freedom, for from that vantage I can observe any guests ascending the wide steps running between the rows of alabaster panthers to the entrance; and can return to my desk before they enter the lobby.

My fingernails done to perfection, I was soon installed in my favorite Morris chair on the Observation Deck, garbed in my mandatory long-sleeved, floor-length lavender dress embroidered with *Leechmont Hotel* on its sleeves. The Great Clock ticked on the wall overhead, a comforting sound, its hands displaying

12:07. I sipped a black Oosian tea from my porcelain cup, quite content to be alone with my musings, reading from Anton Trombone's *Beyond Yonder*, occasionally gazing out across the amorphous, constantly changing chaos to the south.

The view outside the Leechmont is not open to the sky but encompassed by a vast granite dome whose cracks can be seen by the naked eye when the coruscating lightnings flash purple, orange, cerulean, and cyan along the whorling horizon. It often rains, and that night was no exception. There is a book in the hotel library filled with theories on how weather can exist within the dome, but I think it unscientific speculation. Despite our current age of skepticism, I hold to the belief taught me as a child, that Evenmere is an infinite mansion maintaining all of Existence; and as such, many of the domiciles and edifices of the countless countries within it, including the Leechmont, contain mysteries we cannot yet comprehend.

I was starting the chapter where Jackoes and Jamoes lose control of the hot-air balloon and sail into Worlds Unknown—a scene still as thrilling as when I first read it—when I glanced out the windows and noticed three figures climbing the seventy-seven steps to the entrance, struggling in the pouring rain to keep the wind from tearing their umbrellas from their hands. I descended to my position at the desk, straightened my dress, and stood ready.

Doormen are not a fixture at the Leechmont, due, I am told, to their tendency to disappear if left outside too long. At any rate, there have been none during my time here; and the three travelers plunged through the oak doors, the gale at their backs, stomping their feet on the rugs before approaching me. Their advancing forms stirred a memory—something about the taller one sent a wave of anxiety through my chest—nonetheless, I tilted my head slightly and projected a welcoming smile wide enough to display my dimples, a stance practiced in my looking-glass. Making a good first impression is crucial since it can color a guest's entire experience. "Welcome, honored travelers, to the Leechmont Hotel."

"Good evening," the shorter man said. "Have you three rooms for the night?"

"At the Leechmont, the rooms are always fully booked, but new guests can always be accommodated," I said sweetly.

Despite the looks the travelers exchanged, I did not engage in hyperbole; the hotel has been added onto many times over the centuries. But my phrasing is in error, suggesting the work of human hands. Rather, the hotel expands, rooms and even whole stories appearing where none were before. More than once I've been summoned by the maids to inspect a new set of chambers. They consider the increased labor wholly inconsiderate, grumbling and glaring at me as if I were somehow responsible. But I am only the night clerk and have nothing to do with the Owners, whom I have never seen.

The three seemed ordinary enough, the taller man slender and fit, wearing a top hat, a greatcoat, and an unusual leopard-spotted cloak. The pleasantly round-faced shorter man sported a dark sack suit and black bowler, and carried a portmanteau and their sparse luggage. The most interesting of the trio, a dark-haired young woman, somewhat taller than average, had an unusual quality of strength about her face. Here, I said to myself, is one who has faced great struggles and come through scathed but unbowed.

I directed them to the register. The shorter man signed for all three. Glancing at the clock, I recorded the time at 11:35 and scanned the names.

To be employed at the Leechmont, one learns to shield one's emotions. Sanguinity is our motto; serenity our placard; but it was with the greatest restraint that I refrained from exclamation, for here were living legends: Carter Anderson, the Master of Evenmere; his butler, William Hope; and Lizbeth Anderson, wife of Lord Anderson's brother, a woman said to have been a prisoner of the Society of Anarchists for several years from the age of twelve. This explained my sense of recognition—I had seen Lord Anderson years before from a distance.

Composure being indispensable, I bowed my head slightly. "Lord Anderson, Lady Anderson, Mr. Hope. It is an honor to be your host."

"Might I ask your name?" Mr. Hope bluntly replied.

Surprised by the question, I flushed, my heartbeat rising. Perhaps it is foolish, but I prefer anonymity. "Rebecca Rios. I am the night clerk." I retrieved the room keys from their cubbyholes, choosing better chambers than those I had originally intended, and rang the bell to summon the porter. A minute passed and then two. I smiled and rang again.

Curiosity triumphed over reticence, for there is opportunity in everything. Pinecoat's tardiness meant a chance to observe my famous guests. I renewed my confident smile. "It appears the porter is delayed. I will escort you personally."

Coming around the desk, I reached for the twin carpetbags, but Mr. Hope forbore me. "I'm used to carrying them."

"You are kind, sir. Please follow me."

As we ascended the Circling Stair with its Monophian scallops, I ventured conversation. "Will you be staying with us for a time?"

"We aren't certain," Lord Anderson said. "We're doing some research." He hesitated and lowered his voice. "We hope to... repair something that was damaged. To that end, we need to consult with someone familiar with the history of the establishment." His voice is kind, without a trace of haughtiness. Having lodged regents, representatives, dukes, diawards, genarchs, and an occasional princess, the humble tone of the Master impressed me.

"There isn't an official historian, but any inquiries can be directed through me," I said. "I hold an interest in the hotel's customs, both past and present."

"We appreciate your offer and will avail ourselves of it."

Encouraged by his words, I grew bold. One does not anticipate the opportunity to converse with the lord of the entire House. "If I might ask, it is said the Inner Chambers look out onto a land which is not Evenmere. Can that be true?"

"Have you been to the Inner Chambers?" Mr. Hope asked.

I grew flummoxed, fearing I had committed an impertinence. We are schooled to be incurious. I fear I even stammered. "I've only heard tales."

From the corner of my eye, I saw the Master smile. "It's true. I lived outside the House for many years in a land called Scotland. But Enoch, the Windkeep, would tell you that even *that* country resides within the House. It's a paradox, but if anyone would know, he would."

"I see." But of course, I didn't. I wanted to ask if Enoch was truly the Keeper of Time. Some doubt that the Windkeep makes time proceed by winding certain clocks, that the Lamp-lighter maintains the suns by lighting various lamps, and that other individuals supervise other parts of Existence, with the Master serving over all. Certainly, Lord Anderson struck me as more than the head of a declining nobility. But I, who am not well-traveled, have no way of knowing the truth of it; I am only the night clerk of the Leechmont Hotel.

Escorting each of them to their individual chambers, I pointed out the various amenities and opened the curtains to display the view. This was met without comment until I led Lady Anderson to her room.

She bit her lip at the swirling clouds. "Such a stark landscape. So much turmoil. How do you bear it?"

"One grows used to it, my lady. Many of our guests find it has a certain splendor."

"Just as many are repelled, I should think." She crossed her arms and shivered. "Why is it so tumultuous?"

"There are forces at play around the Leechmont often in conflict with one another. The hotel tends to draw important guests such as yourselves, individuals with great power. If you would prefer, I can exchange your room for one facing north. The view in that direction is less turbulent."

"That is kind but unnecessary." She smiled sadly. "I have faced chaos in other forms before."

"Very good. If there is anything you need, the Leechmont is at your disposal. We pride ourselves on being unlike other establishments. Our guests sometimes require extraordinary resources to accomplish their purposes, and we do our best to supply them. You need only ask."

She furrowed her brow. "Truly? At times, my brother-in-law has required whole armies." Her words would have smacked of condescension in another, but she spoke guilelessly, stating a fact as if weighing the possibility of my producing a battalion.

Both amused and puzzled, I replied, "Perhaps not armies, but we go beyond supplying the occasional forgotten toothbrush. Few come here to idle their days."

She smiled, a glint in her eye revealing she recognized the humor. "I will be mindful of it. Thank you."

As I closed the door, I noticed she had turned back to the window. There was something strikingly compelling about her. Were our stations different, I believe we might have become friends.

✧ ✧ ✧

NIGHTS AT THE Leechmont can seem endless. When I returned to the desk, I saw the time was only 1:04. I took up my book again but was unable to concentrate, finding myself hoping for further conversation with our new guests, who were nothing like I might have imagined. There were many questions I wanted to ask about the work of the Master: his duties, his perspective on the House, the Words of Power he was said to wield. I once read a book claiming he had tamed the great dragon in the attic and destroyed a false House built by his enemies. I knew he was married and wondered what his wife was like. Though he wasn't as dashing as some men, the more I thought of him the better I liked his demeanor. Perhaps he wasn't married after all. Perhaps he would take an interest in a humble night clerk at the Leechmont Hotel. What girlish fantasies! But I can surely be forgiven such thoughts—we are all fascinated by the powerful and famous.

I gave up the book and returned to my desk. Ichabod, the night mailman, came in on the blowing wind, his heavy sack on his back, stamping his feet and muttering against the chill. We conversed while I sorted the mail into its cubbyholes, he being ever eager for conversation. Delivering the mail is trying at best and fatal at worst, and his stories are often intriguing. I gave him hot tea, and we stood together before the great fireplace while he set down his truncheon and warmed his hands.

"There's something about," he said. "Best you keep wary."

"What is it?"

He shook his head, making his gray hair quiver at his shoulders. "Can't rightly say."

"Something summoned?"

He barked a laugh. "Who knows, lass? I can feel it, though, just in the last hour, deep in my bones."

"The head of the House has come." Understand, I do not gossip about our guests, but Ichabod is a friend.

"The Master?"

"Lord Anderson himself."

"I don't believe it. Did you see the Tawny Mantle? The Lightning Sword?"

"He wore a spotted cloak. He didn't carry a weapon."

Ichabod frowned. "What would he be doing here?"

"They say he is far-traveled."

"Yes, but. . ." He abruptly downed his cup. "I best be off."

"Because of him?"

"Because of him. If he's here, there's a reason. *Someone* has sensed his arrival, make no doubt. More than one of your guests considers him their enemy. Prudence, I say. I'll hasten to finish my rounds this night. Keep warm, keep dry. Don't wander the halls; stay close to your desk."

I walked him to the door. Fairly leaping onto Nightshadow, he gave a wave and cantered off along a side path. His intuitions, born of experience, were not lightly dismissed.

✧ ✧ ✧

THOUGH IT IS against policy, I admit I sometimes doze at my station. When the wind roars over the eaves, it sings a song of slumber. I have noticed, however, that I never dream there—I cannot remember when last I dreamed at all—and am awakened, alert and refreshed, by any unusual noise. Nor am I ever startled awake, as I surely might have been when the porter bounded down the stairs. He did not shout; he never shouts, but rasped with clear urgency, "Miss Rebecca! We have a problem."

I straightened myself, assuming my professional air, but seeing his face, I knew this was no ordinary difficulty. Pinecoat is gaunt and middle-aged, with jet hair springing upward as if in a perpetual gale. His chin is weak, his nose, bulbous, his eyes, keyhole slits. He lacks any perceivable personality. He has served at the Leechmont from a lad, and his thoughts are slow as drying towels. He never has an original idea, knows no jokes, laughs at none told him. He occasionally drifts into monologues about carpets or lamps or the woodgrain of chair legs. He is a connoisseur of polish. I am extremely fond of him, like a favorite slipper, worn but comfortable.

"Tell me," I said.

"The Master's butler is missing."

"Who is missing him?"

Pinecoat hesitated. "Why, the Master."

"You mean William Hope?"

"I don't know the Master's name."

I maintained my patience. "The Master's name is Carter Anderson. Many people somehow know that. The man who accompanied him is William Hope."

"Well, William Hope is gone and the Master ain't happy." Pinecoat spoke with an aggrieved air, offended that any should besmirch the reputation of the Leechmont by disapproving of a guest's disappearance.

I rose, loathe to abandon my post for the second time that evening. "Remain here. If anyone comes in, try to be pleasant."

"I'll give them my best." To illustrate he produced a skeletal rictus.

"Do so, but don't smile."

"No, ma'am."

Comfortable footwear is so important when working at the Leechmont. One often makes many steps per night. Shoes must be elegant but discreetly supportive. I buy mine from Drice Shoes and Suits, shipped from the country of Far Wing. Delivery is sometimes difficult. This pair was new and not quite broken-in; I hoped I wouldn't have to travel much.

Upon arriving at Mr. Hope's room, I found Lord Anderson dressed and pacing the chamber, and Lady Anderson, sleepy-eyed and still in robe and dressing gown. Without wasting time on inquiry, I went to the braided rug beside the bed. Kneeling, I gave it a dainty sniff.

I kept my voice casual. "I apologize for the inconvenience. I'm afraid Mister Green has taken your butler." I rose, brow furrowed with practiced concern. "He especially likes rugs. We're not certain why. No doubt you were alerted by a splashing sound and Mr. Hope's cry. He must have stepped on the rug and been pulled in."

Lord Anderson's face paled. "I sensed a rush of Chaos. Chaos and Order fluctuate greatly here, but this was extreme. Where was he taken? Is he alive?"

"Let me assure you he lives. We've never had a casualty in these cases. I will see that he is returned. It may require a day or two."

"This has happened before?" When I say the Master's eyes blazed, I am nearly not exaggerating. His voice was quiet but ominous. I admit I took a backward step.

"Only once since I've been here," I replied, "but there have been other instances. We have an excellent procedure for lost guests."

"Why do you leave rugs about if this Mister Green comes through them?" Lady Anderson demanded, tears springing to her eyes.

"We don't know exactly what he is, my lady. There was an attempt two centuries ago to remove the carpets, but he just soaks through somewhere else. Such circumstances occur here on occasion. We are always prepared to deal with them."

"Carter!" Lady Anderson cried. "Where is his carpetbag?"

Lord Anderson glanced around the room and strode over to check the wardrobe. "That's why he was abducted. He has the fragments of my Lightning Sword."

"Then the tales of your sword being broken are true?" Curiosity overcame my discretion, I'm afraid.

He studied me, his eyes calculating. "Where did you hear that?"

For an ordinary-looking man, there is something about him, a command that brooks no disobedience. It wasn't in his voice, which remained low, but there is power in the Master, and I have never witnessed its like before or since. "I meant no disrespect. It is a rumor. Nothing more." I sought to regain my composure. "If you give me a complete description of the carpetbag and the weapon, I will see it is returned."

"This requires my personal involvement," Lord Anderson said. "Mr. Hope is more than our butler. He is our friend. And the sword isn't an ordinary blade."

This was an unanticipated difficulty, one I perceived might require exemplary tact. "My lord, there are certain dangers involved—"

"I am not a stranger to peril."

"Of course." The look on his face was enough to assure me there would be no chance of mollifying him with vain mouthings. I curtsied, an act surprising to myself. "I shall report to the Night Manager immediately."

"We will accompany you." He lowered his voice. "I never should have brought him. If anything happens to Will. . ."

"He wanted to come," Lady Anderson said. "You go, Carter. I'll change my clothes and meet you in the lobby."

Lord Anderson stopped at his room to retrieve a worn leather backpack before we proceeded down the hallway. I hurried to keep up with his long strides, directing him to the steam elevators to bring us sooner to the Night Manager's office. We quickly reached the Emerald Wing, labyrinthine corridors adorned from floor to ceiling with baize fabric green as a billiards table. Despite our haste, it took several minutes before we stood outside the onyx doors.

"He doesn't make himself accessible," Lord Anderson said. "Does he fear assassination?"

"Few would reach a correct conclusion so rapidly," I murmured, knocking on the door, hoping my superior was in an agreeable temper. A voice within responded, and we stepped into an office dimly lit by a single corner lamp. The Night Manager lifted his head from his expansive desk, his face umbral even among the shadows.

"Miss Rios," he rasped, remaining seated.

I introduced Lord Anderson. Neither man offered to shake hands. I explained the situation in the succinct manner my superior likes best.

"I will summon the hotel detective at once," he said. "Miss Rios will send a description of Mr. Hope to the head housekeeper of every floor. The detective will locate Mister Green."

"You must not notify the housekeepers," Lord Anderson said. "It could put Mr. Hope's life in further danger. His knowledge of the mechanisms of Evenmere makes him a target for our enemies. Nor must anyone outside this room learn of the loss of my Lightning Sword."

"Lord Anderson, all of our guests are required to abide by the Leechmont's Rules of Deportment," the Night Manager said. "Violence is not tolerated."

"Apparently, however, kidnapping is. This must be kept quiet. Has your detective experience with this Mister Green?"

"Not personally, but he knows the procedure."

Lord Anderson glanced at me. "Does Miss Rios know the procedure as well?"

"All our staff are well-trained."

"Then she will do."

"It would require summoning her assistant, who has other duties," the Night Manager said. "Surely—"

"Then summon her," the Master replied. "For the good of the House."

I admit I trembled. No one ever questions the Night Manager. Certainly no one save the Owners gives him orders. A bead of sweat broke on my brow during what seemed a lengthy silence.

"Very well," my superior at last agreed, reaching to pull a black bell cord to call my replacement.

We returned to the corridor, where the Master asked, "How many arms *does* he have?"

"I've only counted five, but others tell me there are seven."

"I didn't catch his name."

"He is the Night Manager."

The Master nodded.

"Lord Anderson, if I might... why did you insist on my guidance? The detective is relatively new but efficient. I am only the night clerk."

"Let us say I see something in you," he replied, enigmatically.

When we reached the lobby, both my assistant, Ting, and Lady Anderson were already there, the lady wearing a white cotton blouse and riding pants. I excused myself to my room to change as well.

Located down the hall from the main desk, my quarters are small but sufficient for my needs. Honestly, I spend little time there. I keep few decorations—a photograph of myself as a child with my parents in Nianar, a locket handed down from my great aunt, a scrolled bookcase with a few precious volumes.

I pondered what I might require. For a first layer, I donned breeches and a woolen blouse containing deep pockets, boots, and a leather, holstered belt. From a wooden case in my wardrobe, I drew my pistol, a pearl-handled 37 Hallister, eight-chambered, with a Corovian glass sight.

Over all this, I put on a floor-length red satin and lace ball gown embellished with velvet bows, high-topped to the neck to hide the clothing beneath. I brushed my hair in the looking-glass before giving it up for a lost cause. The boots, hidden by the dress, made me feel like a farmer in a tent, but I might need them later, and there was no way to carry them with me.

I returned to the lobby as Lord Anderson was finishing describing the Night Manager to Lady Anderson.

"Proof of your speculation that the farther we travel from the Inner Chambers, the more bizarre life may become," Lady Anderson replied.

"Which suggests other worlds and other life," Lord Anderson said. Catching my puzzled expression, he explained. "Clearly your Night Manager is from a world—or a dimension—much different than our own." He paused, brow furrowed. "We are far from the Inner Chambers, Miss Rios, deeper in Evenmere than even I have ever been. I've no idea what we may face, but I'm trusting you to be our guide."

I swallowed hard. I am too hidebound to comprehend metaphysics, but Lord Anderson's appointment of me as their cicerone left me uneasy. I am the night clerk, not a pathfinder. Nonetheless, I raised my chin. "I will do my best. Follow me, please, to the ballroom." I glanced at the Great Clock. The time was 12:06. "The dance began at midnight. There are some there who might help us find Mister Green."

We passed down the Frond Corridor, treading the acanthus-leaf carpet. Along the way I spied a chip in the wainscoting and a failed hallway gas jet, which I noted in a small pad I carry always with me. *Elegance through Vigilance* is a precept of the Leechmont.

We soon reached the twelve-foot doors of the ballroom. The two doormen opened them for us, slight surprise in their eyes to see me wearing a gown rather than my customary uniform. Dubaku, my friend and maître d', hurried to our side, eyebrows raised, grinning. A handsome man, I always admire his perfect demeanor.

"Welcome to the Grand Ballroom." His voice is silken and pleasantly low, and he bowed with his palms and head, an open-handed lift. "Refreshments will be brought to you shortly." Turning to me, he said, "Miss Rios. How lovely you look."

"Thank you, Mr. Osei." I glanced at the bandstand, where the musicians stood waiting, fingering their instruments. "Are we between numbers?"

Dubaku's expression lost none of its composure; only the eyes revealed his concern. "The band leader is uncustomarily late. I've sent someone to find him."

For reasons beyond my comprehension, musicians are delightful but perpetually unreliable. The guests would soon be restless, nor did I wish Lord Anderson to perceive further evidence of inefficiency. *Perception is Reflection.* I looked the musicians over. "I believe I can help."

Striding to the bandstand, I targeted the lodatone player. He is tall and thin with bulging eyes and a long face. "Fish, you aren't playing."

"Sorry, Becky, can't do it. I already told Dubaku. Guild rules. Banks will skin me if I start without him."

"And when you and Banks, grinning like little boys, were caught in a lie by the house detective, did you appeal to the Guild?" I asked sweetly.

He looked down. "No, Becky. We're both still grateful."

"There are important people here tonight. Consider it a personal favor."

He looked around, catching the eyes of the other musicians. "And a-one, a-two, a-three, a-four."

The ombo player produced a slithering melody, and the band took off. Guests began leaving their tables for the dance floor. I returned to my charges and a smiling Dubaku.

"Enjoy your stay at the Leechmont," Dubaku told them, flourishing his hands once more. Walking past me, he murmured, "You're a wonder. How did you do that?"

"Charm," I whispered back.

"What now?" Lord Anderson asked impatiently.

"Now you and I must dance."

He raised his eyebrows.

"Bear with me, please. There is a procedure to be followed."

He gave his sister-in-law an uncertain look but led me to the dance floor. Dancing being a requirement for one in his position, I had no doubt he would be competent. I was surprised, however, by his proficiency. He leads well, with great precision.

"Why is this necessary?" he asked, as we began with the simple *colaar*.

I retrieved a previously prepared slip of paper from my sleeve. "Subtlety is important in these matters. I will send out feelers and see what we get."

During a turn, I passed the note to a minor dignitary from Keedin. By the end of the first dance, I had four notes in return. There is an art to holding missives in place, reading them, not dropping them (disastrous!), writing another if necessary.

"What do they say?" Lord Anderson asked.

"One is from an anarchist asking why you are here. The—"

"Anarchists, here? Did you tell them who I am?"

"No, but your face is not unknown. Many factions, including

the anarchists, nihilists, and others, have permanent reservations at the hotel in order to conduct various business."

"There is more to the Leechmont than I expected. What do the other notes say?"

"A contessa from Garvin wishes an introduction to you. The remaining two are inquiring about your identity. My answers will be tactful, rest assured."

The band took up the five-step waltz, a number Lord Anderson accomplished beautifully.

"Is this the way the hotel detective would handle the case?" he asked.

"You and he would probably not be dancing. You asked me to do this, heaven knows why. I must use the connections I have."

He studied my face with his piercing blue eyes. "I made the right decision."

I blushed and looked down, my chest warm with pleasure. Truthfully, I might have found another way to approach the problem, though this seemed the most expedient. But perhaps my emotions clouded my judgment. There are few in Evenmere who can say they have danced with the Master of the House.

When the band broke into a *troate* several minutes later, a number requiring a constant changing of partners, I discovered my message had borne fruition. To Gladstone, the anarchist, I whispered that Lord Anderson was simply visiting those parts of Evenmere far from the Inner Chambers. I kept my gaze guileless, knowing he wouldn't believe it but needing him to believe I believed it. When Lord Anderson was gone, I would still have to deal with the hotel guests and must appear impartial.

He spun me away to an ambassador from Pyton Lakes, who desired an invitation to the Inner Chambers for his daughter. He passed me to a wealthy young gentleman wanting to know what the fuss was about. On the dance went, some knowing who I was, some not realizing my position. Invisibility is both the goal and the curse of those who serve. I have a gift for remembering names and was able to recognize all but one. Regular guests are easy, of course, transient travelers less so.

When the circle brought me back to Lord Anderson, I said, "The whole ballroom is abuzz about you, my lord."

"This is the very thing I wished to avoid. It endangers my

original mission. Both the anarchists and nihilists would happily murder me if it suited their purposes. The nihilists, in particular, have pursued me of late."

"If I might be so bold, could you tell me why you are here? It would help me unearth the correct information."

He hesitated. "You will tell no one this. My lightning sword was broken in a battle with a poet. After three years of research, Mr. Hope discovered it can be reforged here at the Leechmont. We came here hoping to learn how that can be accomplished."

"Do you often fight with poets?"

"Only when they try to dismantle Reality."

The dance took me into the arms of other men, some of whom gave me information or clues concerning Mister Green. When the number ended, we made our way back to Lady Anderson's table.

"What fun that looked!" she said. "Both in the dancing and the skullduggery. Do you practice often?"

"Not regularly," I replied, taken aback by her perspicacity.

Lord Anderson drew my chair for me, seating me as if I were an equal. I wondered if he was simply playing the role or if he treated everyone so graciously. He had called his butler his friend.

"What do we know?" he asked.

"A moment, please. I must sort this out." Placing my hands to my temples, I closed my eyes, recalling what I had learned. "My initial message concerned Mister Green, a simple inquiry on his location. More than half the replies were interrogatories about you. Gladstone, the anarchist, told me his people had seen Green this evening in the billiards room. That room was recently closed for renovation, however. He was clearly lying, wishing to obfuscate the matter. I don't know why."

"Any goal I seek, the anarchists routinely oppose," Lord Anderson said.

"I see. Colonel Derringer, who is retired military, heard a peculiar whistling this evening, seemingly emanating from the room beneath his own. There is no room below his; he is on the first floor; but such noises are said to be a trademark of Mister Green passing from room to room. The colonel's chamber is number 172, forty rooms from Mr. Hope's. His hearing the noise twenty minutes after your friend's disappearance suggests our quarry traveled that direction. According to the calendar, tonight is a full moon, a time of the month when Green seems to prefer the West Wing, confirmation of the colonel's observations. I think our inquiries should begin there. But you should be aware that even my mentioning Mister Green suggests he has taken someone, and any enemies you have in the ballroom will be more than curious."

"I will be mindful of it," he replied.

We left the ballroom by a servants' side door. Once away from public eyes, I reached back, unbuttoned my gown, and pulled it over my waist and shoulders.

Lord Anderson gave a startled exclamation behind me, and I realized my failure to mention I had other clothes underneath. I looked back to find him turned the other direction, his face scarlet.

Lady Anderson laughed. "It's all right, Carter. She's decent."

"My deepest apologies, Lord Anderson." My face burned as well. "I should have warned you. We shall be traveling in places unfit for finery. However, you prove yourself a gentleman of the first water."

He gave a sheepish grin. "The error was mine."

My pocket watch said 3:47 by the time we reached the West Wing. It was going to be a long night. We found the Wing Manager, Miss Fedorov, ensconced in her office worrying a set of ledgers. She looked up, frowning. "You've come about Mister Green?"

"How did you know?" I asked.

"He's been traveling through the wing, popping his head up here and there, frightening the guests. Someone said garlic would drive him away. We scattered it in the hallways."

"I noticed the odor," I replied. "You should have asked. Neither it nor any of the other two hundred thirty-two rumored remedies work."

She shrugged. "Management likes us to take initiative."

"True. Where was he last seen?"

"Corridor Seven, near the mechanical room. I can accompany you."

"Unnecessary," I said. "You have your own work."

She gave me a grateful smile. Though an excellent employee, she seems always crushed by the weight of her duties. I consider it a personality trait.

Yellow fleur-de-lises adorn pink wallpaper down the walls and runners of Corridor Seven, a style considered fashionable to the Duchess of Veth six hundred years previously and revived in the Modern Regal movement of the last century. Untutored by the fashionable elite, to my mind it has the appearance of runny eggs on a sow.

Every corridor has a mechanical room, filled with steam boilers, central gas pipes, bell linkages, and an assortment of machinery of such antiquity as often defies recognition. The Leechmont boasts a battalion of steam and mechanical technicians, hired as apprentices at the age of thirteen, but over the centuries some learning has been lost and many controls cannot be traced to their source.

Using my master key, I opened the mahogany door. Turning the valve controlling the gas-jet strikers revealed a room of moderate size. By engineering legerdemain, beyond the boiler lay a maintenance tunnel set lower than the mechanical room floor.

Lord Anderson's gaze swept the room. "Strange. This reeks of both Chaos and Order. It's as if—." His eyes widened. With amazing celerity, he drew a pistol from a pocket of his greatcoat. Yet when he leveled the weapon, he hesitated. I whirled to see a figure standing in the tunnel, only visible from the shoulders up.

According to the records, Mister Green can appear in various forms: a green knight, a green man made of leaves, an archer with a green face; but most often he is dressed as a gentleman in a stylish suit, its color the same hue as his skin. In this case, he had added a bowler hat. My astonishment at seeing the legendary creature was heightened when I recognized his face as that of Lord Anderson's butler, William Hope.

"Will?" the Master called.

The figure laughed, waved, and rushed into the tunnel. Without hesitation, Lord Anderson vaulted over a pair of steam pipes, dropped the five feet into the channel, and sprang in pursuit. I shouted a warning too late, met by a clattering and his cry of pain. Following after, Lady Anderson and I found him sprawled where the light of the gas-jets faded to total darkness, fallen head-first over an unseen cross-pipe.

"It was Will!" he exclaimed as we helped him rise. "We have to go after him!" He tried to walk but could only limp about.

"Wait, your nose is bleeding." Lady Anderson handed him a

silk handkerchief. "You need a moment."

He scowled but nodded his head and pressed the handkerchief to his nostrils.

"Despite the resemblance to your butler, it was Mister Green," I replied. "His color."

"Oh, William!" Lady Anderson moaned. "What has been done to him?"

"Some horror, no doubt," Lord Anderson said vehemently. "We have to save him."

"Not horror," I said. "That much is clear. Mister Green never abuses them, but I fear for our mission, Lord Anderson. He always returns his captives; I don't know what he might do if we pursue him. There may be unforeseen consequences."

Lord Anderson closed his eyes and placed a hand to his forehead, the anguish of indecision written on his brow.

But Lady Anderson said, "No. We can't wait."

He gave her a questioning glance.

"I know what it is to be abducted and imprisoned," she said. "No captor is benign. Whatever his intentions, Mister Green is a criminal. Not only has he taken William, he has the Lightning Sword. Why did he take it? What are his intentions? Does he serve someone who wants it?"

At her words, a chill gripped my chest. These were matters beyond my station. Yet *Service at Every Moment* is our motto. "His taking the sword *is* a mystery. He borrows people, not objects. Yet many factions with various agendas stay at the Leechmont, and alliances are constantly made and broken. Still. . ." I hesitated, remembering what I had read of the abductor. "It doesn't quite fit. Mister Green has never been known to delve in such machinations. He is considered a fairly innocuous member of a. . . certain class of guest inhabiting the lower levels. I don't mean the regular workers. A hotel of this size requires near self-sufficiency, much of it occurring unseen by its guests: gardens, docks, a slaughterhouse, a host of necessities. All the delivery services are at the back. But the designs of our permanent guests are unknown. Whether they are stray travelers stopping here for a century or two, or creatures serving the hotel in some manner, only the Owners might say."

Lady Anderson looked to the Master. He nodded his assent.

"We will require lanterns," I said. "I'll fetch them while you remain here, in case he returns."

With some effort, I climbed out of the channel and proceeded back to Miss Fedorov's office. "I need two lanterns and a map of the tunnels. Send a message to the Night Manager telling him where I've gone."

Goggle-eyed, she searched a cabinet and produced the map. A storage closet provided the lanterns.

"God Speed," she croaked as I left. I wondered whether she expected to see me again.

Retracing my steps with graceful alacrity, I found Lord Anderson somewhat recovered. We lit the lanterns and proceeded, striding into the darkness. My pocket watch showed 1:13. The tunnel was wide enough for two to walk abreast, separated by a wide pipe suspended on occasional concrete stanchions at knee height. Other pipes, such as the one that had tripped the Master, extended at intervals to the gray limestone walls, forcing us to surmount them. Even more pipes ran along the sides near our heads. A comfortable warmth emanated from them. The air smelled of limestone and moisture.

At first, I thought the passage silent, as one would expect in an underground way, but as we hurried briskly along, I became aware of the creaking of the manor above us, gentle but continuous as the quiet hum of the steam pipes. I imagined the tons of wood and stone weighing down upon us, threatening to collapse from its own weight, crushing us in its demise. I told myself the Leechmont's foundations were deep, that it had stood from time immemorial, but it failed to reassure me. I noticed perspiration on Lord Anderson's brow, but whether through concern for his friend or a dislike of closed places, I could not tell. I would have expected one such as Lady Anderson to be terrified by the journey, yet she moved confidently, almost joyfully, within the tunnel. You would have thought it a stroll through her home in the Inner Chambers.

We traveled some distance before reaching an intersecting passage.

"I was afraid of this," Lord Anderson said.

"Can you use your Maps?" Lady Anderson asked, a question I first thought directed to me, but Lord Anderson replied, "For some reason, they don't work here."

It is said the Master controls an inner compass, allowing him to always find his way through the infinite corridors and passages of the great House. But though the Leechmont is within Evenmere, it is a special place.

I drew forth the map I had brought, and we studied it together. As we looked, I was startled by something running over my foot. I shrieked and grabbed my pistol, causing the others to jump. A rat scuttled away, passing out of the lantern light. I put my hand to my chest and gave a deep exhalation. I do not care for rodents.

"My pardon." I was embarrassed, but Lord Anderson said, "Does the night clerk commonly carry such a weapon?"

"Only if she must play house detective in lieu of her usual duties."

He chuckled grimly and held out his firearm for my inspection. "It's just that yours is similar to my own, which is military issue."

"It was given to me," I replied. "I scarcely know how to shoot it. It's a wonder I didn't blow off my foot."

He gave me a curious look but did not press the matter. Lady Anderson patted my wrist, and we went back to the map. I pointed along it. "Two of the tunnels terminate in nearby dead ends; the way to the right leads to a central hub containing an underground water well. I believe we should go that way."

We turned to the right and had gone scarcely a hundred paces when we reached a circular chamber. A tall pumping mechanism stood in the center of the room, water pipes extending upward from it. On the opposite side, the tunnel continued beyond our lantern light. The room was damp and smelled of mildew. Mister Green stepped from behind the pump, his form faintly phosphorescent, and bolted into the tunnel.

We gave chase, scrambling around the pump and over pipes to reach the passage. For an instant, I thought I detected a glint of green far down the way, but was uncertain. Once again, cross-pipes at knee height barred our path, but Lord Anderson and I vaulted over them, leaving Lady Anderson behind. We halted at a *tee* branching to left and right, momentarily perplexed.

"Which way?" Lady Anderson asked, coming from behind.

I was about to unroll my map once more when I noticed a strand of faintly glowing green on the stone corner, a single cloth thread at shoulder height. I pointed to it.

"This way," Lord Anderson said.

After only a short distance, the tunnel ended at an open door. Stepping through it, we discovered a service stairway.

"Lookin' for somet'n'?" The voice startled us. A figure sat on a wooden stool, his face and form mostly lost in shadow. I raised my lantern higher. Though the light shone upon him, he remained an adumbral mystery, as if darkness emanated from him.

"Did Mister Green pass this way?" Lord Anderson demanded.

"'at he did."

"Up or down?"

"'e only go down from 'ere."

"What is below?"

"Nuthin' good."

The darkness around the figure seemed to gradually expand in a disturbing way, taking up more of the room. I put my hand on my pistol.

"Thank you," Lady Anderson murmured.

"Ain' nuthin'." The creature shrank back to his previous size, seemingly mollified by her social graces. I suppressed a shudder.

"What was he?" Lady Anderson asked, when we were out of earshot.

"A wandering vagabond, I suspect," I said. "Not everyone who dwells at the Leechmont is a guest or an employee, especially down here. Some are very old and best left alone."

We descended metal steps, painted black save where rust had taken hold, the twisted wrought-iron handrail cold to the touch. A stillness fell, the creaking of the Leechmont no longer heard, as if we had crossed a muffling threshold, the only sound our echoing footsteps, likewise chill and metallic on the stairs. After perhaps half an hour, a mist arose, turning our lantern light dim.

"Have you been this way before?" Lord Anderson asked.

"Not by this stair, but soon after beginning my employment I was taken to the level where we warehouse our supplies. The mist was present then, too. It's important for us to stay together." I refrained from mentioning that one of the footmen had disappeared into the fog on that occasion. A flattering drawing of his likeness appears alongside others in the Central Staff Room near a board displaying the number of days without an accident.

All three of us drew our pistols.

Although we could see neither the walls nor ceiling, our voices pattered away, indicating a large chamber. Rows of boxes on either side formed a narrow lane. As we passed down it, scents of wood, oil, cloth—and once, the smell of peanuts—rose from the crates. My pocket-watch said 3:25.

"Can you turn on the lights?" Lord Anderson asked.

"That's impossible, I'm afraid."

"Surely there is a master control."

I cleared my throat. "I'm told Management decided it best to leave the lights off for the sake of. . . morale." I fear I was unable to put the Leechmont's best foot forward but had to respond lest my guests think us wholly incompetent. The problem lies with certain *entities*, for want of a better word, who have infiltrated the lower levels, the sight of which is said to disturb one's mental equanimity. But the manual provided the night clerk contains facts not given to Warehousing, and I will say no more even in this personal journal.

"How can you store your materials without lighting?" Lord Anderson asked. "The workmen must be miserable. It reminds me of the black chambers of the Mere of Books."

"You have been there?" I asked. "I've heard of it, of course. What is it like?"

"As bad as this," he said, annoyed.

Lady Anderson had remained silent for some time; I asked if she was well.

"Well enough. I don't fear the dark. It has often been my friend." I wondered at that moment if her courage exceeded my own.

We passed an interminable time walking between the rows of boxes rising out of the mist, never once meeting a side door or stairs. Lord Anderson occasionally climbed onto a stack, holding his lantern aloft to see what lay beyond.

"If Mister Green can pass through walls and floors, he could be anywhere," he said after his last such foray. "How do we know we're going in the right direction?"

"We can't be certain, but I've studied his history," I said. "In past cases, his guests are invariably found far from their starting point but with little deviation in the direction of his route."

The rows of boxes gradually diminished, replaced by stacks

of furnishings. An establishment as venerable as the Leechmont tends to accumulate things, especially furniture old and new. Articles are broken or become outdated; guests leave personal items that are never claimed. Many such objects are eventually discarded, but others find their way into Storage and are forgotten. It is the disadvantage of a nearly endless space. But I must admit even I was surprised by the variety that appeared before our lantern light: pottery from the Minasian era, lamps from the early fourteen-hundreds; a tattered fainting couch from the days of Escobar the Third. More than any other paraphernalia, there were scores of looking-glasses.

Lord Anderson stopped to stare into the depths of the first one we encountered. His reflection, with his top hat and thin face, looked drawn and gaunt; Lady Anderson, much smaller behind him, resembled an angel or a waif. I, the farthest away, half my face lost in shadow, stared back one-eyed like a master criminal.

"As if the place wasn't eerie enough," Lord Anderson said. "They could at least turn the glass to the wall."

"What time is it?" Lizbeth asked. "I feel like we've been walking for days."

"I've quit consulting my pocket watch," Lord Anderson said. "The presence of so much Chaos makes time erratic."

Lizbeth turned to me. "How do you keep track of the hours?"

I stared blankly at her. "I don't know what you mean."

Lord Anderson studied me. "It's possible you've been here long enough to become synchronized to the Chaos, leaving you unaware."

Lizbeth patted my shoulder, leaving me further confused.

We continued past more mirrors showing ghostly images of ourselves. I kept my finger off my revolver's trigger, lest I fire, fooled by a reflection.

A noise arose above us, not unlike the sound of a file scraped across a kitchen countertop. We raised our weapons to the sound but could see nothing among rafters hidden in darkness.

"We must move quickly and quietly away," I whispered.

"What is it?" Lady Anderson asked, matching my volume.

"Trillers. Think of flying piranha." I am proud to say I kept an even tone. I can testify to the truth of the adage that, like the piping cry of a gargoyle on the eaves, you can mistake other sounds for those of a triller, but when you hear it you do not doubt its origin. The response to its cry is wholly instinctive.

Both my guests reacted as one would expect from experienced adventurers. Lord Anderson drew his legendary Tawny Mantle about his shoulders, and though I could still see him as a vague outline, I would have passed him by if I hadn't known he was there. Lady Anderson put both hands on her pistol, the better to direct it. They hurried along, almost entirely silent, though she the quieter of the two, moving in an extraordinary manner, a movement of feet and legs like both a spider and a stalking wolf. I realized that even her stylish footwear was made of a material intended to abet stealth. There was much to this woman. I sought with some success to emulate her.

The trilling continued, sometimes directly above us, at whiles some distance away, never numerous, for stealth is also *their* virtue. I'm told they gather into a swarm before attacking.

There is great comfort in love and friendship but little in terror shared. The moments crept by while I sought to avoid contemplating being eaten alive. The odd thought ran through my mind that my demise would leave the desk staff short-handed. I wonder if I am perhaps overly preoccupied with my work.

The trilling increased in number and frequency. Gooseflesh covered my arms, for how could we outdistance a flying enemy?

The attack began with a single triller darting agile as a swallow in flight. Before I could react, it took a lock of my hair, cutting it neatly away, carrying it clutched in its mouth. The creature, seen through the shadows as a blur of motion, appeared to be leathery green, wide-mouthed with angular wings. A pair of antennas rose a finger's length from its head. The lock of my hair drifted down from the heights, discarded as inedible. I put my left hand to the side of my cheek, hoping to protect my throat and eyes.

As if the triller had signaled the attack, all the creatures cried at once, a cacophony echoing off the mist-drenched timbers and stone walls. They dropped from the shadows of the ceiling a few yards in front of us, a flood beyond counting. I raised my pistol, knowing it would be ineffective.

Lord Anderson stood two steps before us, facing the horde. I will never forget him standing there, a ghostly outline in his Tawny Mantle, the trillers swooping down toward him, a mass of wings and maws, his arms raised above his head in defiance, not even bothering to point his firearm.

He spoke a single word. I will not write it even here.

It is commonly known the Master of Evenmere possesses Seven Words of Power. They are his greatest weapons, each producing a different effect. No one can wield them save him; only a few know their names or what they do. The Word sent a wave of golden light before him, though *light* is an incorrect term since it was a physical force.

To the trillers, fragile as they were, it meant death. They dropped by the scores, shaking the floorboards from the impact of so many striking at once.

The following sounds were indescribable, the simpering of the injured and the dying, the most pitiful noise I have ever heard, a cross between a crying child and a suffering cat. Had my own life not been threatened, I would have sympathized with the creatures, who only acted according to their nature.

Lord Anderson turned toward us. "Quickly now. There may be more, and the use of a Word drains me."

We had to walk over the bodies of the trillers. The wounded snapped at our boots, sometimes burying their small, sharp teeth into the leather, forcing us to kick them away with our other foot. But we were soon past them.

"How can you run a hotel with such monsters about?" Lady Anderson asked.

"Upon returning to my desk, I will contact the exterminators," I replied.

"Exterminators!" she exclaimed. "Those were hardly bedbugs."

"Thank heavens for that. *They* are so difficult to eradicate. You must understand, Lady Anderson, the Leechmont is unlike other establishments. I will, of course, have words with the Master Building Inspector to find out why the trillers were allowed to become so numerous; someone has failed to do their job and the Night Manager will hear of it. But there are Powers at work throughout the hotel. Some must be repressed, some ignored, some catered to." I gave Lord Anderson a pointed look. "Some are even guests."

"They should tear the place down and build elsewhere," Lady Anderson said.

"I don't believe that's possible," Lord Anderson said. "The longer we remain, the more I suspect the Leechmont serves some part in the Balance between Order and Chaos. There are primeval forces at work here."

A green glow emanated from a stairwell to our right, the first exit we had encountered. Reaching it, we discovered a message etched in cursive script onto the first stone step. *Green is taking the sword to the Quilted Woman.* I felt the blood drain from my face.

"That is Mr. Hope's handwriting," Lady Anderson said. "It's unmistakable. But what does it mean? William couldn't have written the letters there; they're burned into the concrete. Green must have somehow done it himself."

"As if Mister Green has possessed Will," Lord Anderson said. He turned to me. "Is that possible?"

It took a moment to answer, for my thoughts were elsewhere. "It has been suggested but never verified. Those Mister Green takes are returned unharmed but confused by the experience. I've read their testimonies, which are often conflicting. Some perceive Green as walking beside them; others describe him as a ghostly cloud surrounding them. Since you say it is Mr. Hope's handwriting, perhaps he isn't entirely under Mister Green's sway."

"If that's the case, who was in control when this message was written?" Lady Anderson asked. "Who is the Quilted Woman?"

I felt my pulse quickening. "She dwells in one of the sub-basements. I've never been that far down."

"We must find her," Lord Anderson said. "Can you direct our path, Miss Rios?"

"I can. But be aware we are going into even more dangerous ways. No one knows who or what the Quilted Woman is, but by the few reports, she is not to be trifled with. Encountering her may be fatal."

Undeterred, Lord Anderson turned toward the stairs, but I hesitated, momentarily fainthearted.

Any sort of employment requires a certain flexibility, a willingness to perform tasks unlisted in the job description; yet one isn't often asked to go so far beyond the normal call of duty. It is one thing to reconnoiter in Storage, quite another to enter the sub-basements. However, I quickly recalled myself to my position. The Leechmont never takes its responsibilities lightly, whether in supplying clean towels or recovering lost guests. As the saying goes, *One must manicure the minotaurs.* I fancy myself willing to go the extra league, though I felt in this case the task beyond my abilities. Failure would mean a loss of face for the Leechmont, wholly unacceptable as a matter of establishment pride, especially when dealing with the personage of the Master of Evenmere. Fortunately, such an occurrence would make my return unlikely and my dismissal unnecessary.

Walking down those stairs was akin to strolling through heavy draperies, a darkness with a *feel* to it, not merely a psychic resistance but tangible, as if we scraped our way through. I cannot completely describe it but recall it as fingers tearing at my face, my ribs, my back. Our lanterns became blue stars, scarcely lighting the way.

The Mumblers came. I call them that, for I haven't any other name. They whispered; they groaned; they spoke of my secret thoughts and fears, of the wrongs I had done, sometimes behind me, sometimes to either side, sometimes right before me, nearly pressing their lips to my own. I heard the word *murderer* echoing around me. Terrible memories arose of holding my pistol, pulling the trigger again and again. My friends fell around me, dying, and one whom I loved with them. I saw the blood on his face and I fled. Yet, the horror continued unabated, a continuous barrage, the voices rising and falling, the scene repeating until I thought I must go mad. How tenuous our hold on our selves; how easily we are provoked to shame and anger and tears when we think ourselves rational beings.

At last, I could no longer continue. I willed my feet to move, but they refused. I stood, knowing myself nothing—useless, meaningless, guilty of the greatest perfidy, worth less than an insect, a vapor amid darkness, no more than a shadow. I felt I would stand petrified until I could stand no more, only to fall to the steps and perish of hunger and thirst.

A firm hand grasped my own, a human touch. I could not think who it might be, who would care enough to seek me. I called my mother's name.

"Shh," someone said, so unlike the other taunting voices. "Follow me."

"I can't."

"You can."

I was gently pulled, led down one step and another. And

then another. Still the voices condemned me, but the other voice spoke calmly. "It's all right. These are lies you tell yourself. You did nothing wrong. You have worth. You are of value. You are worthy of love and respect."

We reached the bottom. The voices ceased. The fingers no longer tore at me. The lantern flared. I found Lady Anderson grasping my hand in her own, Lord Anderson's in her other. A faintness took me; I nearly fell, but she supported me. The Master sank slowly to his knees.

"Lizbeth," he croaked, "how did you do it? I saw the well I was thrown into as a child, the walls and darkness, the water closing around me. I couldn't even concentrate to use a Word of Power. How?"

Though he asked the question, she addressed me. "I told you I don't fear the dark, for I was so long within it. I recognized the voices, for they were the ones from my own thoughts during my captivity. When you have walked far in darkness and lies, you realize that somewhere, though you cannot see it, there must be light."

We sat several minutes, regaining our strength and courage. I wondered if I would ever be the same. Lord Anderson drew a bit of dried beef from his pack and gave us water from a flask.

"You came prepared," I said.

He laughed grimly. "A lesson hard learned. Journeying through sparsely inhabited countries in the House, I've been hungry more often than not."

From an inner pocket, I withdrew my own supplies to divide among us, having brought enough sandwiches for everyone. I normally take my lunch at three in the morning. My pocket watch said 2:52.

Lord Anderson chuckled. "You are also an experienced traveler."

"Not at all," I demurred. "I've scarcely been anywhere beyond my desk."

We rose and continued on. This was not a spacious chamber as on the level above, but a wide corridor. Thankfully, the mist failed to penetrate this far down. Though the walls were gray stone, red and blue tile covered the floor, creating whirling patterns which never seemed to repeat. There were neither boxes nor furniture stored there.

"How can we find this Quilted Woman?" Lady Anderson asked.

"The appendix of the Leechmont *Manual of Rules of Deportment* states she occupies a suite some distance down the corridor. The implication is that we will know it when we reach it."

At the first door we encountered, a nondescript, unnumbered, steel-framed entryway, Lord Anderson gave me a questioning look, but I warned that trying doors at random would waste time and perhaps prove dangerous.

After nearly an hour we encountered quilts of various kinds laid over the floor tiles and hanging on both walls. Halting, Lord Anderson held his lantern high to better survey them. The floor quilt extended beyond the light, the largest I have ever seen, patterned in alternating yellow and white squares. Those on the wall displayed various animals and men, the left side leaning more toward butterflies and other insects. They appeared almost three-dimensional, as if the creatures were poised to slip from the fringes of the quilts.

I bent down to feel the material. "This is sturdier than cloth."

"At least we won't have to remove our shoes," Lady Anderson quipped.

"Curious." I inspected the wall quilts. "These are ordinary fabric." Yet I misspoke, for the figures looked even more lifelike up close.

Lady Anderson stepped daintily onto the floor quilt, and we followed, proceeding along it for several hundred paces.

"There is power here of a kind I've never before encountered," Lord Anderson said. "Peculiar, leaning toward Order, yet possessing a singular randomness, like a book with Chaos compacted within its folds." Unconsciously, I think, he tapped his side where his Lightning Sword normally hung.

At times, he paused to inspect the figures on the walls. "Men in anarchist gray, soldiers from Kitinthim, East Wing, Veth, Aylyrium, a dozen other countries, some in uniforms I've never seen before. Here's one of our White Circle Guard. Quite detailed."

We came to a door covered in quilting of a leathern sort. Unlike the other doors, this one had a slight step up, also covered in a patterned quilt.

"I'll go first," Lord Anderson said.

I signaled him to wait. Motioning Lady Anderson out of the line of sight of the door, I stepped forward. Whatever awaited us, I would not have the Master of Evenmere placed in harm's way. The Leechmont protects its guests. I think I surprised him, for he opened his mouth to protest but said nothing.

Holding one hand close to my pistol, I gave three firm knocks. My palms were damp with sweat. I heard approaching footfalls. The door slowly opened.

The semblance of a woman stood before me, her figure slender but matronly, her hair gray, her eyes a stunning blue. She wore a full-length silk dress composed of the most vivid colors.

Her face and hands were quilted.

Seams ran vertically from forehead to chin in front of her ears. Another seam ran down the center of her face, bisecting her nose and mouth. Her head was rolled, as if by batting placed in horizontal strips beneath her cloth-like skin, which was the tan of old parchment. Her hands were likewise seamed and rolled, making her fingers appear large and clumsy.

I stood my ground, resisting the urge to flee.

"Hmm," she hummed. "Visitors. Please come in." Her voice had an inviting quality like cotton and lace. She stood aside, holding the door.

Seeing no immediate danger, we stepped across the threshold to discover the kind of modest sewing room found in any village. Quilts hung everywhere; lamps stood on the mantelpiece and side tables; a couch and two comfortable chairs decorated the chamber. To the credit of my training, I introduced myself and my companions with the aplomb of encountering one's great aunt, stressing my position as an emissary from Management. For her own name, she said only, "I make quilts. Please be seated while I bring tea."

We complied. I glanced at Lord Anderson. His face ashen with fear, he pushed himself deep into his chair, as if recoiling from a roaring flame, clearly sensing something neither Lady Anderson nor I could perceive. Lady Anderson appeared watchful but poised. Their reactions prompted me to focus my whole being on signs of peril.

The Quilted Woman brought tea in delicate Corovian cups on a fabric-covered tray, then seated herself on a stool before a hand-cranked sewing machine. Though I kept my pistol by my side, she never once turned her eyes toward it.

I studied the room more closely. Again, everything seemed innocuous; shelves held fabrics of every kind and color; a worktable stood in one corner.

"I receive few guests these days," she said in her warm voice. "I should probably get out more, but I'm a homebody. It's so good of you to come."

"Where do you get the material for your quilts?" Lord Anderson asked, irrelevantly I thought. His eyes held a fervor I could not comprehend.

"Ramo Particus sends them to me."

I literally twitched in my seat. If my finger had been on the trigger, I might have put a bullet through the upholstery. The name of Doctor Particus is mentioned only in hushed tones.

"What kind of materials are they?" Lord Anderson asked. "Of what are they made?"

The Quilted Woman laughed in a motherly way. "Why, the fabric of the universe, of course."

Lord Anderson's expression became one I do not think he has often worn, the look of a man facing a being of incalculable power.

After a pregnant silence, he blew a heavy exhalation and lifted his head, seeming to surrender against an irresistible fate. Seeing him so, I decided if the Master would not exert his authority, I would at least try mine. "As a member of the hotel staff, I brought these guests to you on the recommendation of Mister Green, who told us he gave you a broken sword belonging to them. Perhaps he also left another gentleman, Mr. William Hope, in your care. We wish to return him to his proper room."

The Quilted Woman smiled maternally. "*Tsk.* Mister Green comes to visit at whiles in various guises. We chat and reminisce of bygone eons when we were both young. I was beautiful once, you know, and loved to dance. He is so *delightful*! I have never quilted him; I don't believe his stitches would hold. Perhaps he was wearing your Mr. Hope when last he came. I couldn't say. But he sometimes brings me items for my use: trinkets and knickknacks, objects and beings. When last he came, he brought me this." She raised the corner of the red quilt folded beside her sewing machine, revealing the shards of the Lightning Sword within a white square, along with figures of knights and men.

"The cosmos is full of patterns," she continued. "Here is the pattern for you. All of you gather 'round now." She beckoned with her fingers as if to children.

I believe Lord Anderson tried to speak a Word of Power. It died in his throat. The three of us rose and stepped forward, helpless to resist the summons.

She turned to her sewing machine while we stood beside it. I struggled to move but my limbs refused to obey me. My gun hung limp in my hand. One by one, she stitched us into the quilt, using a process I now remember only in a dreamlike way. I saw her hands reach for me; I felt my body lifted. I witnessed the cranking of the machine, the rise and fall of the needle. It was entirely painless, the stitches a slight tapping along my frame.

Being two-dimensional is unpleasant, though we were not truly that, because in two-dimensional space I should have perceived my comrades only as lines. Nor to my surprise was I immobilized but could move forward or backward along the material. Still, my perceptions were greatly changed. I was turned sideways like the engravings on an ancient Minasian temple, the fabric of the quilt preventing me from perceiving my left side. When I tried to swivel in that direction, I found myself unaccountably upside down, my right side still showing. Though I was looking at my companions' feet, I did not feel as if I hung in the air.

The experience was less like being imprisoned in the cloth; rather, we had *become* fabric, delicate as a cotton kerchief. So terrified was I, I could scarcely muster my thoughts.

Wordlessly, we gathered around the shards of the sword. Being relegated to a single hand, Lord Anderson could only grip two of the four pieces. When he grasped the hilt, it radiated a dim light, turning the cloth around us golden, much as the morning sun colors a counterpane. Lady Anderson and I each took a remaining shard.

We stared helplessly at one another. Odd thoughts passed through my mind: I wanted to weep yet feared doing so lest the water soak into my fabric; I wanted to flee but couldn't imagine accomplishing it with one visible leg; I longed to clutch my companions' hands yet lacked a left arm to do so.

From the corners of our eyes, we became aware of the Quilted Woman's gaze upon us.

"That will do. That will do. I believe this one is done." She lifted the quilt, studying us more closely. "I will call this my Master quilt."

"Wait!" Lord Anderson exclaimed. "Please! You must release us. For the good of Evenmere."

She bent her ear close to him. "What's that you say? It's hard to hear you in there."

Lord Anderson appealed to her again, shouting this time. His voice, and ours, had the same woolen quality as her own. She smiled ruefully as if to suggest that such was life, then turned her head thoughtfully. "Here in my quilting room what is to be will be. In this place, the more doors you go out of, the farther you get in."

With this paradox, she hung us on an empty wall rack and stepped back, admiring her work, her blue eyes dreamy. Satisfied, she left the room.

"What *is* she?" Lady Anderson asked.

"Part of the Balance I can neither control nor withstand." Lord Anderson turned toward me. "As Master, I hold authority over Chaos and Order. If either exerts too much influence, I correct it. The Quilted Woman is more fundamental. . ." His voice fell away in awe. "The question is, what shall we do?"

"Her last statement sounded as if she were giving us a clue," Lady Anderson said. "Could she be trying to help us? That's illogical."

"Perhaps not," Lord Anderson said. "I suspect she is, like Chaos and Order, a personified Force rather than an individual, more akin to a burning sun or a raging sea. If so, her behavior might appear irrational to us. She spoke of doors out being doors in, suggesting we should go deeper into the quilt."

"In the hope of doors in being likewise doors out?" Lady Anderson asked.

"Something like that. Your thoughts, Becky?"

My own vanity occasionally surprises me, for even in that desperate hour, a thrill ran through me at his familiar abbreviation of my given name. How foolish we are, always children wanting to be admired by the Great. I cleared my mind. "Since we're unable to step out of our prison, I see no other choice but to go forward. Assuming we can."

"Being inside a comforter, we shall at least keep warm." Lady

Anderson surprised me again with her ability to banter when others would despair.

Logic dictated that being turned sideways would preclude traveling deeper into the fabric, yet when I attempted it by pushing to the left with my right foot, I turned in that direction. Setting out toward the center of the quilt, we found ourselves moving through endless whiteness, accompanied by a peculiar sense of receding. If you have ever walked through falling snow, you may have some idea of our journey. Looking behind me, an action rotating me upside-down again, I saw the other quilt figures hanging as if in air, gigantic from our perspective, and the room beyond even larger. As we journeyed farther, however, both were lost from sight.

A dread came upon me, a fear of wandering this waste for eternity, perhaps made immortal by its transforming properties. It gave me some comfort when my leg began to tire, suggesting the passage of both time and physical strength, even while it implied the possibility of starving to death. I looked at my watch and found it continued to tick. The time was 5:35; the night was drawing to a close. We had been walking almost continually throughout most of it, and I blessed the fit of my Drice boots.

We stopped to rest at Lady Anderson's request; I believe Lord Anderson could have walked a hundred leagues without complaint, so stolidly did he go. She removed her shoe to massage her visible foot.

"This place could use some decoration," she said. "Besides ourselves, I mean. Some paint on the walls, if there are walls, a few end tables, a four-poster bed."

"With satin sheets," I added, "and a looking-glass and dressing table. Maggedwin rugs would be nice, my lady."

"Blue, I think," she said. "But since we are in this together, you must call me Lizbeth."

I raised my eyebrow but otherwise hid my surprise and delight. She is a great lady. There are no loftier stations in Evenmere than those surrounding the Master. Even dukes and barons throughout the countries of the House defer to it. I should have demurred the commendation; it was too grand an accolade for the night clerk of the Leechmont. The Night Manager would have been appalled to see me lower my gaze and reply, "An honor. . . Lizbeth."

We chatted as women do, adorning the emptiness with imaginary ornamentation until Lord Anderson laughed.

"You find us amusing?" Lizbeth asked.

He shrugged. "Only an observation. We are at the heart of a mystery, in great peril, yet a woman is a woman regardless."

"And a man is a man, even if Master of Evenmere," Lizbeth answered sweetly, "all business and little decor. Or decorum, comes to that. Yet, if we ever get out of this, I suspect it will be because we are men and women working together, complementary in our kindred souls and varied viewpoints."

"I trust you're right," he said. "We need every possible advantage."

"At least we found the sword," I suggested, glancing at the shard I still carried. I hadn't thought to examine it previously and found myself abruptly awed. I was *holding* part of the Master's Lightning Sword. It tingled almost imperceptibly in my hand. Its makeup is neither iron nor steel. I ran my thumb lightly over the jagged blade, careful not to cut myself, for it is exceedingly sharp.

"It's wondrous," I gushed, forgetting myself.

"It's ancient, passed down from Master to Master through many generations," Lord Anderson said. "I thought it unbreakable. Mr. Hope tells me it isn't as old as Evenmere, though. Our records show the Masters have carried other weapons: pikes and spears, various swords; one used a brass mace lost when he died fighting a Nameless Thing in the Rainbow Sea. Each was more than a simple weapon, and like the Lightning Sword, received its unique power at the Leechmont, but there isn't any record of one being recast."

"So this is a gamble," I said.

He smiled ruefully, only half of his face perceptible. "I think of it as a necessity. To survive, I require a better weapon than a pistol. I must have this one remade or a new one empowered. Either way, it can only be done at the Leechmont."

"You possess the Words of Power. Aren't they enough?" I asked.

"The Words are specific. I can use them to dispel illusion, to seal and unseal doors, to find secret passages, to walk the world of Dream, and other tasks. At whiles, something blunter is needed." The man spoke of legendary power as I might talk of scheduling the maids.

"Someone is approaching," Lizbeth said.

I rotated to see a crimson-armored figure moving toward us, two-dimensional as ourselves. Recognizing him from the appendix to the *Manual of Rules of Deportment*, I drew a startled breath.

"Who is it?" Lord Anderson asked.

"A Nihilist Paladin."

"The Nihilist Assembly," he replied. "Their organization broke off from the Society of Anarchists five years ago and is even more fanatical. The anarchists seek to remove pain from the world by rearranging Reality; the nihilists believe life is utterly meaningless and wish to abolish all physical laws."

"After you checked in, Ichabod, our postman, warned of the rising of an unknown danger," I said. "It is an assassin, a Summoning with a brief life and terrible power."

"The nihilists must have sensed our arrival." Lizbeth pulled on her shoe. "I think it best we avoid this creature."

My mind churned. Every tale told of the paladins was one of horror. Could even the Master of Evenmere stand against it? In desperation, I ventured, "You mentioned secret passages. Could there be any in a quilt?"

Lord Anderson lifted his eyebrow. "Very perceptive. I'm able to sense when they're nearby; we've been approaching one for some time. I didn't want to raise your hopes by mentioning it. It's close enough now for me to make it visible." His expression changed; he spoke a Word of Power. Our surroundings popped and shook like a sheet hanging in the wind. The fabric rose, a wave throwing us upward, helpless as matchsticks. Fortunately, the quilt being soft, we landed easily, though strewn in every direction.

Lizbeth scrambled up. "That was exhilarating."

I pulled myself up from my hand and knee and looked about, hoping to see a doorway, but only the whiteness remained. The paladin drew closer.

"Quickly now," Lord Anderson commanded.

Snatching up our things, we broke into a run. A strange dash it was, for I felt only the pressure of my right leg, and our two-dimensional state caused us to move in jerking motions. Lizbeth and I struggled to keep up with the Master, who traveled like a younger man, his eye fixed on the horizon. I kept glancing back at our pursuer, flipping up and down to do so. He continued gaining on us.

When we began our flight, I felt I could go for leagues, but in less than a minute I began to flag. My leg stiffened, my breath grew ragged. Still, I vowed not to disgrace myself. Recalling running at other times when my physical condition was greater, I pressed on. Nonetheless, my vision narrowed with faintness before Lord Anderson called an abrupt halt. I bent over, hand on knee, gasping for breath. "I don't see anything."

To my chagrin, Lizbeth appeared scarcely winded. She is no coddled woman spending her time in endless drawing room conversation. "Only the Master can discern the effects of the Word of Secret Ways."

Lord Anderson reached toward something invisible to me. He knelt, feeling with his hand. A muffled click sounded; a door covered in red fabric appeared. He grasped the brass knob, then recoiled. "It's locked and sealed."

A fiery dart whistled past my head. I rotated toward the paladin. It was close now, running at full speed. Drawing back its arm, it flung another missile from its gauntlet. Flipping around, I pulled Lizbeth down, instinctively shielding her with my frame. The dart passed where she had stood, landing several paces away, a burning blade that blackened and scorched the "air" of the quilt.

I whirled to a kneeling position, bottom-up once more, and fired my pistol. I judged the shot fell short, though it was impossible to tell on the white field. I fired again, this time catching the paladin in the center of its chest. My Hallister revolver is a much higher caliber than most pistols, so much so it was difficult to control the recoil with one hand, yet the paladin did not even pause.

Memories of other times I had used my pistol flooded me. Of faces falling before me. Of those I had betrayed. Of those I had destroyed. My hand began to shake. I struggled to contain a rising panic even while I fired.

"Stand back," Lord Anderson ordered. "I must use the Word Which Seals."

In my torment, I scarcely heard him, though I remember wondering how a Word Which Seals could unseal a door. The Master spoke it, rocking the quilt again. The paladin, nearly upon us, was sent tumbling. As it regained its footing, I gained control of myself once more and emptied the chambers of my weapon at it, trying to pierce some vulnerable spot. I am an excellent shot but failed to get past the armor.

At Lizbeth's urging, I turned right-side up and hurried toward the door. Lord Anderson shook the brass knob. "It's unsealed but still locked." He spoke with incredible calm. I suppose that is why he is the Master. He drew his pistol, intending to shoot the lock, a plan that works wonderfully in stories and less well in real life.

"Wait!" From a pocket of my blouse I drew a set of lockpicks. Without waiting for his consent, I knelt and went to work.

Picks are so useful at the Leechmont that my initial training included several hours practicing their employ. One never knows when a key might be lost or an emergency occur for which my master keys are insufficient. In this case, however, I was hampered by the of use only one hand.

I realize it sounds mere hyperbole to say the paladin's breath preceded it, but it is the truth. I hope never to meet another creature of its ilk, one whose sheer *otherness* was palpable. Its exhalations were more than a stench, for it breathed ignominy, horror, despair. For an instant, my fingers refused to function; I saw no reason to go on; all the world, my life, my days of service at the Leechmont, seemed vain. I could hear the monster advancing, its footfalls heavy even in the quilt. In my mind I saw its face, its head that of a lion, a serpent, a shark, the pincers of a venomous spider, seen all at once.

I would have failed had Lord Anderson not placed his hand upon my shoulder.

Whether a display of the Master's might or simply the power of a human touch, I do not know. I rather think the latter—that there is strength beyond understanding in the compassion of another person; that one touch, one kind word, one sympathetic glance, can roll back great darkness. My despair fell away; my focus returned to the lock and my pick, my gaze narrowing to a tunnel, even my fear subdued by my concentration. Time slowed in a way I had only experienced in battle. Though it was but the barest instant, the moment stretched long before me.

The lock clicked open; I turned the knob even as the paladin loomed above us, a blazing sword in hand, prepared to descend and destroy.

I leapt through the door, going first lest I block the way. Lord Anderson and Lizbeth crossed the threshold together. The paladin's sword crashed down where we had been, rolling the fabric of the quilt and the door itself. The awful head gazed upon us.

Lord Anderson threw himself against the door, slamming it shut. The portal vanished.

None of us moved, too dazed by our encounter. My heart pounded; my hand, so steady when working on the lock, trembled uncontrollably.

This was quickly followed by a tremendous feeling of expansion, like a pillow being fluffed, as I became once more three-dimensional. I could see my left side. With an effort, I contained the urge to weep.

When we recovered, I reloaded my pistol, and Lizbeth and I handed our shards of the Lightning Sword to Lord Anderson, who placed them in his pack. He gave her a wry smile. "You were right; it required all our varied gifts to win through."

"But where are we now?" she asked me.

Looking about, I groaned. "These are the Luxury Suites." I consulted my pocket watch. It was seven minutes till midnight. We were making good time, but I wondered if we would survive the night.

There is only one Luxury Hallway, twenty feet tall and equally wide, lined on both sides by oak wainscoting and doors stretching nearly to the ceiling. The doorknobs, proportional to the doors, were twice the size of an ordinary fixture. A dull gray light emanated from a floor-to-ceiling stained-glass window at the end of the hall.

Lord Anderson craned his neck to the pinnacle of the doors. "Do giants dwell here?"

"We haven't registered new guests in the Luxury Suites since I began my employment," I said. "Nor have I met any of the current residents. The records show most as occupied, but neither the maids nor the service people come here for any reason." I did not add that I dreaded the day I might have to enter one of the rooms.

"There is someone down the corridor," Lizbeth said.

Turning my gaze in that direction, I saw a comfortable nook furnished with a fireplace and chairs. The air in the corridor was chill, and Mister Green sat warming his hands before the fire.

Lord Anderson stiffened. He raised a finger to his lips for silence and gestured for us to remain where we were. Drawing his Tawny Mantle about him, he seemed to become one with the wainscoting.

Lizbeth and I pressed ourselves against the wall. I vainly attempted to follow the Master's progress but was only able to imagine it, measuring the distance with my eyes. When I thought he must surely be at Mister Green's heels, there was still no sign. By this, I knew he traveled with exceeding stealth.

Despite the Master's efforts, Mister Green must have sensed his approach, for he abruptly leapt to his feet. Momentarily, he struggled with his unseen opponent, only to bolt down the hall.

"Come on!" Lizbeth ordered.

We broke into a run. By the time we reached the fireplace, we could scarcely see Mister Green speeding along the gloomy corridor. Lord Anderson remained invisible to us, but we heard his footfalls ahead.

We sped past oversized paintings set at a level higher than the eyes of any human, abstract art depicting neither country scenes nor men of renown, only splotches of color forming geometric and random shapes. We were gaining on Mister Green when he halted, turned back toward us, and took a single step forward.

"No!" I shouted, raising my pistol.

With a tip of his hat, he melted into a braided rug lying before a doorway, flowing into it like candle wax. Lord Anderson appeared at the rug's edge, and we trotted up beside him.

When we had caught our breath, the Master turned to me, "What now?"

I did not answer, for my eyes were fastened on a nameplate, long as my arm, beside the door of Luxury Suite #1. I pointed toward it, struck speechless.

"Doctor Particus," Lizbeth read. "The Quilted Woman mentioned him. Who is he?"

"A permanent guest of the Leechmont," I replied. "By all accounts, he has dwelled here since the hotel was first established. Like all the residents of the Luxury Suites, he pays his bill directly to the Night Manager."

"One of the long lived." Lord Anderson spoke without detectable skepticism in his tone.

"What else do you know of him?" Lizbeth asked.

"Only that he is never to be disturbed," I said. "Ever. Five years ago the anarchists chose to ignore that stipulation by slipping a calling card under his door. Firmly against our policies, of course; one does not approach another guest without a proper introduction. The next day, their pelts were found tacked to the hotel fascia."

After a momentary silence, Lizbeth asked, "Isn't. . . skinning another guest against your Rules of Deportment?"

"Though not directly mentioned in the manual, it *is* implied. A number of the staff felt the doctor should be expelled, but they were overruled by the Owners, who have a broader perspective. Having only been employed a few short months, I found it both disturbing and regrettable."

Lizbeth cleared her throat. "Unless you happen to know the doctor, perhaps we should be on our way."

"A moment's consideration," Lord Anderson said. "Is it coincidental that Mister Green brought us straight to his doorstep? He directed us to the Lightning Sword. William may be influencing him to help us."

"Or perhaps Mister Green has plans of his own leading to our destruction," Lizbeth said.

"I can only speculate," I replied. "Hotel Management considers Mister Green a mischievous sprite, a fixture of the establishment known as little more than a nuisance. There aren't any reports of his causing permanent harm to individuals. Particus, on the other hand. . ." I shivered.

"We can't know where Green has gone, can we?" Lord Anderson asked.

"Not at this point, I'm afraid," I said.

"Then this is our only lead. I shall attempt the door."

I tried to sound courageous, though I spoke with all the hope of a spider before a dust mop. "I can't allow you to do that alone. We already know what happens to guests lacking an introduction. However, as a member of the staff, there is a chance my credentials might make an intrusion acceptable. But, Lord Anderson, you are taking a terrible gamble."

He looked at me with grave concern. "I am used to such risks, but I regret imperiling you." He then added, "Lizbeth, you must stand back. If we don't survive, you're to serve as Steward until the House chooses you or another as Master."

Lizbeth opened her mouth to demur, then bowed her head and stepped to the side of the door. I raised my eyebrows at his words. Apparently, she was the assumed heir to the title of Lord of Evenmere, though his phrasing of the House doing the choosing struck me as obscure.

He and I stepped around the rug, being careful not to tread upon it. Lord Anderson placed his hand on the door.

"Another new sensation," he said. "Blends of Chaos and Order such as I've never felt before." He glanced over at Lizbeth, his eyes troubled. "I never should have brought her, either. We thought it a simple errand. Foolish of me."

He straightened his back. "I'm ready."

Somehow, his misgivings gave me courage. I hesitated only an instant, contemplating the proper tact. If one must broach the threshold of destruction, I thought it best to do so with authority. I knocked boldly, calling in a loud voice. "This is the night clerk of the Leechmont. The Master of Evenmere, Lord Carter Anderson, respectfully requests a word with Doctor Particus."

We waited, I nervously counting the time, hoping I wouldn't need to risk impertinence by having to knock again. Twelve seconds passed, then twenty, before heavy footfalls sounded within the chamber, the tread of a titan. The door opened wide.

No one stood before us. I had directed my gaze upward, assuming Particus nearly as tall as the door frame. Dropping my eyes down and farther down again, I discovered a man scarcely a foot tall, dressed in a silver material bright as a tea service, with ebony shoulder pads and shoes. His hair, likewise dark, rested on his shoulders.

"Carter Anderson." His voice was many-toned and pleasantly harmonic. "I have and have not been expecting you."

The shock in Lord Anderson's eyes could not have been greater. Not because Particus recognized him, I judged, but because of what the Master recognized in Particus.

"Please come in," Particus said. "Even she who stands behind the door."

Lord Anderson groaned, but Lizbeth peeked from around the architrave, and we three complied. The similarity between his invitation and that of the Quilted Woman intensified my anxiety.

If I must face monsters, I prefer they appear without disingenuous politeness. I clutched my pistol, fairly certain it was useless.

"What are you?" Lord Anderson asked. A shiver ran up my spine at his use of *what* instead of *who*.

"I am many things," Particus said.

"I suspect I've heard of you by other names," the Master said. "Foley's Shade, the Double One, the Smallest."

Particus chuckled, smiling only with the left side of his face. "Foley's Shade, the light which casts two shadows. That is one of my attributes. But it's a jest, a bit of fun."

"We have come—" Lord Anderson began.

"Through Mister Green and the Quilted Woman," the doctor said. "You have ridden the Fabric of the universe. You seek to mend the Lightning Sword. A pretty stickpin, that."

Sweat trickled down Lord Anderson's forehead. Even I, who understood none of it, felt we stood before a Power. The stories I had heard of Doctor Particus were as nothing compared to the pervading energy radiating from his diminutive form.

"I can and cannot repair the blade," the doctor said. "I am an artist of the highest and lowest degree. I paint with the strong and the weak brush, with great gravity and radiating decay, my landscapes both attractive and repellent. Do you wish to see my work?"

Lord Anderson's lip trembled. "Must we?"

"What artist doesn't long to be appreciated? I insist, and it is the way you must go."

Lord Anderson bowed his head and closed his eyes as if accepting some unspeakable doom. "Why should these two suffer my fate? I am the Master of Evenmere; the duty is mine. I beg you, if you have any mercy, spare them."

Particus laughed, his many-toned voice ringing in the chamber. "Nary a shred. I am cold, Carter Anderson, and burning hot. Right this way."

Lord Anderson's inability to resist the doctor terrified me. I wanted to run, at least taking Lizbeth with me, but something prevented me—loyalty to my position and the establishment, unwillingness to act the coward, I suppose. And I have never retreated before—oh, but I cannot lie, not even in this diary no one will ever see.

Particus led us to a door as tall as those in the hall. So powerful was his presence, I do not recall whether the room we were leaving was even furnished. The door opened of its own accord, revealing an endless darkness. A cold, soundless wind blew from it, chilling my soul.

Particus waved us within. Lord Anderson went first, vanishing into the blackness. Lizbeth grasped my hand and we entered together like frightened schoolgirls.

I could see nothing, not even light from the room behind us. Lizbeth's fingers evaporated beneath my grasp. I called her name at the same instant she uttered mine. I reached out but could not find her. I stood still, awaiting I knew not what. Gradually, however, I recognized a blue, luminous pathway beneath my feet, receding far into the distance. Beside it stood a series of paintings framed on stands like floor mirrors.

The voice of Particus emanated behind us. "I leave you to it. You will recognize the landscape you need when you see it." The door slammed, booming through what sounded like a vast chamber, its echoes impossibly long.

Though I hadn't seen him before, I discerned Lord Anderson standing in the path ahead of me, his face grave in the blue luminance.

"What does it mean?" I asked.

"As Master, I know more of the nature of existence than others do, facts our scientists have yet to discover. A civilization can only assimilate so much information, so I keep such matters to myself. Particus is. . ." He bit his lower lip. "Though I've never seen him before, I recognized him at once as a representation of primeval Force. Unlike Order and Chaos, he isn't under my authority. I can neither control nor resist him."

He hesitated, studying me. "I don't want to overwhelm you, Becky."

"I've seen many oddities in my tenure as night clerk."

"Very well. You know that the universe is made up of objects too small to see. But at the tiniest level, they don't follow the ordinary laws of science. I mentioned Foley's Shade, a metaphor for a single object occupying two places at once. That is only a fraction of the strangeness. Particus represents—no, he actually *is*—a physical manifestation of that lowest level."

His words were beyond me, yet I understood why he, who held much power, feared the doctor. "What shall we do?"

"What he has sent us to do," Lord Anderson said. "Study his paintings and hope for the best."

"Is it possible he wants to help us?" I asked.

"*Wants* is meaningless when you speak of him," Lord Anderson said. "But he may also answer to the Balance, or perhaps a greater Balance, in ways I can't conceive."

So saying, he approached the first painting. It was beyond any work of art I have ever seen, for the images moved, their coruscating energies traveling simultaneously in upward, downward, and sideways cascades. Its great depth made it appear incredibly lifelike, and it seemed to be telling me something, imparting information I could never comprehend. I drew closer and felt myself falling into it. Startled, I wrenched my eyes away and found I still stood on the path.

"This isn't the one," Lord Anderson said.

We moved to the next painting, completely different from the first, done in shades of red and orange, depicting endless rows of minuscule blocks constantly trading positions. The figures possessed a disorienting quality suggesting a fourth dimension, filling me at once with an unbearable sense of the unfathomably *alien*. I looked away and we moved on.

Down the path we went, past painting after painting. The farther we traveled, the more the way widened and the larger the canvasses became, until they towered above us, our heads little higher than the ornate bottom frames.

We reached a painting possessing a shimmering quality. Gigantic, shadowy shapes moved within it. Though I could see nothing clearly, something about it was so foreboding I cried out a warning.

Even as the words left my mouth, Lord Anderson was abruptly pulled into the frame as if by an invisible hand. He gave a brief shout and was gone.

Lizbeth shrieked and sprang forward. I seized her arm lest she, too, be taken.

"Let me go!" she insisted. "Oh, let me go! I must follow him."

"You mustn't!" I replied.

A low moan sounded nearby. We both froze, then began searching for its source. Hearing it again, we ran to look behind the enormous frame. Lord Anderson stood with his back to us, head down, arms hanging limp by his side.

"Carter!" Lizbeth swept to him, placing her hand on his shoulder. "Are you all right?"

"I. . ." His voice faltered. I held both hands over my mouth to suppress an outburst of emotion.

"Carter?" Lizbeth said.

"I. . . uh. . . I." Seeing he did not respond, she seized his shoulders and turned him. His face was slack, his eyes, vacant.

"Speak to me, Carter!" She cast an imploring gaze toward me. "What's happened to him?"

A shiver ran through me. "He's been halved."

"Halved? What does that mean?" For the first time in our adventures, she sounded near panic.

I took a deep breath. "It's an old tale whispered throughout the Leechmont. He's been divided. Half of him went through the painting, leaving this half behind. We have to find his other half and reunite the two."

"Where has it gone?"

I hesitated. "It's. . ." I sought to regain my composure long enough to remember a brief paragraph in the back of Typhon's *Leechmont History for Dimwits*. "His lost half will travel in a more or less straight line. We must intercept him."

Her eyes went wild. "What kind of madhouse is this?" Bursting into tears she threw her arms around him.

His expression grew troubled. He lifted his hand to pat her shoulder, his words tenuous. He gave a *tik* with his lips before speaking, as if struggling to think. "Lizbeth, what's wrong? Don't cry, dear. Don't cry."

She studied his face. "Can you understand me?"

"*Tik*. . . I can't seem to. . . Everything's. . . foggy."

She looked imploringly back at me. "He is the father I never had. We must save him."

I steadied myself, trying to display an assurance I did not feel. "We shall do so."

"How, when we don't even know where he's gone?"

I considered the situation. "Particus said we would recognize the painting we needed. Perhaps it will lead us out of here. Once back in familiar corridors, we can find his other half."

The look she gave me was bleak as any I have ever seen. This was clearly a moment requiring reassurance. "I am the night clerk because I have a knack for solving problems. Intuition often leads me. You think our odds impossible; we shall make them possible." I admit my words bordered on braggadocio, but appearances must be maintained, and I do have some skill in unraveling conundrums. "Have courage. We shall prevail."

My words had the desired effect. She lifted her shoulders and thrust her chin bravely forward. "Very well. We should make haste."

This proved more difficult than expected, for Lord Anderson could not be hurried. Lizbeth had to take his hand and lead him shuffling along, her attempts at urgency in vain. We struggled so for several minutes, passing more paintings, each unique, some bizarre, some portraying halls and chambers unfamiliar to me. At last, we stopped before one depicting a room I recognized. "This is the one, I think. It's the Mirror Room, lying adjacent to the aviary on the first floor, not far from the Grand Fountain. From it, we can travel through its mirrors to other parts of the hotel."

"We may find a better choice farther on," Lizbeth suggested.

"*Tik*. . . This one." Lord Anderson pointed with a shaking hand. "Take. . . this one."

"It's possible he senses his other half," I said.

"I shall go first then, in case I, too, am divided," Lizbeth said.

"Lady Anderson. . . Lizbeth," I said. "The responsibility for your safety is mine. I must precede you."

"Me," Lord Anderson said.

I swallowed. "I'm sorry, but that is impossible. If you were halved again and survived, there would be two of you for us to find."

"Then it must be me," Lizbeth said. "You are the only one who can lead us. Should you be halved, we would be left without a guide."

Her logic was unassailable. I nodded. "If it allows you through, you mustn't turn back with any part of your body. The result could be disastrous."

She nodded and pulled herself onto the lip of the gigantic frame, took a deep breath, and stepped through into the room beyond. Turning, she spoke to us, but we could not hear her.

Lord Anderson and I went through together. Despite his affliction, he followed my directions without hesitation.

The Mirror Room is a high-ceilinged chamber filled with hundreds of looking-glasses. Despite having been there many times before, I was unprepared for the extent of its heights, nor were the mirrors gargantuan obelisks when last I came.

"The room has grown!" I exclaimed. I gave Lord Anderson a questioning look, but his thinking had become too slow to be of use.

"Remember how the path widened and the paintings grew successively larger?" Lizbeth asked. "I think rather we have shrunk."

I stared at her, trying to rationalize the possibility. Judging by the size of the mirrors, we were two to three inches tall.

"Carter's earlier talk about Particus answers for it," Lizbeth said. "He has spoken to me before about the unusual aspects of Reality. Our bizarre host commands forces relative to one another, size surely being one of them. Either he shrank us intentionally, or we shrank as a repercussion of passing through his gallery."

For me, that moment—Lord Anderson incapacitated, the two of us diminished—was the darkest since our journey began. I took several deep breaths and forced what I hoped was a brave smile. "The resources of the Leechmont are at our disposal. We shall carry on."

As if in answer to my attempted resolve, I caught movement in the nearest towering looking-glass. Still in the form of William Hope but small as ourselves, Mister Green stood grinning and beckoning in front of it. With a laugh, he leapt onto the frame and plunged through the glass.

"Should we follow?" I asked, uncertain.

"Follow." Lord Anderson spoke with greater energy than before, and when he walked, he moved more quickly with longer strides as if accustoming himself to his condition.

Nearing the frame, I could not help but notice our reflections. Despite our hardships, Lizbeth looked fresh as an orchid. My hair was a catastrophe; I should have tied it back from the start.

We climbed onto the ledge formed by the frame and passed through together, Lizbeth and I helping Lord Anderson along. There being no frame on the opposite side, the step proved a large one, jolting me to the bone and causing Lizbeth to fall to her knees. Wobbly as he was, Lord Anderson somehow managed to stay upright.

I sighed. We were still in the Mirror Room, surrounded by

looking-glasses on every side. Lizbeth gave me a questioning glance.

"Nearly every glass leads somewhere," I said. "Some always go to the same location, others change over time. A guide map is provided, but we are too small to reach the Information Desk."

"Why would Green bring us here?" Lizbeth asked.

"If he's trying to take us somewhere, we might have to step through several mirrors to get there. Which means. . ." I scanned our surroundings and pointed. "There!"

Mister Green raced toward a distant glass.

We followed. He paused at the corner of a frame to peer back at us, grinning like a jester before darting behind the mirror. By the time we reached it, he was standing in front of another one. Catching our eyes, he bounded over its frame like a boy.

When we pursued, we found ourselves in an alcove just off the main room. Four or five mirrors stood within. The walls were painted a light peach with white baseboards. Mister Green had already reached another glass and was leaning on it like a leprechaun smirking by a pot of gold. Tipping his hat to us, he vaulted the frame.

We followed in haste. Crossing over, my feet touched rocky ground. I gave a startled exclamation.

"Where are we?" Lizbeth asked.

We appeared to be outdoors, for a mist shot through with flashes of color surrounded us. I turned around to find the mirror vanished, replaced by a wall of interlocking beads. When I surveyed the ground, what appeared to be solid earth was composed of the same latticework structure.

"See how the mist moves," Lizbeth said. "It darts, patches of it in one place suddenly rushing to another."

"*Tik*. . . Smaller," Lord Anderson rasped. "Particus." He struggled unsuccessfully for further words.

"Smaller?" Lizbeth asked. "We're smaller? We've continued to shrink?"

"Yeesss." He breathed the word and slowly swept his hand toward the sky. "Smaller than atoms."

Unable to bear the ramifications, I set my mind on practical matters. I studied the ground, hoping to discover Mister Green's footprints. Boots upon beads—it was hopeless.

"There is nothing to guide us," Lizbeth said. "Should we set out at random?"

"In such a region we might become irredeemably lost," I said. "I suggest we wait in the hope of Mister Green's return. He has led us this far."

"Let's eat, then," Lizbeth said. "I'm famished and we will need our strength."

I took some cheese from my diminishing supply. Lizbeth helped Lord Anderson sit. As we ate, I watched the coruscating energies pass back and forth in a multitude of hues, beautiful in its way. Yet the bolts were not made to be seen by human eyes. Imagine a lightning flash where each part is momentarily visible, like flowing drops of water.

Lizbeth treated Lord Anderson with the loving diligence of a daughter, helping him eat, seeing he got enough, giving him most of her share, deep concern etched upon her brow. She turned to me, tears in her eyes. "He must be made whole."

"We won't rest until he is."

She studied me. "I believe you're right. I trust you."

"You are kind."

She shook her head. "It's more than that. *He* trusts you. From the very first he has told you facts the Master does not normally reveal, information only those in his inner circle know. He explained the Words of Power and the Lightning Sword to you, revealed aspects of the universe he tells to only a few. He sees something remarkable in you."

I dropped my eyes, my cheeks burning. "He doesn't know me." My facade of professionalism nearly crumbled. I felt a fraud. We were in territory beyond my experience, facing questions I could not answer, ones that might mean the life or death of my charges. I recalled, too well, another time when I had failed.

With an effort, I rallied, reminding myself that though I am only the night clerk, mine is the face of the Leechmont. *Confidence through Competence*, as the Night Manager reminds us. I tried to think. "Lord Anderson spoke of Foley's Shade, suggesting a single object could exist in two places at once. The Master has been halved. He now exists in two places, yet when twin shadows are cast by two lights, one is often dimmer than the other."

"Unlike the objects of Foley's Shade, Carter isn't wholly himself, you mean," she said. "Something has been taken from his essence. Presumably it now resides with his other self."

"Yet that other self is still Lord Anderson. If he can, he will seek the same goals he did before."

"But he doesn't have us to help him. He might not be able to reason."

"Or he may be the brighter shadow," I replied.

We fell silent, both considering. I thought of the greater and lesser Powers existing in the hotel, and of the path we had taken: Mister Green, the Quilt Woman, Doctor Particus. I believed they were related: the green man who rises out of rugs, the seamstress who stitches the Fabric of the universe, the tiny creature dwelling in and perhaps regulating the smallest motes of that fabric. I explained my musings to Lizbeth.

"Evenmere is like a pocket watch, all its parts necessary to its movement," she replied. "There is a Great Machine I have seen, one level down if you will, which is the mechanism allowing Evenmere to exist—the casing of the watch. But these creatures we have encountered must be part of the whole, regulating in some fashion the watch's internal workings. It makes me wonder: could the Leechmont be the underlying foundation upon which the entire House rests?"

I frowned. "Your metaphor suggests matters beyond my comprehension. However, it's true that these beings keep a permanent residence in the hotel."

I returned to our original subject. "If Mister Green truly desires to aid us, wouldn't he help the other Lord Anderson? Is he perhaps doing that now?"

"If so, that would explain Green's absence," Lizbeth said, "assuming he can't also be in two places at once. We should wait until he brings the other Carter here."

"No," Lord Anderson said.

We turned to him. He closed his eyes. "*Tik.*" He raised a slow arm to point into the mist. "*He* is out there."

"You mean Mister Green or your other self?" Lizbeth asked.

"Both. I sense him."

"Then you must lead us," I said.

He nodded slowly and set out.

As we proceeded, objects tall as trees appeared out of the mist, again formed like latticed beads, forcing us to pick our way around them. Between those and the fog, we could see only a few feet before us.

"Chaos," Carter murmured as we walked. "*Tik*. . . Chaos."

I could not help but agree. Our every step revealed new aspects of the region. Hazy clouds—orange, pink, and blue—surrounded tiny, indistinct spheres. The spheres themselves both moved and remained in place, one version veering away, leaving its duplicate, and behind that, another copy. They traveled constantly, yet never seemed to touch one another, their discharging energies creating a high-pitched, incessant drone.

And then the ghosts appeared.

The first one glided out of the mists, peering at us from beneath a shroud, its face a ghastly, vacuous ruin, its eyes empty orbs, its arms hidden in its dark robe. I aimed my pistol at it, and it flickered away, emitting a noise like crackling rice paper.

We froze, waiting. Then Lord Anderson led us forward again. Almost at once, more of the crackling sounded to our right, its source hidden from our eyes. We veered left to avoid it, moving steadily away. It grew gradually dimmer, leaving me to hope we had escaped the specters.

We reached a clearing large enough that the mist hid the taller latticeworks, creating a beaded plain. We had scarcely begun crossing it, however, when more of the ghosts appeared before us. We retreated, only to find them behind us as well, dancing in a circle, holding hands, their individual forms randomly flitting in and out of existence. Crackling moans came from them, the most hideous sound I have ever heard.

How easily we are transformed from rational beings to superstitious children. I am a person of reason, yet their aspect triggered something primitive within me. Their dead, empty faces, their emaciated limbs. I grew panicked. I could not even think to raise my weapon. Perhaps it was some power they wielded, for Lizbeth seemed equally quailed. Our pistols fell from our trembling hands.

In horror, I realized the circle was narrowing, yet as it did, their numbers remained the same, as if they each grew smaller to accommodate the space while *appearing* no smaller. Ever closer they came.

I could not move. Finally, they were within arms' reach. One seized my hand in its talon, icy as the tomb. Another grasped my other hand. They did likewise to Lord Anderson and Lizbeth.

We danced with the ghosts while their dreadful moans filled

the air. And in the movement of the dance I lost myself. I was no longer the night clerk of the Leechmont. I was a single spark, a speck, a bit that could be anywhere and many places at once. I bounced through the ether; I split and divided; I touched other sparks such as myself. I was two, then a hundred Rebeccas, but not Rebecca at all. I traveled through suns; time and space meant nothing to me. I was a sole bit of matter, a tiny flame in a vast universe.

We danced with the dead.

But they were not really ghosts, only creatures of an alien region far different from our own.

The dance ended. We stood under a gray sky like molten rock. I remembered who I was. My breath filled my lungs; my heart beat in my chest. I was the night clerk of the Leechmont Hotel. I straightened my blouse, pushed my hair behind my ears, and looked about.

A man sat on the edge of a wishing well of smooth gray stone. Its bucket and rope stood on its lip. He was a thin, angular creature, dressed all in black. His face appeared made of the same gray stone as the well. Nearby stood Mister Green, smiling out of William Hope's face, his eyes filled with glee, the other half of Lord Anderson beside him.

"Did you enjoy the dance?" the stone-faced man asked, his voice deep as an avalanche.

I was speechless, but Lizbeth answered, "It was entertaining." An understatement beyond admiration, with her poise the woman would have excelled as a dinner hostess.

"I am Tractus," stone-face said, smiling coldly. "I have awaited you." His teeth were gray stone, too. "The little Lord of Evenmere and his assistants. Charming. You are being pursued, you know. A Rider comes after you, summoned by those who wish you ill. The Master has enemies he does not even know: chaos supplicants, monarchists, perpetualists—the list is long."

I had never heard of Tractus. Though I did not know with whom I was dealing, I stepped forward. "I am the night clerk of the Leechmont. These are our guests. The use of any form of force or coercion are strictly forbidden according to the Rules of Deportment and will be met in the strongest manner."

Tractus laughed. "Such cheek! But when the game grows serious enough, law is suspended." He turned to Mister Green.

"Thank you for bringing them." Green waved a hand in return and hurried into the mist.

"Will!" Lord Anderson shouted, but the creature was already gone.

"We have been betrayed," Lizbeth said. "He never meant us well."

Tractus studied us, then nodded his head as if reaching a decision. Lifting his hand, he beckoned to us. Once again, as with the Quilted Woman, a force surrounded us, pulling us forward. There was no question of resisting it any more than I could have stepped off the hotel gables and kept myself aloft. He closed his hand when we stood at the edge of the well, halting us.

"You must descend," he said.

Both Lord Andersons groaned.

"Please, sir." Lizbeth's voice was suffused with agony. "Take me if you must, but spare Carter. I beg you. He was thrown into a well as a child. Don't murder him in this fashion."

Astonishment spread across Tractus' face. He threw back his head and laughed, and I swear his booming merriment shook the earth. I clutched the edge of the well, terrified.

"It isn't water," he said. "This is a gravity well."

He flicked a finger and we fell into darkness.

May I never again know the agony of being torn to pieces one fragment at a time. I saw the source of my destruction, a single, minuscule dot. I spread around it, was absorbed within it, became part of it. In any normal situation, I would have fainted from the pain. There was no such relief. My consciousness remained. At that moment, I learned that when one enters the world of torment, it lasts an eternity.

Finally, the anguish ceased. I rested there, happy for the end of my suffering, content to be a single grain of sand on an endless shore.

✧ ✧ ✧

I SEEMED TO awaken, though I had not been asleep. When I opened my eyes, I found I was lying on my stomach, my head turned toward a great sea. But *sea* is only a word, for its composition was not that of water, though it moved in waves on a beach of whispering granules. Raising myself to a sitting position, I saw

Lord Anderson and Lizbeth making their way toward me from farther down the shoreline, the Master striding like his old self. To my other side, Tractus sat on a blue beach chair. The sky was the color of ripe peaches, illuminated without evidence of a sun.

I rose to my feet, somewhat dizzy. "Lord Anderson, are you recovered?"

"I am whole." His eyes held a light difficult to describe, the expression of a man who has seen wonders and terrors. Tears sprang to my own eyes. I wanted to hug him, but deportment is a watchword at the Leechmont, so I was surprised when he grasped my hand, squeezing it briefly between both of his own. He turned to Tractus. "Why was it done? Why do you bother? Any of you, the Quilted Woman, Particus, yourself, could destroy us with a gesture."

Tractus smiled. "And yet the Master needs his Lightning Sword. Haven't you found that it is the obligation of the powerful to help the weak? Are not we, who serve the House which serves its inhabitants, *their* servants? Gravity must both obey and be obeyed."

"But what *is* the Leechmont?" Lizbeth asked. "It seems apart from Evenmere itself."

"And yet it is central to the running of the House, the bedrock on which the Balance between Order and Chaos stand," Tractus said. "A hotel is a place of constant transition, its guests arriving and departing; luggage moving from lobby to room, room to lobby; sheets and towels, food and supplies diminishing and replenishing; its staff gradually turning over, never static, never the same. The Leechmont is Evenmere's Fount of Unresolved Possibilities, the negotiation of probabilities before a choice is made and the waveform collapses. It is the instant of change when one thing becomes another, whether it be chemical properties, light to heat, energy to mechanism, mechanism to energy. Whenever there is change, those energies are redistributed. That is why those such as the anarchists keep rooms here, to steal bits of power during such transitional moments, utilizing it in ways they sometimes call magic. At the Leechmont, power can be made manifest. And swords can be recast."

"What place has Mister Green in this?" Lord Anderson asked.

Tractus laughed, making the beach quiver. "That imp! He is a happenstance serving without knowing he does so." He pointed toward tall hills bordering the beach. "You must go to the Valley of the Montromorrs, great beasts that even the Words of Power cannot overcome. Approach them only when the moving particles create a storm, for the lightning is their food and the thunder their lullaby. Should they awaken, they will destroy you. Nor should you stand still for long, lest the lightning strike you. Set the shards of the sword on the anvil at the valley's center and wait until a bolt strikes the blade, remolding it. Return here once the weapon is whole."

I felt I must speak. "You are sending us into great danger. But you are, if I understand it, the Master of Gravity. Can't you take the sword for us?"

"I am not gravity's master. I *am* gravity. I can aid you, for gravity is sometimes helpful, but I cannot do the work for you."

"I should go alone," Lord Anderson said. "There is no need for anyone else to risk their lives."

"That is incorrect," Tractus said. "You have been brought here; and this moment, for good or ill, belongs to the three of you. You may die; I cannot say, but the task is before you, and each of you must decide if you will undertake it."

"I will," Lizbeth said, her jaw set.

"I am the night clerk of the Leechmont Hotel," I said, "ignorant of Forces and Powers, but one does not desert a guest requiring clean sheets or tactical support. I only wish I had my pistol."

"Weapons are useless to you now." Tractus raised his hand and vanished as if he had never been, shaking the ground in his passing.

Lizbeth and Lord Anderson exchanged glances. After our journey through the well, even her faultless hair was a tangled disaster; mine was surely worse. The Master looked worn and weary. Yet there was a strength of love between the two, a father to an adopted daughter, and I could not help but think their strength would get us through. I believe I am a realist; I knew we were in dreadful danger, but we had passed through tremendous difficulties already, and it seemed at that moment that love brought peace; and peace, clarity of mind; and clarity of mind, truth. And truth, the power to overcome. A silly rumination occurring in an instant, but it gave me fortitude.

We headed away from the beach, ascending hills made of an

iridescent, constantly quivering substance. The climb took longer than expected, and we were breathing hard by the time we reached the apex. The ground ran level for some distance before sloping downward to form a deep vale.

A rumbling arose overhead, making us instinctively duck. Energies passed in jagged bolts across the empty peach sky, tessellating the horizon like cracked glass before fading away.

"The storm comes," Lord Anderson said. "We must hurry."

We trotted along, still breathless from our climb, then gained our second wind. The rumbling grew, followed by a dimming of the unseen illumination, turning the world to gray twilight.

We were nearing the valley when we heard a noise behind us. I cast a glance backward. Something was coming, ebony in the dusk, a figure riding a tall steed akin to a horse but with twice the legs.

Lord Anderson bade us halt. "It's the Nihilist Paladin. We can't outrun it. Our enemies seek the sword for themselves. Or my death. Or both. They will do anything to disrupt the established order of Reality."

We spread out, preparing ourselves. How I longed for a rifle. Though my pistol had proven ineffective against it, I believe I could have taken it at a hundred yards with the right weapon.

The paladin carried a ball and chain instead of a sword, its spiked head glowing with red energy like a fallen star. Lord Anderson was clearly its target, its steed thundering upon him with such speed that I scarcely had time to cry a warning. But Lord Anderson threw his Tawny Mantle about his shoulders mere seconds before the enemy struck, vanishing, and the rider's flail passed harmlessly through empty air.

The paladin's mount did not pass unscathed. Unknown to me, Lord Anderson carried a knife. While still invisible, he thrust it into the steed's shoulder, causing the beast to scream and buck. The rider pulled it from the animal's flesh and cast it aside. It bounced across the ground near me. Without thinking, I scooped it up.

Despite its pain, the paladin regained control of the beast. Turning, our enemy lifted its head. Its eyes and mouth, seen through its helmet, radiated an orange jack 'o lantern glow. In that light, Lord Anderson stood visible.

The rider charged. I ran toward the Master.

Once again, the enemy wielded its flail. Lord Anderson moved to the side to avoid it, but the chain lengthened, seeking its target, striking him on the shoulder, throwing him to his knees.

I saw this only from the corner of my eye, for as the paladin passed its target, I leapt.

I had calculated my trajectory correctly, but the paladin's steed turned at the last moment. I struck the animal behind its saddle and sought to scramble up. The paladin pushed me away with one hand, thrusting me flying backward.

As I fell, I cast the knife, aiming for the rider's exposed throat. The steed rolled past. I struck the earth, losing sight of my enemy.

Jarred, it took me a moment to recover enough to turn and see. Our foe continued on, apparently unharmed. Then its flail left its hand; it slouched to the side and dropped from the saddle.

Lizbeth sprang toward the paladin, weaponless but intent on preventing it from rising. I did not know how she could do so. I rolled to my feet to help. We reached it at the same time, only to see it turn to ashes before our eyes. Its mount whinnied once, then crumbled, too.

Without pausing, Lizbeth hurried to Lord Anderson. He clutched his shoulder and struggled to rise. "How bad is it?" she asked.

He grimaced in pain. "I don't know."

"Let me look," she said.

Thunder rolled above us. In the distance, a bolt struck the earth.

"There isn't time," he said. "The montromorrs will soon be sleeping."

We descended through the quivering, iridescent landscape into the Valley of the Montromorrs. Like the rest of the country, it was barren of vegetation, nor were there any boulders, forcing us to crawl on hands and knees to avoid detection. We soon spied the montromorrs below us, and the sight of their thousands of hulking forms brought us to a halt, for they were still awake.

The storm grew in intensity. A bolt struck the valley floor, and then another, each producing a deafening roar. The discharges increased like a coming hailstorm while we sat, easy targets on the bare ground. Hugging myself in fear, I set my concentration on the montromorrs.

They began yawning their cavernous mouths. One sleepily pawed the shoulder of another with its iron talons. Two others playfully butted heads with bone-powdering force, assuring me our discovery and demise would provide them a delightful but trifling diversion.

One by one, while the heavens rolled, the montromorrs slept, soothed by a cacophony so dreadful I clamped a hand over my mouth to keep from shrieking each time a bolt struck. My ears ached; I trembled like a puppy beneath the storm.

Finally, Lord Anderson rose and gestured for us to follow. It sounds foolish to say we kept absolutely quiet beneath the thunderous energies, yet we did not know how sensitive the montromorrs' hearing might be. In a land where tumult was commonplace, a human voice might be akin to the noise of a prowler on a wooden floor. So we crept along in silence.

The montromorrs' bodies, lying close together, formed a maze. We moved among them, more than once having to slip beneath the horns of their heads while their ozone breath blew upon us. They whimpered and moaned in their sleep, dreaming whatever dreams such creatures have. I will never forget their massive forms, the parapets of their scales, the doors of their faces, the cauldrons of their nostrils.

Not far ahead, a lightning ball struck one of the beasts. I tightened my fists, expecting it to rise, but instead the energy diffused across its body. It bellowed contentedly, squeezing its great lids together in pleasure, feeding on the blast.

The minutes passed, each second an eternity. If an eye opened, we knew we must perish. Gradually we made our way toward the valley's center. There, we found the enormous anvil, high as my chest and wide as a tabletop. I wondered who had originally placed it there.

Drawing the shards of his weapon from his pack, Lord Anderson laid them upon the anvil and gestured for us to stand back. I watched the shards, unconsciously holding my breath.

When the bolt struck, I wished I had closed my eyes; it blinded and deafened me. Lizbeth and Lord Anderson must have been wiser, for when my vision returned, I found them standing at the anvil's edge, looking at the result.

Drawing near, I saw the Lightning Sword made whole, though welded together with rough, unattractive beads. It burned with a red light as if aflame, and Lord Anderson's eyes blazed with it, his mouth set in determined, satisfied lines. He held his hand above the hilt, aching to touch it, knowing it was too hot. Yet it cooled with amazing celerity, as if it absorbed the heat. He grasped it, and we hurried back the way we had come. My hearing gradually returned; the thunder lessened. I studied the sky. The storm passed, the flashes diminishing in both strength and frequency. The montromorrs made rousing noises. We broke into a run, darting among the creatures' limbs. One montromorr rolled onto its side, nearly crushing me.

More than once, we found our way wholly blocked, forcing us to backtrack. On one occasion, Lord Anderson led us over a monster's paws, using its glistening, green talons to maintain our balance. Its hide was rough as a rock wall.

We passed the final creature and were close to the top of the valley when we heard a bellow. I glanced over my shoulder. A montromorr galloped toward us.

We broke into a wild sprint. I have never before run so fast, desperately hoping the monster would turn back at the valley crest.

It did not.

When it was nearly upon us, Lord Anderson turned to meet it, while our momentum carried us on. I looked back, knowing I could do nothing to help.

The montromorr charged. The Master leapt to one side with admirable celerity, striking at it with his sword. The beast swung its head to the left, and the blade struck one of its horns. Energy erupted from the Lightning Sword, permeating the montromorr's body. The creature collapsed, dropping as if its legs had been cut from under it.

I laughed in relief. The montromorrs fed on energy during slumber; it had instinctively fallen asleep, its hideous face dreamy.

No other montromorrs pursued us. We sped back to the beach and found Particus, rather than Tractus, awaiting us.

"You have succeeded." He gave his half-faced smile. "Yet you have not been wholly successful. More work is needed. Give me the blade." He held out his hands, palms upward.

Lord Anderson grimaced at the sword's unsightly welds before laying it on Particus' tiny hands. Particus gazed upon it, seemingly doing nothing, but the Lightning Sword was instantly whole, the welds melting into the metal, leaving it bright as spun gold. He handed it back to Lord Anderson.

A new expression came onto the Master's face. He gripped the hilt of the jagged blade and closed his eyes, savoring its feel, holding it so hard his arm trembled. With great solemnity, he raised it over his head, golden as the sun, its point to the sky. His visage became golden as well, his whole form radiating with the power of the blade. At that moment, I truly saw the Lord of Evenmere in his glory.

Tears streamed down Lizbeth's eyes. She wiped them quickly away with the back of her hand. "What now? The sword is whole, but must we remain forever minuscule?"

Particus bent down, touching the strange grains of sand. A frame rose from it, bearing an image of the Third North Corridor. He gestured toward it.

Lord Anderson bowed at the waist. "We thank you, Particus, and Tractus as well. What of Mr. Hope?"

"He is the concern of others," Particus said.

With nothing else to be done, we stepped one by one into the painting and found ourselves full-sized once more, standing in the North Wing. A figure came walking down the hallway.

"Will!" Lizbeth dashed to meet the butler of Evenmere, only to hesitate when she drew near. "It is you, isn't it?" When he answered in the affirmative, she ran into his arms in a most surprising display of affection for one of his station.

"Now, now," William Hope said, his face crimson. "All's well. I'm back."

Lord Anderson hurried to clasp Mr. Hope's hand. "Are you all right?"

"Right as rain but weary. Mister Green sent me scurrying all about the place. He borrows bodies, you know, in order to experience our thoughts and feelings. He's much different than we, a strange creature from deep in Evenmere. He believes he's the last of his kind."

"It must have been dreadful," Lizbeth said.

Mr. Hope's round face twisted, but he cheerfully replied, "Oh, it wasn't so bad as that, rather like sharing a coach with a stranger, both hard and easy. He isn't evil, only profoundly curious. When he realized who Carter was, he wanted to seize *him* but was afraid to do so. He feared taking you would arouse the interest of Powers less congenial than yourself. Once he had me, he became fascinated by our quest to mend the sword and decided to help. That's why he took it."

"Do you remember everything that happened to you?" I asked. "Most don't."

"Having experienced many unusual situations in Evenmere probably helped," Mr. Hope replied. "I was never really afraid for myself, but Green is capricious as a mischievous boy, and I feared where he might lead you, so once I realized what he was about, I decided my best course was to befriend him." Despite his words, his smile looked forced.

"But why did Green lead us on such a chase? We saw him with Tractus. Why couldn't he simply have brought us and the sword there?" Lord Anderson asked.

"He could have, but he wouldn't have found that as amusing. It was sheer sport to him. His leading you to Particus by way of the Quilted Woman was no more than a fanciful whim."

"How did he know we would find the hidden door out of the quilt?" Lord Anderson asked.

"Through me, he understood your abilities; he knew there were doorways in the Fabric of the universe and that you could use the Word of Secret Ways to find one. Assuming you thought of it, of course."

"A gamble with our lives," Lord Anderson said.

"Yes, but you succeeded. The rest followed thereafter. He didn't know about the Nihilist Paladin, but it wouldn't have changed his plans. I tried my best to get him to pursue the least dangerous course; he concocted even wilder schemes you couldn't possibly have survived."

"Since we're still alive, you must have influenced him greatly," Lizbeth said.

Mister Hope shrugged.

"Becky has been an immeasurable help, too," Lord Anderson said. "We wouldn't be here without her."

I fear I blushed. To hide my discomfort, I said, "Here at the Leechmont we are always happy to accommodate our guests." I took out my watch. "I see it's almost midnight. I really should return to my desk. Though I'm certain Ting is doing an excellent job, she is relatively new. May I lead you back to your rooms?

You must be exhausted."

"I believe we can find our way," Mr. Hope said. "Mister Green taught me a great deal about the hotel."

I left them there, returning through the hallways to my station. Nothing untoward having happened during my absence, I was soon back on the Observation Deck overlooking my desk. I tried to resume my reading of *Beyond Yonder*, but my mind kept returning to the night's adventures. The book soon slipped from my hands, and I fell asleep for a time, more spent than I knew. I awoke at 2:15, chagrined at having slumbered so long.

✧ ✧ ✧

LORD ANDERSON'S COMPANY chose to check out at 5:32 in the early morning hours of my shift. I had finished *Beyond Yonder* and was beginning *A Short History of the Masters of Evenmere* when the three travelers appeared, once more carrying their own luggage. Descending from the Observation Deck, I gave Pinecoat a reproving glance. He responded with a helpless shrug.

"I trust the remainder of your stay proved uneventful?" I asked.

Lizbeth and Mr. Hope exchanged enigmatic glances.

"Quite. . . restful," Lord Anderson replied. There seemed to be some unspoken concern among them, but it was not my place to inquire.

"Shall I order a coach?" I asked.

"Our transportation is already arranged," Mr. Hope said.

"How do you stand this eternal night?" Lizbeth abruptly asked.

I laughed uncertainly, puzzled by the question. "The nights *are* long, I admit, but one adjusts."

Lord Anderson studied me before speaking, uncustomary hesitation in his voice. "I'm not a storyteller as some I've met, but do you have time for a short tale?"

My eyes widened in curiosity. "Of course."

He cleared his throat. "There was once a young woman who, desiring to serve the House, enlisted in the military. Being intelligent, courageous, and gifted with the ability to make rapid decisions, she rose quickly in the ranks and soon became a sergeant in the White Circle Guard.

"During the Poetry War, her unit was sent to hold the Winelderwist corridors, little knowing they would face an enemy four times their number. It was a disaster. Her lieutenant was killed; her captain, wounded. She was suddenly in charge. In a textbook maneuver, she created a diversionary tactic and brought her men to defensible hallways. She then held them against a superior force until reinforcements arrived. For her actions, she was awarded the Medal of Valor and promoted to lieutenant. Wounded, she was given light duty near the Inner Chambers. One day she vanished, being last seen in the Portrait Gallery. She was sought but never found.

"The paintings in the gallery are unusual. There is an exceptionally compelling representation of a benighted mansion surrounded by brilliant energies. The piece is called *The Leechmont Hotel*."

My heart lay frozen within me. At last, I said, "How did you recognize me?"

"We came here to find you," Lord Anderson said. "Being a fastidious man, Mr. Hope discovered how to enter the portrait while researching a means to repair my blade. We hadn't any way of knowing if you had gone through the portal, of course. We only hoped. We would have sought you even if we couldn't have repaired my sword."

I fear my decorum momentarily failed. My voice choked. "And did Mr. Hope's research discover that the young woman was in love with the lieutenant who died?"

An awkward silence followed. At last, I spoke. "So that's why you asked me to help you instead of the hotel detective. I wondered." The moment had come. There was no escape; I was found out. I cleared my throat. "Am I to be taken back a prisoner?"

"Why would I do that?" he asked.

"For desertion." I stiffened my trembling lips. I could not look him in the face. My voice broke. "And. . . for the murders."

And then he did a strange thing. He took my hands. I looked up and there were tears in the corners of his eyes. "You murdered no one. You made the correct choices and saved the lives of your company. Your comrades died at the enemy's hands. Not yours."

I dropped my gaze. "I couldn't save them all. If only I had—"

"Look at me," he commanded. Reluctantly, I did so. One does not disobey such a man. "You think you cannot be forgiven for a crime you did not commit. Very well. Then I tell you, in the name of the House and by the names of those who perished, I, the Master of Evenmere, who have slain men and sent soldiers to their deaths—who bears more blood on my hands than I can ever wash away—forgive you. And I will tell you a secret. At the last, if we can accept it, love and forgiveness is all we have."

He squeezed my hands. "Becky, in our journey we have faced our fears together. You've proven your worth both as a soldier and a human being. Let this be the beginning of your healing. You will never forget those who died; they will remain with you forever. But if they could speak they would not require your penance. You have hidden yourself here, fleeing from an unwarranted guilt you've placed on yourself for deaths beyond your control. I deeply regret not helping you more after the battle. When you decide to leave this ghastly hotel and return to the White Circle Guard or to private life, you will be welcomed. You haven't deserted; you have taken an indefinite leave of absence granted by an edict from the Inner Chambers. Should you choose the Guard, I guarantee you a captain's rank. If you do not come within six months, one of us will return to see about you."

I could not think what to say. Lizbeth came around the desk and hugged me tightly. Mister Hope shook my hand, a friendly grip. And then they were gone, clutching their umbrellas, traipsing past the rearing statues of the winged lions in the central fountain into the rainy night.

I returned to the Observation Deck and watched them descend the seventy-seven steps running between the rows of alabaster panthers. Coruscating energies lit the clouds in every color. The icy wind tore at their garments, its shrieking audible through the panes of glass.

Reaching the last step, they approached the narrow gate I had passed through upon first arriving at the hotel. Set in the south stone wall, nearly hidden by twisted ivy, it is an exit no one except me ever seems to perceive. Mr. Hope opened it, and they stepped over the threshold, vanishing one by one like ghosts, returning to the Portrait Gallery in the Inner Chambers.

I resumed my place at my desk and sat a long time pondering. At whiles, I wept. Other guests arrived: a diplomat from South Lowing, a duchess from Rassee, a scholarly entourage from the Order of Subsuming. I greeted them, gave them their keys, and saw to their comfort, doing my best to serve them well. When they were gone, I glanced at the Great Clock. It was 11:35.

Though it seemed like hours had already passed, my shift was only beginning.

But I didn't mind. It is my place, at least for now. For I am the night clerk of the Leechmont Hotel.

✧ ✧ ✧

AFTERWORD

A NUMBER OF years ago my wife and I were traveling through several small towns when we needed to stop for the night. Our choices were limited to a motel originally built in the 1950's, its doors opening to the outdoors. It was a less-than-stellar experience. A unique feature of the establishment was a decorative facade displaying hundreds of cubbyholes. Over the years, swallows had nested in the niches, filling nearly every available space.

I like swallows. Every year, a pair builds their nest on our back porch. They're fascinating birds, fun to watch. However, I had never seen this many together, and entering the office was like stepping into a scene from Hitchcock's *The Birds*.

When we prepared to depart, I walked outside to return the room key to the office. Just as I was about to turn the corner, the entire flight of swallows took wing, passing directly in front of me, startling me. I momentarily thought it was a swarm of bats.

As we drove away, I commented something like, "So ends our time at the Leechmont," coining the name on the spot.

My wife and I laugh about that experience, but the name stuck with me. When I decided to write an Evenmere novella, I knew it had to be about the Leechmont Hotel. I sat down one day and typed the first paragraph of the story, certain the narrator would be a young woman but having no idea about either her broken heart or the murders.

Those lines were all there was for a time. I wanted to plot it as I went—not the most efficient way to write a story but a method filled with both trepidation (Can I finish this thing?) and the thrill of discovery. I think the swallows are the inspiration for the *trillers*. Writers take whatever gifts they find.

CHRISTMAS AT HOSTAGE CANYON

FOR HOURS THE family rolled like tumbleweeds through the flat expanse of West Texas, past pumpjacks and pastureland, fields of winter wheat and empty reaches of harvested cotton. Now, with a sudden turn, they descended into darkness.

"Hey, we're goin' down!" Eric yelled.

"I told you where they live," his mother said from the front seat. "Remember us talking about the Caprock Escarpment?"

"Oh. Right." After driving through one of the largest tablelands in the country, they were entering a canyon at the edge of the plateau, one of a series of ravines marking the Caprock boundary.

"What's this canyon called?" Eric asked.

"She already told you that, dummy," his brother, Daniel, said beside him in the back seat. "Hostage Canyon, 'cause this is where the Apaches met to ransom their captives back to their families."

"Don't call your brother a dummy," their father ordered, dimming the car lights. "You guys look around. They really decorate for Christmas here."

The sedan made its way along the steep incline and curved around a boulder-strewn hill. Along the headlight beams, Eric glimpsed mesquite, prickly pear cactus, and yucca.

As they rounded the bend, Eric gaped as a fairy valley opened before them. Houses, decorated with lights of every color, huddled around a small lake. Electric stars hung over garages; bulbs covered pines in Christmas-tree splendor. Shepherds and Smurfs, wise men and snowmen, mangers and Power Rangers stood on the lawns. Banners proclaimed the season. The lights shimmered off the water, and in the darkness it was hard to tell which was real and which, reflection.

"Look at that!" Eric shouted, pointing at a mechanical Santa waving from a rowboat in a front yard.

"Don't yell in my ear!" his brother warned.

"Sorry." In a departure from his usual good humor, Daniel had recently joined the vagabonds drifting along the borders of teenage moodiness. Though Eric never consciously expressed the thought, his brother's faltering desertion from childhood left him uneasy.

As the car wound its way around the lake, they encountered other vehicles going both directions, creeping along to see the lights. Their Ford slowed to a crawl. More cars came up behind them, and it became a parade. Inflatable choirs on the lawns generated music, providing both band and audience. Eric lowered the window and shouted, "Merry Christmas, everybody!"

"It's too cold to have the window down," Daniel complained.

"Better roll it up," their mother said. "You might catch a chill."

"Bunch of Scrooges," Eric said, annoyed at his brother's treason.

"He's right," Dad said. "Leave it down, son. We're here for Christmas."

Eric was wise enough not to look at Daniel. With a four-year age difference between them, he had learned long ago not to celebrate his triumphs.

They passed a plywood display running the length of the roof of a Colonial—Santa in his sleigh pulled by the reindeer.

"There's Rudolph," Eric said.

A man walking his German Shepherd passed beside the car, his breath a cloud in the cold.

"Merry Christmas!" Eric called.

"Merry Christmas to you, son," the stranger replied, smiling, the lights making his face clearly visible.

"Nice people," Eric said.

They were forced to stop a few minutes later as the drivers paused to observe a particularly festive house, its roof a sea of bulbs, its seven pine trees crowded with twinkling lamps, its Chinese elm and desert willow dipped from trunk to tips in illumination. Eric bounced in his seat in anticipation of drawing next to it.

"Calm down, can't you?" Daniel said.

Eric cut his efforts in half to suggest compliance. He glanced beside the car. Beneath the shadows of a row of oaks sat a figure on the curb, face shining dead-white. Eric studied the creature, thinking it must be a mannequin. To his shock, the figure stood and stepped into the street, a man with a long, thin head and sneering elven features. His face shone with a zombie light. Was it a mask? Some kind of paint?

The creature looked at Eric with pale, piercing eyes that made the boy shudder. There was something animal about him, like an elf gone bad.

The stranger leapt into the air in a fluid movement, twisting his body in a way that seemed physically impossible. He pirouetted, rising over the ground like a ballerina. His clothes were blood red and the dark green of stagnant water.

Inserting a finger of each hand into the corners of his mouth, the elf stuck out his tongue, pulling his mouth wide and then wider, impossibly wide, hideously wide, until his whole face was contorted beyond anything Eric thought imaginable.

"Death," the elf said, looking right at Eric, his voice high and grating.

Under that dreadful gaze, Eric froze. The elf reached a clawed hand toward him. With a shout, the boy pushed the button to raise the window.

The glass went up; the car moved forward. The elf ran a hand against the rear window, cutting long scratches in the glass with two-inch fingernails.

"Did you see that guy?" Eric yelled.

But his parents were talking and pointing out lights, while Christmas music droned from the car speakers. Daniel ignored him.

"What is it, honey?" his mother finally asked.

"That man! See him?"

Eric turned to where the elf had been, but he was gone. He vainly searched the shadows beneath the trees.

"I don't see anyone," Mom said.

Eric kept his eye on the back window until they reached their aunt and uncle's house.

✧ ✧ ✧

AUNT LAURA AND Uncle Gregg lived in a sprawling Victorian on the south lake shore. Eric's uncle, full of stories, loved to play chess and checkers; his aunt did crossword puzzles and read romance novels. They didn't have any children, which Eric thought a shame.

Everyone stayed up late the first night, talking and drinking hot cider around the burning logs of the ornate fireplace. Eric's parents brought the presents out of the trunk of the car and placed them beneath the Christmas tree, a real pine bedecked in golden bulbs with a ceramic angel atop the highest branch. The brisk aroma of the needles tickled Eric's nose.

At bedtime, Eric was led to his room upstairs, which had an ebony dresser and queen-size bed. The blinds covering the long picture window were closed.

"There's a flashlight on the nightstand if you need one," Aunt Laura said, "or I have a night-light if you want."

"I'm too old for night-lights," Eric asserted a little uncertainly, glancing at the shadows crowding the corners of the high ceiling.

He was tired but unwilling to turn loose of the day, so he played with the flashlight a while, casting the beam to different parts of the ceiling, illuminating the portrait of a sailing boat, and the carved faces of monks and angels on the antique dresser.

Downstairs, the grandfather clock struck midnight, the sound humming through the walls of the house. He counted the long, slow strokes of the witching hour.

With the sounding of the last chime, he heard a snarl outside, a high throaty cry like a child in pain. His whole body tensed. He shone the light at the window, then remembered cats sometimes made such noises. Despite that reassurance, he lay in bed, the covers around him in the winter chill, waiting. When the noise came again, he rose, gripping the flashlight, and crept to the window. Lifting one slat of the blinds, he peeked out.

His room overlooked the backyard, which sloped down to the water's edge. A canoe and kayak were moored to his aunt and uncle's narrow dock. It was a moonless night, but the lights from the far shore illuminated a figure dancing across the frost-kissed lawn, the elf Eric had seen on the street, his pale face shining.

The creature spun in a circle, leapt high into the air, somersaulted across the grass, came upright, did a handstand, pushed himself up by his arms, and landed on his feet. He slid toward the water without moving his legs, like a skater on ice. Turning, he danced backward, then rushed forward and did a roll that brought him just beneath Eric's window.

Landing on one knee, arms outspread as if awaiting applause, he leered up at the boy. His lips were crimson. Even at this distance, Eric could see the hunger in the glistening glare.

The elf dropped one arm to his side, pointed straight at Eric, and with a voice clearly audible through the glass, cried, "Death on Christmas Eve!"

Eric gasped. The elf sprinted back toward the lake, bounded forward, and vanished. Eric searched, thinking he must have leapt into the water, but the surface remained undisturbed.

Grasping his flashlight, Eric bolted down the hall toward his parents' room.

✧ ✧ ✧

"Just a bad dream," his father said, helping Eric back under the covers. "Too many Christmas treats late at night. Happens to the best of us."

"It wasn't a dream, dad. I promise it wasn't. I saw him in the street, and I saw him again. He was like a big elf, but evil!"

From the glow of the hall light, Eric rested beneath the study of his father's thoughtful eyes. Eric's dad was one of those parents who believed his children.

"I'll talk to your uncle in the morning about it. It's probably some local prankster in makeup. But look, we're on the second floor. You saw how high the windows are. No one can possibly climb up here, and Laura and Gregg have a security system, so your elf couldn't get in without the alarm sounding. Go to sleep and we'll figure this out tomorrow. I'll sit by your bed a minute."

Under his father's scrutiny, Eric drifted off to sleep.

✧ ✧ ✧

By the next morning the incident seemed more dream than reality. Having placed it in his father's hands, Eric dismissed it, for it was Christmas Eve, and there were games to play and pies and candy to eat, and a light snow that started at noon.

"A white Christmas after all," said his uncle.

That night they drove around and looked at Christmas lights again, though Daniel didn't really want to go. Only then did Eric remember the elf. He found himself searching the shadows, looking for the creature, but they covered the route along the canyon without any sign of him.

"You're awfully quiet," his mother said. "Aren't you enjoying the lights?"

"He's afraid of ghosts," Daniel said.

"Am not!" Eric grimaced, feeling betrayed. His brother must have heard him last night and ferreted out the story from dad.

"Maybe they'll let you have a night-light tonight," Daniel said. "Just don't get any ideas about sleeping with me."

Eric hunkered down. Older brothers have all the power.

Home again, they played dominoes on the kitchen table.

"What do you think Santa's going to bring you, Eric?" Uncle Gregg asked.

Eric smiled and looked innocent. On the Christmas Eve of his sixth year, when he and his brother were going to bed, Daniel had casually said, "You do know mom and dad are just pretending when they say there's a Santa Claus, don't you?"

"Yes," Eric had replied, his voice quavering slightly. Idolizing his big brother, who sometimes teased but never lied to him, Eric, not without a period of mourning, thereafter realigned his theology.

Still, adults had to be placated in this planet-wide game of pretend, so Eric said to his uncle, "I want Santa to bring me a baseball bat and a *Monster Hero* video game."

"Are you sure you've been good enough for that?" Gregg asked in feigned surprise.

"He's a pretty good boy," Mom said. "But who knows what Santa will do?"

Having found where his mother kept the unwrapped presents two weeks before, Eric had a fairly accurate picture of the intentions of the Claus organization.

Once upstairs in bed that night, Eric turned on the flashlight and shone it around the room. He sighed. He would never go to sleep; the night would last forever, and it was going to be seven centuries before his parents let him get up to open presents.

With images of *Monster Hero* dancing in his head, he drifted off sooner than he would have thought possible.

The chiming of the grandfather clock roused him. He counted the beats—eight, nine, ten, eleven, twelve. It was only midnight. Hours to go before morning. He groaned and rolled over. Dumb old clock! If it hadn't woke him. . .

A crash came from downstairs, the splintering of wood, the breaking of glass. Eric sat up in bed. Remembering the dark elf, he lay back down and pulled the covers close. Maybe something had fallen downstairs. Maybe the Christmas tree had toppled over. Any minute, he expected to hear his dad's feet padding down the hall to check. He strained to listen, but there was only the screeching of metal on wood floors, the thuds of falling objects.

What if his dad went downstairs and the elf was there? Would even his father, a veteran of Desert Storm, be able to stop him? Dad always kept a gun at the house, but he didn't have one here.

For an instant, Eric lay frozen, afraid of what would happen next. Afraid for his father. Afraid for everybody. *Death on Christmas Eve*, the elf had said. His parents slept with the door closed. Maybe they couldn't hear the noise.

When Eric was five, Daniel had accused him of being afraid of the dark, a brutal denunciation since it happened to be true. Ashamed and angry, Eric had refused to turn on the light any time he walked into his bedroom, stepping fists swinging into the blackness to wallop the waiting monsters. So he had beaten the dark, mastered it, brought it to leash. But lying in bed listening to the chaos downstairs, he knew his conquest had only been temporary.

He got up, grasping his flashlight but not turning it on. It was a black night; no moon peeked through the blinds. He stepped into the hall, the floorboards creaking beneath his feet despite his feather-light efforts.

Daniel's room was closest to his, but he passed it by, going straight to his parents' door. He reached for the knob, but it wavered and eluded him—surely a trick of the dark. He snapped on the flashlight and tried again. The knob bulged inward, avoiding him. He tried to knock, but the wood danced away from his fist. He called, softly at first, but with increasing volume. He waited a lifetime, but no one came.

Eric!

He jumped. A voice ethereal as mist beckoned from below.

Eric!

He rushed back to Daniel's door and ran straight at it, straining to reach the knob. It receded, ten yards, twenty, thirty, the door frame stretching like rubber. He halted and found himself standing in the hall before the closed door.

Eric! Come down!

The voice, an insistent humming in his head, sounded louder now.

He clinched his fist and gripped the flashlight. He passed Laura and Gregg's room without even trying the door. There was no one to help him, and it wasn't fair! He was the youngest, the littlest, and it wasn't right for the elf to pick on him, for him to be punished just because he was the one who had seen the creature.

As his hand touched the newel post at the top of the stairs, a dim glow rose from below. The sounds of violence ceased.

He crept down the steps, shaking with dread. At the bottom lay the remains of the outside door, splintered wood and broken glass sprawled across the kitchen floor. As he descended, step by step, looking over the banister rail, more of the living room came into view. The fireplace was lit, soft patter of flickering flames.

Heart pounding, he reached the bottom. He had to step over the shattered door, avoiding nails and diamond-glistening glass to reach the living room carpet. A silverware drawer lay upended onto the coffee table. Slashes crisscrossed his uncle's recliner, leaving strips of hanging cloth. Torn presents were scattered around the room; the baseball bat Eric had asked for lay in the middle of the floor, half-covered by the Christmas stockings from the mantel.

Eric sucked in his breath to keep from screaming.

The elf stood by the front window, behind the Christmas tree, peering out from between the branches, razor nose crinkled, mouth gaping a grin, like a kid playing a game of hide and seek.

With deliberate slowness, he stepped from behind the tree, raised one hand toward the boy, and displayed the decapitated body of the Christmas angel.

"Come to me, little one," the elf commanded, beckoning with his other hand. His eyes twinkled like broken glass.

"Who are you?" Eric demanded. He tried to sound brave, but his voice came timorous and thin. "This isn't your house. What do you want?"

The elf laughed. "Such cheek! Such courage in the face of disaster. I am an ancient nemesis of your people, locked out of your world centuries ago. Tonight that will change. This very evening, your blood will permanently secure the passage between my dimension and your own."

"I called the police," Eric said. "They'll be here any minute. You better go."

"You called no one," the elf sneered. "Do you think I can't overcome your childish technology? You haven't any idea. What fun I shall have, playing with you poor mortals."

Eric stood shaking, wanting to run, to flee through the broken door into the cold night. He glanced into the darkness of the yard.

"Don't bother," the elf said. "Even if you chose to desert your family, you couldn't leave the grounds any more than you could enter your parents' room."

The elf stepped forward, backing Eric against the wall. "Do you know what night it is, little one?"

"Ch. . . Christmas Eve." Eric stammered.

"That's right. It is also three days after the Winter Solstice, the longest and darkest night of the year. There are principles and dominions of which you know nothing, Eric, powers which humans can neither imagine nor cope with, creatures too terrible for mortal understanding."

The elf glanced at the fireplace. "There are awful places in the world, places with dreadful names. Auschwitz, the Colosseum of Rome, the Solovki Gulag. Wherever your pitiful human lives have been cheapened, wherever the darkness of human hearts manifests itself, the barrier between my dimension and yours is weakened. This is Hostage Canyon, a minor outpost in your long history of atrocities. I began crossing over on the night of the solstice, but it takes three days to fully manifest."

The elf glanced at the fireplace again. "It is a shame to slay one so young." The creature's long fingernails gleamed like knives in the firelight. "Let's at least have a bit more light, so I can do the job efficiently."

Leaving the boy pressed against the golden wallpaper, the elf threw a heavy log in the fireplace. The flames blazed, making the shadow of the Christmas tree dance.

"Much better." The elf returned to Eric. This close, Eric could smell him, an oily odor, sickeningly sweet. While the child watched in petrified terror, his breath coming in strangled gasps, the elf touched the tip of his fingernail to Eric's throat.

"A single slice and it's done."

Eric howled, shouting for his father and big brother, but his yells echoed uselessly around the room. He fell into quiet sobbing.

"Are we done?" the elf asked. "Good. I like to work without distractions."

Eric closed his eyes, waiting for the terrible pain. The grandfather clock ticked away, second by second, while he anticipated the first cruel cut. The elf's fingernail tapped against his throat. His whole body shook.

The moments passed; the stroke did not come. The creature abruptly withdrew his hand. Eric's eyes fluttered open. The elf looked at him thoughtfully.

"I don't want to do this, you know. So young! Such a tragedy! It's necessary, but I don't like it."

He put his hand to his cheek in thought. "There is another way. It isn't often done, but it could be, in a special case. I could use a substitute instead of you. Someone else. Would you like that?"

Tears running down his face, Eric nodded, too frightened to even speak.

"Hmm," the elf said. "Who would serve? Let me think. Who could I possibly use?"

The creature closed his gleaming eyes in concentration. He opened them and snapped his fingers and said with a smile. "I have it. Your brother will suffice."

A short cry escaped Eric's lips.

"Now understand me, little one. I would be quick. Just slip up to his room and do the deed. He wouldn't know it was coming. It wouldn't be like you, standing here awaiting the blow. He wouldn't feel a thing. A pillow over the face and he's gone. And your parents would never know. Natural causes, they'd think it was. And Daniel would go to heaven to be with the angels."

"Please don't take my brother," Eric said, shaking his head.

The elf glanced at the ornamental bells on the Christmas tree. "Now let's not be irrational. It has to be one of you; you haven't any choice in that. But let's think about it. Your brother has had a lot longer to live. And he hasn't always been kind to you, has he? Oh, I know he isn't one to hit you, but isn't he always bossing you around, telling you how to act, as if you're supposed to be as old as he? And lately he's been distant. Listening to loud music, ignoring you. Talking to his friends on his cell. You've admired him, it's true. You've looked up to him. But you know in your heart you'll never live up to what he is. He's stronger than you, smarter than you. All your life you'll stand in his shadow. I can take care of that right now. You say the word and I'll slip right upstairs. It'll be so much easier."

Eric's tears abruptly ceased as he realized the elf was *asking* permission to kill Daniel.

"There isn't any other way, Eric. One of you has to go. There are rules you know nothing about. And think of your mother. Hasn't she always told you how precious you are, how special? Don't you know in your heart you're the most important one to her? She'll miss Daniel, of course, but not like she'd miss you. The grief might kill her. Kill her dead."

Eric thought. Though his mother never actually said she loved him more than Daniel, he was sure she thought him extra-special. Wasn't he the compliant boy, her good little man? If there wasn't any choice, if one of them had to die. . .

"I can see by your look you're coming around to my way of thinking," the elf said. "Come now, Eric, let me finish my job. For your mother's sake. It's the right thing to do."

Eric faltered, for in mentioning what was right, the elf had stirred something within him. Eric's parents always told him to do what was right. His mother insisted on it. His dad said a man was measured by it. It was like the heroes in books, like Captain America in the comics. Cap didn't let someone else die in his place. Besides, when the older kids in school tried to pick on him, didn't Daniel stand up for him? Shouldn't he do the same for his brother?

A log in the fireplace popped and the elf started and whirled toward the sound, his whole body twitching.

He's afraid of something, Eric realized. As powerful as he is, he's afraid.

For the first time, Eric found his courage, as if he were again swinging his fists in the blackness of his bedroom, facing the darkness. He had to stall until he figured out what the monster feared.

"I need to think about it," he said.

"No need to think, and no time for it, either," the elf said smoothly. "You know what you should do." He brought his hand back toward Eric's throat. "Death is dark, Eric, filled with darkness. Unending darkness. Darkness forever and ever."

"You said Daniel would go to heaven."

The elf's eyes blackened but immediately grew softer. "That's Daniel. Big brothers are different. If you decide to let me take you instead—why, that would be like suicide. And suicide is bad, Eric. Everyone knows that."

"I don't know how that works. Can you explain it?"

The elf shook his head. "No, I can't, Eric. There isn't time. Your time is up. Your brother or you? Which is it?"

Eric felt the sharp edge of the fingernail against his neck, pressing, cutting.

With a sound of collapsing air, the fire went out, plunging the room into darkness.

"No!" the elf shouted out of the blackness. "It was nearly done!"

A figure stood beside the mantle, a tall shadow in the ebony. Broad. Powerful. Eric choked back a cry, thinking it must be something awful, perhaps something even worse if the elf feared it. Perhaps the monster's terrible Master.

There was light. A single shaft at first, rising to a silver glow. Eric blinked against the brilliance, and when he could see again, he discovered the newcomer had drawn a long sword, a blade capturing every stray illumination in the room: starlight from the windows, lamplight from the houses across the lake, the shine from the refrigerator panel in the kitchen, focusing it into a dazzling radiance.

The figure was a man with ruddy cheeks and an ivory beard, broad-shouldered, easily a head taller than Eric's father. He wore a red suit with white fur fringes, and his eyes were as piercing as the sword he carried.

But the creature had drawn a weapon, too, an ebony blade darker than darkness.

Eric had only one thought. There *is* a Santa Claus, and the elf is going to kill him.

But this wasn't the Santa of the old stories, with a belly that shook like a bowlful of jelly. He was big, but there was nothing fat about him, and his suit wasn't felt, but crimson body armor polished to an exquisite sheen. Not Santa Claus at all; Saint Nicholas come to slay dragons.

Without a word, Santa darted forward, his speed belying his size, inserting himself between Eric and the elf, his blade a wall protecting the boy.

They struck swords. The fighting was furious, swifter than Eric believed possible. The elf attacked with savage desperation, and Santa parried, blow after blow, incredible impacts so deafening Eric clutched his hands to his ears. The noise boomed through the house, rattling the walls, sending pictures clattering to the floor.

Back the elf drove Santa, until he pressed him against the wall. Eric's hopes fell. It looked as if it would be over before it began.

With a savage roar, St. Nick began his counter-offensive, his face a gray grim mask, his eyes merciless and terrible. Two of his blows nearly beat through the elf's defenses, sending the creature stumbling back. Santa was on the attack.

They destroyed the living room, splitting the coffee table like a tomato, sweeping the lamps aside, slicing hunks out of the couch. The Christmas tree fell; ornaments and Christmas presents rolled and bounced across the carpet.

Back and forth they fought, grunting with their efforts, neither speaking as they dueled. Eric did not understand what it was about; he only knew his family's lives depended on the outcome.

Santa took a bad stroke to his side, and though his armor held, the blow slowed him. The elf closed. For an instant, they fought face to face, blade to blade, one arm locked against the other. The elf pushed with all his strength, and Santa slipped and fell.

The dark blade whirred above Claus' head. Santa's own sword was down, caught beneath his enemy's booted foot. A triumphant grin lit the elf's blood-red lips, the exultant anticipation of victory.

The baseball bat Eric had wanted for Christmas lay at the elf's feet. The creature kicked it away and repositioned his foot for the final blow, rolling it to where the boy stood.

Without thinking, without a plan, without considering the power he was up against, Eric snatched the bat, pulled it to his shoulder like Daniel had taught him, and swung with all his might. It was a stout blow against the elf's back, a solid thump.

The elf swept his blade backward, a streak of darkness, and Eric was holding the bat handle while the rest of the bat clattered against a wall. For an instant, he thought his fingers had gone with it, but they were all still there. His eyes passed across a label taped to the handle: *To my little brother. From Daniel.*

Puny as the effort had been, it was enough. Santa freed his sword and blocked the elf's stroke. Claus scrambled to his feet, striking right and left, moving the blade in a dance of death, while the light from his weapon grew to brilliant intensity. Unable to recover from the change in fortune, the elf parried poorly. Santa's blade tore through the creature's upper body.

The elf's eyes widened in shock. He gave a whistling gasp, a shrill whine ending in abrupt silence. Then the monster was gone, vanished in smoke and steam, leaving only an oily stain on the carpet.

Eric and Santa stood facing one another in the ruined room, the warrior bent, hands to knees, panting for breath from his exertions. Eric looked into those fierce blue eyes, as terrible and frightening as the elf's, and burst into tears.

At first, Santa merely stared, until Eric was certain the warrior would turn his wrath on him. But Claus' dreadful glare softened.

"Here, now," he said in a deep voice, between gasps. "What's this? And after fighting so well? It was a blow well-struck. I owe this victory to you, Eric."

Still breathing hard, Santa knelt at eye level and placed a hand on the boy's shoulder. Eric started, but the powerful grip rested gentle as a child holding a sparrow.

The light from the warrior's blade was waning, but before it failed completely, Claus glanced around, and with a wave of his gloved hand, caused the candles on the mantel to emit a soft flame.

"Better," he said. "You have seen enough of darkness this

night. Enough darkness for a lifetime."

At this bit of magic, wonder replaced Eric's fear. "Are you really Santa? I didn't think you were real."

"Perhaps it were best if you still believed so," Claus said. "Such horror as you have witnessed is not for little boys. Yes, I am Father Christmas, Saint Nicholas, Hoteiosho, Papa Noel—Santa Claus."

"Do you have a sleigh with reindeer and everything? Is there really a Rudolph?"

"I sometimes use a sleigh pulled by reindeer, but Rudolph is a legend. Reindeer noses cannot glow, you see." Santa gave him a wink. "I was an ordinary man once, Eric, but was chosen long ago—the why and how need not concern you. When the forces of darkness seek to enter our dimension, it is my task to prevent them. The struggle is fierce and continuous. The moment the elf appeared I knew of him, but he was little more than a phantom until this evening, when he attempted a permanent transition into this world through a blood-sacrifice. I was nearly too late—other powers sought to prevent my coming."

"He wanted to hurt Daniel."

"Daniel was always the target. In the land mortals call Faerie—though it is far, far more, both darker and brighter—there are rules to such encounters. The elf could only strike through the youngest sibling. He couldn't have killed you—he deceived you about that. He wanted to destroy both you and Daniel, your brother through death, you through guilt and remorse. Such is the way of these folk. But you resisted, Eric. You were willing to sacrifice your own life for Daniel's, and that gave me both time to reach you and power to aid you. Your tiny resistance was all I needed to break through. The lit fireplace was but the elf's foolish attempt to create a further barrier against me."

"He said I'd never be as good as Daniel."

"The elf spoke many lies, some close to the truth because those are the most deceptive," Santa said. "I, who am far-sighted, tell you this, Eric, you will not be the high school quarterback, the football star your brother will become. You will never possess his easy, athletic ability. Your heart is turned toward books and contemplation. And you will always be the little brother to him, even when you are old, so that sometimes you will long for him to treat you as an equal. But you will be special as he is special, and you will love one another though you have nothing in common save the odd fact of growing up in the same house. And it will have to be enough."

Eric looked into the wise, thoughtful eyes. "You're nothing like the stories."

"No, I suppose not. My task is battle. I am the Defender against the darkest of all nights. No doubt it makes me grim."

"Do you really bring presents?"

Santa laughed, a deep, pleasant rumble. "The gifts are a legend from long ago. All year long I gather my strength for this night. But there are more than presents to be had in this world. There is good done to others. And I think we have exchanged presents tonight."

"Huh? Oh." Eric remembered his manners. "Thank you for saving us."

"And thank you for what you did for me. Not many children can say they saved the life of Santa Claus."

The warrior glanced around the room. "It is best if no evidence remains of this battle." He waved his hand and the scattered objects in the room inching back to their places. The shattered glass of the door quietly reformed, piece by piece. The coffee table and couch mended themselves. The Christmas tree slowly rose, and the Christmas angel, head intact, returned to the topmost branches.

"By morning all will be as it was," Santa said. "You do understand that no one will ever believe what happened? Best not try to tell them. Especially Daniel."

Eric smiled. "He'd really make fun of me."

"Goodnight, Eric. Go back to bed. Tomorrow is Christmas and I must go. There are other evils to defeat before sunrise. I have to do it all in one night, you know."

Santa stepped to the fireplace. He turned, gave Eric a final laugh, and was gone, sliding up the chimney like water.

Under the vigil of the angel at the top of the tree, Eric watched as the living room gradually returned to normalcy. He picked up the bat, now whole, and studied his brother's printed inscription.

Sleigh bells sounded outside. Still clutching the bat, Eric ran to the window. Through the blackness, he caught a glimpse of animals large as bison pulling a mighty wagon into the sky.

"Merry Christmas," Santa's voice rang through the terrible darkness. "Merry Christmas."

✧ ✧ ✧

AFTERWORD

WEST TEXAS IS flat and semi-arid. When the wind blows hard in the Spring, we have occasional, unpleasant dust storms. Maps locate this part of Texas in the classic region of Tornado Alley. Summers are hot and bring severe thunderstorms and hail. The inhabitants continually hope for rain. Trees exist only where they've been planted by human hands.

I love it. I grew up in a similar landscape in the Oklahoma Panhandle. I'm a child of the Great Plains, from a small town where a kid can learn to write books because there's little else to do. I have no desire to live anywhere else; I intend to die in this country. I love the sound of the wind in the trees, the hot summer days, the smell of the air when the lightning comes.

These days, I live in another small town in a canyon created by the Caprock Escarpment mentioned in the story. I was walking my dog one night around Christmas. Cars were driving by, filled with families looking at the lights. It struck me how bizarre it would be to don a hideous mask and go lurching about like Quasimodo, peering into the car windows. I didn't do it, of course; I am, at least on the exterior, an adult; and who wants to scare a little kid at Christmas? But the story soon followed.

Gordon Van Gelder was kind enough to allow me to include a dedication to my older brother, Bob, "*who fought a courageous 14-year battle against the darkness called cancer.*"

The story is about him, too.

THE FIRST EDITIONS

IT IS SAID that every person's life is a book unto itself, a statement that is true, as I learned while on a business trip to find a source of latching gears for my coatpin factory.

Departing from my home village of Giom, located across the border from France, I took the train through our tiny country of Aquitanita and soon arrived in Dumon, the capital city. It is always a pleasure to journey there, to see the moss-encrusted *haciendas*, the splendid palaces, the soldiers in their royal garb.

My quest for raw materials proved successful by the second day, and I was in high spirits when I chanced to hear of Yon Diedo, a gentleman rumored to possess the largest library in all Dumon. As I am also an ardent collector of books, I determined not to leave the city without paying him a call.

Messages were exchanged through the hotel concierge, and the following evening I found myself riding in a post chaise beneath the shadowed archways and ancient walls of the great city. Wide avenues turned to cobblestone streets that gave way to dusty roads as the carriage moved farther and farther into Dumon's outskirts. Storm clouds covered the sky, so that darkness had fallen by the time I reached the entrance of a vast stone mansion enmeshed in cascades of ivy. A servant, wearing the brown, loose-fitting garments of his caste, stepped from beneath the doorway.

"Good evening, sir. Welcome to the manor of Yon Diedo." Without waiting for my comment, he turned to the coachman. "You can be on your way. Return transportation has been arranged."

I gave the servant a questioning glance.

"It is the custom of my master," the man said.

"That is very gracious and highly unexpected."

The servant shrugged. I paid for my fare and followed

through halls rich with the scent of burlwood and roasting meat. To my delight, for my ride had left me ravenous, I was led into a small chamber with a claw-foot table loaded with a repast of wild boar, sautéed potatoes, herb bread, and Antierian wine.

My host soon entered, wearing a scarlet cape and short yellow doublet. A powerful man with deep-set eyes and a heavy brow, he bore seven individually-braided mustachios. He had a deep, smooth voice and an accent I could not place, but which I assumed originated in the South.

"You will forgive the lack of festivity," Yon Diedo said as we shook hands and seated ourselves at the table. "I am a scholar. Entertainment for me is solid food and the silence of study. Alas, I am also a bachelor, so there are none of the tender sex to provide lighter diversions."

I shrugged. "I am unmarried myself, though my sister shares my household. Your home is both beautiful and inviting." Yet, even as I spoke, I realized his manor was neither. And despite his pleasant voice, something about his eyes made me uneasy.

"Ah, but you are young," Diedo said. "There is plenty of time for marriage."

I smiled at the compliment. "I have had my share of living in my thirty-odd years."

"Then you must tell me of it," he said, raising his glass, "for I am a student of the lives of others."

Wine, the great pacifier, soon washed away any disquietude I felt toward my host. Yon Diedo was a man who knew how to draw others out. I was soon telling him of my youth in tiny Tien Manaar, of my father's work in the copper mines there, and of my own labor within those same mines until my rebellion at fourteen, when I set out to join the army in Itlan with but a water flask and half a loaf of bread. I told of returning home after serving in the war, of working in the factories of Oscoga, and of eventually founding my own factory in Giom.

My story told, the last shred of boar eaten, I set my glass aside.

"I have gone on far too long," I said, waving my hand. "I fear I've been tedious."

"To the contrary," Yon Diedo said with great earnestness. "You have lived more in the last fifteen years than many men do in sixty. You should write a book."

"I fear my love of literature does not include the penning of it. But perhaps, if we might. . ."

Diedo smiled. "Ah, my library. Yes. I have kept you waiting long enough. Come this way."

We stepped through double-paneled doors into the largest and most beautiful library I have ever seen. Its walls, floors, and shelves were of burlwood. It was built like a great wheel, with a circular central chamber and dozens of outlying rooms—small alcoves really. An enormous hearth, decorated with stone minotaurs and Aquitanitan cherubesques, curved along one side of the main room, its stones glowing from the heat of a happy fire.

Yon Diedo smiled smugly as I gaped.

"So many volumes!" I cried. "Unbelievable."

"There is no love like that for the printed page."

I strode to the nearest shelf. "You have Kephrin! And Invaldres! This volume, I dare not even breathe upon it. It is priceless."

"Yes, those are quite valuable. But I have books beyond value as well, one-of-a-kind volumes kept in a special section. Come and see."

I followed into one of the alcoves, an agreeable nook with a small hearth, a quilted rug, and a spacious, comfortable chair with reading lamp and table alongside. A peculiar buzzing noise arose when I first entered, as if an insect circled the room, a sound that subsided too quickly to be located.

"These are my special treasures," Diedo said, "shown only to those I deem worthy. I often retreat here to lose myself in my reading."

I studied the volumes, but my brow soon furrowed. The spines displayed only the writers' names, not the titles. "Yon Diedo, forgive my ignorance. I recognize none of these authors."

"Nor would I expect you to. Only one copy exists of each of these books. Sit and I will show you."

I sat in the chair, which seemed to wrap itself comfortably around me. Each of the volumes had a single eye looking out from the spine, but despite that uniformity the books were of all colors and sizes, some ornate, some plain, some of leather and many of cloth.

Yon Diedo eyed me carefully. "Each volume is an autobiography of the most personal kind, all unabashedly frank, revealing those secrets most would never tell. The writers bared all, withholding nothing."

"Truly?" I asked, disappointed. Such *faux*-biographical books, supposedly relating the adventures of a real person, were quite common. But I had anticipated more than the ribald tales so popular with the unlearned.

"You are unimpressed." His face twisted with unexpected rage as if I had committed some unpardonable effrontery, the change in his demeanor so violent I recoiled in the chair.

He instantly mastered himself, his voice smooth again, but the suddenness of his return to good humor chilled me even more than his anger. I abruptly realized how vulnerable I was, seated, my host blocking any escape from the alcove. I remembered how far I was from home.

Yon Diedo chuckled and shrugged. "Should I expect you to be impressed? No, not at all. But perhaps you will be more interested if I tell you I am a sorcerer."

I laughed uneasily. "Yon Diedo, you make sport of me because I am from a small village. Such superstitions—"

My words remained unfinished. Diedo made no movement, spoke no spell. A flash of jade light passed over his eyes.

My sight grew unsteady. I found myself lying on my back in the chair, my head level with Yon Diedo's knees. Chuckling, he reached toward me, his groping hand covering my vision.

Then Yon Diedo picked me up and held me in his grasp. I found myself looking down at his feet, unable to see his face.

"You have told fascinating tales of your life," he murmured as if to himself. "Yet, you will tell me so much more."

I felt the pressure of his hands upon my sides. And then he *opened* me. I heard a soft creaking, the slight shuffling of paper. With numb horror I realized I had been transformed into a book.

"Yes," he said, pleasure in his voice. I could not see his expression but could feel his eyes upon me, studying my contents. "You will make a worthy addition. I have given you a great honor, Jakob Mamolok. The chance of a lifetime. How fortunate you are."

I screamed; I cursed; I implored him to change me back. If he heard, he gave no answer—my voice had become no more than a shuffling whisper emanating from somewhere between the pages.

He shut me; I felt my sides snap together as I closed. He pulled me upright. From the single eye on my spine I could see his arm and face once more, but the hand that held me, being too close, was blurred. He lifted me somewhat higher than his head, and I felt pressure on both of my sides. Releasing me, he stepped back, leaving me at what seemed the edge of a precipice. Seeing dark wood above and below, I realized I had been placed on a shelf with the other volumes.

He beamed at me like a child, apparently pleased at my presentation, heedless of my supplications. And yet, a moment later, his face writhed as if in torment.

"My collection," he half-whispered in a tone of dread or disbelief.

He turned and rushed from the room.

I wept in fear, trembling like a dog terrified of the thunder. There were other sounds around me, but I was too agitated to hear. I do not know how much time passed—an hour, half a day—it was all one to me in my pain, but finally I grew calm enough to recognize a woman's voice arising from nearby.

"Please," she crooned, "I know it's a shock, but you must calm yourself. You are not alone. We're here. We are all here."

"Who are you?" I demanded. "Where are you? I can't see you."

"I'm right beside you. You can feel me touching your side."

"I. . . Beside me?"

"Yes."

She was right. I *could* feel her against me, a gentle warmth.

"I am a fellow prisoner, Janine Laroque."

"Why has he done this?"

"Because he is a collector of stories. And what greater ones than those of a human life laid out in detail? In the evenings, he comes to read one of us."

"This is madness. It can't be happening."

"You will discover it is quite real. You will learn to accept it."

But despite her efforts at consolation, I was too overwhelmed to listen. Nor could I bear to learn of the particulars of my circumstance. Fortunately, though no longer human, I still retained the ability to sleep, and I soon blotted out the horror of my condition by escaping into the sanctuary of a deep slumber.

I awoke to the sound of Janine singing *Two Silver Pesatas*, a popular tune from four years before. She had a lovely voice, and for a moment I thought myself still in my comfortable inn in the heart of the city. Only when I opened my single eye and stared out at the narrow alcove, my vision flat and one-dimensional, did I recall my situation. From my vantage, I could glimpse a patch of morning sun emanating from an unseen window, warming the burlwood walls in the library's main room, but my vision was otherwise restricted to the surrounding shelves.

I moaned.

"Hello," Janine said. "Are you better?"

"How can I be?" I asked.

When she did not answer, I said, "I'm sorry. It is a shock."

"It is," she agreed.

"What will become of us? What of my work? My business. I need to return home."

"You must forget your home. You can never go there again."

"He can't keep us here forever!"

"Books and sorcerers share one thing in common: they can both be destroyed, but they never die. I have been here for only two years, but there are volumes in this library seven hundred years old."

"What can we do?" I asked, horrified.

"We can become friends. You haven't introduced yourself."

I told her my name.

"Very well, Jakob Mamolok. You have a good feel about you—a strong cover and a stout binding. You're a dark-green leather, you know."

"What do you look like?"

"You can tell, as long as we're touching. We see not only with our eye. Feel my cover against you? Concentrate on it."

No sooner did I comply than I realized I could indeed sense her. An image more tangible than any ordinary mental picture rose in my mind. I saw gilded pages and red leather embossed with ornate scrollwork, a magnificent book, one a collector such as myself would have lusted to own. She was beautiful, this Janine Laroque.

She laughed sweetly as if sensing my thoughts. "I think we will become good friends."

After a moment's silence, I asked, "All these books, all of us, are here solely for Yon Diedo's entertainment?"

"For his pleasure and for our degradation."

"What do you mean?"

"Look inside yourself. No, I mean no common metaphor. You are a book now. Look inside yourself. You can do so, even as you were able to see me. Shut your eye. Turn inward. Concentrate on the center of your being."

At first, I did not comprehend what she meant, but after several tries I saw within my own pages. I could scan the words; I could skip from page to page. Everything was there: my thoughts my dreams—and my humiliations and cruelties. Nothing was omitted. I inwardly blushed to see my lowest desires in print.

"Yon Diedo will read me?" I asked.

"All of you," she said bitterly.

✧ ✧ ✧

THE FIRST DAYS in the library were the worst. I spent every waking hour seeking a way of escape, and when its impossibility became clear I thought I would go mad. Perhaps, if not for Janine's guidance, I would have. She helped me deal with the limited depth-perception brought on by having only one eye. She showed me how to move by rippling my cover, an action that propelled me forward by the barest fraction of an inch. She taught me how to feel the musty air of the library, the warmth of the surrounding books, the dark wood of the shelves. But most of all I was aware of her cover lightly touching my side.

Hers was a sweet, discerning nature. She was talkative, and unlike myself, little given to brooding. If she had not entirely accepted her lot, she had learned to deal with it, day by day.

The other volumes welcomed me as a new friend—fresh pages, they called me. I received greetings from everyone. I could only converse with the books immediately surrounding me—even our loudest shouts were minuscule—the buzzing I had heard when I first entered the library had been the books crying out to warn me—but the library had a system of passing messages from volume to volume, so that books from every part of the alcove sent their best wishes. It was impossible to learn everyone's names at first, although I assumed I eventually would. A library has nothing but time.

I quickly became acquainted with the books around me. Major Tamwidge, who had hunted in Namibia, sat to my right with a shelf support standing between us, so we did not touch. Beyond him stood Professor Andover and Ernest Dawkins. Arturo Villareal rested to Janine's other side, and I could not help but wonder, with a twinge of jealousy, whether their covers pressed as closely as did ours.

On the shelf immediately below us stood the Bonne triplets, a trilogy of older women with theosophic leanings. To their right was Katrina Voletta, a reformed lady of the evening, though whether she reformed before or after becoming a book, she did not disclose. Beyond her rested Parson Niemoller, (literally a man of the cloth now). On occasion Miss Voletta was caught in the midst of furious debates between the parson and the triplets.

The books generally slept from midnight until dawn and would drowse again through the heat of the afternoon, waking at evening when Yon Diedo came to read. He would light the lamp, choose a volume, and prop himself in the comfortable chair for two or three hours, often chuckling as he read. Occasionally, he perused non-living books and was a great enthusiast of Baron Karkonolf, an author I consider unbelievably dull. Sometimes he would not read at all but would sit contemplating his collection, rising to dust a volume, to tap it gently into place, or simply to hold it, his hands caressing its cover and spine, his expression rapt in admiration.

Contrary to my expectations, he did not begin reading from me at once, and I began to wonder if he intended to do so at all. To my surprise, the thought made me resentful. He had, after all, brought me into his library. Was I to be nothing more than an unopened volume? Yet, I dreaded the idea of him reading me as well.

When he at last took me from the shelf, I found it ghastly. Bad enough to be handled by his smooth, meticulous hands, I had not realized that as he scanned me I would feel myself being read, hear the words in my mind, know exactly what part of my personal life he plundered. I struggled to shut myself until his fingers trembled against my efforts.

"My friend," he finally said, "the fireplace is at my feet, and a book can be easily burned."

For an instant I considered letting my pitiable existence end. Yet, I feared the flames, and by that time I had taken some comfort in the society of the other volumes. I ceased my struggles and he finished his reading.

I sighed in relief as he closed me. He turned my spine to face him, and I saw tears glistening in his eyes. He ran his hand along my cover.

"Jakob," he said, his voice taut with emotion. "I must apologize. I am truly sorry. I shouldn't have threatened you. It's just—you have such a beautiful cover. And such wonderful words. Your phrasing. . . all my books are so beautiful. So lovely. You should be satisfied here. You *will* be satisfied. Think! How often have you longed to spend your days in such a library, in the company of good books? And these are the best of books. You can read them; they can read you. Idyllic. The slow turn of library days. I have given you what you always dreamed."

He beamed at me, his face childlike as a cherub's. But his expression crumbled, taking on a haunted look.

He glanced across the shelves, his lip curled. "Filthy collection. Filthy books. Would I had never seen them."

As he returned me to my place, violated, humiliated, I had no doubt we were in the hands of a madman. He departed immediately after, but not even Janine's kindness could cheer me.

"Has he read you often?" I asked.

"Nearly every night at first."

"Did you ever get used to it?"

"Never," she said. "And pray you never do, Jakob. Among the books are those who learn to enjoy it. Let us never become as those."

Perhaps I was not as interesting as some of the other volumes, for Yon Diedo soon wearied of me. But it may have only been that his attention shifted to a new prisoner. He led her into the little room exactly as he had done me, an extraordinarily beautiful woman, who I later learned was the Contessa du Maurier. She and Diedo spoke warmly, even flirtatiously. I thought perhaps he intended to court her, but instead, once he had seated her in the comfortable chair, a jade light enveloped her. Her laughter died into the dusty corners of the bookcase. She became a slender volume with brightly colored pages.

"Such a shame," Janine said. "She was so lovely."

"No more beautiful than you," I said.

"Oh, Jakob, how would you know?"

"Why, by your cover, of course."

She laughed to conceal her embarrassment, but I felt her turn warm against my side.

✧ ✧ ✧

THE DAYS PASSED and my affection for Janine grew. She was my oasis, my sanctuary. One would imagine our being constantly together would grow tiresome, yet her wit, vitality, and good nature always pleased me. There came an evening, after Yon Diedo had spent his hours dipping into a seventeenth century Englishman who had served under Oliver Cromwell, that she and I did not sleep, but talked late into the night. Moonlight through the window in the main library illuminated a section of its floor, leaving our bookshelves in shadow. The library lay silent, save for the settling of boards and our own, papyrus-small voices.

"I suppose this is to be our lives," I said, staring into the shadows with my single eye. "You and I moldering together on the shelves?"

"You won't mold," she said. "Yon Diedo is careful with his collection. And if a bookworm comes for you, I will squash it between my covers."

I laughed. For the first time since beginning my strange imprisonment, I felt suddenly contented, as if I were a man again, the library's owner rather than its captive.

"Perhaps it won't be so bad," I said, "sitting on the shelf, spending my days here. As long as you are by my side."

I felt the heat of her blush. "You make too much of me, Jakob. You have been through a terrible ordeal. I was the one who helped you through it, that's all."

"It goes deeper than that," I said, lowering my voice so the others could not hear. "You have become more than a friend—at least for me. I wish we had met outside these walls. What adventures we could have together."

"You mustn't talk this way."

"Have I misread us?"

"I. . . you don't understand. I have loved my time with you, but it can't last. The sorcerer occasionally shifts the entire collection to provide us with variety."

"Because he cares so much for our well being?"

"We are his obsession. But whatever his motives, a day will come when we will be separated. You mustn't expect too much."

"I see," I said, stunned by the thought. "I don't want us to be parted."

"Nor I, but we must anticipate it."

After a moment's silence, I said, "Then let's at least enjoy this evening. Tell me all about you. I want to know everything."

She hesitated. "And I, you. Perhaps. . ." Her voice faltered. "I would be willing. . . would you, perhaps. . . like to read me?"

The question surprised me, for I had already learned that allowing oneself to be read was singularly personal. This differed from reading *to* another book, which was done all the time, sometimes to all the surrounding volumes as if one were giving a recital. Janine and I had read to one another several times. But to actually read a companion's pages was an act of deep friendship or love.

At my hesitation, she blurted. "I didn't mean all of me, you know. Just select passages. I'm sorry. I shouldn't have—"

"No," I said, embarrassed. "Please. It would be an honor. It's just, I don't know the custom or even how it's done. Do we take turns?"

"It can only happen when two books are touching. We do it together. You must think of the pages you wish me to read, as will I. It just happens then. It's all quite natural. Just concentrate on a single page at first."

I looked inward and found a humorous incident from my childhood on page twenty-three.

"Perhaps this one," I suggested.

She gave me her page ninety-seven, an account from her adolescent years. I gasped as her page sprang to my mind, vellum-white with golden letters—Janine was beautiful inside and out.

We read together, a brief passage, and it was the most intimate experience I had ever known. Her soul lay before me, captured in lines rhythmic as poetry. More than the words, it was the order and the shape, the letters and punctuation, the sentences and paragraphs, the way her thoughts rose and fell. It was an ecstasy, holy and wonderful. At the same time, I felt her partaking of me. She murmured in delight as she read me; I basked beneath her approval; our thoughts intertwined in the reading. Our covers touched lightly; I felt the passion of her soul.

Her page finished at the end of a sentence.

"I want to see the next one," I said.

"No, not that one."

"Please. We could—" I concentrated, trying to turn her page. She struggled to hold me back.

"No, Jakob. You're hurting me."

"Please, Janine, I—"

She gave a cry, abruptly ending the contact. I felt sudden mortification.

"I'm sorry," I said. "I didn't mean to. It was so overpowering."

She said nothing.

"Forgive me," I pleaded. "Please."

She eventually replied, her voice calm. "The fault is mine, Jakob. I should not have allowed it. It was too soon. Come, let us speak of other things. I read of your childhood. Tell me of it."

We talked until the moonbeams climbed high up the far wall of the central chamber.

✧ ✧ ✧

THE DAYS PASSED and our love grew. After our first awkward encounter, we read regularly from one another, and as our trust increased we enjoyed more personal passages. Not all, of course. The only one who ever read everything is Yon Diedo. Only he has seen my page 126. Bad enough that I burned crimson as he scanned the text, but he laughed as he read.

But I did not show page 126 to Janine, and she kept her own secrets as well, saying a woman must have her little mysteries.

As the weeks passed, I gradually began to accept my new life. Sitting on a shelf sounds dreadfully dull, but as long as the company is good, books possess a wonderful capacity for repose. I found myself looking upon my former life philosophically, wondering about my constant hurry and impatience. I enjoyed reflecting on my own text, seeing how the path of my life, which had appeared random before, now seemed orderly, almost planned. But perhaps its being written down only made it appear so. I tried not to spend too much time looking within, however.

More than one volume had become obsessed to the point of narcissism, living within itself, no longer interacting with the other books. Only in the library of Yon Diedo could one learn everything there is to know of one's self.

I participated in grand discussions, sometimes with one or two other books, sometimes with nearly the whole library. These latter could last for days, with points and counterpoints being passed from book to book all around the library. It sounds tedious, but it was exhilarating. So many fine minds! Some of the books were learned, some less so, but Yon Diedo had chosen his library well, and there were no vapid volumes. I mingled with orators and princes, theologians and philosophers, scientists and socialists. Others, despite having little education, were treasuries of experience, wisdom, and wit. A poet from Arana, an Ottoman mercenary, a Persian merchant, a former slave from America. A library of great books.

Out of all the wonderful volumes, the one exception was a large book of battered leather, bare of any name. We called it the Gray Book. It never spoke to anyone but muttered almost continuously to itself. None knew its history, except that it had been there longer than any of us. Some said it was a sorcerer Yon Diedo had conquered. Some said it was his first victim, grown mad through the centuries. Diedo never placed it beside another book but kept it apart between two plain, wooden bookends. Everyone, even the earliest captive, agreed that Yon Diedo never read it. In fact, he seemed loathe even to touch it.

After several weeks of captivity, the dreaded reordering of the books occurred. Our captor arrived early and began moving the volumes with studied care, humming as he worked, sometimes addressing us.

"Ah, Minuet," he said to one fat volume. "Petite Minuet. How lovely you look this morning. What a beautiful young woman you were when I first acquired you—how long ago? Five hundred years? Has it been so long? If not for me your beauty would have faded. But here you are, as comely as ever. And such good stories! Perhaps I will dip into you later this evening. But for now, what if I place you beside Mr. Whitbourn? He tells the most devilish tales! I think you and he will get along splendidly. And your *confidante*, Lady Albrecht, can sit to your other side."

"All my old friends," he muttered, picking up another volume. "I want you to be surrounded by the most pleasant of company, so you will be content."

When he came to us, he seized Janine first. I struggled with all my bookish strength to hold her, as if I still had arms. The results were pitiful; I could do no more than wriggle my covers. I shouted in my loudest voice, a bare flutter. He lifted my love high into the air, then brought her down to the lowest shelf at the end of the nook. When he seized me; I burned with such hatred toward him I thought it must surely scorch his hand, but he paid no heed. I was placed on the highest shelf, far from my beloved.

"I will put my two newest acquisitions together," Yon Diedo said. "Perhaps you will find something in common."

I stood between two other books, our covers lightly touching. I recognized the volume at my front as the Contessa du Maurier. The other turned out to have been a captive longer than any other volume save for the Gray Book, an elderly tome, twice the thickness of the others, entitled Edward Dawson, though everyone knew him as Captain Steed. We were close to the Gray Book—only one other volume stood between it and the Contessa, and even from my position a foot away, I could sense the malevolence pouring from that unholy tome.

The library had a custom, after what we called The Shuffle, of reintroducing ourselves to our neighbors on every side, after which we were each expected to relate one story from our past. In deference to his age, Captain Steed was asked to begin, and told an absorbing tale of his passage as a young midshipman to Easter Island. The book on the Contessa's other side, Archibald Winters, took his turn next. He, too, had been to sea and related a fantastic episode of an encounter with a kraken. In the midst of his telling, the Contessa whispered to me, "Believe none of it. I was a row above him before. A notorious fabricator."

"Really?" I was surprised. He had a sonorous, genuine manner.

"Can a book as slender as he have lived such adventures?"

"Actually, I can't see him."

"I have. He is no wider than a little finger." Her pages rustled, which is the laughter of books. "Don't be fooled, my friend."

The Contessa told a charming story of her triumph over a particularly wicked rival in Paris, and I gave an account from my military days. I would have enjoyed these tales immensely, if only I had been able to share my delight with Janine. As it was, our separation left me heartbroken.

✧ ✧ ✧

THE DAYS THAT followed were not as those before. Janine and I tried calling to one another, but it was impossible; I could scarcely hear her, much less continue the intimate conversations we had previously enjoyed. We passed messages, but it was not the same.

Captain Steed, while affable enough, was several centuries old and prone to repeating himself. But the Contessa proved a most interesting companion, and we spent many hours together. She had a droll wit and a way of leading people into conversation, making them feel that she held them in high esteem. Though she lacked Janine's sweet nature, she was much more sophisticated. Nor could I forget how beautiful she had looked when she first entered the library.

She often spoke of escape, especially after being read by Yon Diedo, a humiliation that made her so furious that her pages curled. At first, I tried to console her, but she only turned her wrath upon me, and I learned to leave her alone at those times.

One evening, following such a reading, the Contessa displayed an unusual fragility.

"Jakob," she said, pressing her back cover against me as if for sanctuary, "we must find a way of escape. I won't have him putting his hands on me, knowing my every thought."

She wept in the only way books can, moaning, her whole frame shuddering convulsively. The cries of a strong woman have always affected me deeply, and if I had possessed arms, I would have wrapped them about her.

"Come now, Contessa," I soothed. "It is all right. He may abuse us, but he can't take away what we truly are. How can I help you?"

"Oh, Jakob. Tell me a story. Let me read your pages."

I had not meant for us to become intimate, but in that moment of sympathy, I let her scan a page of my text, and she gave me a page of her own. And then we were reading one another hungrily, taking in every letter and mark of punctuation. Hers was a world filled with the marvelous and cosmopolitan.

Thus, the Contessa and I became lovers in the only way books can. And if I felt guilt at giving myself so soon to another after my separation from Janine, I reflected that I was but doing what I must to survive in that bizarre prison.

In the nights, the Contessa and I sported together. Competitive, she loved proving her superiority, sometimes at my expense. Nor did she hold a high opinion of the other books, despite having met so few of them. But in the day, she often spoke to Archibald, the volume to her other side, the one she had earlier labeled a braggart. When I asked about him, she simply gave the bookish equivalent of a shrug (the slightest movement at the top right-hand corner of a page).

"It means nothing, dear Jakob. He thinks he impresses me, not knowing how I scorn his pomposity. One must find amusement where one can in this dreadful place." Despite her assurances, I burned with jealousy.

In response, I pushed to read more of her, as if by doing so I could utterly possess her. Sometimes she allowed it; sometimes she refused, pretending no interest. Or perhaps it was not pretense. Whatever the case, it felt like punishment. Only my pride kept me from begging for her attentions, for I knew that if she ever reduced me to that point, I would become an object of her ridicule.

One evening, when she had treated me with particular neglect, I heard her and Archibald talking far into the night. The light flooding through the window into the main chamber attested a full moon. Despite being unable to discern what they said, I despaired, thinking I had lost her affections. I was drifting into a black, mournful sleep when I became aware of the sounds of movement. Rousing, I found the Contessa stirring beside me.

"What is it?" I asked.

"You're awake," she said. "Excellent. Help us push."

"Push what?"

"Archibald. We must move him toward the Gray Book. It's the only way."

My pages fluttered. "Why does he want to go there? What—"

"Help us," she ordered. "I've no time for questions."

Time being our greatest commodity, I thought that a peculiar answer. Nonetheless, I pressed with all my paper might.

Movement is difficult for a book, but we set our pitiable

strength to the task. It proved a grinding effort, as we struggled through the long hours. Finally, when the moonbeams slanted into the farthest corner, I heard a delicate *whoosh*.

"What was that?" I asked.

"We've done all we can," the Contessa said. "Archibald has tipped against the bookend holding the Gray Book."

"Why are you doing this?"

"Because we require an ally if we wish to escape. Why does Diedo keep the dark book separated from the rest of us? If it were once a sorcerer, as some say, it might help us."

Though unable to make out the words, I could hear Archibald speaking to the Gray Book and the volume answering with guttural replies. To captives, tiny rebellions take on great significance, but I could not help but wonder if our actions had been wise.

"Read me, Jakob," the Contessa demanded. "I want to celebrate tonight's victory."

I read her far into the morning hours.

✧ ✧ ✧

BY DAWN, THE entire library knew what had happened. Through messages passed along the shelves from volumes with a better view, we learned that Archibald remained upright, leaning lightly against the bookend, the top of his cover touching the Gray Book. The two of them conversed continuously, but Archibald ignored any questions from the rest of the shelves. The books fell into furious debate, some arguing that he should withdraw at once, others wanting him to discover the truth concerning the mysterious volume.

"Has anything like this ever been tried before?" I asked Captain Steed.

"None of us were ever placed close enough to reach the Gray Book," he replied gruffly. "And it shouldn't have been done now. The book is evil. I would have tried to stop you if I had realized what you were doing."

Yon Diedo did not come to the library for the next two days. This was not unusual; like all men he pursued his hobbies when time allowed, but it was unfortunate.

In the afternoon following the day Archibald first spoke to

the Gray Book, he began to whimper in an animal whine.

"What's happening?" I demanded.

"I don't know," the Contessa replied.

We called to Archibald, but he did not answer. And still the Gray Book murmured to him, its voice increasingly caustic.

By the second night, Archibald began screaming, a frail, thin noise like that of a book being eaten by silverfish. The entire library began shouting, begging him to push away from the vile text, but if he heard he gave no answer.

"If only he'd stop," the Contessa moaned. "He's driving me mad."

Eventually, Archibald did cease his cries, but only after his voice reached a continuous wail ending in savage abruptness. Into the silence rose a shuffling sound. From the corner of my vision, I saw a pair of objects flash past, the bookend and Archibald. My eye involuntarily shut at the impact of his body slamming to the floor.

Nor was the ordeal over, for its contact with Archibald had roused the Gray Book, and the Contessa soon gave a choking whisper.

"Jakob, the book tries to reach us."

Nothing happens quickly in a library, and this was no exception. Throughout the night, we listened, sleepless, as the Gray Book struggled, emitting a rustling, whining noise I hope never to hear again, a cross between the grunts of a pig and the screams of a horse.

Around three o'clock in the morning, the noise grew louder. Apparently, something had impeded the Gray Book until then; it had either been marshaling its strength or had needed to overcome some type of restraint. Whatever the case, it now moved toward us.

"You must protect me," the Contessa urged. "You must."

There was little I could do, but I spoke to Captain Steed, sending word down the line to see if there were room for flight. We had some difficulty; Van Gelder, the fourth volume down, was a metaphysical nihilist who insisted we were in no danger since nothing really existed. (Perhaps not an extreme philosophy for one turned into a book.) But at last we convinced him to comply. With four inches of space between ourselves and the side of the shelf, we began a slow retreat, hoping to buy time until

Yon Diedo appeared.

The night passed; the pale light of sunrise tipped the library walls, and still we fled. All the while, I felt a palpable aura of malevolence emanating from the direction of the Gray Book.

"Tell them to hurry," the Contessa cried, over and over. "It's getting closer. Oh, you must save me."

Some of the others, discouraged by our shuffling flight, would have faltered completely except for Captain Steed, who proved himself a true leader. Through encouragement and remonstrances, he spurred the volumes to their greatest efforts.

The Contessa and I required no such incentives. The Gray Book was so close we could hear it whispering. Though the phrases it spoke were nonsense, they filled us with indescribable dread, as if at any moment they might become words too horrible to bear. If, I thought, in some obscure age the book had once been human, it must have given itself to such complete evil as one never meets in the sunlit streets of the world.

At last, toward evening, our flight ended. Word came down that we had closed the gap; there was nowhere left to run. The Contessa, nearly mad with fear, kept crowding against me, as if to bury herself in my cover.

The murmuring of the Gray Book was closer now. Although I could not see it, I imagined it towering above the Contessa's corners, looking down upon us. I felt sick with the weight of its malice.

"Trade places with me!" the Contessa demanded. "Shield me, Jakob. Don't let it get me."

She, who had always appeared strong, panicked. Despite my fear, I would have tried to help her, but getting between her and the Gray Book was impossible. Even if there had been enough shelf space, it would have taken half a day.

The next hours were a purgatory. My mind began to wander; dreadful visions assaulted me, horrors I will never attempt to describe. I did not believe there could be such hatred in the world.

As the evening sun faded from the library, a bitter cold pierced my spine.

"Jakob!" the Contessa screamed. "It touches me. Oh, please, make it stop."

At that moment of despair, Yon Diedo entered. A buzzing cry

of alarm went up from the entire library, loud enough to startle the sorcerer. He hurriedly lit the lamp above his chair and turned to examine the alcove. When he spied the Gray Book pressed against the Contessa, his brow grew inflamed.

He picked up the awful volume as one might grasp a serpent, touching it only with his thumb and forefinger, moving it safely away from us. Retrieving poor Archibald, he thumbed through him and set him aside, then picked up the Contessa and read her final three or four pages.

"Vile witch!" he cried. "You think *me* evil, who am but a collector."

He picked me up next and scanned my last pages. Only then did I realize that our stories did not end when we were changed into books; we grew to include our experiences in the library.

"Poor dupe," he said to my open pages. "But not so foolish as Archibald."

He returned me to my place and picked up Archibald's silent form. Opening his pages, Diedo furiously displayed them to all the books, walking up and down the aisle, turning from side to side so everyone could see.

Every page was blank.

"This," Diedo shouted, tears of rage and sorrow in his eyes, "is the fate of those who encounter the Gray Book. It drains the life from its victims. Did you think I kept it separated from you for any reason other than your protection? Archibald is ruined! Ruined! Such a magnificent volume!"

He took Archibald, and laying him carefully upon the fireplace grate, built a pyre and consigned him to the flames. Removing Pastor Niemoller from the shelf, Yon Diedo read aloud from him as the book was consumed. His voice broke more than once during the ceremony, and when it was done he sat in the chair, weeping with his face in his hands. But whether he felt pity for Archibald or merely mourned the loss of a rare volume, I could not tell.

When he had grown calm once more, he rose stiffly and addressed the library in a subdued voice.

"I am sorry, my friends. The fault is not yours but mine. The Gray Book, for reasons I will not divulge, must remain in the library. But I was careless, leaving it too close to some of you. I had thought. . . I had hoped. . . that the kindnesses I have shown you would be appreciated: the way I rearrange you so you can experience a variety of companions, my careful placement to prevent any book from being too crowded, my constant vigilance against foxing, mold, and insects. I mend your pages; I watch for your safety. But not all appreciate my efforts. I can understand that some of you are new here, but I tell you, sometimes I grow weary. A collection is not an easy burden. A little consideration would be appreciated, a little policing of yourselves so I do not have to do it for you."

He strode from the room, leaving the books murmuring.

The library held a memorial service of its own immediately after. Archibald had made many friends, and wonderful eulogies were passed around the shelves. Under the Contessa's influence, I had apparently misjudged him, whose stories may have been more true than she had suggested.

The Contessa, overwrought by her terror, demanded to be comforted. That night I read her again but with a new eye, realizing for the first time that despite her protestations she was one of those Janine had spoken of, who enjoyed being scanned by a man with Yon Diedo's power and wealth.

✧ ✧ ✧

I COULD NOT be content, thereafter, but longed for the days spent with Janine. I still found the Contessa compelling; despite her self-absorption, she was a vibrant, extraordinary woman. Men are not always wise in these matters. But the evil of the Gray Book made me long for the goodness of my friend.

To make matters worse, we were shuffled a week later. Any small group of people creates its own society, and in our library those societies rose and changed with each rearrangement. Some were gracious; others less so. Some turned acerbic.

I was placed between a watchmaker from Stockholm and a dancer from Vienna. For Diedo to have chosen him, the watchmaker must have possessed a rich, inner life, but it was one he never displayed. Sullen, withdrawn, he scarcely spoke a dozen words in all the time I knew him. The dancer tended toward an unfathomable esotericism wrapped around her art. She also had a streak of cruelty and a dagger-tongue that spared no one. Only a bright young boy on the shelf below and a circus acrobat from the shelf above made life bearable. But altogether, we were a sullen group. Having lost even the amusement of the Contessa's company, I began to despair.

Two weeks of this convinced me that I had to take action. I decided to work myself forward until I stuck out enough to draw Diedo's attention. Noticing me, his curiosity would surely compel him to read my final pages and discover my desire to be with Janine. If he had pity, he would place me beside her. But if he proved cruel, I might find myself exiled from the others or even given to the fire.

Still, I was determined. I began early in the morning, pushing first with my left cover, then my right, waddling my way forward. By the time Yon Diedo arrived that evening, I had succeeded in writhing out almost an inch. His hands wandered over the shelves as they often did, preparatory to his choosing a volume. To my dismay, he casually patted me back into place. I roared in frustration, but if he heard me he gave no sign.

Three days in a row I followed my plan, but each time he returned me to my original position.

I decided my scheme had not been bold enough and resolved to push myself until I careened to the floor. Yon Diedo would surely read me then. This was a dangerous strategy, however, as I had no way of knowing if I could survive the fall.

I began in the early evening, while Diedo was still reading, knowing I would not be far along by the time he left. He departed without noting my efforts, and I spent the rest of the night creeping toward the edge. I ignored my companions' inquiries, especially those of the dancer, who had been particularly disdainful of my previous efforts.

"Message from Janine," a book on the shelf below called to me in the early morning light. *"What are you doing, Jakob?"*

I glanced across the shelves. The last reshuffle had brought Janine and me only slightly closer. She was positioned on the third shelf up at the far end of the alcove, while I sat higher, in the middle section.

"Getting Diedo's attention," I said. "Trying to reach you."

As I continued my exertions, I heard my message passing down the line from book to book.

"Jakob, don't do it," her reply came back. *"You'll be killed!"*

I laughed sardonically. "You call this living? But I won't die."

I tried to sound more confident than I felt. She implored me, but I refused to give up. Others sent messages as well, words to encourage or dissuade me. A few feared upsetting the sorcerer. Captain Steed informed me that several books had made similar attempts in the past only to suffer broken spines or dented corners. I thanked everyone for their concern and kept to my task. Shortly before Yon Diedo's normal hour of return, my weight shifted forward and I toppled, top down.

Though the fall took the barest second, it seemed an eternity before I bounced onto the floor. The pain was not as dreadful as I had imagined, more akin to a bad dive into a pond. My spine tingled, but I could still see, and my edges remained uncrumpled.

Janine's voice flowed down from the heights.

"Jakob? Can you hear me?"

Momentarily forgetting what I was, I tried to raise an arm in triumph, an effort that caused my cover to flap the barest fraction, bringing cheers from my fellow books. I shouted my reassurances, then lay waiting for our captor's return.

Perhaps the sorcerer was not as insightful or as curious as I had suspected, for upon seeing me on the floor, he clucked twice, showing none of his expected anger. His moods, always unpredictable, ranged daily, even hourly, from sullen to exuberant.

"Jakob Mamolok, what are you doing? Do you think you can run away from home? Where would you go?"

Chuckling, he picked me up and examined my spine. "No harm done," he proclaimed, placing me back on the shelf.

"Read me!" I yelled. But he gave no sign of hearing.

I fumed that evening while he browsed the pages of a trader from Cathay. But before Diedo departed, I began creeping forward again.

By the next morning, I noticed Janine doing the same.

"You shouldn't try it," I sent to her. "You could be hurt."

She did not listen.

I fell first and was again unharmed. She followed shortly after. She took a bad bounce that brought her less than a foot away, spread pathetically open, her pages showing. At first, I thought she was weeping.

"Janine?" I called. "Janine, are you. . . are you. . . laughing?"

"Oh, Jakob. That was fun! I haven't had such a thrill since I was a child."

I admired her courage. After the fear of the fall, her laughter became infectious. We lay there, flat against the floor, helpless in our mirth.

✧ ✧ ✧

BY THE TIME Yon Diedo returned, anticipation had erased our levity. When he saw us on the floor, he did not appear amused as before, but annoyed.

"Again?" he said. "And who is this?"

But he did what I desired. He read my back pages and then Janine's. We waited in trepidation.

His eyes flamed with anger. "I try to be considerate. I try to make everyone happy. But I will *not* have my books dictating their positions *to me*. I will *not* have the niceties of my collection, my careful arrangements, ruined by two seditious volumes. You especially, Jakob, have caused far too much trouble."

He put us each back in our places, and then, having dealt with our tiny rebellion, went about his usual reading.

Overwhelmed by grief, I asked the books beside me to pass word to Janine, expressing my regrets. By return message she said she did not blame me, but rather, admired my determination.

But the battle was not over, for something in our story touched the inner pages of the library that night.

"Don't worry," the lad on the shelf below me said. "We'll find a way to get you near her."

Many offered encouragement. Messages passed back and forth. Oaths were made. Cries of unfairness rang out.

"Diedo hasn't the right," the dancer declared. "He hasn't the right."

A great murmuring rose from the books, louder than I had ever heard before. This lasted for some time before Captain Steed's deep bass finally called for order.

"There has been much talk, but talk is inadequate," he said. "Is it your wish to take action against Yon Diedo, even if it means punishment, or even. . . destruction?"

"Yes," the books cried. And "Yes!" again.

"Then there is but one course, if we have the courage," the captain continued. "We must disarrange ourselves."

"We will do it!" the dancer shouted. "We will show the big man."

✧ ✧ ✧

THE NEXT EVENING, when Yon Diedo came to read, nearly every book, except a handful who refused to join the revolution, lay scattered on the floor. The sorcerer gaped; his eyes turned bleak with concern, then red with rage. He lifted his foot to kick the books before him but held himself back, not daring even then to harm his collection.

"Where," he hissed, "is Jakob Mamolok?"

He waded among the volumes, moving carefully even in his wrath. He pushed books aside until he found me. Taking me up, he set me on the fireplace mantle, lit the fire, and lifted me high in the air. A gasp came from the volumes.

"This is your hero?" he shouted. "This, your dissident? I—why! I'll show you what happens to those who oppose me. I'll show you!"

He brought his hand back to send me into the flames. His face burned red as the fire itself. I imagined the heat searing my pages; I prayed it would not hurt too much.

In the midst of releasing me, Yon Diedo hesitated. His hand trembled violently. He clutched me so hard I felt his fingers grinding into my cover.

"I can't!" he shouted, dropping me to the floor. "I can't do it."

He burst into tears. "If only I could burn it all down! Every book. The entire house."

He collapsed into the chair, overcome. After several minutes he looked up, his face red from weeping. "I'm sorry. Forgive my outburst. I didn't mean what I said. You are my friends, the only friends I have in the world."

He lifted me to the side table.

"This cannot go on," he murmured. "I must consider."

Without another word, he left the room. But I did not know whether he spared me because he was not a murderer or merely because he could not bear to burn a member of his collection.

The library buzzed with speculation. All agreed the sorcerer had never acted so erratically before. Some suggested he was going insane. But I wondered how many such discussions had occurred over the centuries, how many times the prisoners had sought to comprehend the actions of their captor, the same way the children of a drunkard vainly seek to understand the aberrant behavior of their sire.

At dawn the next morning Diedo returned, eyes set. Without speaking, he began replacing the books on the shelf. It took half the day to finish because he must have them just so. But he left me where I was, and I wondered if he intended to consign me to the flames in a public execution.

With all the other volumes back on the shelves, he stood at the front of the alcove and addressed us.

"I want my library to be happy," he said softly. "This. . . this insurrection cannot continue. I could take steps against a random number of you." He glanced at the fire and I shuddered.

"But that is not the way of Yon Diedo," he said. "I am a connoisseur of books, and you are the greatest collection in the world. You should be proud; you should be honored to be a volume in this library. I have chosen each of you carefully. Some of you, I traveled hundred of miles to find. Others came into my hands by chance. Yet all of you I have treasured. Many of you have outlived your entire generation, your words and thoughts given immortality. Would you leave here only to turn to dust?"

Low whispers came from several of the older volumes.

"Is it such a bad place," Yon Diedo continued, his voice imploring, "sitting in quiet conversation with the company of interesting people? I keep you dusted; I move you about to give your lives variety. I allow no man's hand but my own to handle you. You can read one another. You have time for contemplation. Is your fate so terrible?"

"Lord Diedo," Colonel Steed said, "we are not all unhappy here. My time is done; you took me when I was old and past my prime. But love has touched our hearts. These two are young. They should be out in the world together. And some of the others should have the chance for a real life."

Diedo sat down in his chair, his fingernails lightly touching my cover.

"Is this what you all wish?"

"We must have hope, my lord," the captain said. "Books are written in hope."

Yon Diedo tapped me gently, his brow furrowing and relaxing as if he were embroiled in some inner turmoil. At last he said, "As I told you last night, for many centuries you have been my only friends. Should friends have secrets? No, they should not. I will tell you everything.

"When I was a young man first learning the ways of magic, I found the Gray Book, which has another, darker name I will not repeat. I ignored those who warned me not to delve into it. After all, I said to myself, how can reading a book harm anyone?"

Yon Diedo fell silent, lost in reverie.

"From it," he finally continued, "I learned the spell for turning people into books. What a wonderful thing it was, to capture all a person would ever be, to delve into every secret thought. And to have it between beautiful covers. It was a collector's dream. But such power is not given without conditions, of which there were three. First, the Gray Book must always be kept within close proximity of the transformed. Second, as a byproduct of the enchantment, the Gray Book becomes animated. Third, the most dreadful, the one I did not know before using the spell, the user becomes obsessed with his collection."

Yon Diedo looked down. "That is right. I admit my weakness. I think of you constantly; sometimes at night I dream of you. I see your covers in my mind. I have not left the manor in years for fear of something happening to you while I am away. Is there no way to break the curse, you ask? Yes. If I were willing to give up my books, the spell would be broken and I would be free. But how can I bear to lose you?"

He raised his hands to us in supplication. "You see how helpless I am. My collection would be ruined. I cannot do it."

He sighed. "But this insurrection. Things cannot go on like this. You have become discontent, all because of the foolish love between Jakob Mamolok and Janine Laroque. As if that were anything compared to the love of a man for his books."

He hesitated again. "But that being the case, I was thinking that perhaps if I could... if I could... release the two of you, perhaps it would give me the strength to give up the other volumes who wished to leave.

A cheer came from the shelves.

"Now, not all at once," Yon Diedo warned, raising his hands for silence. "It would take some time. I could not be rushed. And I need to read Jakob and Janine a moment before making my final decision."

He took me up and perused me from the time I had first come to the library. He seemed particularly interested in my relationship with the Contessa. At last, with a rueful smile, he set me aside.

"It is not as simple as I first thought. Having read between Jakob's lines, I see his love is not so pure. Therefore, I will free this book and one other, the one Jakob chooses. For three days, I will place him between the Contessa du Maurier and Janine Laroque. Let him then decide."

I groaned. Though Yon Diedo was willing to let me go, he would also punish me for the trouble I had caused.

✧ ✧ ✧

BEING PLACED BETWEEN Janine and the Countess proved awkward for me. I scarcely knew what to say to either of them. But an advantage to being a creature of pulp and paste is that one can hold private conversations to either side without the opposite volume being privy, the left side of a book not always knowing what the right is doing. The Contessa addressed me the moment Yon Diedo departed.

"What an opportunity for you, Jakob. I congratulate you. You have played a dangerous game and won. You will soon be free."

"It appears so," I said.

"Do you know what I would do if I were you? I would take a coach to the coast. I own a marvelous little chalet overlooking the sea, a cozy cottage for relaxation and healing."

"Unfortunately, I do not own such a chalet."

"Still, you should do something of the sort."

Over the next two days, she told me more of the things she would do if she were in my place, of sea voyages and dinners with royalty. She talked of how glad and grateful her father would be were she the one leaving. In short, she reminded me that she was wealthy, beautiful, and powerful, fully capable of rewarding her friends. I must admit her words affected me. She was, as I have said, an intriguing woman.

How different were my discussions with Janine, the conversation of two friends whose interests met at so many points. She never mentioned the matter of my decision until I brought it up.

"Jakob," she told me. "You shouldn't take me with you."

"What do you mean?"

"There are others here, such as the boy, who deserve their freedom more than I. Take him, instead. He's a bright, cheerful lad, who deserves to live his life as more than a book."

"Yon Diedo said I must choose between you and the Contessa. He might allow none of us to leave if I demand the boy. And you have been a good friend to me. More than a friend."

"Don't say it, Jakob. Here among the books, I have a lovely cover, embellished in gold. But in the outer world... I don't deserve you there. I'm not a beautiful woman—"

"You are too modest. Every woman thinks herself less lovely than she is."

"The Contessa doesn't. But I'm not being modest. I know what I am, Jakob. I come from common stock. I have two beautiful sisters, but I am not beautiful or even pretty. I'm plain, with too long a face and mousey hair. If you have to choose between us, you should choose the Contessa. I know you have... feelings for her. She can give you so much more."

"My little mouse, then," I said, trying to cheer her.

She burst into a fluttering of book tears. "I can offer you nothing, Jakob, neither money nor beauty. At least among the books, I wear a pretty face. You are the only one who ever thought me beautiful. Leave me here, where you will always remember me that way."

I am not without vanity. The thought of being with the Contessa fascinated me. A woman of such beauty on my arm—and wealth besides. Men judge other men by the loveliness of their wives. I had struggled in business. With the Contessa's fortune, I would struggle no more. Yet, how could I leave my friend among the books? It was a hard choice.

✧ ✧ ✧

IMAGINE YOURSELF IN a prison with the power to free one person. Think of how the other captives would treat you. I found my name on the lips of many, some of whom I scarcely knew. What good friends we had been! What wonderful talks we had shared!

I ignored them all. I did, however, meet with a committee formed on the shelf above, representing a number of books who wanted me to bring armed guards to rescue them once I attained my freedom. I promised to do what I could.

The night before the announcement of my decision, the Contessa woke me. Or rather, she roused me from my brooding as I had scarcely slept at all.

"Jakob, I don't know what you'll decide, but for tonight, let us read together one last time."

"No, I—"

"Please, Jakob. Do this for me. Haven't we been friends?"

I complied, though it shamed me to do so. I had avoided reading either Janine or the Contessa while making my decision; such an intimate act seemed inappropriate.

"I will show you a passage I've never shared with anyone else," she said.

The story, from her childhood, showed a side of the Contessa I had never seen before. She had not been born of wealth. Her father had been a drunkard who cowed her mother. Her life would have been wretched save for a schoolmistress in Dumon, who took pity on the girl, taught her to read, and showed her the ways of society.

At the age of twelve, in an attempt to escape her condition, the Contessa befriended a coach boy about her own age. Through him, she caught the notice of a nobleman. Undoubtedly, she had been a beautiful child. She told him her parents were dead, and the man and his wife eventually adopted her.

My heart went out to her as I read of her struggles to overcome her hardships.

"You were tenacious," I said.

"I did what I had to, to survive."

"What happened to the schoolmistress and your parents? And to the coach boy?"

She gave the book version of a shrug. "I never went back. It was all too painful."

I did not easily return to slumber after that, knowing the next morning I would decide the fate of two women, both of whom had struggled in their own way. I fell into an uneasy sleep, still uncertain which to choose.

Yet, when I woke with the dawn, I had made my decision.

✧ ✧ ✧

YON DIEDO ARRIVED at mid-morning that day, undoubtedly curious. I had assumed he would change me back into a man and demand my answer. But, of course, that was not his way. Instead, he picked me up and read my final page.

He nodded slightly, whether pleased or displeased, I could not tell. He made the slightest gesture and my world shifted. My vision expanded; I looked out of two eyes instead of one. I glanced down at my now-human form, amazed at the wonder of my own hands.

Something stirred to my right. A young woman stood there, dressed in red velvet with gold brocade.

"As you can see," Janine said, her eyes downcast, "I told the whole truth."

She was not beautiful. She lacked the high cheekbones, the wide eyes. Her face was too long for beauty. Her hair was straight and mousy. Yet, when she spoke, it was the voice of my friend. I took her hand and kissed it. "I have looked between your covers and seen the beauty of your soul."

A murmur of approval rose from the shelves. Together, Janine and I turned and faced our fellow captives.

When the small approbations died, I detected another, more strident tone, the voice of the Contessa. To my surprise, I found books entitled Janine Laroque and Jakob Mamolok still sitting on the shelf beside her. I glanced inquiringly at Yon Diedo.

He shrugged. "They do not live. But if a man can't own a first edition, a second will have to do."

I grimaced. The sorcerer would still be able to read the details of my life. But at least I would not be there to suffer the humiliation.

I addressed the Contessa. "I'm sorry I—."

"You fool!" she cried. "I could have given you everything. Everything! You. . . little man!"

"You must go now," Yon Diedo said. "This is no longer your place."

We left the library feeling helpless, knowing we could do nothing to aid our fellows.

"You have chosen wisely," Yon Diedo said as he escorted us to the door. "I have read both women from cover to cover. You may never be wealthy, Jakob Mamolok, but you will be happy."

I knew he was right, for the Contessa's story had the opposite of its intended effect. True, she had suffered great hardships, but she had never inquired concerning her parents or the schoolmistress and coach boy who helped raise her fortunes. If I had chosen her, she would have discarded me as one beneath her station. I had read enough of fairy gold to see the common stones beneath. A man becomes more evil—or more good—one step at a time.

"Do not try to find this house," Yon Diedo said. "Or try if you must, but you will never do so."

"Will you free the others as you said?" Janine asked.

"I will. . . try. This is a first step. I will see if I can take another."

Janine and I exchanged shy glances. I took her hand. We walked away.

"Janine! Jakob!" the sorcerer called after us.

We turned. He stood at the doorway, his expression tortured, one hand lifted in farewell.

"I will miss you, my friends."

We left without another word.

✧ ✧ ✧

Forty years have passed since our release, and Janine and I have remained together.

We have searched for Yon Diedo's house, but true to his word it is not to be found. Yet, half a dozen years ago while on business to Dumon, I felt a tap on my sleeve and found the Contessa standing there. Her beauty had failed; she had grown heavy. Her clothes were shabby. It took a moment to recognize her.

"You are Jakob Mamolok," she said, her voice trembling.

"Contessa! Diedo set you free!"

She grimaced. "No thanks to you. He set us all free eventually, except for those who wanted to stay. It took years for him to overcome the power of his obsession. I returned to find my fortune gone, my connections ruined."

"I am truly sorry. I—"

"I wanted to make certain it was you."

She slapped me twice as hard as she could, then turned on her heel, muttering, "Nothing but a ten *sou* novelette."

As for my little mouse and me, we have been happy, though as Yon Diedo predicted, we have not grown wealthy. Still, we are comfortable and have raised good children. I often regret that I did not read Janine's entire story when we were together as books, so that she remains somewhat a mystery even now. Though she is not beautiful to others, she is beautiful to me.

In the evenings, we sit together by the fire and read to one another out of our little library, which does not include a single first edition. But we never, ever mistreat a book.

✧ ✧ ✧

AFTERWORD

I'M NOT ONE of those writers who can sit down and purposely create a short story out of the air. Or rather, I might be able to, but it wouldn't be any good. My stories always begin with an idea. They come to me at random, usually when I'm doing something monotonous like shaving. Most of them I mentally discard; a few I jot down so I can remember them. Of the latter, the majority remain unwritten. The ideas that resonate either soon become stories or simmer, sometimes for years, in the back of my mind, occasionally plaintively calling to me.

If there is a lesson for aspiring writers here, it's that ideas come in silence from the subconscious mind. In a world of constant noise, someone who wants to come up with anything original—whether to solve a problem or create something new—must seek times of quiet and solitude.

I like reusing characters. The Contessa du Maurier also appears as an antagonist in the third Evenmere novel. In my novel, *The Back of the Beyond,* Joiwend explains that the Contessa was her sister-in-law, who caused her to be exiled to Faerie. From the evidence, after tricking Joiwend, du Maurier wound up in Evenmere, then later left there to return to Aquitanita, only to become part of Yon Diedo's library.

By the way, as an aside to those readers fluent in grammar usage: while preparing this collection for publication, I noticed that in the originally-published version editor Gordon Van Gelder chose to capitalize the title 'countess' throughout, doubtless to emphasize her position. This, despite the "rule" stating that titles should be capitalized only as part of a name or in direct address, i.e. Countess du Maurier. I kept with his original choice in this volume. Writers and editors often break the rules for creative purposes, but both Gordon and I *do* know the difference.

The First Editions was written shortly after I came up with the idea. It appeared in *The Magazine of Fantasy and Science Fiction* and was later included in *Year's Best Fantasy 9*, edited by David G. Hartwell and Kathryn Cramer.

DAY OF THE SHARK

SO SINGS THE poet, Voa, playing on shell and bone:

We lived under the ocean, a great people, and if history has forgotten us and time veiled our existence, this song must set the matter right.

I sing of great evil, monsters of the Deep, battling armies, the love of a woman, and a quest to the bottom of the sea.

I sing of Thalassa.

In the fourth year, the Time of the Descending Stream, in the migration of the bluefins, the beginning of spring.

✧ ✧ ✧

THEY CAME IN the evening, nineteen weary warriors, to the Third Mark of the Vercan Rift—ninety fathoms down, much deeper than they had ever been before—far from the land of Ooanga in the reefs.

Arc lifted his eyes and gaped up at the translucent expanse of the ocean above, feeling its massive weight upon his chest and shoulders. He turned his head from side to side to draw extra water over his gills as he made a bleak survey of his fellows, who sprawled listless with fatigue on the backs of their manta rays. The waning light at this depth turned the pearl inlay on the hunters' shark-skin armor dull gray.

He glanced at Shartoom, but even his older brother, the best of the company, sat dejected, staring along the haughty lines of his aquiline nose, his usual blue-gray skin ivory-pale with weariness and despair. Still, he caught Arc's gaze and managed a ragged smile. "An hour's rest, brother. Then we will continue the pursuit."

If this had been Geerd or even mighty Iteemon, Arc would not have been discouraged, for Geerd was wise but lazy, and Iteemon loved his sleep, but Shartoom was a moray wedged deep in its hole; he did not relent. If he said rest, then rest they must, though it shook Arc to his soul.

But he nodded and replied, "It's cold here. The mantas can't keep up the pace."

Arc rubbed the cephalic fins of his mount, Whisper, close to the eyes where she liked it best. Her wingspan, the widest in the tribe, spread ten and a half arms. Old Uncle Uyo, now lying dead back at the crèche, had given her to him at the boy's coming of age on his thirteenth birthday.

Despite Arc's attention, the manta kept her cephalic fins scrolled close to her head, a sign of agitation. The vast sweep of her wings lifted and fell in strokes ponderous with exhaustion. The parasite-hunting remoras attached to her belly had eeled away, driven back to warmer waters after the company crossed into the cold layer at seventy fathoms. Under any other circumstances, the hunters would never have driven their mounts so hard or so deep.

"I say ride them till they sink," Shartoom replied, his lips tight.

"They can't go another league," Arc said. "Won't we need them, after?"

Shartoom gave Arc a bitter look, no doubt thinking none would survive the journey, but he replied, "You may be right." He pulled himself from his riding net and unfastened the halter straps from around the shoulders of his mount.

This surprised Arc, for his brother, six years his senior, did not listen to him often; some said he did not listen to anyone at all. Shartoom passed the word to the others, and one by one the Ooangans dismounted and released their mantas.

The creatures did not mill around their masters in the normal way but slid upward in a clump toward Thin Blue, pumping their wings against the pressure, only their long gill-slits and white underbellies visible from below. Arc watched Whisper go, knowing he might never again ride her through the canyons of coral.

Arc's twin sister, Ayita, joined her brothers. Her red locks, which normally glistened in fiery splendor when close to Thin Blue, looked black as Arc's own in the depths. Her face mirrored his distress.

"This day is accursed," she said.

"It is," Shartoom agreed, seating himself on a rock outcropping along the ocean floor. Arc and Ayita slid to the ground at his feet, and the ooze rose around them, momentarily blinding them in its fog.

They sat in silence, all three lost in memory, for this was the fourth anniversary of the death of their father, who had been taken by a Great White. A shark will seldom attack a man, but this one had, and Arc had seen it all. The memory remained cold and clear, the massive jaws, his father's screams. He still could not bear to think of it.

On that day, at the age of eighteen, Shartoom had replaced his father as crèche lord. Arc and Ayita had been twelve. Their mother was gone as well, taken by a wasting disease when they were four. Arc remembered her face as soft, misty lines and little else, but Ayita recalled her better and spoke of her often. After their father's death, they were raised by Shartoom and all the aunts, uncles, and cousins of the crèche, most of whom, on this anniversary day, had been captured or slain by the bandit, B'tat.

"It's my fault," Shartoom said, his voice low so the others would not hear. Arc looked up in wonder; Shartoom did not usually admit his mistakes, and Arc idolized him too much to want to hear him do so.

"You couldn't have known," Arc said. "We were gone—"

But Shartoom waved away his defense. "You tried to warn me yourself, but I wouldn't listen. B'tat came to us, an outsider, full of stories of foreign waters, flattering me while learning our weaknesses. I knew he was smooth, that his eyes lied, but I took him in anyway. He told me of great kingdoms, said we, too, could become a great people if we allied ourselves with such as he and followed his foreign gods. Forgetting my duty to the crèche, I coveted the wealth and power he offered. I have acted like a gobie, dancing at the grouper's jaws." Shartoom fell silent, staring across the sea. "Why could you see so clearly what I could not?"

Arc shrugged. "He was *ingat*, alien. It's like father said, we can't trust anyone except our own people. It's always been that way."

Shartoom nodded. "I shouldn't have forgotten."

Throughout their long pursuit, Arc had tried not to think about the women and children in the clutches of the raiders.

Outland lords like B'tat had a reputation for cruelty. While Shartoom and his hunters had been away hunting, B'tat's bandits had battered down the crèche doors and carried away the men's families, slaughtering those too old to be useful.

The hunters had returned home to find the crèche deserted, its four doors waving wide. The guards had laid down their lives in long rows for Shartoom's wife, their crèche lady; the hunters had found their bodies drifting in the rooms, their blood floating in the chambers. Shartoom had vowed upon the names of the dead to find their slayers and rescue the captives.

Of all the women, only Ayita, who was with the hunting party, remained free. Arc shuddered, thinking that if she had been in the crèche she would have surely fought and died. He did not think he could bear it if anything happened to her.

The dolphins, who are a friend to everyone, had told the Ooangans the whole tale. In their rattling tongue, they spoke of following B'tat, scolding him as they went until he turned and drove them back. The dolphins know only two numbers—one and many—and could not give a count of the enemy.

When the avengers first started their pursuit, the dolphins followed for a time between making trips back to Thin Blue for air, chattering about the attack until the party entered the Vercan Rift. As the walls of rough stone covered in sea urchins rose higher around the men, the dolphins fled, for the Dread Ones dwelled in those canyons.

Arc's people feared the rift, but Shartoom inspired them to descend, for despite his vanity he outshone every other man in the tribe. A born leader, he could out-fight and out-think any of his companions. At times he seemed larger than life. Though he and Arc had lived, laughed, and hunted together all their lives, Arc often felt he did not truly know his brother.

Sometimes he thought Shartoom touched by divine hands. Many in the crèche might have agreed.

✧ ✧ ✧

Once tied around rock formations, the hunters' riding nets doubled as sleeping pouches to keep the occupants from drifting. They slept on their backs, floating inches above the sea floor, looking up toward the dim, diffused glow of Thin Blue, taking comfort in its light. They did not post sentries, for no one had the strength to stay awake, and their enemies were still far ahead of them.

Arc's thoughts churned until slumber claimed him. He wondered if they were doing the right thing. The implication of B'tat having passed this way filled him with dread, for none intentionally sought the Dread Ones. Not without design. . .

Arc woke at Geerd's touch. He looked up at the kind face. Geerd was old, nearly forty, but not too ancient to hunt. Like all the people of Thalassa, his upper body, made for swimming, was amazingly muscular; his waist was thin, his legs strong. He still had many years of life in him.

"How long?" Arc asked.

"Not long." Geerd tied the braided strands of his golden beard along his neck with a kelp cord to keep it from floating into his eyes. Some of the reef people possessed facial hair—others such as Arc and Shartoom did not. "It's hard to judge the time this far from the light, but I think we've slept little more than an hour. Rise quickly. We must be sharks."

Arc nodded and repeated the motto of the hunt: "We must be sharks." The saying arose from the legend that Lord Shark never slept but sought its prey with endless, precise fury. Because of the way his father had died, Arc seldom used the expression.

The company arose and drifted into the hunting formation, the *denary*, a four-sided wedge with Iteemon at the point and Shartoom directly behind him. Because so many ocean creatures attack from hiding, the lord's best warrior always led, leaving the master protected on every side by his men. Only during the charge was the leader permitted to slip to the front to make the kill. The custom was old as Arc's people. Arc and Ayita swam side by side above and slightly behind their brother.

Once in position, the hunters quickly fell into a smooth rhythm, arms and webbed feet stroking with the fluid grace of dancers, the whole company moving in instinctive symmetry.

As the denary descended, following the sloping rift floor, the pressure increased. Colors had gradually deserted the hunters throughout their journey: first orange, then yellow, finally green; now the water faded to the midnight blue of the twilight regions. The last vestiges of coral had vanished twenty fathoms before, leaving only barrel and tulip sponges, anemones, and waving clumps of sea pens, emptied of hue, gray shadows in the gloom.

Gone, too, were the schools of fish, the mollusks and crustaceans, the starfish and sea cucumbers, the thousand inhabitants of the reefs. Arc spied a single squid propelling itself out of the denary's path, ghostly in the dimness. Finger-length hatchet fish drifted by, their faces like wizened men, their eyes clouded with blindness, the bio-luminescent glow of their sides turning their backs silver, their bodies iridescent. Black shrimp sailed by. Nothing broke the silence except for the hunters' muttered conversations, not even distant whale songs, dolphin chirps, or croaker cries.

Grottoes lined the rift walls. Arc shuddered as he looked at them, wondering what creatures might dwell within, species his people did not know. With each stroke, every hunter turned his head sharply to the side, watching for danger, ready to alert the denary. Darkness was never safe for the people of Thalassa, for the predators woke—shark and barracuda—and the night sea contained too many perils for an unsheltered human. They kept above the ocean floor, for sand creepers lurked at these depths, large enough to snap up a man.

Arc, who had the best eyes of all the hunters, sighted something below him. He slipped between the forms of his fellows, drew beside Shartoom and pointed, and the crèche lord called a halt. The hunters floated down to the ocean floor; Iteemon, the first to land, swept the sand with his spear for creepers. Arc's bare feet sank into the ooze.

A bone spear protruded upright from the ground, its flint point driven into the detritus as if thrust there intentionally. A swirling symbol etched into its end boasted the sign of B'tat's house.

Beyond the blade the rift fell sharply, dropping into an even more oppressive gloom. Above the descent, a shoulder of rock jutted out, carved into the massive head of an octopus, staring with malignant eyes. Runes surrounded the carving. Having no written language, the hunters could not read the words, but they stood like lost children, heads down, not wanting to see, for here began the Fourth Mark, the boundary of the Dread Ones' country.

They had not expected it so soon; perhaps they traveled more quickly than they thought. When Arc saw it and knew how deep they were, a wave of panic swept through him; the pressure of the water against his chest seemed suddenly unbearable.

He glanced at Shartoom. Though his brother was surely as frightened as any, he gave a rough smile that restored Arc's courage. He felt the air filtering through his gills once more.

Yet Geerd's words terrified him anew. "They are lost," the old warrior murmured. "B'tat has taken them to the Dread Ones."

A horror fell upon the whole company. Even Shartoom faltered. They sank to their knees upon the sand, one by one, eying each another in despair.

"What can we do?" Iteemon asked.

"Why would B'tat do this?" Ayita asked. "The Dread Ones will surely seize him and his men." She pulled on the abalone rings of her twelve hair locks with fierce strokes, a habit when upset.

"If we want to find out, we have to follow them," Shartoom said softly.

The hunters fell silent. Finally Geerd said, "We will all be killed. Our kin are as good as dead; how will it help for us to die with them?"

"He's right," Iteemon said, his dark eyes hollow sockets in the gloom. "The Dread Ones would destroy us."

Shartoom surged to his feet. "I will not desert my wife and children! I will go, even if it means death. What do we know of the Dread Ones, anyway? None of us has ever seen one."

"My father told me they are twice the height of a man," Otoon said, "and dark as morays peering from their holes, with burning, yellow eyes."

"And your father heard those tales from his father, who learned them from your great-grandfather," Shartoom said. "All we really know is that B'tat has given them our kin."

Arc looked at his companions huddled together in a tight circle, their gill slits trembling with excitement, their faces fierce with fright.

"I won't force anyone to go," Shartoom said, "but I am going. Do as your heart tells you."

One by one the older members agreed, even Otoon, who had no children and did not like his wife much, and the younger ones like Belo and Enivir followed their example. As one, they rose from the bottom, scarcely disturbing the ooze.

"Very well," Shartoom looked down his hatchet nose at each of his followers, meeting their eyes, his own glistening in approval. "Before we go, we must examine the area to ensure B'tat isn't leading us into a trap. I don't like that beckoning spear. Perhaps he placed it there to lure us down, then took the captives upward."

The hunters murmured their agreement. They searched the area carefully, Iteemon even passing deeper into the rift, where he found a single footprint in the sand and a piece of shark-skin jerkin torn by a jagged stone. The hunters discovered no other signs, but by these they believed the bandits really had descended.

Geerd, who had been searching close to a gaping grotto, moved to its mouth.

"Where are you going?" Arc asked, alarmed. Anything might hide in a cave.

Geerd raised his hand. "A moment. I see something useful."

He disappeared into the opening while the hunters milled anxiously at its mouth, spears ready. A light bloomed from within, and everyone tensed, thinking something stirred, but Geerd returned carrying a handful of glowing bio-luminescent algae. "We'll need this for our lamps."

They took their conch lamps from their squid-skin packs and followed Geerd back into the cave. The passage twisted immediately to the right, but a pale orange glow rose from around the corner.

Beyond the bend, the walls were covered with the algae, glistening golden and scarlet. The luminants the hunters had carried with them had long grown dim, so they poured them out, scraped the algae from the wall with bone knives, and refilled their conch-shell lamps, which used polished quartz-crystal prisms placed at the mouth of the conches to amplify the glow. The rays of the luminants shone pink through the shell walls. Such lamps cast only a little light, but it was enough for the Ooangans' large eyes.

They descended deeper into the rift. The ground angled downward for a quarter-league, then abruptly fell away, leaving the hunters swimming into what appeared a bottomless abyss, as if they descended into the Deep, where no man could survive.

The canyon walls closed in above them, turning the light of Thin Blue into a faint gash. Scattered finger-size lanternfish appeared, phantoms slipping through the sea, silver in the luminous light emanating in rows along their bellies.

Still the hunters went on, seeking the bottom. Arc craned his neck to keep Thin Blue in sight; he feared losing it, lest he lose his courage as well.

By the time they reached the bare stone of the rift bottom the pressure bearing down upon them made their blood throb in their veins. Arc could feel his skin tightening against his face and a sharp wedging in his ears like a slow spear thrust. Slender Thessen, two years younger than Arc's fifteen, seemed most affected. He drifted to the bottom and was unable to rise. The tribe gathered around him, many hands raising him up.

"Leave me, Shartoom; I'll only slow you down," he said, though his eyes shone with the horror of being deserted. "I'll find my way back."

"You wouldn't be able to," Shartoom said, squeezing his shoulder. "Brave Thessen. Any farther and none of us will be able to go on. But we may not need to descend much more. Gather your strength."

They momentarily rested. Arc, who had half-expected the Dread Ones to attack the instant the Ooangans entered their region, took comfort in still being alive. Perhaps Shartoom was right; perhaps they were not the gods men called them. Certainly Arc's people did not worship them as such.

He glanced around.

"What are you thinking?" Ayita asked.

He managed a smile. "Something foolish. If this were a journey for exploration, I would probably enjoy it."

"No one comes here for pleasure."

"No, but there are fish down here I've never seen before. Aunt Ferocious used to describe them to me. I'm finally seeing them."

"Aunty came this deep?"

"Deeper, once, when she was a girl."

"I didn't know." Ayita's voice caught, for their aunt was a captive with the others.

"She's been where all the fish are luminescent. She said they were beautiful but terrifying. When I was little, she promised to bring me down someday."

Ayita sighed and took Arc's hand. "I guess she has."

Arc squeezed his sister's fingers. "Other than the pressure, it isn't as bad as I expected. It's almost peaceful." He looked across the ooze toward the bare stone walls. A few crabs grazed along the rocks; otherwise the rift looked deserted. With so much life on the reefs this wasteland seemed strange.

The company continued on. To their surprise, they soon came across a Great White floating dead. Being ever eager to observe any aspect of nature, Arc spied the body first, portions strangely black, bobbing half-hidden beneath the overhanging projections of the rift wall. Tiny crabs and starfish covered the shark, drawn out of whatever deep crevices where they dwelled; hags slithered in and out of the body. Clouds of miniature sand sharks bickered for the remains.

Fire being unknown to the Ooangans save from the volcanic vents that spewed liquid flame, they stood puzzled until Ayita said, "It was burned by the Devouring Light."

At her words, Arc understood the charring of the body and recognized the searing scent that accompanies lava, an aroma he had smelled only once before. He looked around but could not find any evidence of a volcanic fissure.

"This shark was unusually far down," he said. "What could have killed it?"

"Only the Dread Ones possess this kind of power," Geerd said.

No one replied, and a new melancholy fell upon them.

Iteemon led them just below the teeming mass of scavengers; the water surged with the sand sharks' struggles. When they were right beneath the body a strange, wavering voice cried out, "Mommma. . . Mommma."

The startled warriors raised their weapons.

The sound rose again, close to the body of the shark.

"What could be crying for its mother in all that?" Ayita asked. "Is there a child?"

"More likely some trick of the Dread Ones," Arc said. "Even if it is a child, it is ingat."

"That's cruel!" Ayita said. "Whether it's of the crèche or not, you wouldn't leave a baby to the hags." Breaking from the denary, she shot toward the sound. Arc thrust after, fearing for her safety; in their frenzy sharks do not always care where they strike.

Together the twins stroked to the shelf, Arc with his spear ready, Ayita anxiously seeking the sound. Shartoom and several others hurried after.

"Mommma!" the cry came again.

Arc waved his spear before him, driving the predators away from the mother's left flank. Blood, hunks of flesh, and the smell of death filled the sea.

Spying a wavering fin, Ayita thrust aside a hermit crab to reveal the source of the sound, pressed close between its mother and the shelf.

"Here it is!" she cried. She put one hand to her mouth. "Oh, no!"

"That?" Arc asked. "It can't be!"

As if in answer, the creature cried, "Mommma!"

"Is it really a Great White?" Arc asked.

"A pup. You should kill it," Ayita said, her sympathy draining away.

The shark, less than an arm long, swam back and forth along its mother's flank. Other than its ability to speak, it appeared no different than any other Great White: the white belly, the sharp fins, the black, soulless eyes and cruel, rending jaws.

Shartoom paddled along beside. "I've heard of these," he said, scowling. "From the times of the Old Wars. The Dread Ones bred them, giving them the power of speech."

"Obviously, the Dread Ones do not care about their servants once they're usefulness is over," Arc said.

The pup pressed against its mother, emitting a strange whining cry, closer to that of a human than a shark. Arc watched it with a mixture of loathing and fascination.

"Sharks don't nurture their young," Arc said. "Everyone knows that."

"These must be different," Shartoom said.

"Wait, what's that?" Arc's eyes caught something glistening within the corpse.

"I see nothing," Shartoom replied.

"There!" Arc waded forward, driving the scavengers back. From within the shark's open belly, something silver reflected the light of his conch lamp. He reached forward, while hags, slithering to escape him, emitted thick mucous over his hand.

Grimacing, he pushed through the dead flesh, seized a heavy handle, and pulled it out of the shark. He lifted it high, and despite the gore, everyone could see it was a short but magnificent sword, little longer than a knife but made of a substance far stronger than bone. His followers gaped as the conch light danced across its surface.

He traced its edge with his left hand; it was sharp as a surgeonfish spine. "A sword beyond compare!" he exclaimed. "A sword from the belly of a shark."

He looked at the other hunters, and all but Ayita had floated back from him, overawed.

"What will you do with it?" Geerd asked.

"It is a sea gift," Shartoom said. "You have to keep it."

The hunters drifted closer again, their eyes on the blade until Arc put it in his belt.

"Momma!" the pup whined again, and everyone, having momentarily forgotten it, turned back to the shark.

Geerd raised his spear. "I'll kill it."

"We have no more time," Shartoom said. "Leave it to starve."

They passed beside the carcass, careful to avoid the scavengers, leaving the pup crying for its mother, a death wail that followed them a long time through the darkness.

The cries finally faded, and their spirits rose again when the rift leveled off, ending their descent. The conch lamps revealed stonefish the color and texture of the sea floor, gaping upward like brooding crones. The hunters avoided them, for their dorsal fins were lined with thirteen poisonous spines. Arc had once seen a man die raving in agony from a single sting. Those who survived an attack experienced tremendous swelling, and their fingers and toes sometimes turned black and fell off. Because of their camouflage, the stonefish were easily overlooked, so the hunters kept above the ocean floor.

The rift narrowed, siphoning them along. They soon approached a rock wall, the apparent end of the canyon, though narrow caves along its face suggested the possibility of further passage. There they saw the Dread One.

It lay like an octopus in its den, in a craggy hole an arm across, its tentacles curled around it, only the top of its bulbous head and its huge, swollen eyes glaring up at them. Indeed, if not for its eyes, it might have been mistaken for a blue-ringed octopus, but those orbs seethed with intelligence.

It slithered with startling speed from its hole, a single tentacle stretching out, then another, then the saclike head. No one doubted what it was; its evil pulsed over them with a force as tangible as a hand squeezing their throats. For a moment the entire party forgot its hunting skills and froze like gobies, every eye upon the creature. Someone gave a groan of fear. Arc's blood ran cold; only his sense of honor kept him from fleeing.

In form it truly resembled a blue-ring; its brown skin was covered with brilliant navy whorls that gave depth to the ball of a face too long and swollen to be mistaken for a true octopus. Where the blue-ring was small, the Dread One stood upright on its appendages, twice human height. Its eyes glowed yellow, the huge pupils flat and merciless. It wore no clothing. Its mass of tentacles, easily three fathoms long, each ending in hoary, clawed hands, danced down the side of the rock face. Arc shuddered, remembering the blue-ring as the only octopus with a poisonous—and lethal—bite.

The denary finally reacted, raising spears and velos-bows. Seeing how easily the tentacles might flick out to seize them, the whole company save Shartoom swam backward. The crèche lord kept his position.

The creature spoke in a hideous voice like the scraping of bone against bone. "Why do the blue-skins disturb our nest?"

Following Shartoom's example, Arc summoned his courage and paddled forward again, though his whole being revolted against doing so. To his surprise, the others followed.

"I am Shartoom Nyin, crèche Lord of the Tula kin, dwelling in Ooanga." Arc's admiration for his brother rose even higher when he heard his deep, unwavering voice. "The bandit, B'tat, has taken our women and children. We followed him here."

The creature kept silent so long Arc thought it had not heard. Its flowing hands groped along the rift floor, moving serpentine around both sides of the hunters. Finally, it said, "No one came here. Depart from us."

Arc swallowed hard, knowing Shartoom would never leave without a fight. And what man could slay a Dread One? He saw the path of honor stretching before them, ending in their deaths.

"We saw signs of their passage, not two hundred fathoms

past," Shartoom said. "You have them. We want them back."

The arms fanned out, nearly enclosing the Ooangans in a half-circle. One tentacle writhed less than the length of two arms from where Arc floated. It had a strange, oily look that made him shudder. He wondered whether his bone knife could cut the dark sinew.

"We have your kin," the Dread One admitted. "They are ours now as is the custom. You saw the shark we destroyed. She was an unfaithful servant. We slew her using weapons you cannot comprehend, magic that could kill all of you now, right where you swim. Seek vengeance against B'tat, who is the least of our servants and no longer here, but do not meddle in our affairs."

The hunters shifted uneasily, looking for the source of the terrible weapon, but Shartoom spoke with eerie calmness, taking on the tone of a man bartering with his neighbor. "But you have meddled in our affairs. Come, be reasonable! Surely you see our position. Give us back our kin, and perhaps we can do you some good turn."

Arc thought of what his brother had said before, about his people knowing nothing of the Dread Ones. Perhaps the hunters could survive if they treated the creatures like men.

The Dread One shifted its eyes to Shartoom and gave a wheezing, death-rattle that might have been a laugh. "A bargain? You offer a bargain? How audacious the blue-skins become! What can you give us?"

"A hundred shark skins by the next hatching of the great turtles," Shartoom said. A few of the hunters gasped. This was a high price, but Arc thought they could meet it if they hunted the sharks through the spring.

The Dread One laughed again. "Shark skins! What are they to us? Do we cover ourselves like you soft ones? We care nothing for shark skins. If we did, we would have taken the hide of the one we slew."

"Ten handfuls of polished chrysolite," Shartoom said. This did not disturb the hunters as much, for they had recently found a vein of that stone in caves near their crèche.

"We do not adorn ourselves in gems."

"Twenty spears," Shartoom said.

"We do not use spears."

Shartoom paused. He looked close to losing his temper.

"There must be something you desire."

Though the Dread One had no discernible features, Arc sensed it relax, as if the point of the discussion had finally been reached.

"You are the leader of the tribe?"

"I speak for the crèche," Shartoom replied.

"The woman and children B'tat gave us are nothing. They will work in our nests until we devour them. They are not as useful as they could be, for those who serve us unwillingly soon perish from our presence. We will free your women and children if you, Shartoom Nyin, and your men, enter our house and promise to serve us faithfully as long as you live. That is something we can use."

"Surely there is something else, some other price."

"That is all we need. Nothing else. But we do not offer mere servitude. The Dread Ones traverse the ocean floor; our emissaries are everywhere. Our servants dwell in great crèches, doing our will. If you serve us well, we will make you masters of multitudes."

"We will not give up our freedom."

The Dread One gave an odd, popping sound that might have been a guffaw. "Your freedom! Your freedom to do what? To eke out a life of bare survival? We have watched you, holed up in your little crèches, the last of a dying race. We, who live long lives remember when your cities covered the sea floor. Now, everyone hates you; everyone hunts you. Where are humans honored? But if you serve us, we can give you the chance to be more than prey. And if the women decide to remain with you, they can stay as well."

Shartoom turned back to his people, and they pulled together into a knot, enfolding him, keeping their spears poised, their velos-bows ready.

"It's a trick," Geerd said.

"Of the worst kind," Shartoom replied. "One we can neither refuse nor accept."

"I'll do it," Ayita said. "Let them take me for your children."

Shartoom cursed under his breath. "I should have known they would want something like this. What do the legends say of those who serve the Dread Ones?"

Thessen dropped his head. "According to Uyo, their spirits

are lost because they grow as wicked as their masters. They never die but become like shadows, doomed to wander the darkness of the Abyssal Plain in the service of Leviathan."

"Everything we have heard about the Dread Ones is true," Shartoom said. "They recruit their followers through deceit. Our souls are at stake this day, yet I would risk mine for my Ineera."

Geerd hissed. "What are you saying? Our families are lost, but we, if we willingly give ourselves to evil. . . We should attack instead. He is only one and we are many."

Shartoom looked around at his followers, catching the eye of each. "No. We cannot fight the Dread Ones and win. Look above us."

They raised their heads and saw the yellow eyes of a dozen Dread Ones staring down upon them from holes in the rocky cliffs, their tentacles swirling in fans behind them.

The Ooangans fell silent in horror.

A desperate, wily look crossed Shartoom's proud features. "But if we barter, we should barter well."

He broke away from the company and approached the Dread One, his strokes resolute.

"What is your answer?" the Dread One asked.

"The price is too high," Shartoom replied. "You ask too much."

The Dread One gave a low rumbling in its throat. "Then depart before we lose our patience."

"Hear me," Shartoom said. "I claim the right of the Trial of the Circle."

The Dread One gave its rattling laugh. "You are unworthy."

"I am a crèche lord as my father before me. I led my hunters here, daring the depths to seek you. I have a keen eye, steady arms, and the courage of ten. I have killed the Great White single-handed. I demand the Trial."

The Dread One remained silent a long while. At last it said, "We grant your request."

Shartoom turned back to his followers, his face lit with triumph.

"What is this trial?" Geerd asked. "I know nothing of it."

"Because you did not listen closely to the old stories." Shartoom was not only strong but wise and remembered the ancient tales almost as well as the crèche chanter. "A trial by combat."

Arc's eyes widened. "Against a Dread One?"

"Against something else, I know not what."

"Come," the Dread One commanded. "The ordeal will be held in the Pit of Confrontation."

The creature moved away, propelling itself by its powerful tentacles, and the humans followed over a high rise and down into a shell-shaped ravine.

"Your followers will remain there," the Dread One ordered, pointing one of its tentacles at the side of the canyon.

"Shartoom, take this." Arc drew the short sword he had pulled from the belly of the shark.

Shartoom eyed the blade. "None of us has any experience with this weapon. I will trust to my spear."

"Take this, too," Arc urged.

Giving his brother a grim smile, he took the sword and slipped it into his belt.

The Ooangans ranged themselves along the slope, looking down at the declivity while Shartoom followed the Dread One to the bottom. Other Dread Ones approached, aligning themselves likewise around the circle of the pit. Arc could see a shelf near the bottom, half-concealing a long slit in the rock's side.

Shartoom drifted just above the floor, his spear held at the ready. A Dread One on the rocky slope raised a conch shell to its thin lips and blew, sending a low resonance through the waters.

In answer, thin strands flowered from the slit in the side of the pit, black lacing filaments fanning outward in a half-circle.

At Arc's side, Geerd gave an anguished cry. "*Tegula!*"

A head poured its way through the opening, followed by a body shaped as a manta but with four clawed hands stretching from its wings. Brown and white and golden shells covered the creature's form, attached one by one from the time of its hatching and held in place by secretions from its skin. With such a lovely defense did the tegula adorn itself, and its filaments branched forth like cod whiskers, seeking its prey, its eyes being a little blind.

It did not seem to swim but blossomed toward Shartoom with jellyfish strokes, and if the warrior had not instantly plunged away, he would have perished at once.

The tegula rushed past, the water through its shells chiming whispered tones, the *O* of its mouth sweetly glistening. The stinger on its tail shone with poisons intended to immobilize its victims.

So quickly did the tegula pass, Shartoom had no time to prepare a stroke. It rolled over in the water, turning to come again. He tried to bring his spearpoint up, but it was upon him too soon, leaving him only time to grasp his weapon in both hands and use it as a shield, thrusting upward, blocking its double rows of teeth. It passed above him, its wide wings pounding him against the floor.

It doubled back, beating above him, trying to crush him with its full weight. The struggle churned silt from the bottom, and Arc lost sight of him beneath the hammering wings. Precious seconds passed. Just when Shartoom seemed doomed, he shot out from the debris, propelling himself from the bottom with a desperate thrust of his legs. As he rose, he gave a heavy stroke with his spear. It bounced harmlessly off the beast's shell mail.

The tegula whirled in the direction of the blow. Shartoom dove, forced to avoid the monster's grasping claws. Its head shot out, catching the spear. With a twist of its jaws, it snapped the shaft in two. While it worried the haft, Shartoom fumbled after the spearhead. He grasped it, and now beneath the monster once more, thrust upward toward the tegula's throat.

Arc's cheer died on his lips. Despite the well-executed stroke, no blood poured forth. The tegula shifted to its side, revealing shells protecting even its underbelly.

Shartoom pushed up again, gaining height. The tegula passed beneath him. Its spiny tail shot out, piercing Shartoom's shoulder. The man writhed away. Arc groaned in agony.

Shartoom twitched twice and grew still. His arms wavered; his hands fluttered uselessly by his side. The spearhead drifted to the floor.

The tegula came round, moving almost leisurely now, coming in for the kill. Its maw opened wide.

At the last instant, Shartoom stroked upward, propelling himself above the tegula's jaws, the short sword Arc had given him, drawn during his pretended helplessness, now clutched in both hands. He cut downward, thrusting into the creature's left eye.

The tegula spun away, writhing, turning in circles in its death throes.

Shouting in triumph and concern, the denary swam to Shartoom's side. They surrounded him, Arc and Ayita close to his head. Blood oozed from his shoulder where the stinger had entered. His eyes were already beginning to glaze.

"For the best," he muttered. "For the best." He trembled violently.

A Dread One rose above them, its tentacles waving.

"The man fought well," it said. "He has courage before the kraken, as we say. If administered in time, there is an antidote for the poison. Swim back."

Cautiously, the Ooangans moved away from Shartoom. The Dread One slid down and wrapped a coiling member around their fallen leader. Arc held his spear at the ready, but the Dread One took the leaves of a plant resembling seaweed and pressed them to Shartoom's wound and lips. At first there was no response, then Shartoom moved his arms. Within moments his strength had returned. The Ooangans gave a ragged cheer and crowded close to their leader.

"Shartoom, you beat it!" Ayita exclaimed.

"They have to let the others free now," Arc said.

Shartoom pulling himself vertical. Looking around, he spied the sword Arc had given him. He picked it up and handed it to his brother, his eyes somber. "It was truly a gift of the sea as I said. May it serve you as well."

Arc took it, grinning.

Shartoom addressed the Dread Ones. "I claim the victory right."

"As you say," the Dread One agreed. "You will serve us willingly?"

"I will follow you to the Abyssal Plain itself," Shartoom said, his eyes cold.

Arc's grin faded. He felt the blood drain from his face.

"My chieftain, no!" Iteemon shouted.

"But Shartoom, you won!" Arc said.

"I won the right to exchange myself for the hostages. That is the meaning of the Trial."

All the Ooangans began talking at once, but Shartoom waved them to silence. "This happened because of my pride. The responsibility is mine; the sacrifice must be mine as well. The crèche lord gives his life for his crèche."

Arc clutched Shartoom's shoulders and looked up into his brother's face. "Shartoom, please! Don't do it. Nothing will ever be right again!"

Shartoom's eyes, always so cold and imperious, softened as he looked upon Arc. "You're right. It won't. But that is the way of the world. Things change, but the crèche will survive. It seems you must bear the burden of leadership even earlier than I did." Shartoom took his brother's hand.

He then beckoned to Ayita. "Little sister."

Ayita drew near and Shartoom placed her hand and Arc's together between his own two hands.

"We'll never see you again," Arc gasped. "You can't go."

"You mustn't try to stop me. And if you ever see me again, flee, knowing I am no longer my own master but your enemies' servant." Shartoom's voice fell to a whisper. He clutched their hands harder, so tight it hurt. Though he smiled bravely, his voice broke. "You are twins, the blessing of the Sea King. Take care of one another for my sake."

He gripped them once more, then turned. The hand of every hunter went out as if to restrain him, but only touched his shoulders, his arms, his back.

"I am ready," he told the Dread One.

The Dread One laughed; its scorn sweeping over the company. "Enter our caves, then."

"Not until you swear by the Olosi to release all the others unharmed."

The Dread One's tentacles swirled as if it had been struck. "That name is forbidden here. What do you know of it?"

"I know when the Dread Ones swear by the Olosi, they keep their word."

The Dread One gave another rumble; its arms beat against the sides of the rock face, sending showers of stones drifting to the bottom, but at last it touched a tentacled hand to its forehead and said, "I swear by the Olosi that your families and these men will swim free. Now enter the home of the Dread Ones, and we will teach you all there is to know of pleasure and pain."

"Our families first," Shartoom said.

The Dread One hissed but said, "Your kin."

It waved a tentacle. One by one the wives and children of the crèche slipped from a cave behind the creature. Once free, they rushed out, whimpering and crying in terror, clutching their men with terrible savagery. Shartoom's wife and children left the cave last, as if the Dread Ones knew exactly whose family they were. Lady Ineera hurried into Shartoom's arms, but he took her by the shoulders, kissed her fiercely, and handed her to Geerd. He hugged his two children, Jessoon and Myrmry, then passed them back as well. The hunters gripped them, knowing what must come next.

"Welcome, Shartoom," the Dread One said.

Ineera shrieked and Shartoom's children wailed as Arc's brother swam to the Dread One, and it was all the hunters could do to hold them back. The other hostages cried out as well, filling the water with their shrieks. Shartoom's face was gray as the stones beneath his feet, but he held his head high; Arc later swore he swaggered before his new masters as he swam across the rock shelf. A lump blocked Arc's throat; salt flowed from his eyes.

When Shartoom vanished into the depths of the cave, all the women and children fell silent, ceasing their struggles. Then Arc knew how awful the nest must be, for he saw in their faces that they would never return there, not even for the sake of love.

The Dread One raised a shadowed tentacle and pointed along the rift. "Go. We have been merciful."

✧ ✧ ✧

THEY MADE THE long trek through the canyon, swimming in formation with the ransomed at the center. Arc sought to take his position at the outer edge, but Geerd said, "No, Arcurian. Now you must swim in the place of honor, for you are the hope of the crèche."

Arc floated dumbfounded an instant. Even when he made his way to the middle of the formation, he refused to take his brother's post so soon, but left a gap where Shartoom should have been. He called Ayita to him.

"Sister, will you swim to my right?"

Ayita bowed her head in acknowledgment, a flush to her face, the place to the crèche lord's right being reserved for his most trusted adviser. They clasped hands, silently sharing their horror and grief, and fell into position. At Arc's hesitant command, the denary moved on.

They quickly came to the shark carcass. The pup still nuzzled against it, crying for its mother.

"Kill that beast," Ayita said bitterly. "Put it out of its misery so we don't have to hear it."

Arc left the formation, his spear raised. The shark moved in slow circles, an ugly, deadly hunter.

"Mommma!" it mourned.

Arc swam above the pup, taking careful aim. Its cold eyes stared up, unsuspecting.

He lowered the spear, let it drift to the bottom, and drew the sword that had killed the tegula. He stared at its glistening edge. "No," he said, his voice sounding to his own ears as if spoken by another.

Ayita, now by his side, raised her eyebrows, her voice accusing. "Will you spare it?"

Arc looked around at the hunters and back at the sword. "Perhaps it, too, is a gift from the Sea-King. I will tame it, instead."

"No one can master a shark," Ayita said.

"No one has ever owned one that speaks," Arc replied.

Ayita looked him full in the eyes. "Are you certain?"

Arc returned her stare, realizing he did not know the answer. He felt foolish and stubborn and angry. All he knew was that his brother was gone, an outcast, alone, without tribe or family.

"We have lost Shartoom," he said as if that explained it, barely controlling his voice.

"But father was—"

Arc cut her off. "Geerd, Thessen, find a way to bind it without losing a finger."

"Are you going to name it, too?" Ayita demanded. Her cheeks were dark, her eyes furious, but he met her gaze. For the first time, the burden of leadership fell upon him, sudden as the bite of a sea snake.

"I will call it Mercy."

"Mercy?"

His voice grew so soft Ayita could scarcely hear the words. "Sister, our tribe needs a symbol of hope. Shartoom turned away the wrath of the Dread Ones; I will grant mercy to a beast that has none. And from this time forth, we will celebrate today not as a day of sorrow, but of sacrifice and forgiveness."

Without waiting for her stunned reply, he swam slowly back to the denary. He did not spare the shark's life for pity; he had none for those terrible beasts. Neither would he show mercy for B'tat once he found him. But on the anniversary of his father's death and the day of his brother's loss, the crèche Lord of the Tula kin took a Great White for a pet.

✧ ✧ ✧

AFTERWORD

IN 2000, I got the idea for a book about a people living under the sea. It wasn't an original concept—there were the Sub-Mariner and Aquaman comics when I was a kid, and Poul Anderson had written stories about underwater races. However, I wanted to write it in a way that portrayed the animals and plants of the ocean in a realistic fashion.

Growing up on the Great Plains, my experience with bodies of water never went beyond swimming pools. I researched the ocean, became fascinated by it, and wrote the first draft of what I conceived as a trilogy. In 2002, I polished up the first fifty pages, sent them to my agent at the time, and met him at a Science Fiction convention to discuss the book.

He worked in Manhattan. It had been less than a year since 9/11, and he was still trying to recover from being so close to Ground Zero. Added to that, the book industry was reeling from the economic devastation caused by the months of American despondency following the attack. We spent most of our lunch talking about his experiences.

Looking back, I wonder if his lack of enthusiasm for the book would have been different at another time. Regardless, he gave it little hope, and I relegated the manuscript to a computer folder.

Several years later, I decided to try rewriting the first chapter as a short story which eventually became *The Day of the Shark*. Deviating from my intention to only include animals based on ones that actually exist, I added the tegula for the action scene near the end. I submitted the story—the editor liked it and wanted to hang onto it. I was working, writing, and raising a family. Time slipped away. After a couple of years, I contacted the editor, who still wanted to publish the story but was making formatting changes to his magazine. More time passed. I occasionally checked with him, often negligently losing track of it for months at a time. Finally, I contacted him only to discover he no longer published fiction. Eight years had passed since I first submitted the work. I believe I may hold some kind of record for the longest time waiting for a rejection.

Eventually, Howard Andrew Jones picked it up for *Tales from the Magician's Skull*. If time allows, I would someday like to return to the novel, perhaps as a single, standalone book.

THE LAST ROADMAKER

FOR THOSE UNFAMILIAR with William Hope Hodgson's work, this story may require an explanation. It was written for Andy Robertson's website, which is dedicated to Hodgson's novel, *The Night Land*. Written in 1912, *The Night Land* is an extraordinary work set in a far future where the sun has gone out and humanity lives in a miles-high pyramid built in a chasm deep in the Earth. Forces of Evil surround the pyramid, waiting for its force field to fail so they can prey on the remaining humans.

Hodgson wrote three other novels: *The Ghost Pirates*, about a sailing vessel assailed by spectral pirates; *The House on the Borderland*, depicting an ancient manor besieged by snouted aliens from beyond our dimension; and *The Boats of the Glen Carrig*, the story of a ship facing monsters of the deep.

In this story, I wanted to tie together *The Night Land*, *The House on the Borderland*, and *The Ghost Pirates* with what I had read of Hodgson's actual life. The title of the story refers to the mysterious builders of the roads depicted in *The Night Land*, roads constructed ever deeper into the chasm as the sun grew colder.

✧ ✧ ✧

Through the whole void of night I search,
So dumbly crying out to thee;
But thou are not; and night's vast throne
Becomes an all stupendous church
With star-bells knelling unto me
Who in all space am most alone!

Grief—William Hope Hodgson

But there was presently, such a power and horror of Monsters and Evil Things in that Valley of Shadow, that the Road Makers were made to go Backwards into the Red Light which did fill the Westward Valley, and came from that low Sun.

The Night Land—William Hope Hodgson

✧ ✧ ✧

"THEY SAY IT'S haunted," Colleen said, pushing a strand of red hair from her eyes.

"My dad says there's no such thing as a haunted house," Will Hodgson said.

"Your dad's a priest; he has to say it."

"Does not."

The two children were standing in a garden overgrown with weeds, gorse, and saplings. Apple and pear trees were scattered over what once had been a grand estate, their limbs grown twisted from neglect, their ruined fruit strewn across the ground. With Will's hound, Pepper, by their side, the children had spent half the afternoon crossing rocky, bramble-filled terrain to the old mansion, drawn there by Will's curiosity and Colleen's determination.

At last, Kraighten House stood in view between the leaves of the ragged trees. It was nothing like Will had imagined, but a fantastic structure built in a rough circle, with pinnacles suggesting leaping flames and bricks orange-tinged with brown, reinforcing the hint of conflagration.

The children had seen flocks of birds on their journey: a host of sparrows, a murmuration of starlings, a murder of crows; cardinals had trilled their sweet song along the way. Pepper had chased a fox, and deer had stared at them from among the vegetation; but here all was still, and not a single piping filled that hush, as if the house had cast a cloak of silence over the wild, uncultivated gardens. It had been easy in the comfort of Will's house to talk of visiting the mansion. Now they stood overawed and not a little afraid.

"Well, this is why we came," Will finally said, stepping forward. His parents having moved to County Galway a month before, he dared not display cowardice before his new friend, who was not only a girl but a year older than he.

Colleen came alongside, and the leaves rustled beneath their feet as they approached the manor. Will tried to walk softly, fearing to disturb the quiet. Even Pepper was subdued, sniffing cautiously among the trees, his ears laid back.

They passed the drive, weeds sprouting between the cobblestones, and approached the massive front door.

"Why are all the windows barred?" Will asked.

"To keep out brigands, of course." She narrowed her eyes in a knowing way. "My mother says it's hundreds of years old. There were bandits everywhere back then."

Deep marks like the claws of a bear scored the door. Will expected it to be locked, but the knob turned easily beneath Colleen's hand, and it swung wide with a scraping rumble, unnerving in the silence. The opening beckoned; the pair exchanged uneasy glances. Pepper whined and brushed against Will's leg.

"I'll go first," Will said.

They stepped into a gloomy hallway smelling of long disuse. Shafts of sunlight pressed through tall windows at the end of the passage, revealing showers of dust motes above floral carpets.

"It's in fine shape for its age," Colleen said, her voice scarcely above a whisper. "Nothing's been disturbed and none of the windows are broken."

They stood in a great-room with high ceilings, Morris chairs, and floral couches. Pictures hung massed along one wall. A wide stairway led to the upper floors.

"Are you certain no one lives here?" Will asked.

"Naw; look at all the dust. Everybody knows it's been empty for years. We could make this our clubhouse. No one would ever bother us."

"You said it was haunted."

"Ghosts only come out at night. We'd be here during the day."

Pepper whined again. Will reached down to pat his head. "It's all right, boy. Nothing to be afraid of."

A soft sighing, like a woman's exhalation, passed through the room.

"What was that?" Will asked, his voice unsteady.

"Probably wind from upstairs. Let's go see."

Will eyed the stairs dubiously but followed after.

The boards creaked beneath their weight. They had gone only

a few steps when Pepper's whine made Will turn. The dog sat whimpering at the bottom of the stairs.

"It's all right," Will said, unwilling to go without the dog's companionship. "Come on, boy."

Reluctantly, the hound ascended the stairs, his tail low, his ears pressed against his head, Will coaxing him at every step.

Past the first landing the air grew surprisingly chill. A long corridor awaited them at the top. It stretched away into darkness, making Will wish they had thought to bring a light. An even deeper silence enfolded them, an uncanny stillness as if they had stepped out of the world: no scraping boughs against the walls; no wind against the eaves; no creaking floorboards beneath their feet.

"Which way should we go, right or left?" Colleen sounded uncertain for the first time.

Will glanced both directions. Neither were appealing, but there was more light to the left, and he chose that way.

They went slowly, unwilling to admit their reluctance. Pepper cowered against Will's leg, not daring to move a single pace from his master. Their feet left tracks in the dust. They passed glaring portraits whose eyes seemed to follow them, and low tables adorned with vases and brass candlesticks. Will wondered why the house had never been vandalized when there was much worth stealing.

Pepper whimpered more insistently.

"Can't you shut him up?" Colleen demanded.

"He's frightened."

"Of what?" But her own voice trembled.

As if in answer, a whispering arose behind them. They whirled, but there were only the shadows and the empty hallway.

"What was that?" Colleen asked.

Out of the obscurity a darkness rose. Pepper growled. Will gave an inarticulate cry.

The children stood transfixed as the darkness lifted ever-higher, until it towered above them in the shape of a figure shrouded in robes of night, its face hidden. It reached an enormous hand toward them.

Shrieking, they turned to flee, only to find another of the creatures blocking their way.

Forgetting everything but his fright, Will scrambled toward the nearest door, Colleen right behind him. He seized the knob. It was locked. There was no way of escape.

The children and the dog pressed together, their backs against the door. Now that his master was threatened, Pepper growled ferociously.

One of the creatures touched the dog, a stroke soft as a caress. Pepper's knees gave way; he crumpled to the floor. Will shouted in anguish and terror. The creature reached toward him, its massive hand large enough to cover his head.

A light bloomed above them, a penetrating glow that cast back the shadows. The creatures of darkness raised their hands to their faces to ward its rays. The light became a ring of fire; time seemed to slow.

The White Circle slowly descended in front of the children. Twin shafts of light radiated from it, one aimed toward each of the creatures. The monsters backed away, driven once more into the shadows.

The Circle drew closer to the children. Multiple eyes stood in symmetric patterns within it, staring with an unwinking, flaming gaze.

Will and Colleen stood frozen, too astonished to move. A silver tendril emerged from the Circle and brushed across the body of the dog. Pepper rose to his feet, tail wagging.

Two tendrils reached the children. Colleen recoiled, flinging herself against the door. "No!"

One tendril withdrew, but the other touched Will's forehead. The boy felt pressure upon his brow. Heat surged through him, a momentary wash of joy.

The White Circle rose, hovering near the ceiling. Will took Colleen by the arm and helped her to her feet. "Let's get out of here."

Clutching one another, the dog staying close, they hurried along the corridor, the White Circle floating above them. They clattered down the stairs and rushed to the front door. Will grasped the knob and the apparition vanished. The children plunged into the daylight and ran wildly through the garden, fleeing the dreadful house. But Will's skin still tingled where the White Circle had touched him.

✧ ✧ ✧

THE YEARS PASSED. It was the spring of 1918 in Belgium, but the only signs of returning life were scattered weeds growing around the edges of the craters. Most of the trees were gone, turned to splinters in the months of fighting, and the ground was pocked as cheese. Not fifty yards away lay a great shell-hole with thirty crosses sticking from it, some barely rising out of the pooled rainwater. Ragged clouds hung in the sky. The roar of gunfire rolled from the southwest.

Having held this position for two weeks, the 11th Royal Field Artillery had carved some comfort among the dugouts and trenches despite the rain. The enemy was hidden by distant hillocks. Two men, a lieutenant and a captain, their uniforms muddy and worn, sat with their backs to a trench wall, eating bully beef and hard biscuits from their kits.

"Word is they've taken Merville," Captain Carver said.

Lieutenant Hodgson glanced briefly in the direction of the town as if to penetrate the thirty-mile distance. "What are we doing?"

"We've sent in the 5th."

Hodgson nodded.

"So, why *did* you reenlist?" the captain asked, returning to a previous discussion. "You've never said. You had an out."

Hodgson gazed across the battlefield before answering. "When they asked what I did in the war, I didn't want to tell them I fell off a horse and broke my jaw. But I swear, Carver, if I had known what that last push would be like I'd have foregone the honor."

"It wasn't the Maypole dance." Captain Carver lit a cigarette and extended another to Hodgson, who waved it away.

"An editor once told me one of my stories was too horrific for his audience," Hodgson continued. "I could give them horrors now. True horrors. And I will, when we finally get out of this."

"Did I tell you I read one of your books during my last leave? Had my wife send it to me. The one about the haunted mansion."

"*The House on the Borderland?* She must have found it in a remainder bin. You've probably doubled my readership. What did you think?"

"I've never read anything like it. You have an uncanny mind, there's no doubt of it. Where did you get the idea?"

Will Hodgson's eyes grew dreamy with that far-away gaze Carver sometimes saw steal over him. He was a short man, but quite muscular, with dark hair, an aquiline nose, and striking good looks. "My father was an Anglican priest. We moved numerous times during my childhood. There was a house at County Galway, close to where we happened to be living at the time. My schoolmate said it was haunted. She was right."

"What happened?"

"Something that changed my life forever." Hodgson looked up with a sheepish smile. "You'd think me daft if I told it."

✧ ✧ ✧

THAT EVENING, WILL dreamed he stood near the forecastle of a sailing ship. It was night and a full moon hung overhead. The vessel creaked; the smell of the sea filled his nostrils.

The deck was deserted. Not a soul stood watch; not a sailor manned the wheel. He recognized the vessel at once as the *Sangier*, the last ship he had sailed on before leaving the life of a seaman. Those had been unhappy times, filled with endless toil, bad food, and a chance for neither learning nor advancement. The years of service had made him hate naval life with such vehemence that when the war came he joined the army rather than serve on a vessel again; yet the sea itself had always lured him.

The wind, still before, abruptly filled the sails; and Hodgson's old training took over, sending him to the wheel. He felt its smooth wood beneath his palms. The ship was sailing west, but where it was going or why, he did not know.

He had experienced such visions many times before and knew this one, which felt real to his senses, was not an ordinary dream. Beginning after the White Circle touched him in the abandoned house, they had made his youth a terror. In the first year, they were always about Kraighten House. When those finally ended, he thought himself rid of them forever, but eighteen months later, after being sent to boarding school, they began again, this time shifting to the far future. He had run away from the school at the age of thirteen, hoping to escape them.

They had driven him to the sea, where he spent eight long

years. For the first six, they left him alone, then began again, driving him from even that rough sanctuary with scenes of a trading ship overwhelmed by ghostly buccaneers. The dreams had been the basis for his books and many of his short stories. Except for Colleen, he had never told anyone, not even his wife, Bessie. Even she wouldn't have believed him. He scarcely believed it himself.

Now, after years of absence, the dreams had returned.

He strode to the port rail by the fore brace-lock and peered across the sea. The moon shone down, illuminating the water several feet under. Something moved there, a shadow among the shadows. Just below the surface lay the black form of a royal-yard, and deeper, the gear and standing rigging of a great mast. And below the mast, far down in the dimness, the immense, indistinct stretch of vast decks. It was not a reflection of his own vessel but the shadow-ship that had haunted his visions during his time on the *Sangier*, visions that made him cry out in his sleep, disturbing the other crewmen and giving Hodgson a reputation as a Jonah.

The old terror fell upon him. From out of that ship the ghost pirates would come, and there was no one to oppose them except him.

He made his way to the captain's cabin. It was unlocked, and a lantern stood on the table, mysteriously lit in the unoccupied room. He searched the drawers until he discovered a serviceable cutlass. His hope for a gun proved vain, though he wondered if any weapon could halt the phantom creatures, who were similar to the figures he and Colleen had faced at Kraighten House.

He picked up the lantern and stepped onto the deck. His years at sea made him uneasy at leaving the wheel unattended, and he hurried back to it, but the ship seemed to travel well enough without his guidance. He kept an anxious watch through the hours of the night, a solitary sailor on empty waters, while the ghost ship kept pace with the *Sangier*.

At last, when the moon lay a third of the way up in the west, he heard the sound of breakers beating on a shore. Alarmed, he strode to the wheel, but upon reaching it, found something wrong with his vision. He looked around and rubbed his eyes. The air twinkled like stars, breaking up, crumbling to pieces.

He looked at his hand. It was dissolving, and the ship and

ocean and sky with it. It became a dazzling, blinding swirl of particles. He closed his eyes.

When he opened them again, he was sitting at a battered desk in a small study. He ran his hand along its surface, feeling its smoothness against his palm.

"Hello, Will." Gooseflesh rose on his neck, for it was Colleen's voice. Grimacing, he turned. She wore a green sweater that made her jade eyes brilliant in the candlelight. Her red hair was pinned back on one side the way he always liked.

A ragged sob escaped him. He rose and wrapped his arms around her, hugging her fiercely, wanting to squeeze her into himself until they were compacted into one body, together forever. "I've missed you so," he rasped, kissing her, feeling the sweetness of her mouth. "I've missed you terribly."

After a few precious moments, she gently extricated herself. They stood gazing into each other's eyes until she took his hand and led him to the picture window. Together, they stared out onto a garden at twilight, wild and overgrown, with tattered trees.

"Why in hell are we here again?" he asked.

"Let's go out and look around." She tried to lead him, but he insisted on going first. They left the study and entered the corridor. It was exactly as he remembered, and he glanced fearfully at the shadows.

Recalling the touch of the White Circle, unable to keep the bitterness from his voice, he said, "If only it had never happened."

She smiled the mischievous smile that was so much her. "It wasn't your fault. I goaded you into going. It was our destiny."

"It's been my curse."

"The monsters would've killed us, sure, if the Other hadn't come," she said. "When it touched you, it placed you under its protection."

"Protection! If that's what these dreadful visions are, it can keep its protection. But I could have stood it, if you were always in them."

She reached over and stroked his face. "But I refused its touch, don't you see?"

He fell silent and they slipped down the stairs and into the twilight. The crickets sang; the air was still, and watery with humidity.

"It hasn't changed in all the years," Will said. "How could. . ." His voice trailed away.

"What is it?" she asked.

He gave a sharp inhalation. "Out there. Don't you see?"

Figures moved at the edge of the grounds. They walked upright, their shapes indistinct in the gathering twilight, but something in the outline of their strange, misshapen heads suggested forms not wholly human. Hodgson counted at least a dozen.

He took Colleen by the arm. "Get back in the house." They hurried inside and Will bolted the heavy door behind them. All the windows on the lower stories were barred, but there were five outside doors, and he tore through the dwelling, ensuring each was secured. When he was done, he went to the gun room, collected and loaded a shotgun and a rifle, and hurried to the great-room. Colleen was there, staring out through the bars of the narrow front window. One of the creatures walked before the pane, holding its head high, sniffing the air. Its face was an unwholesome shade of white; it had a grotesquely human mouth and jaw but almost no chin. Its long snout, sloping forehead, tusks, and pointed ears gave the semblance of a wild boar. But the eyes, glistening almost to the point of glowing, bespoke a shrewd intelligence. With a grunt, the Swine-Thing dropped to all fours, scented the ground, and gave a baying howl answered all around by the others.

Hodgson touched Colleen gently on the arm, startling her. She shrieked.

"Sorry," he said.

She put her hand to her breast and exhaled sharply. Her face was pale; her voice trembled. "How dreadful they are! Months of dreaming of them, and you but a boy. Oh, Will, how did you stand it?"

"I don't much like sleeping. You must never look into their eyes." In the year following their encounter with the White Circle, his almost nightly visions had been of the Swine-Things besieging the house. But Colleen had never been in any of them until now.

"Can they get in?"

"The doors are solid oak. It should hold them a while."

She took a seat in a floral chair, her gaze still fastened on the window.

"I started writing about it after you... left," he said. "I thought perhaps that was the point, my getting it down, but I've never understood the meaning of it all. Is there anything you can tell me?"

"I know no more than you." She laughed mirthlessly. "I probably know less. I don't even know why I'm here. In all your journeys to the house, have you ever seen the Other?"

"The White Circle? Not a hint of it."

A knocking began on the front door, gradually rising to a pounding. It went on and on, becoming a steady thunder. When it seemed about to shake the house to pieces, it abruptly ceased. More snuffling sounds rose from behind the window.

Hodgson sat down beside her and clasped her hand, staring intently into the green eyes he had thought never to see again. His voice trembled. "Can you... can you tell me where you've been?"

She shook her head, rose, walked behind him and stroked his temples. He kissed her fingers. "It isn't allowed, Will. But I can tell you there is no such thing as death; there is only separation."

His voice caught; he struggled to control himself. "I've missed you so."

✧ ✧ ✧

HE WOKE WITH a start. He had been asleep in a dugout, and the smell of earth and soldiers filled his nostrils. Half-light filtered through the rectangle of the opening. Carver was shaking him by the shoulder.

"Morning, Sleeping Beauty. The Huns are coming for a visit. HQ says we fall back to Ypres."

He leapt to his feet in confusion, looking for Colleen. He had deserted her again, leaving no one to protect her. Momentary panic filled his chest, quickly replaced by reason. She couldn't have been real. Yet he wasn't certain; he often suspected his visions were glimpses of other realities.

"You all right?" Carver asked.

"I—Yes. I'll be there momentarily."

Alone in the dugout once more, he buried his head in his arms and wept. Seeing her again had reopened the old wound. He had kept in touch with her after his family moved from

County Galway. During his days at sea he had written to her from ports around the world and visited her whenever he could, and their friendship had eventually turned to love.

After leaving the service, he had started a Physical Culture club in Blackburn, mostly training policemen. Colleen had gone to visit her family in County Galway, and he was to meet her there and ask her father's permission to marry. But when he arrived, he learned she had gone for a stroll the evening before and never returned home. Her mangled body was found in the early hours of the morning. The constable reported that a wild dog had killed her, but the claw prints had not been those of any earthly animal.

He often wondered where the White Circle had been when she needed it most. It had saved them both before; why had it deserted her to that dreadful, lonely death?

He stepped from the dugout, trying to escape the pain. He was in a deep trench, its bottom muddy from the recent rains. He scrambled up the back side. Everywhere around him men were making preparations, mere shadows in the half-darkness. Soldiers hooked the artillery to teams of horses stamping and snorting in the morning chill.

Within an hour, they were on the move. The rains left the battered ground soft, and the equipment soon bogged down, forcing the men to push and dig. By mid-morning, they had scarcely made two miles. As Hodgson urged the men on, he found himself growing increasingly agitated. Distant sounds of rifle fire rose to the north. The air was still, sultry, almost electric. Jumpy and short-tempered; he wondered if his nerves were going.

"Something's coming," Hodgson murmured to Captain Carver. "Something terrible."

"What do you mean? What's coming?"

Hodgson hesitated. He forced a smile. "Don't mind me. I'm just sick of mucking in the mud."

But the feeling only grew stronger, as if in naming it he had brought it to reality. Something *was* coming. Something worse than the Germans.

✧ ✧ ✧

IN HIS DREAMS that night, he stood once more by the wheel on the *Sangier*, still holding his lantern and cutlass. The moon hung exactly where it had been before, but this time the vessel traveled east rather than west, and he wondered what it meant.

He glanced down on the starboard side and spied the black mass of the ghost ship moving abreast his vessel. Black forms moved up the masts of the shadow ship toward him. As one of them drew near, it detached itself from the darkness. He thought it a trick of the eye until the figure pulled itself over the railing, its shape that of a man in bulky robes, carrying a cudgel.

With a roar of fear and rage, Hodgson leapt across the deck, cutlass raised, lantern swinging in his other hand. He slashed at the pirate, who reeled backward, attempting to dodge. The blade lit with a fiery glow, a supernatural light bright as day. Will felt a surge of power run through him, an almost superhuman strength.

The sword struck home, passing through the creature, cutting it in half at the waist. An unholy scream erupted from its lips. It toppled to the deck.

The head of another invader appeared above the railing. Hodgson thrust, stabbing it between the eyes with the tip of his blade. The sword swelled with energy, a blinding flash that sent the shadows scattering.

He turned a half-circle, seeking more enemies. The decks were empty. He glanced over the rail. The water lay still; the pirate ship had vanished.

He laughed aloud in triumph. It was as if the power of the White Circle had returned to inhabit his blade. For the first time, he had a weapon against the darkness.

Yet even as he exulted, a voice called, "Wait!"

He spun around. Another specter had pulled itself up to the rail, a shadow among shadows. Hodgson lifted his cutlass.

"Do ye want to have her back?" the ghost pirate asked. "The one who died? We can return her to life. She could love ye again."

"How?" he asked.

"All things are possible to them's I serve."

Emotions ran through him: loathing, hope, fear, the heartsick loss of losing her again. "What do you want in return?"

"The house. Give us the house."

Hodgson stood, open-mouthed, overwhelmed. It was too much to consider.

The vision faded, falling apart; the brightness filled his eyes.

When his sight returned, the scene had changed, but instead of waking in Belgium, he walked a road winding down a canyon wall in a series of switchbacks. The cold, windless air bit like iron. The color was washed from the sky, leaving it nearly white. The rift down which he traveled was surreal in its immensity. Its slate-gray walls stretched miles below, losing themselves in a gloomy haze. Close to his position, the two forks of the canyon met at an angle of nearly ninety degrees. The sun shone at the horizon down the western branch, a crimson ball in the dusk, its rays illuminating the walls for hundreds of miles. The northern fork lay cloaked in shadow.

"The Great Bight," he muttered. Then, quoting from *The Night Land*, a book he had written years before from other visions, he said, *Yet am I to my pen again; for of late a wondrous hope has grown in me, in that I have, at night in my sleep, waked into the future of this world, and seen strange things and utter marvels. . . And surely it is all so strange and wonderful to set out, that I could almost despair with the contemplation of that which I must achieve.*

The road before him was narrow, formed of an unfamiliar material without a mark upon it. He was alone in a place hundreds of miles and millions of years from Belgium and the war; and he thought how incongruous he must look, dressed in his helmet and uniform, his Enfield rifle in hand, a soldier from a forgotten civilization. There were no signs of life—not a bird or fox, not an insect crawling across the road, only the cold, the awful desolation, and the tramp of his boots on the road.

He trudged along, trying to absorb what was happening. But his thoughts kept returning to the pact the ghost pirate offered. In all the years, one vision had never led directly to another until the last few days. He had always thought of them as separate stories. *But are they?* he wondered. *What if the creature could give Colleen back to me?*

"I swear I would deal with the devil himself," he muttered.

With such thoughts, he occupied his time, the monotony of his trek gradually filling him. He found himself humming. What was the song? Some variation from Kipling. He began to sing, a marching tune.

To the legion of the lost one, to the cohort of the damned,
To my brethren in their sorrow overseas,
Sings a gentleman of England, cleanly bred, machinely crammed,
And a trooper of the Empress, if you please.
Yea, a trooper of the forces, who has run his own six horses,
And faith he went the pace, and went it blind,
And the world was more than kin, while he held the ready tin,
But today the Sergeant's something less than kind.

Back to the Army again, sergeant,
Back to the Army again.
Don't look so hard, for I haven't no card,
I'm back to the Army again.

The road continued, making sharp bends as it wound down the side of the canyon. He had never seen the Rift in daylight; in his previous visions Earth's sun had flickered and died eons before, leaving a land of utter darkness, with scattered fires, terrible monsters, and a pyramid seven miles high containing the remnants of besieged humanity, a vision of the far future. Now, through gaps in the haze below, he saw the outline of a city on the canyon floor to the south.

He grimaced. He had been walking for hours and the sun had not moved. With a sinking in his stomach, he realized it never would. In this age, the Earth's rotation had ceased. The daystar would remain where it was, lighting the canyon through long eons, growing ever dimmer until it was only a smoldering coal; then that, too, would fail, leaving darkness.

Where is England? he wondered. *Lost topside in the cold wastes. Oceans frozen or long evaporated. Lifeless. The land we shed our blood for. The war isn't even a memory now.*

Tears sprang unbidden to his eyes. He wiped them savagely away. *It's only a vision like the times before. I'll wake back in the trenches.* He gave a grim laugh. *As if that were the better horror.*

He rounded a bend and discovered a village built within a cutout in the canyon wall. This amazed him almost as much as his first sight of the Rift, for the excavation, burrowing for yards into the stone, was clearly the work of machines capable of melting and fusing rock to a glassy sheen. The buildings were pyramidal, made of the same imperishable material as the road.

He raised his rifle. Nothing moved around the nearer structures, while those farther back lay lost in the shadow of the shelf. He gave a *halloo* and waited expectantly. Moments passed. He stepped closer to the buildings.

Beside one of the pyramids lay scattered bones. A human skull stared at him with empty sockets. He backed away. Gun trained on the village, he continued along the road. The legendary Road Makers had built this path through hundreds, even thousands of years, paving the way for the last vestige of humanity to reach the warmth of the canyon floor; no doubt the villagers had eventually followed. Were the bones the remains of a hermit, living alone in the heights? He would never know. He took another hairpin turn onto the next switchback, losing sight of the village.

He wondered if the bottom of the Rift were his true destination, and if so, why he was going there. It would take days to reach it.

✧ ✧ ✧

HE WOKE BACK in the trenches. A soft rain pinged against his helmet.

That day was spent positioning the guns. The bombardments to the south and west were drawing closer. Despite the work and the war, Hodgson brooded over Colleen, the ghost pirates, and his march into the Great Rift.

With the artillery in place by mid-afternoon, he and two subordinates, Corporal Stephens and Private Ridley, were sent out as forward observers. They traveled on foot, leading a pack horse, stringing telephone wire behind them. In danger from their own artillery, targeted by an enemy hoping to blind the English gunners' eyes, an observer's job was perilous. Nonetheless, Hodgson had volunteered for the work. He was good at it, and his efforts saved British lives.

By twilight they reached a hill overlooking a wide plain that had been forest before barrages leveled the trees. Hodgson studied the ground with his field-glasses. Two layers of British trenches ran across the plain; beyond them, past the barbed-wire barricades, stood the German excavations. Will studied the area with a practiced eye, looking for signs of the enemy massing for an attack beneath the cover of the trenches.

They made camp behind the protection of the hill, eating cold biscuits from their kits, avoiding lighting a fire. The night was clear; the stars burned down in all their magnificence. He thought of how the sky would someday be utterly empty.

He slept fitfully, as he always did at his observation post, but soon found himself once more on the *Sangier*, exactly where he had been before, though the ship now traveled west. He kept guard along the railing, watching the shadows beneath the vessel. There was no sign of the phantom ship.

The night passed. A shrouding mist arose. The sea remained calm. Morning turned to afternoon and afternoon to evening. The mist faded, revealing the setting sun. The moon rose; the vessel sailed on, guided by mysterious hands.

He grew morose. His life was nothing but a vanity, moving from place to place, always trying to escape the visions, always failing. He wondered why so many of the characters in his dreams, the monsters, even the heroes, were both nameless and faceless. Were they figments of imagination brought on by his own lack of identity? He had been an unhappy sailor, a failure at Physical Culture, a hack as a writer. Now he was playing soldier in a war it seemed no one could win. Nothing he had ever done had mattered. And it was all because of the White Circle. Why wouldn't it leave him alone?

And yet. . . and yet. . . Colleen had come back, at least in the vision. And how could he not wish to see her again? But he did not know if he ever would, unless he could find his way once more to Kraighten House.

The familiar dissipation of the vision overtook him.

✧ ✧ ✧

HE WAS SITTING in the same chair as when he had left her. Someone touched his shoulder from behind. Looking up, he found her there. He closed his eyes and took her hands in his own, pressing his forehead against them, holding them tightly. "I'm sorry I was gone. I don't want to leave you, but I can't control it."

"You've been right here," she said. "We were talking when

you got the strangest look on your face."

"I've been away for hours."

"You haven't."

The last rays of the day still shone outside the barred windows. The Swine-Things still snuffled around the house.

"Come into the kitchen and I'll brew some tea," she said. "You can tell me where you wandered."

He did so, and despite the lurking horrors beyond the walls, they sat and talked as they had not done in years. Time seemed to slip backward, returning Will to the days when they had been young and in love, and had spent many such evenings in sweet conversation. He told her all that had happened since they parted—of his failed business and his writing, his meeting with Harry Houdini, his enlistment when the war came, and of some, but not all he had seen there.

She watched him talk, her eyes dark and very lovely in the shadows. Finally, he paused, and laughing, said, "I've gone on and on about myself."

"You've talked about everything, except your wife."

He looked down at his wedding ring, his face burning. "I. . . guess I haven't. Not much to say, really. I—"

"What's her name?"

"Betty Farnworth. I call her Bessie. She worked for a magazine. We met because of my books."

"A fine thing, to be a writer. You always had a way with words. I'm proud of you for that."

"Colleen, I—"

"But I see the truth now, sure as the world. You've been unfaithful, Will."

"I haven't," he cried, his voice filled with passion. "It wasn't like that! I always loved you. I've never forgotten you. Not even for a moment. You have to understand. You were gone. I was lonely. But even after we married—"

"It's Bessie you've been unfaithful to."

"I—" His mouth fell shut; he could not speak. A strangled noise escaped his throat.

As was always her way when a point was made, she said no more, only kissing his forehead and walking from the room.

✧ ✧ ✧

HE WOKE IN Flanders to the beginning of the brutal campaign later named the Fourth Battle of Ypres. The town had been a strategic center throughout the conflict—poison gas had first been used there—850,000 men would die to control that blighted piece of ground.

Hodgson was kept too busy that day to think about his visions. Typical strategy called for heavy shelling before a surge from the trenches; and though the German troops directly before him remained in their places, at mid-morning an almost continuous barrage of enemy artillery erupted to the southwest. Using his compass as a guide, Hodgson triangulated the position between the German and British guns, and telephoned the sector information back to Captain Carver. When the 11th Royal Field Artillery responded, Hodgson watched the shells fall and relayed corrections.

In combat, there is never enough time for sleep. At midnight, with only sporadic sounds of gunfire, Hodgson wrapped himself in his blanket, leaving Corporal Stephens on watch. Drifting off, he thought of Colleen and Bessie. Faithful Bessie, who had been his friend and companion, though they hadn't actually spent that much time together. They had met and married in 1912, four short years before his enlistment. Had his intentions been as pure and honorable as he claimed, running off to war for God and country? Had he ever truly committed to the marriage?

In his dreams, he was soon sailing east through the darkness, a stiff wind filling the *Sangier's* sails. He wondered how many hours he was compacting in a single day, living his life in Belgium, the ship, the house, and the Great Rift. He didn't feel any more exhausted than usual—one was always weary in war—so he supposed the time spent in the visions didn't affect his physical body. He wondered what would happen if he were wounded or killed in the dream.

The hours passed peacefully without any sign of the pirates. Late in the night the vision changed, and he walked the eternal twilight of the road again, winding his way clutching his rifle, still high above the canyon floor. Disoriented by the change, he sat on the road to gather his thoughts. He had noticed a pattern: when the ship went east, it took him to the road; when it journeyed west, it brought him to Kraighten House, as if transporting him from vision to vision, traversing both time and space. He realized the ghost pirates had initially sought to prevent his passage. Yet someone—presumably those who caused his visions—had given him the sword for a weapon. For what purpose?

A bark pulled him from his brooding. He glanced around, surprised to think there might be dogs in this epoch. But, of course, there must be, for in later eons when they sun had flickered and died there would be the monstrous, mutant Night Hounds.

A barking, thin-legged mongrel sprinted up the road. Will rose to his feet, staring blankly at it.

When the dog was within twenty feet, he said, "Pepper?"

The hound bounded to him, bouncing its forepaws against his thighs, nearly knocking him over.

What a reunion that was, a long-lost boy and a long-dead pup on the imperishable road, on the dying earth, in the Rift that would become the last sanctuary for humankind. His fur was soft as down; he licked Hodgson's face as if to lick it off. Will laughed, the long, happy laughter of childhood. Not since Odysseus and Argos had there been such a meeting, and he wondered if all the dead would return to him.

The idea sobered him. Were his visions true? Or only the hallucinations of a lunatic? Many times he had asked himself if the Great Rift and the Night Land were real. He had never found a satisfactory answer.

Sitting on the road with Pepper beside him, he studied the panorama stretching before him. On the canyon floor, he could see the towers and domes of the town that would someday be known as The Quiet City. The sound of distant machinery reached his ears, and he wondered if perhaps the generations of Road Makers were still at work.

He patted Pepper again and rose, clutching his rifle. "Come along, old friend. I'd like to finally meet the ones who made these roads."

They traveled deeper and deeper along the switchbacks into the chasm. Will hummed a marching song, and the road went on and on through hours that stretched to days. Thinking of Colleen and Bessie, he reached a resolution.

✧ ✧ ✧

WHEN NEXT CAME the flashing light and the breaking of the image, he was once more aboard the *Sangier*, his cutlass in his hand, the ship traveling west. He fetched the lantern, for the moon had set and the night was black.

A rustling rose among the masts. He searched the darkness above him. At first, he saw nothing, then spied, where there should have been stars, a patch of emptiness shaped like a man. He raised his sword. The form descended the rigging but stayed out of reach of Hodgson's blade.

"We've given ye time," the ghost pirate hissed. "Time for thought. We ain't attacked the house. But we needs our answer, y'see."

"What are you?" Hodgson demanded.

"A pirate and a murderer, and I make no shame upon it. I'm captain of me ship."

"What is the house to you?"

"Naught. But them's I serve, they wants it, and they'll have it in the end, whether ye would or no. They'll have ye, too, if ye don't bargain. And yer pretty woman with ye. They ain't pleasant with them that displeases 'em."

Will raised the lantern higher, so it shone on the phantom's face, but saw only a pool of darkness where the features should have been. The specter turned its head and growled, troubled by the light.

"What bargain did you make with them?" Hodgson asked. "What did they promise you?"

"That's naught to such as ye."

"What was it? Treasure? Immortality? What did you get? A shadowy purgatory, an unending life as a slave?"

With an animal roar, the pirate leapt from the rigging onto the deck, but Will danced back, avoiding the creature's grasp. He made a quick slash with his blade, forcing the ghost away. The phantom hesitated, cowering from the cutlass.

"Tell your masters I'll give them nothing," Will cried, driving the pirate back. "Now get off my deck or I'll cut you in half."

Snarling, the ghost backed its way to the railing and dropped without a splash into the sea.

Will stamped across the deck, a furious sentry. He trembled with anger, his heart pounding against his chest; he flourished the sword and ached for the phantom to return so he could finish it.

His rage passed, followed by an empty despair. He didn't understand any of it; he didn't comprehend this game in which he was only a pawn. And where were the Forces of Good who had presumably given power to his blade? Why did they remain aloof?

An hour passed. The vision faded.

✧ ✧ ✧

HE WAS BACK in the kitchen at Kraighten House, overlooking the wilderness garden. The house was quiet. He was about to call to Colleen, but something made him hesitate. He picked up the rifle off the table and made his way upstairs to the study.

His wife, Bessie, stood beside a Morris chair, gazing out at the gardens. She turned at the sound of his approach. Her hair and eyes were brown; she was a handsome woman.

"Hello, love," he said.

"William?" She ran to him. Guilt swept over him as they embraced. No matter how much he loved Colleen, no matter how much he wanted her back, only a fool trades the living for the dead.

"How did you get here?" Bessie asked. "Where are we?"

"I'm in Belgium and you are lying safe in your bed at home. We are meeting in an odd sort of dream."

"Impossible."

"Nonetheless, true."

He led her to the couch. They sat holding hands.

"What does it mean?" she asked.

"It means you and I need to have a talk," Hodgson began uncertainly, unsure what he would say. "I think I should tell you that I haven't loved you as I should, and that I'm very sorry. I have allowed the past to color our relationship. But I intend to change that. When I return home, I want to be the best husband I can to you."

"But you've been wonderful, William. We've had marvelous times! The days in France; our lives in England. You've been everything I ever imagined."

"But not everything I should. Trust that will change, my dear."

"I'm afraid," she said, biting her lip. "This dream. Don't such things portend some terrible happening? I fear for you constantly."

"Don't be frightened. I have passed through the dark of the Night Land and the shadows of the ships at sea."

She smiled. "Oh, William! Your literary allusions."

"Silly me," he said.

They spent a long hour talking until the dream ended.

✧ ✧ ✧

HODGSON STARTED AWAKE to the sound of an explosion. Clods of dirt showered down upon him. When it ended, he glanced around and called to Stephens, "Corporal, what's happened?"

From where he and the private crouched behind the hill, the man called back, "Stray shell, sir."

Will pressed closer to the hill, waiting to see if more would follow. Several blasts sounded far behind them, none close. The shelling went on for over an hour, then ceased. He drifted back into slumber.

✧ ✧ ✧

AGAIN ON THE ship, traveling west toward the house. Would he find Bessie there, or would it be Colleen? And if the latter, what would he tell her?

In the early hours before dawn, the ship began to fade. Even as he closed his eyes against the blinding light, he heard the captain of the phantom vessel call out. "Wait!"

He turned and tried to look. The brilliance faded.

The ghost had pulled itself over the rail. Hodgson lifted his cutlass.

"None o' that, now," the captain said. "I just needs a bit of parlay."

Without a word, Will stepped forward and slashed at the specter. The glowing blade caught the creature in the shoulder, and it leapt cursing into the sea.

As if that had been a signal, cries erupted from high in the masts and on every side of the ship. By the lantern light, Will saw shapes skittering over the riggings and sliding over the rail. Unable to stand against so many, he sprinted toward the stern.

When he was nearly there, two knife-wielding pirates disengaged from the shadows and rushed toward him. He took the first with a neat cut to the head. The second slashed at him, a raking blow that caught his bicep; but his blood was up and he did not feel the pain. He jabbed the phantom in the throat. It went down with a gurgling cry.

Other ghosts closed in, but he reached the stern in two strides, threw himself into the captain's cabin, and bolted the door. Ghostly hands hammered against the frame.

He stepped back, his breath rapid, his heart pounding. Dark blood oozed from his wound.

He heard the roar of the captain's voice. The pounding ceased. A silence fell, broken only by Hodgson's inhalations and the creaking of the timbers.

The full weight of numerous pirates crashed against the door. It shuddered but held. Will heard the clatter of feet upon the deck; they struck the door again. The captain cursed, urging his crew on.

At the third hit, the door began to splinter. There was no way of escape. Hodgson could meet the assault best at the doorway, though he couldn't hold out for long.

Another crash. The door was falling to pieces. He prepared himself for his first stroke.

The top part of the door fell away, revealing the phantom shapes beyond. Even as they drew back to strike again, the vision faded.

✧ ✧ ✧

HE WAS IN the house once more, standing in the kitchen. This time, he hadn't returned at the exact moment of his leaving. The rifle he had taken from the gun-room lay on the table where he had left it.

He heard Colleen's scream and the staccato of running feet. Turning, he saw her rushing up the hall, her face a mask of terror, two of the Swine-Things loping behind her.

Snatching up the rifle, he took quick aim, but Colleen was in the way. She came through the doorway, saw his weapon, and dodged to the left.

His military training served him in good stead, for he hit the first creature square in the center of its chest, crumpling it to the ground. The second one tried to swerve, but Hodgson took it with a bullet to the head. It fell nearly at his feet, lying bloody and twitching.

"The drawing room!" Colleen shouted. "They came through the side door."

He bolted down the hall, running with all his strength, arriving breathless and panting at the drawing room. A half-dozen Swine-Things were crossing the threshold into the house. Without pausing to aim, he fired three times in rapid succession. One of the creatures fell, but the others came at him from two sides, forcing him back down the hall.

Rushing to the kitchen, he found Colleen still there, a shotgun in her hands.

"Run!" he ordered, grasping her arm.

They sped through the house. The grunts of the monsters rose behind them. Glancing back, he saw them loping steadily after, almost at their heels.

Sprinting into the main room, they saw more of the beasts at the front door, their faces pressed against the barred windows on either side.

They turned toward the upstairs staircase as their pursuers entered the room. Colleen, who had hunted with her father as a child, raised her shotgun and fired. The creatures dropped back, howling in pain.

They took the steps two at a time and rushed into the hall. One part of Will's mind reminded him that they were going to the place where they had first met their enemy as children. He led her into a bedroom and locked the door.

"I'm sorry, Will!" she cried. "They made me open the door. I was looking at the window and one of them was staring at me. I wanted to turn away, but its eyes held me. The next thing I knew I was throwing the bolts. As soon as the door opened, I came to myself."

"I won't let them have you again," he said.

He had chosen this room because long windows covered one wall, a possible means of escape, but looking out showed a sheer drop to the ground and more Swine-Things waiting below.

The doorknob rattled.

"Help us!" Will cried to the heavens. "You helped us before.

Please!"

But if the White Circle heard, it did not answer.

Multiple claws scratched against the door.

Guns ready, Will and Colleen faced the entrance. Noticing the dried blood on his shirt where the pirate had cut him, Hodgson realized his question was answered: he could die in this vision. But even that would be all right if he could save Colleen.

The scene began to fade.

"No!" Will shouted, dropping his gun and wrapping his arms around her. "Take us both!"

She looked into his face, her eyes brave and green as jade. "I love you, Will."

The room fragmented; the light blinded him. When he could see again, he was back in Flanders. His arms were empty.

✧ ✧ ✧

HE WOKE TO the cadence of a bombardment. The dawn was breaking; the enemy guns were a continuous roar. Corporal Stephens was on the telephone. Private Ridley was at Hodgson's side, holding the field-glasses.

His heart leaden, he nonetheless rose, took the glasses, and ascended the hill, Ridley following.

Even as he made his way, he realized the ghost pirates had outwitted him, keeping him on the ship long enough for the Swine-Things to lure Colleen into opening the door.

Lying down, he peered through his glasses at the enemy lines. The German artillery, hidden by distant hills, lit the morning sky. Their guns were shooting long, over the heads of the British trenches, but would soon get the range.

"Send word back," he ordered the private. "Sector 81 under heavy fire. Assault anticipated." He consulted his compass and gave further coordinates. Ridley repeated them and scuttled down the hill to the telephone.

Hodgson looked through his glass again, and an exclamation escaped his lips. His mouth went dry. Behind the German lines loomed a twisted house, unbelievably enormous, built in a circle. He lowered his field-glasses and could see the structure easily with his naked eye, though it had not been there before. It seemed to stand above the Huns like a general guiding its troops;

Hodgson could feel emanations from it, the pulsing power of its *will* radiating outward, directing the Germans, feeding them its malefic energies.

It was Kraighten House, looming many times its original size over the Belgium countryside, a phantom manor standing above the German lines. There was no chance of his going back to rescue Colleen. His heart lay dead within him.

Private Ridley clambered up the hill and knelt beside him.

"Do you see that?" Hodgson asked.

Ridley's eyes raked the distant field. "What, sir?"

"That—that structure. That house."

"Where, sir?"

"Right there, man, plain as your nose. Above the German trenches."

The man squinted to see. "I'm sorry, sir. I don't see anything unusual."

"My mistake," Hodgson lied. "I must have had something in my eye."

✧ ✧ ✧

THROUGHOUT THE EARLY morning, the house stood over the battlefield, stretching across the horizon, its doorway beckoning, its lights flickering off and on. Clouds were visible behind its translucence, which turned their colors a pale green. Unaware of its existence, the Germans maneuvered always beneath it, obeying its directives.

He couldn't understand. Could an Evil Force be behind the intent of a nation? The Germans weren't a wicked people, despite what the propagandists said. No war was good; yet there were surely just wars. He liked to think the English side was just.

And where are the Forces of Good? he asked the sky. *Where were you when I needed you to save Colleen? And if this thing comes against us, who stands for England?*

A particularly deafening barrage landed behind the trenches.

". . .you, sir?" a voice said.

"What?" Hodgson turned to Ridley.

"I said, is there anything I can bring you, sir?"

"No, that's all right."

✧ ✧ ✧

BY MID-MORNING THE assault had begun. The Germans charged under cover of the guns, crossing the deadly No Man's Land between the armies, sprinting into the sights of the British rifles while the English fired from the protection of the trenches. Thousands would die as they always did in a charge.

The German artillery did not cease as was usual in an attack but began firing farther behind the British lines. Suddenly, the shadow of the house grew long across the battlefield. Will felt its dreadful malice reaching over the distance, groping for him.

It was there to destroy him. He did not know why this should be so, but he felt it with certainty. In the process, the forces controlling the house would cut through the English army, severing it from its supply routes to the sea. It would mean German victory.

He sprinted down the hill and ordered his men to move out. They hurried the gear onto the pack horse and hurried away, scarcely leaving the hill before the German artillery found it. Hodgson glanced back to see it obliterated by the impact of shell after shell.

He led in a zigzag pattern across the landscape. The bombardment followed wherever he turned. Nightfall found them ensconced at the bottom of a deep crater.

"I've never seen the like, sir," Corporal Stephens said. "Shells everywhere we went. You're a good luck charm to bring us through, and there's no doubt of it."

But Will wondered if he should give himself up to death, so the house would leave the battlefield before whatever power it supplied the Germans resulted in disaster.

He sat down to rest, and exhaustion caught him before he knew it. Even as he fell asleep, he wondered how he could prevent the ghost pirates from finishing him. At that instant, he didn't care if he lived or died. Perhaps better for England if he perished.

✧ ✧ ✧

HE WAS BACK in the *Sangier's* cabin, holding his cutlass, and the door had been nearly torn apart.

"Now I'll have ye," the ghost captain called from the other side of it. "We have the house and we'll take ye, too. Ye'll be well-paid for the stroke ye gave me."

Will blew a ragged breath. This was it. But he wouldn't give up without a battle; he'd try to take the captain with him.

The pirates slammed against the door again. It fell in with a crash. The phantoms poured through in a rush. Hodgson braced himself.

No sooner were they in the room than they recoiled. With shouts of fear, they pressed themselves against the wall, trying to force their way back through the doorway.

Something glowed overhead. The White Circle hovered directly above him.

The pirates fled. The captain thrust his head through the doorway, cursing, but dared not enter.

Hodgson had no spirit left for exultation. The only thought that ran through his brain was, *You rescued me now. Why couldn't you save her?*

He stayed in the cabin beneath the White Circle's protection. The hours stretched by. The vision faded.

✧ ✧ ✧

HE WALKED THE gray road above the vast Rift, Pepper at his side. His previous treks had brought him past the clouds of mist, and the whole canyon lay visible below him. What he saw made him gape, for in the shadow of the Rift, a hundred yards from where the road ended far below, appeared a house where none had been before, a mansion of enormous proportions, a twisted version of Kraighten House, recognizable only by its unusual gables.

He halted, studying it. Pepper whined, as if sharing the chill that ran along his neck and arms. Sitting down on the road, he tried to imagine the Night Land as he remembered it from his dreams, the way it had looked through the telescopes at the apex of the Great Pyramid. He stared across the miles at the place where the Great Bight fell into shadow. The snaking roads built by the Road Makers ended close to where those shadows began. Something about that seemed wrong, but he couldn't remember why.

He followed the line of the last road, past the house and into the umbra cast by the Great Bight. The bottom of the Rift stretched into that gloom, flat and bare save for scattered shrubs and lank trees, then the ground descended into a deeper cleft. When the sun was at last extinguished, that would be known as the Great Slope, leading through utter darkness to a land of volcanoes and strange vegetation.

He glanced again at the house. Its windows reflected crimson in the red twilight. He measured the distance with his eyes. It was hard to be certain. Yet, if the walled town to the south was indeed the Quiet City. . .

He ran his hands over Pepper's warm coat.

"The House of Silence."

He stood, walking back and forth along the road, staring at the Rift and the house, and perspiration beaded his forehead. Pepper circled him, puzzled by his excitement.

According to the ancient stories of the Last Redoubt, the House of Silence, the most evil structure in the Night Land, had been built by Gosil, a hero in the age before the Great Pyramid was constructed. Hodgson now saw this was untrue. Rather, the wandering tribes of humans, driven to find shelter from the encroaching monsters as the sun failed, had found Kraighten House standing upon the plain and tried to make it their own. But they hadn't succeeded; the house had proved *unsuitable*; wasn't that the word the old texts used?

Hodgson grimaced. Unsuitable indeed! A hell house if ever there was one. And eventually, the Forces of Evil had taken their home back from humanity.

He left off pacing and strode down the road.

✧ ✧ ✧

He reached the canyon bottom at last after many long hours. There, he hesitated, uncertain what to do next. His gaze traveled upward to the walls of rock rising around him, mile upon mile, their peaks lost among the overhead vapors. He was still leagues from the shadow cast by the Great Bight. He saw no sign of another living creature.

Glancing toward the end of the road to the north, he looked upon the house and shuddered. Machines lay scattered around it.

Could Colleen possibly still be alive, held captive? But if the Swine-Things were there, how could he overcome them alone? He considered the Quiet City to the south. He might find inhabitants there, allies who could help him.

But when he left the road to go toward the city, Pepper growled behind him. He gave the dog a puzzled look.

Pepper sat on the road, eyes firmly fixed on his master.

"Come on, old boy. Let's see what we can see." Hodgson turned again, expecting the hound to follow, but Pepper began barking and refused to obey.

Hodgson hesitated. Once before he had ignored Pepper's cries of protest. How different his life might have been had he followed the counsel of his old friend.

"All right." He returned to the road. "Which way should we go?"

Pepper rose, wagging his tail, and headed toward the house.

"Apparently one of us knows where he's going," Will murmured.

✧ ✧ ✧

AFTER MORE LONG hours, he came to the end of the last road of the Road Makers. It halted in an abrupt smattering of material several furlongs from the house, as if those who made it had been driven off. Paving machines, tall as locomotives, stood quiescent nearby, their silver sides reflecting the light of the red sun. Metal steps led up to the drivers' seats, which were open to the air.

He sat on the steps of one of the machines. Pepper climbed up beside him, and they looked toward the sun which would gutter and die but never set.

He ruffled the dog's ears. "Well, old boy, you brought us here. What now?"

Pepper licked his face and lay down.

"We wait? Is that all you've got?" Hodgson chuckled. "If you're not the most empty-headed captain I ever followed, you're the most reticent."

He looked back to his right toward the dreaded house, and beyond it to the shadows cast by the Bight; and he thought of the visions of the Night Land that had assailed him night after night for an entire year. *If the House of Silence stood over there, the Great*

Pyramid would have been back to the south. It was hard to measure the distances in the light. The road halted half a mile from where the house had appeared. And it ran. . .

He hesitated, realizing what had troubled him before. In his visions, the road had not stopped here but had circled the House of Silence and run to the edge of the Great Slope. It was as if the Forces of Evil had brought the house through time to prevent the road from being completed.

As if in response to his thoughts, Pepper began frantically barking. Hodgson looked around for signs of danger, but the dog's eyes were fixed on his own.

"What is it, Pepper? What is it, boy?"

The dog sprang up the steps of the machine and bounded back down to Hodgson, then up the steps again, stopping at the top to look over his shoulder.

Hodgson stared at the dog, who whined and barked and tossed his head, beckoning. Will ascended and joined his friend. The mechanism was simple enough, little different from that of a motorcar, except it used an azure sphere to control direction. He moved his hands over the sphere. The machine emitted a faint hissing and lifted a foot off the ground. Pushing the sphere forward sent a gray material swirling from the nozzles at the back of the machine. The paver advanced, laying the road, continuing the abandoned work.

He laughed grimly. *Brought through millions of years to be a common laborer. I could have driven a taxi in London to better purpose.*

The machine inched its way along. Hodgson drove for an hour, spreading the material in a wide line, his eyes fixed on the door of the house, looking for signs of the Swine-Things. Nothing moved around the structure; the windows stared blind-eyed onto the plain.

Something about the scene was familiar, something about the house and the canyon walls. "God in heaven help me!" he muttered, realizing what it was. Among the many visions he had seen concerning Kraighten House, one had been of a vast plain bathed in a red, twilight glow, with the house at its center. And above the house, perched on nearly limitless crags, had peered the old gods of myth—Seth, Anubis, Chemosh, Dagon—hundreds of them, swine-headed beasts and vulture-headed monsters, dragon forms and animal shapes—some he had recognized and others he had not. All of them eternally watching the house.

He looked upward toward the top of the Rift, hidden scores of miles above him by clouds of mist. Were there carved upon the upper reaches the heads of those vile gods? And if so, what did it mean? Were all the world's Evil Forces focused on that dreadful manor?

He shuddered at the awesome Power he faced.

✧ ✧ ✧

HE WOKE WITH a gasp. He was lying at the bottom of the crater. Corporal Stephens was sitting by the telephone; Ridley was asleep.

Hodgson rose and pulled himself to the crater's lip. The east glowed with a pre-dawn light. Through his field-glasses, he saw the Germans had broken through the British lines. Rather than engaging the English to either side, they were marching furiously toward Hodgson's position.

There could be no doubt; the house was seeking him, using the unsuspecting Germans, manipulating them in a charge that made no strategic sense.

"Corporal," Hodgson said, "I want you to relay the following to Captain Carver: Turn all guns on section Seventy-four and maintain fire. Tell him it is of the ultimate urgency if we want to halt the enemy advance."

The corporal came up beside Hodgson and stared onto the field. His brow furrowed. "Sir, we'd be aiming far beyond the enemy artillery."

"I am aware of that and of other information you do not know. Relay the message at once."

"Yes, sir."

Carver will think me mad, Hodgson thought. *Even though he can't see the enemy, he will know how far off the sector is. But will he do it? And will shelling have any effect on the immaterial house?*

An explosion ripped the earth a hundred yards from where he crouched. He dropped back into the crater. The enemy guns were seeking him again. He wouldn't be able to stay there long.

The British artillery came alive. Shells roared over Will's head. He clambered back up to the crater's mouth. *Good old*

Carver! I should have known I could count on him.

He looked back toward where the British artillery lay hidden behind rows of hills. There, riding high in the sky above Carver's guns, hung the White Circle, grown huge, glowing in the morning light. The English bombardment would not be in vain! Shells were already striking the house; several landed in its upper stories, rending it, sending wood and glass splintering across the battlefield. A cheer escaped his lips.

"What is it, sir?" Ridley called.

Hodgson dropped to the bottom of the crater, hopeful for the first time in days. Before he could give an answer, a German shell struck at the back of their sanctuary.

The blast threw Will off his feet. Everything went black.

✧ ✧ ✧

FOR AN INSTANT, he was back aboard the *Sangier*; he felt the wind on his face and heard the mast creaking beneath the stars. But the vision faded as quickly as it began, and he was again atop the machine within the Great Rift.

The White Circle spun rapidly above the paver, coruscating flames tinged with sparks of green, looking unreal in the twilight. It turned its gaze to Hodgson, its many eyes piercing as knives. He recoiled beneath their sharpness.

Tendrils extended from the Circle, aimed toward the house, a command to go on.

"Why?" Hodgson demanded, feeling a rising anger.

When the Circle did not respond, Hodgson said, voice faltering, "I want to know. Did *I* make all this?" He raised his hands to indicate everything around them.

A thought entered his mind, like someone answering, though the White Circle did not speak audibly. *You did not.*

"Then why?" Hodgson's voice poured out his anguish. "Why did you give me the visions? Why did I have to go through it all?"

The Circle thrust its tendrils again toward the house, yet still Will refused to move. He had been a pawn from the beginning, and they had abandoned Colleen, forced *him* to abandon her when she needed him most.

The Circle spoke again. *Will you trust me?*

He looked into its terrible eyes. They were deep wells, unfathomable. "Why didn't you help her?"

Will you trust me?

Pepper whined and nuzzled his nose against Will's arm, urging him to move the machine forward. Pepper had also been touched long ago by the Circle, a touch that had saved the dog's life.

"I'll trust you," he said at last, "for the sake of England."

He drove the paver forward, pouring the road inch by inch.

As he neared the house, its doors burst open. The blood drained from his face, for within lay only darkness, Silence, limitless power, infinite hate far greater than that of the Swine-Things or the phantom pirates. Not even the White Circle could stand against it.

This was what the old gods intended, to transport the House of Silence from millions of years in the past to the Great Bight and establish their dominance long before humanity was ready to face them. It would taint the life in the Great Rift, bending it to its ends, bringing a swift finish to the human race. Nothing could stop it. Hodgson hung his head. This was what he had always dreaded: his dreams of Kraighten House, the Ghost Pirates, and the darkness of the Night Land given form.

There came a flash of light and the vision faded.

✧ ✧ ✧

HE WAS BACK in Belgium, lying on the ground after the shell's impact. He rose and staggered forward, trying to rub the smoke from his eyes. Ridley lay dead, eyes wide to the sky. Stephens was nowhere in sight.

He climbed to the top of the crater, feeling surprisingly light and strong. He rubbed his eyes, uncertain what he was seeing. The house stood radiating sheer evil, the shells falling around it, its walls the color of green jade in the morning light. But behind him to the south, thousands of soldiers came rushing across the battlefield toward the German lines.

Reinforcements! Something inside him said he had to be part of that belligerent charge against the seen and unseen foe. He seized his rifle and sprinted across the battlefield, filled with an unaccountable exhilaration.

He joined the charge slightly in advance of the other soldiers, practically leading them. They sped over the broken plain, shouting unintelligibly at first, a cry that changed into a long shout. *"For England!"*

Their bayonets fixed, their rifles blazing, they hurled themselves against the Germans. To Hodgson's surprise—for the Huns had never lacked bravery—the enemy threw down their guns and fled on every side.

The soldiers crossed the plain unopposed. The house stood before them, a gargantuan, gaping edifice. British shells were landing around them now, striking at the manor.

Between the men's shouts and the pounding blood at his temples, he did not hear the slow silencing of the barrage at first, but gradually became aware of his boots striking something harder than bare earth. He was running on a gray surface, and the air was tinged with crimson. He was back in the Rift and the army with him, racing on the road he had fashioned for their passage.

He glanced at the man to his left. It was Ridley. Without slowing his pace, the private gave him a grim salute. Will looked to his right and saw a French soldier whose death was etched forever into his memory; behind him charged a North Hampton lad he had seen perish at Ypres. He gaped back down the road at an endless line, thousands of the dead of Flanders' fields. There were German soldiers, too, once foes, now allies in the fight, marching against the final enemies of the Earth.

They approached the White Circle and Pepper upon the machine; and Will was surprised at not seeing himself at the helm. There was no time for speculation, for out of that gaping doorway the house reached its invisible tendrils, attempting to pull the army into its endless Silence, to smother the soldiers in its Emptiness. Will gave a choking cry.

At first, the sheer terror of the house quailed them, for it pressed upon them with its dark will, and had its power not been diffused over so many, they would have been destroyed. Yet even as it sought to entrap them, the White Circle moved to a position above the soldiers' heads, a cascading luminance shining from it, bathing each of them in its radiance; and all of them, including Hodgson, became pinpoints of light bright as the Circle itself, every man feeding off its energy, taking strength and resolve from it. Washed in that tremendous glow, Hodgson was possessed by a terrible ecstasy of love and light and power to perform justice.

We must reach the machine, the Circle's command rang through their minds.

Their individual forms blurred into one; the soldiers doubled their pace, a spear aimed at the heart of the house, every man singing a song of Humanity.

The army met the awful hush projected from the house, stumbling into a stillness far greater than the absence of sound—the Silence Incarnate that existed before the making of the worlds, the ultimate desolation. Within its terrible emptiness, nothing could exist. Will felt himself being torn apart, broken down atom by atom. He looked at his hands; they were disintegrating; he could see his blood pulsing through his veins, feel his frame crumbling. The men around him were dissolving into meat and bone. He screamed a silent scream, one of defiance, not fear. If he would die, he would die for Colleen and Bessie, for England and the whole world. And he and those around him would take the house with them if they could; would show the uncaring universe that men could strike back.

In their desperation, their song became one song, unheard at first, then gradually rising. It burst forth, breaking the Silence:

Take up our quarrel with the foe;
To you from failing hands we throw
The torch; be yours to hold it high.
If ye break faith with us who die

And beneath the power of that song, the soldiers' forms grew whole again, once more an arrow against their enemy. Along that shaft of light they swarmed around the paving machine, shaken but unbowed in the very shadow of the great eaves. Gasping and drained, some scarcely able to keep their feet, they managed a rough *hurrah!* And Hodgson cheered with them.

But the White Circle's thoughts echoed like iron across the plain. *There is no time! The road must be finished, the Road Maker protected. Will you sacrifice more than blood?*

A cry of assent erupted from the soldiers. The tendrils of the White Circle touched Hodgson's head as it had touched him so many years before.

Will's vision shifted; Time became tangible. He looked through Space and Time as if it were a continuous line. Glancing behind him, he saw the Road extending back along the canyon floor and backwards through Time; he saw The Quiet City, and the Quiet City being built, and the empty plain before its building. The farther he looked, the more his vision telescoped. The Road went on, back to Ypres, so he knew that even as the house was a Doorway for the Forces of Evil, he had become a Portal for the army of Flanders. And beyond that, he saw his journey to Belgium, and his journey through life, and even farther back to sailors fighting phantoms on a ship at sea, mariners lost in an island of seaweed, and even farther, to Kraighten House standing beside a great chasm; and beyond that, the manor throughout the ages, and the dark gods who possessed it looking on.

Turning the other way, he saw how the Road led to the porch of the house standing in the Rift; and he knew it must be finished, that Time might follow its original course. With a shock, he realized he was ordained for that moment; that he was *Road Maker, Paver of the Way, Seeker of the Path.* The course of his life had been down but a single road. He realized the Forces of Good had used the Passage created by the house, following the Road through Time, exploiting that which had been created for evil in order to thwart Evil's intent.

Despite being so weary he could scarcely put one foot before the other, he staggered up the steps of the paver, and the army placed itself between him and the House of Silence, pitting their spirits against its own. A wall of white light, the strength of their combined wills, rose between them and it. The White Circle spun above the wall, adding its own strength, its rotations so rapid it roared.

With Pepper licking his hand, Will cut a wide swath around the house, pouring the road, yard upon yard in the endless twilight, following the vision that showed where it must run.

But the House of Silence would not be so easily vanquished. It extended its will toward Hodgson, trying to reach him with its dark intellect. And ever the soldiers and the Barrier of Light stood between him and destruction. Yet the house reached through the Barrier in places, pulling men clattering over its porch, across its threshold into the darkness of its doorway. Entering there, their voices fell silent, dying in the air like poppies before the frost.

Hodgson kept to his task. With every inch of the road he laid, he saw Time quiver and change, the permutations narrowing, strange futures falling and fading into the Never-Have-Been as the new chronal lines created by the materialization of the house collapsed.

He passed into the shadow of the Great Bight.

More and more of the soldiers were swept into the House of Silence. Will felt its malignant will pushing through the Barrier, drawing closer to him. He heard it calling, ordering him to stop the machine. He lowered his head and pressed forward, weeping as he went, trying not to hear the cries of his comrades. But before they fell into the Silence, they sang a valiant song that echoed off the walls of the vast canyon, rising up through the leagues to the dead surface of the world, a final hymn to the glory of the lost civilizations of the Earth:

I am the enemy you killed, my friend.
I knew you in this dark; for so you frowned
Yesterday through me as you jabbed and killed
I parried; but my hands were loath and cold.
Let us sleep now. . .

At last, when Will thought the power of the house would destroy him utterly, he saw just ahead a final future of a world of endless darkness lit by strange fires, and a Great Pyramid standing in the midst of the plain. He reached the Road's end, where the Road must end, at the top of the Great Slope that would someday lead down into darkness. The machine emitted a final burst of material, and—devitalized at last—fell quiescent. Hodgson could go no farther.

A stirring filled the ether. He felt the glaring malice of the old gods beating upon him. Then the air cleared; the terrible pressure from the house ceased. The pagan gods were gone. Their terrible presence had deserted the house, leaving it no longer the House of Silence, but only the shell of Kraighten Manor.

He stepped down from the machine. Three-quarters of the army of the dead were gone. Those who survived saluted as one man before winking out, one by one, leaving the mortal plain for the last time, their final duty done.

Within minutes only a few dozen remained. These drew together, facing Hodgson and the White Circle. From their midst stepped Colleen.

Tears welled in Hodgson's eyes. He took her hands. "I never thought to see you again. I couldn't get back to you. I wanted to, but—"

"You would have died before your time if you had. It was a terrible ordeal, but the White Circle protected my soul from destruction, and I was not left alone."

"But. . . Bessie. I promised—"

"I'm sorry, Will." She kept her eyes fixed on his own. "Some promises cannot be kept."

"Then what was the point of my confession?"

"The struggles and choices we make give us the strength when we need it most. Your time with her, your voyage aboard the *Sangier*. . . these were necessary."

Will found he could not speak.

The White Circle's thoughts rumbled through the air. *By foiling the assault, we have gained millions of years for the human race. But there is always more to be done.*

The Circle bathed the entire company in its light. Beneath its glow, the soldiers, including Hodgson and Colleen, grew tall and thin and regal as kings, glowing white with a holy light.

The light died, save where it haloed Hodgson. The White Circle said, *You will lead these, the best of the brave, to protect the Future. And you will have an old name that is new, and will hereafter be called "Hope," for you will bring hope in the coming darkness.*

And Hodgson finally knew that though there was great evil in the world, there were Forces of Good to oppose them.

Colleen gently squeezed his hand. "We've work to do, my love. The work of Eternity."

✧ ✧ ✧

CAPTAIN CARVER STOOD stone-faced, listening to Corporal Stephens.

"I had just moved back to the telephone, sir. There was a blast close-by, and the lieutenant and Ridley were thrown back. There was nothing to be done for either of them."

Carver nodded his head. "Did he say anything at the end?"

"He was mumbling something, sir, about the dark land and the silent house, I think it was. It didn't make any sense. He was a brave man. One of the bravest I've seen."

"He was certainly that. If he hadn't had us retrain the guns, the Germans would have broken through. He may have saved the army and the war. We won't meet his like again."

"No, sir."

The corporal left and Carver stared across the battlefield. It was November 19, 1918. In the fields of Belgium, William Hope Hodgson lay dead, cut down by a German shell.

But millions of years in the future, when the sun is no more, white warriors walk the Great Road and the desert places of the Night Land, defenders against the Forces of Evil. And among them are two who always travel together. Legends say they are sometimes seen holding hands. And a great hound accompanies them, who never leaves their side.

✧ ✧ ✧

AFTERWORD

WILLIAM HOPE HODGSON was a fascinating man. We know only a little about his life, much of it from his published letters: his seafaring apprenticeship at a young age, his interest in "Physical Culture," his death in 1918 in World War I when the German's shelled his forward observation post. The main liberty taken in my story comes from his poem, *Grief*. It suggests that before he married his wife, he was once in love with a woman who died. This bit of speculation rings true to me, though it may be completely incorrect.

I read *The Night Land* when I was sixteen. Fantasy novels were rare before Tolkien created the modern genre, and I read any of them I could find. Hodgson purposely wrote *The Night Land* in an archaic and redundant style that gives the book awe and majesty. (The closest I've found to his writing is in *The Travels of Sir John Mandeville*, written in the fourteenth century.) As a teenager, I was too hungry for fantasy to be bothered by his stylistic choice, and I still consider it one of the Great Novels. In order to bring it to a wider audience, I rewrote it in a more accessible style some years ago under the title *The Night Land, A Story Retold.*

During the writing, I was in communication with Andy Robertson, a passionate fan of *The Night Land* and editor of the Night Land website. I sent him a copy of my rewrite. Andy could have excoriated me for daring to rewrite the author he valued most; instead, he wrote a kind and fair review of my version. He was always encouraging. Our conversations led me to write *The Last Roadmaker* for his website. I was saddened to learn of his unexpected passing a few years ago.

In my original version of this story, when Hodgson is transmuted to the Night Land at the end, he became a Silent One, one of the mysterious creatures depicted in *The Night Land* who walk the roads. With the ardor only a true fan could display, Andy insisted that the Silent Ones of Hodgson's work were evil, and Hodgson *couldn't* become one.

I quoted references where Hodgson suggests the Silent Ones weren't truly malevolent. (Not to be confused with the House of Silence, which is utterly wicked.) "No," Andy insisted. He was willing to publish it but would place it in an area for stories not part of the official "canon."

Such are the debates of true fans. I relented and rewrote the scene, amused but unwilling to have the story exiled to a different web page. At the time, I thought I would return it to its original ending if it was ever republished. But the years have passed, and I prefer to respect Andy's wishes.

THE STAR WATCH

For my part I know nothing with any certainty, but the sight of the stars makes me dream

—van Gogh

I WAS SIXTEEN when I came to the Tower of Astronomy in the great house, Evenmere, and there is no place I would rather have been. Because of this, I was a tremendous disappointment to my father, who farmed on the great Terraces. The earth between his hands and a son to carry on the tradition was all he ever wanted. I, myself, found the work tedious. I listened to his discussions of rain and beetles and warm sunshine on green leaves—our household was full of such talk—but I would not hear. The earth did not move me, for I wanted the stars.

The stars! I would stand in my father's fields at night and stare up at the sky. I knew all the constellations and the individual names of many points of light. The sight of them left me aching with a nameless yearning, for in my mind they lit the path to all the mysteries of the universe, being somehow connected to God.

When I turned twelve, I sent a letter to the Grand Astronomer, and to my wonder, he replied. I asked foolish questions, but he answered them all. Thereafter I wrote him four times each year. He was kind and once sent me a star chart etched by his own hand. I nailed it to my wall and stared at it for hours.

At the beginning of my sixteenth year I petitioned to apprentice in the Astronomy Tower for a summer, to see if I possessed the necessary qualities for the work. I was nearly overcome with delight when the Astronomer gave his permission.

I will never forget the look on my father's face the day I left. Both my parents sought to reason with me, he talking of the long summer's work to be done and of how the land would all be mine some day; she saying how much it would mean to father if I stayed. I paid no heed, for all I could think of were the stars. And because my father was a gentle man, he said no more on the day of my departure, but clasped his arms around me in a husky embrace. He smelled of warm earth and sweat, and that is the way I always remember him.

"You will come back," he said. "The earth will draw you home. It is in your blood. You must be careful. They say the Towers are tall; do not be falling from them." Though he spoke bravely, his eyes were filled with a sorrow that I, at my young age, did not comprehend. How strange that we can look into the past and see events more clearly than we could at the moment they occurred.

I walked the long corridors of Evenmere, down gas-lit passages of floral carpets, dark oak wainscoting, frescoed ceilings, and flying buttresses carved with apostles and angels. This being my first time away from home, I marveled at the endless variety of the enormous mansion and considered all the scholars said concerning it: that it is God's mechanism for maintaining the universe; that its clocks must be kept wound and its candles lit lest time and the stars run down like children's toys; that it is a symbolic representation of all the universe—a thousand such stories crowded my mind, many completely contradictory. Having grown up within Evenmere's halls, I had taken its strangeness for granted; only by traveling through it did I finally glimpse its mystery and majesty.

I passed through the passages of Cosing and into Aylyrium, a country of towering domes and silver-splendored mosaics, with long, sweeping hallways and immense, majestic statues. After seeking directions from the inhabitants, I found my way up the winding stair leading to the Tower, where I entered a circular chamber draped in floral rugs, with Morris tapestries of peacocks on acanthus backgrounds concealing brick and mortar walls. A fireplace curved along one side, surrounded by desks, end tables, and fat chairs with threadbare arms. Plaster angels stared down with hollow eyes from the cornices as if in judgment of me.

There, I met the Astronomer, a rotund gentleman of great age. He had a warm, honest face, and as was the custom of all who worked in the Tower, wore a white robe with a heavy hood. By his side stood a young man only slightly older than myself, whose robe loomed so large it nearly swallowed him, leaving his face peeking out as if from a stone crag.

"Edwin," the Astronomer addressed me. "This is Forth, my son. He knows much of the stars and will be Grand Astronomer after me."

Forth grimaced at his father's words. He was dark-haired with brooding green eyes. I suppose he might have been handsome had his nose not once been broken. He walked with a slight limp as well, I assumed from some accident.

The Astronomer guided me to the Mechanical Room above the circular chamber, but Forth, begging other duties, did not accompany us.

The chamber, or actually, series of chambers, was the beginning of wonder for me, a world of levers and dials, gauges and gears, whole apparatus of which I had no specific understanding, though I knew their ultimate purpose.

The Astronomer uses them to regulate the stars.

From telescopes of every size around the chamber, the Grand Astronomer watches the heavens. The uninformed believe he actually keeps the stars in their courses. Of course, this is gross superstition. No man, even with the number of assistants employed by the Tower, could watch every star. Rather, his duties are to monitor the heavens and set right that which can be set right. Some tasks are within his power, others are not.

As we stood in that room, he lectured in his pleasant, patient voice about the working of the brass controls, but after the passing of an hour I could withhold my eagerness no more and interrupted by blurting, "Please, sir, may I see the Nine Towers?"

He smiled at this with an understanding that told me he, too, remembered being young.

"This way then, my friend. I forget how dreary it is to a swift, new mind, dwelling too long upon a single topic. The Nine are best seen from the Central Tower."

He led through a heavy oak door along a narrow stairway winding itself up and up. We passed several doors before at last exiting into another circular chamber with polished wood floors, oriental rugs, and a garrison of fainting couches, chairs, and side tables heavy with knickknacks. Paintings covered nearly every inch of the walls in Victorian style. I thought that a shame, for the walls, being curved burlwood, seemed too beautiful to conceal. Seven double windows wrapped in floral curtains stood at identical intervals around the room. The Astronomer strode to the first of these, threw the curtains back with a flourish, unlatched the window, and pulled it open.

"Come see," he said, gesturing to me.

I drew near and froze in amazement. Nothing I had read, nothing my mentor had told me, could have prepared me. Outside the window three towers were visible, reaching high into a sky black as deepest space. Around those towers hung the stars.

Red, blue, yellow, green—such names give no justice to their hues. In appearance, their size varied from that of a child's ball to seething orbs larger than the chamber in which I stood, all suspended around the towers like inset gems. The sparkling pearls of the Milky Way shimmered in a net across the highest spires, and stars hung beneath us as well, as if the Earth had vanished, leaving only the towers and the celestial lights.

There is no certain explanation for it. From our observation point I should have seen blue sky, not the black velvet of space. And how can stars revolving in their massive orbits also be jeweled ornaments on the Nine Towers? But Evenmere is a strange house, as I have said.

Regardless, I stood mesmerized, scarcely able to catch my breath, for here at last hung the objects of my yearning, I, like a lover within reach of his beloved, paralyzed in awe before the beauty of her soul.

✧ ✧ ✧

SO I CAME to live and work in the Tower of Astronomy. Of all the scores of assistants the Astronomer employed, I was the youngest, the rest save for Forth being ten years my senior. Most lived outside the Tower, and with these I formed no friendships.

Forth proved a poor companion. At first I thought we would be confederates, but when I tried to speak of the stars, he showed an astonishing lack of interest for one destined to be Grand Astronomer. In fact, he scarcely spoke at all on any subject, and his expression remained perpetually morose.

I used to walk the stairs of the Towers at night. I can never forget those early days: the creaking of the floorboards, the smell of wood and carpet, the smell of *stars*! Others have scoffed at me for this, but I swear I smell them, acrid and hot, sweet with burning blazes. It was the best time of my life—to cross a room and look out, to see the stars suspended. Oh, how I loved that place!

My duties proved both interesting and dull, for though they often varied, I was sometimes required to spend long hours alone monitoring the various instruments. Because of my enthusiasm, the Astronomer took greater interest in me than in any of my fellow workers. In this, he may have erred by demonstrating procedures earlier than was customary. It is easy to equate a quick mind with wisdom; I had the first but lacked the second.

Many times he assigned me a star to monitor. And though the vigil might last long hours, I remained diligent, observing until the luminary reached a predetermined location in the heavens, when I would call the Grand Astronomer to manipulate the brass levers and knobs in ways beyond my understanding. Despite my ignorance, I watched diligently, and even in those early days, began to suspect more art than science in the work.

✧ ✧ ✧

BECAUSE FORTH AND I were his favorites, the Astronomer often paired us together. At first, I thought this an opportunity to learn, until Forth's father began depicting me as a model to his son. Whether this was done intentionally or otherwise, it did little to improve Forth's attitude toward me.

"The Star Watch," the Astronomer often said, "is like fishing. Have neither of you been fishing? Of course you have! It is a matter of finding the proper water, whether the still pool or the running stream, of trimming the line, setting the bait, making the cast. It is discovering the proper currents and watching the cork bob, then the moment of the nip, the taking of the bait, the struggle—the tightening and loosening—the bringing of the quarry to the shore. Such is the Star Watch. I do not simply observe the instruments; I sense the powers at work; I listen for the ebb and flow of the star tides, discern the rushing solar winds, and perceive the slow, grinding orbits of the suns."

This was useful instruction, but he often added such remarks as, "Edwin, I see in you the Gift of Astronomy. I notice the way the movement of the stars fascinates—you understand the art. Forth, you must benefit from Edwin's example. Learn to be the patient fisherman. Only then will you become a great Astronomer."

But Forth was not patient; his thoughts rippled constantly across his brow. And at his father's words, he glared at me. Certainly it did not help that I was the younger. At those times, I believe he hated me.

✧ ✧ ✧

THERE CAME A day when Forth's father assigned us to the Middle Reaches of the Sixth Tower. "You are proceeding well," he told us. "I never allow apprentices your age to ascend beyond the first levels, but between the two of you, you will perform splendidly. There is a pair of stars in Centaurus requiring minor adjustments."

He led us down several corridors, then up the circular stair of the Sixth Tower. On such excursions, the rotund Astronomer proved remarkably robust, for in the hour we climbed, Forth and I required frequent rests, but he never seemed to tire.

As we ascended, the stars outside the windows grew nearer. My heart raced, not merely from exertion but excitement as I imagined drawing close enough to warm my hands against their heat, to reach out and touch them!

Scarcely a third of the way up the tower, we at last attained a circular room filled with various mechanisms. The Astronomer led us through one of the six doors encircling the chamber, onto a gray stone rampart surrounding the outside of the tower.

We stood as if in the depths of space, and before us flamed the stars!

The nearest, hanging only a few yards away, could be reached by a stone bridge passing from the Sixth to the Seventh Tower, a span five feet wide without balustrades. The slow rotation of the stars made it seem to sway.

"This way," the Astronomer said, leading down the span.

For a moment I faltered. Though I have never feared heights, the infinite abyss unnerved me. Forth, having undoubtedly accompanied his father countless times, gave me a mirthless grin. "What's the matter? Does the farmer fear the sky?"

He could have said nothing to provoke me more. I gritted my teeth in what I hoped was a confident smile—probably more a terrified rictus—and followed Forth over the bridge.

Strange thoughts flood a man in high places. The Void is terrifying yet compelling. One has only to step off. . . I glanced into the abyss only once, then despite my irritation at Forth, hurried to draw closer to him.

Even through my apprehension the stars compelled me. A few feet overhead hung a red beauty—pulsing with light, the heat dancing off its surface. Below the bridge hung another, nearly ice-blue, its rotation slow, its flames wisping away in tendrils.

The Astronomer stopped beside a pair of twin yellow stars hanging directly beside the span at chin level, each no more than a foot across. He gave a boyish grin made radiant by the starlight. "This is your subject," he said. "These revolve around one another, dancing like a young couple consumed with love! Their orbits will soon require correction. Your task is to observe and to summon me at the proper time."

I reached out my hand to grasp the roaring sun, but the Astronomer stopped me with a warning tap. "You must never touch them."

"Would I be burned?"

"I am uncertain, as we are not consumed though we stand so near. Probably you would, but even worse, you might affect their orbits."

"Sir," I asked. "Are we really standing among the stars? Why can we look upon them with unshielded eyes? How do we breathe in airless space? And why are we larger than the suns?"

He smiled again. "I will answer only the first question, for the rest proceed from it. We *do* stand among the stars, and yet we do not, for this—" he waved his hands to indicate all around us, "this is a metaphor, an allegory. But the mechanisms we use truly control the heavens. It is a paradox; life is full of such. And I repeat, you must not touch the stars."

"I understand," I said.

Thereafter, we returned to the circular chamber from where we would monitor the twins. With his usual precision, the Grand Astronomer showed us our task, ordered us to contact him when the gauges reached the appropriate levels, and departed.

Our vigil proved longer than I anticipated. We lived in the chamber for days, eating the food brought us and taking our turns at the monitors. At first, I grew anxious, expecting the gauges to unexpectedly leap to their places, but gradually I recognized the ponderous nature of the suns. *Star work is slow work*, as we say. Only being able to step onto the rampart and study the burning brilliance of the luminaries kept me from going mad with boredom.

For Forth, it was surely a nightmare. He sighed; he slept. He produced an illustrated book entitled *The Great Gliders* from inside his heavy robe and pored over it for hours.

I have often wondered if the Grand Astronomer simply assigned two lads to a task, or if in his wisdom he sensed Forth's resentment toward me and forced us together to see if we could be friends.

Whatever the case, being young, we had not yet developed an aptitude for hoarding a grudge. As the days passed, we came to know one another. For my part, I had less to overcome—Forth had seldom treated me with intentional cruelty. Eventually I asked him about the book. He shrugged as if it meant nothing, but a fire like a touch of starlight winked in his eyes when he looked upon it.

"It's only a book," he said.

"About what?"

He glanced down shyly. "About those who build air gliders, machines to ride the wind in the land of High Gable."

"Is it dangerous?"

His eyes flashed madly. "Sometimes. But I rode one once, two years ago, and there is nothing like it. They experiment with them all the time and talk of adding motors to make them fly like paddle boats on a river. I want to be part of it, to become an aviator. That's what they call them. I want to move to High Gable and work there."

"An aviator." I rolled the unfamiliar word over my tongue. "But you are to be the Grand Astronomer! You would have to leave the Star Watch."

"I hate the Star Watch!" His vehemence seemed to startle even himself. "My father talks only of stars, as if he were a shepherd and they the sheep, but I hear nothing he says! He knows them by names I can never remember. These twins we watch—I don't even know *their* names."

"Rigelius and Thollamai."

"You see! You are the one my father calls gifted. *You* should be the Grand Astronomer."

"I?" I replied, both embarrassed and pleased. "You've been here all your life."

"And hated it!"

We sat silent a time, I baffled that anyone could want other than to work in the Tower of Astronomy. But at last I said, "Does your father know?"

"How could I tell him? He has craved this all my life."

"My father wished me to be a farmer, but I cared nothing for it. I used to believe I could make myself carry on his work, but it was *his* work and not my own. When your father took me into his service, my father accepted it, though he was not pleased."

"My father would *never* accept it," Forth said, but a hint of hope crept into his voice.

That afternoon Forth poured out his love of gliders to me as if the words, dammed so long behind his teeth, finally broke through with my ears the reservoir to receive them. It stunned me that this quiet lad could speak with such passion about anything. Certainly he had never before told anyone of his dreams. He showed me his book and withdrew from between its pages scraps of tattered papers depicting his own glider designs. I in turn related my elation at finally following the path I loved.

"How strange it is," he said, greatly moved. "You are doing the thing I despise, yet it is your greatest ambition."

Later, we went out to look at the twins. Standing on the rampart, we gazed, I happily, Forth with a brooding eye.

"Does the Void frighten you?" he asked.

"A little."

"It doesn't frighten me. Nor my father. He is extremely ancient, you know, older than anyone because he spends so much of his life between the stars. He once told me time does not pass here, and if a man stays on the rampart he requires neither food nor sleep."

We sat in silence again, I pondering this new bit of wonder while the suns crackled all around. Eventually, Forth said, "I fell once, fifteen feet from one of the towers onto a stone ledge. That's how I broke my nose and leg." He slapped his thigh for emphasis. "A few feet over and I would have dropped into the Void."

"That must have been terrifying." I retreated a step from the edge.

His eyes held a strange light, "You would think so, but it wasn't. The moment seemed to last forever, as if I were flying. Ever since, I find myself imagining what it would be like to spread wings and go drifting into the darkness. What a ride that would be, sailing on solar winds!"

I shivered. "Not for me, thank you."

✧ ✧ ✧

DAY AND NIGHT meant nothing to us, with the black abyss before us and scores of suns in the sky. We kept constant watch, taking turns during the hours normally considered night.

When Forth roused me for breakfast the next "day" he seemed excited. When I asked why he had failed to wake me for my shift, he replied, "I spent the night thinking. Besides I wanted you to rest, for you must keep the watch alone today. I am going to tell my father I want to be an aviator."

I stopped eating. "Are you sure?"

"I am." His face was set with a glorious certainty.

✧ ✧ ✧

BECAUSE OF MY concern for Forth, the time crawled by, and I found myself pacing the chamber. He returned six hours later, his face pale, his expression ragged. I did not need to question him, nor did he explain except to say, with an effort not to weep, "Now I know my duty."

He was not the same thereafter, and the watch became once more a dull, companionless affair. But as the hour for the adjustment drew near, I became more and more fascinated by the twin stars. Perhaps I, who had prompted Forth's ill-fated confrontation with his father, grew obsessive to avoid blaming myself for my friend's silence.

Whatever the case, I became absorbed not only in the stars themselves but in the adjustment mechanisms. During the time Forth had been communicative, I had asked him many questions about the instruments. Despite his denials of astronomical skill, his quick mind fathomed more than perhaps even his father realized.

But there remained certain matters concerning the controls

that neither he nor I understood, and in those hours of Forth's new silence their mystery became my fixation.

The answer came to me in a flash, causing me to cry aloud.

"What is it?" Forth asked, perhaps thinking I had injured himself with the instruments.

"I understand!" I almost shouted. "The linear mechanism! It makes sense!"

He drew near despite his melancholy, his interest aroused.

"Explain," he said.

"These levers control what your father sometimes calls the Engines of Apogee, and these," I grasped a pair of rotating knobs, "affect linearity and rotation. It is the combination of the two that actually makes the adjustment! By moving the levers together when the gauges both read one-hundred sixty-five, the suns can be moved oh so slightly!"

"I don't understand," Forth admitted. "How are the two related?"

"It's exactly as your father says," I continued, nearly blind with joy. "It's the art of it! Don't you see?"

Sometimes in his enthusiasm a young man grows unintentionally cruel. The Grand Astronomer was correct in suggesting I had a gift for the stars, as many are gifted in matters beyond my own comprehension. Having made an intuitive leap, I failed to see why anyone else could not do the same.

As Forth stood staring at me, his look became gradually more dire. Finally he said, "I understand nothing."

"You will!" I said. "You will, when we make the adjustment!"

His expression turned to astonishment. "We, make the adjustment? You've lost your mind! We are to call father. *He* will make the adjustment."

"But don't you see, we don't have to!" I said. "We can do it ourselves. It's simple. Anyone could do it. We'll save your father the trouble of a trip. He'll be proud of us."

"He'll be proud of you!" Forth spat.

"No, of both of us!" I was filled with inspiration. "Don't you see we have the opportunity to feel the power of the stars themselves? Oh, Forth, I know once you've tasted what it's like to be a true Astronomer you'll want it for yourself."

I said this and much more. I was persuasive, perhaps more so than ever in my life, either before or since, and my final argument lit a light in my friend's eyes, for he did want to please his father. It was manipulation of the worst sort, but I believed my own words at the time, and he fastened to them with the talons of desperation.

Two hours later found us waiting at the controls, I manning the levers within the room, Forth on the rampart dealing with another apparatus consisting of a large corkscrew valve. That an experienced Astronomer could have done the procedure single-handedly shows how little we truly knew.

The gauges inched toward the required measurements. In my vanity, I neither doubted my own ability to control the stars nor considered the consequences of failure. I burned with concentration, my eyes darting between the twin suns and the intricate mechanism beneath my hands.

More than scientific precision guides the Astronomer. If he is gifted, he senses the moment when the change must be made, feels the shifting star fields, the fluctuations, the variations in heat and light. Perhaps he perceives them in his soul; I cannot say. But I felt the balance between the forces and elements with such fierce intensity I did not even need the gauges to recognize the moment.

I moved first one lever, then another. I closed an outlet; I raised a switch. I felt the power of the Grand Astronomer within my own fingertips. My face flushed with triumph.

"The valve!" I called to Forth. "Open it!"

"Now?" he shouted back. "Are you certain?"

I was on my feet at once. "Yes! Yes! It must be now!"

The Gift lay so strong upon me I thought Forth must surely sense its urgency.

I think the look in my eyes frightened him, for he yanked the valve with all his strength, then gaped at me in horror. "It's stuck! I can't open it!"

Neither of us had thought to test the mechanisms beforehand. I scrambled across the chamber to help.

Before I could reach Forth's side, a rumbling arose, sending the towers trembling as if the twin stars outside the chamber scraped against one another. I stumbled and fell, but Forth held onto the valve. Despite the tremors, he scrambled up beside it onto the balustrade itself, and with his back to the abyss, pulled with all his might. The valve opened with a loud hiss even as the tremors doubled in intensity. Thrown off balance, Forth tumbled from the rampart into the darkness.

At that moment, I must have finally realized that whole stars were at stake, for despite my horror at Forth's disappearance, I rushed to the valve and completed the turn. The tremors instantly ceased. I leaned over the parapet and looked down.

Forth clung to an iron bar, his robe, loosened by his struggles, billowing in the Void.

I dashed inside, retrieved a rope, tied one end to the valve, and tossed the other to Forth. He caught it, pulled himself up to where his feet found purchase on the bar, and rested there, panting from his exertions.

"Oh, Forth, come up!" I cried, stretching my hands toward his. I was overwhelmed with elation at seeing my friend alive and the tremors ended. "We did it, Forth! We did it! The stars moved at our command!"

Perhaps it was the triumph on my face, the joy in my eyes, the ferocious wonder that turned his expression to stone.

"No, Edwin," he said softly. "You did it. The stars moved at *your* command."

"We both did. Take my hand!"

"My father was right. You *are* gifted." His eyes searched my face with a keen hunger; we momentarily seemed frozen in time. Gradually, his expression changed to one of intense exhilaration, as if a tremendous revelation suffused his features.

"Standing here," he said, "I can feel the solar winds blowing beneath the rampart."

He was right, for his robe swelled hugely, making him look like a great bird. I could hear the hot, whispering sun tides. Shadow and light played across his brow, transfiguring him. He looked holy, immortal.

"You were born to be the Grand Astronomer," he said passionately. "And I to fly. Oh, Edwin, I will follow my dream. I will *be* an aviator."

I stretched my hands even farther to reach him, but he smiled and released the rope.

He did not fall. He glided. He swooped, drifting farther and farther down between the stars. And as he descended, he shouted with a joy that seemed to go on forever. I watched in horror until he vanished from sight.

✧ ✧ ✧

THE GRAND ASTRONOMER did not live many years thereafter. He blamed himself, even as he forgave me. He was that kind of man. And before he died he appointed me his replacement.

It is harder to forgive oneself. Even though the young boy of those days, fresh from the farm, meant no malice, even though his only crime lay in loving the stars and his Gift too much, I wonder how he could have been so blind.

I seldom speak now, especially to the young, without considering my words, and I go often, even after all these years, to the Sixth Tower to stand before the stars. If, as we believe, time does not exist within the Void and neither food nor sleep is required, Forth has become immortal. It was the contemplation of that eternal fall that killed his father.

But at such times when my guilt ebbs, I do not share the Astronomer's grief, for I heard Forth's shouts of delight echoing between the stars. In those moments I see him gliding forever. Laughing. The supreme aviator lost in exultation.

✧ ✧ ✧

AFTERWORD

EDITORS HAVE ALWAYS been kind to me. I've honestly never had a bad experience with one.

I was doing a book signing at a convention after my novel, *The High House*, came out. Gordon Van Gelder, then editor (now publisher) of *The Magazine of Fantasy and Science Fiction* introduced himself, said he liked the book, and asked if I ever wrote short stories. Stoked at having my first book released by a major publisher, I told him I was more focused on writing novels. We had a friendly chat and he left.

Sitting there, it dawned on me I had just turned down an editor who *invited* me to submit to his prestigious magazine. Mentally slapping myself multiple times on the forehead, I resolved to write something for him. Fortunately, being the gentleman he is, Gordon didn't hold my smugness against me; he accepted *The Star Watch* and shepherded several of my later stories through publication over the following years.

Years before writing *The Star Watch,* I used to read a terrific small press publication called *Empire: For the Science Fiction Writer.* Inspired by an article by Barry Longyear about maintaining a writing career by interconnecting one's stories, I set *The Star Watch* in the same universe as *The High House.* I would later use Edwin Phra, the narrator of this short story, in *Evenmere,* the third book in the novel series. As a reader, I've always loved when a writer makes such associations.

ACKNOWLEDGEMENTS

As always, to my wife Kathy, my first reader and greatest enthusiast. To live with such a supportive life-companion is a gift beyond measure. Lon Mirll, Kreg Robertson, and Joe Trent have critiqued and honed the majority of the stories herein, and I treasure our hours together sharing stories and life. Friend and fellow writer Dr. Robert Finegold edited *The Leechmont* for me in his usual, meticulous manner, and Joel Eidsath gave me invaluable insights to improve it.

I am equally grateful to the editors I've worked with, who always encouraged me to make my writing better.

And a large thank you to those who have read my books, especially the ones who have emailed me over the years, correspondence that means more to me than they can possibly know.

ABOUT THE AUTHOR

James Stoddard's short fiction and articles have appeared in publications such as *Amazing Stories* and *The Magazine of Fantasy and Science Fiction*. His short stories, *The Battle of York*, and *The First Editions*, appeared respectively in *The Year's Best SF 10*, published by Eos Books, and *The Year's Best Fantasy 9* from Tor. His novel, *The High House*, won the Compton Crook Award for best fantasy by a new novelist and was nominated for several other awards. He taught Sound Recording at the college level for many years before leaving to write full time. He and his wife live in West Texas.

Further information can be found at:
www.james-stoddard.com

PUBLICATION HISTORY

"The Perfect Day" originally appeared in *Amazing Stories.* (1985) | "The Star Watch" (2002), "The Battle of York" (2004), "The Star to Every Wandering Barque" (2007), "The First Editions" (2008), "Christmas at Hostage Canyon" (2011), and "The Ifs of Time" (2011) all originally appeared in *The Magazine of Fantasy and Science Fiction.* | "The Last Roadmaker" (2011) first appeared in Andy Robertson's *The Night Land* website currently located at https://nightland.website | "Day of the Shark" (2018), and "Cage of Honor" (2020) originally appeared in *Tales from the Magician's Skull.* | "The Leechmont" (2022) appears here for the first time.

Also by James Stoddard

THE HIGH HOUSE
THE FALSE HOUSE
EVENMERE
THE NIGHT LAND, A STORY RETOLD
THE BACK OF THE BEYOND
LIBERTY BELL AND THE LAST AMERICAN

Music by James Stoddard

EVENMERE, A SONG CYCLE
BASED ON THE NOVEL
THE HIGH HOUSE
Available as a download on many streaming services

Visit www.james-stoddard.com to learn more about the author.
To contact James Stoddard email: evenmere@gmail.com

www.ingramcontent.com/pod-product-compliance
Lightning Source LLC
Chambersburg PA
CBHW030651260626
47157CB00007B/2592

* 9 7 9 8 9 8 8 6 6 8 0 0 8 *